M. L. WHITE

Shifter Awakened

First published by White Wolf Publishing 2025

Copyright © 2025 by M. L. White

All rights reserved. No part of this publication may be reproduced, stored, or transmitted in any form or by any means, electronic, mechanical, photocopying, recording, scanning, or otherwise without written permission from the publisher. It is illegal to copy this book, post it to a website, or distribute it by any other means without permission.

This novel is entirely a work of fiction. The names, characters, and incidents portrayed in it are the work of the author's imagination. Any resemblance to actual persons, living or dead, events, or localities is entirely coincidental.

M. L. White asserts the moral right to be identified as the author of this work.

M. L. White has no responsibility for the persistence or accuracy of URLs for external or third-party Internet Websites referred to in this publication and does not guarantee that any content on such Websites is, or will remain, accurate or appropriate.

Designations used by companies to distinguish their products are often claimed as trademarks. All brand names and product names used in this book and on its cover are trade names, service marks, trademarks, and registered trademarks of their respective owners. The publishers and the book are not associated with any product or vendor mentioned in this book. None of the companies referenced within the book have endorsed the book.

Second edition

ISBN (paperback): 9798899713316
ISBN (hardcover): 9798896926658

Cover art by SeventhStar Art

This book was professionally typeset on Reedsy.
Find out more at reedsy.com

*To my Danny,
None of this would have
happened without you.
I love you.*

Contents

Chapter 1	1
Chapter 2	16
Chapter 3	21
Chapter 4	34
Chapter 5	50
Chapter 6	59
Chapter 7	73
Chapter 8	93
Chapter 9	109
Chapter 10	115
Chapter 11	140
Chapter 12	158
Chapter 13	186
Chapter 14	209
Chapter 15	226
Chapter 16	239
Chapter 17	255
Chapter 18	268
Chapter 19	280
Chapter 20	290
Chapter 21	314
Chapter 22	325
Chapter 23	335
Chapter 24	342
Chapter 25	357
Chapter 26	370

Chapter 27	383
Bonus Chapter	396
Bonus Chapter	413
Bonus Chapter	429
Series Order	449
About the Author	450
Also by M. L. White	452

Chapter 1

I ran.

Faster and harder than I had ever gone before.

I ducked under branches barely able to see in front of me. My flashlight sucked, making the chance of tripping on a tree root or rock so much higher. Vicious snarls sounded behind me, getting closer and closer, my heart racing as I darted to the right in hopes of putting more distance between us.

A large wolf was hunting me. I had never seen one that large before. I was lost in the woods, and 100 percent in *his* territory.

I felt his hot breath seconds before his jaws snapped just behind my ear. I screamed as a chunk of hair was ripped from my head. Tears clouded my vision but I shoved through the dark brush anyways. I had to get away. I couldn't *finally* get my one chance for a better life only to die like this!

I slid in the grass as I abruptly changed directions, hoping to shake the wolf off, and landed on my right hip. Pain rippled through my body, and I swore under my breath. I sucked in a breath as I waited for it to sink its teeth in my neck, but was utterly surprised when it didn't happen. The wolf skidded past me and into a nearby tree. Relief washed over me, but I froze when he snapped its jaws again.

I jumped to my feet and ran as fast as my legs would let me go. A burning sharp pain had replaced the achy tired feeling in my legs, and I knew I'd collapse soon. I couldn't find my cabin or even a tree I could climb. Most of the branches around me didn't dip low enough for me to reach, and honestly I don't even know if I had the strength to pull myself up anymore. I was running out of breath and options.

My ragged breathing and heavy footsteps were the only thing making noise in these woods. The woods had gone silent as I turned left and ran faster. Then I heard something that made my heart drop. Another howl. It was followed by more, and soon I couldn't tell how many there were. *I bet it's the pack!* I thought to myself. I felt so stupid walking in the dark all alone in the first place. I should have just slept in my truck, but no... I thought I could just walk home in a strange place I had never been before. *Good work, Shanely!*

My sneakers were soaked as I ran through a shallow stream. The only thing I could hear was the sound of my pounding heart, and no matter where I looked, I *couldn't* find the wolf. *Where did he go?!* I wondered as I stumbled in the creek. My clothes were quickly becoming soaked as I ran down the creek, hoping it would mask my scent, but I shivered as a breeze rolled through. This sucked. *What in the world do I do now?*

My sneakers slipped on a wet rock, and I went tumbling to the ground. My head rebounded as it slammed against a large boulder. My world shifted as I lay in the cool water, my head bleeding where I hit. I blinked, hearing the loud howl once more. As my vision began to grow dark, I wondered how everything went so wrong today. Honestly, my whole life has been nothing but one massive mistake after another. *No reason to just blame it on today*, I suppose.

This was supposed to be my escape though, my fresh start, and a chance to learn about the family I never knew. Instead, it's become the death of me— *literally*.

My eyes closed as I drifted back to this morning when I pulled my beat up RAM truck into this tiny town deep in the Washington Mountains. It was a beautiful evening, and my leg bounced anxiously as I drove the long winding road through the mountains. I was finally about to arrive after the insanely long drive from Indiana. 34 hours of nearly non-stop driving in a truck with no AC. My stomach grumbled as I searched the small gas station plastic bag I had filled with snacks for the road. I rolled my eyes when I found nothing but wrappers inside. *Doesn't matter*, I thought to myself. I was so ready to get out of the truck and stretch my legs, but I still had a

CHAPTER 1

little ways left to go according to the maps I bought at the gas station. But I was close.

I rolled down my window and inhaled a deep breath. *So this is where I'm from*, I wondered to myself. A thousand questions ran through my mind as I wondered how my life would have been had I known my family. I grew up in the foster system, bouncing from one broke home to the other, and I never knew who my family was. It wasn't until I got a call from a lawyer one day, explaining how my grandmother left me a cabin in her will. When I tried to explain that he must have the wrong person because I had no family, the lawyer cut me off and said he wasn't wrong. He and the lawyer from Diablo, Washington had painstakingly done their research, and I indeed had family. Family that knew about me enough to leave me a cabin and land in the mountains. As frustrated as I was for being cast aside like I had been, that woman saved me from the life I hated. I now have a fresh start, and I was not going to waste it.

I shook off the hallowed thoughts before it ruined the good mood I was in. *He* wasn't here, and he would never find me again. *I made sure this time.* He and everything else was in my past, and that's where they'd stay.

I took another deep breath and felt the scent of pine and thick foliage relax me to my bones. The mountain air smelled so good, and even though I had never been anywhere outside of Indiana, it just felt like home here. I smiled softly. Home. That felt more surreal to me than this whole thing really. I finally found a place that *feels* like home.

A small town came to view and I slowed the truck to take a look around. It was way smaller than I was used to, but it had a charm to it that I couldn't put my finger on. Like this place was plucked from reality, and everyone just seemed happy in their little bubble. Few heads turned my way as I drove on through, following the map to the right up the mountain further. The road made its way deeper into the mountains and was surrounded by woods on both sides. It was beautiful driving through the thick foliage, and the further I drove away from the town of Diablo, the more I realized how far away this cabin was from everything.

My grandmother lived up here alone? I wondered to myself, curious how she managed it. From what the lawyer said, she was pretty frail in her last days.

All I knew was that she had died in her sleep, and she lived her whole life in these mountains. The lawyer had very little to go on as another lawyer had originally drawn up the will for her, but anything new he uncovered, he'd send my way. There wasn't anything else in her will either. Just the cabin, and the 10 acres surrounding it, and everything was left to me with only my name and last known location. He said it took him a bit to track me down, but once he contacted the foster care system, they thankfully had a paper trail that led to my last known family, which led to me. I was surprised my foster mother even gave the lawyer my number. My guess is she assumed I was in some legal trouble and was all too happy to help out. I rolled my eyes when he told me that.

At least living up here would be quiet and safe, I thought to myself. Far from Peter who had no idea I had even left. Out of all my mistakes, he was by far the worst. How that man qualified to be an officer was beyond me. The town loved him, which baffled me. Peter was the town's beloved football captain that grew up to become a police officer. *You should just be grateful our Peter even took an interest in you.* The old biddies sure had a way of making me feel small when they'd come into the diner where I worked. Just thinking about it made me want to puke.

Good riddance.

I blinked rapidly as my mind came back to the present. *God, becoming a new Shanely was going to take some time*, I thought to myself. I made myself focus on the road then. My drive should be coming up, and I didn't want to miss it.

Another fifteen minutes later, I saw my driveway. *315 Hemingway drive*, I thought to myself as I turned left past two wolf statues that were beginning to crumble. I sat on the edge of my truck's seat, anxious to take it all in. I couldn't believe that this was all mine. Everything here belonged to me, *just me*, and I didn't have to share it with anyone. I was safe, and for the first time in my life, I felt excited for the future.

The drive was rather long, I realized. This cabin was deep in the woods,

CHAPTER 1

which meant out of sight to any prying eyes. No one would know I was even back here as there was nothing around for miles. My smile grew wider. It was perfect!

I grabbed my necklace, twirling the pendant between my fingers as I took it all in. This necklace was the only thing left to me when I was a baby, and it became sort of a fidget toy over the years. It was a simple wolf pendant and was worn thoroughly and chipped in the corner, but I didn't care. It was the only thing left of my real mother, and I never took it off. The lady from the agency, who processed my paperwork and took me in when I was first left on their doorstep, made sure it stayed with me especially during each family transfer. I always appreciated that woman for looking out for me and was crushed when she finally retired. I gripped it tightly, wondering if this cabin was where my mother grew up. I couldn't help being curious about the family I never knew, my own flesh and blood. Maybe living here would finally give me answers.

I parked my truck and slowly got out to stretch my legs. I took a moment before the small rustic cabin to appreciate the simple beauty before me. A small front porch with a wooden railing, and one main window to the right of the massive wooden door, the cabin was plain and simple. It wasn't grandiose or obscenely large. It was perfect for just me.

I cocked my head to the side when I noticed the carvings above the front door. *More wolves*, I thought to myself. *My grandmother must have a thing for wolves.* The wolves ran together in a pack above the door. Whoever did the work, they had talent.

I quickly grabbed my keys and the two bags I brought with me before bolting up the creaky steps. The door unlocked with ease, swinging wide open and clattering against the wall. I winced as the wall shook, but thankfully nothing seemed broken.

The cabin was small, only two bedrooms, a kitchenette and dining room, and a living room with a fireplace. *Unlike any home I had ever been in, that's for sure*, I thought as I remembered all the foster homes I had been before.

I dropped my bags at the front and looked around the living room. The cabin was furnished but had sheets covering the furniture and loads of dust.

So much I could see it floating in the air. It was pretty inside though and looked in decent condition. All it needed was a good cleaning, which was something I was good at.

I walked past the couch on the right and stepped right into the dining room. I ran my hand across the beautifully finished oak table with matching chairs. *This was custom made*, I thought to myself as I took a closer look at the pretty carvings on the side. Turning to the right, I saw a somewhat dated kitchen. It didn't bother me one bit though because it was *mine*. I could organize it the way I wanted to, and no one could tell me otherwise.

I paused at the sink, looking out the window behind it. A creek ran right through my back yard with wild flowers and green grass as far as the eye could see. The corners of my mouth rose as I realized something wonderful. If I didn't feel like doing the dishes that night, I could leave it for another day, and no one would blow up on me over it. I wouldn't be in trouble for skipping out on a chore because this was *my house*.

My house.

I gently tapped the counter with my fingers and turned around. Just past the kitchen on the left was a hallway, which I assumed led to the bathroom and two bedrooms. I'll check those out in a bit. I was dying to look at my backyard and quickly moved to the right of the table to open the double doors.

The view took my breath away. Nothing but trees *everywhere* and that babbling creek looked straight out of a fairy tale. *I wouldn't even need to use the white noise machine I brought*, I thought excitedly. I could just open my windows at night and listen to the water move down the creek bed. I inhaled deeply, filling my lungs with as much fresh air as they could handle. It was the end of summer, and the weather was beautiful.

I looked around and saw a swinging bench that sat off to the left. Walking over, I double checked the cable, making sure it wouldn't break under my weight and plopped down. I had a thousand things to do before nightfall, but I just wanted to enjoy this moment. *Just a little longer at least.* I pushed off with my feet, listening to the swing creak above me. I closed my eyes and let my mind wander to the many things on my task list. I barely had

CHAPTER 1

any savings left, and I needed a job. That would be first on my list of things to do, but at least I didn't have a house payment. I owned the house and the land, so it was a huge thing off my list. But the utilities were another issue. And food. And clothes, and anything else I might need like a new phone. I had to ditch my old one when I came here.

Suddenly, a twig snapped loudly, causing me to jump in my seat. My eyes shot open, and I scanned the backyard as my heart rate rose, but there was nothing there.

I rolled my eyes. *It was probably just an animal*, I thought to myself. I lived in town with Peter, so all I heard was constant traffic and train horns when they went by frequently. This was going to take some getting used to.

"I better start getting used to hearing all sorts of stuff," I muttered to myself. My eyes darted back and forth across the yard nonetheless. I couldn't shake the uptight feeling in my chest so I rose and went back inside.

I clicked the lock in place before looking at my watch. It was already 7:37 pm. I groaned loudly, realizing my mistake. Unpacking will have to wait because I needed to make my way *back* to town. *Such a waste of gas*, I thought as my stomach grumbled again. I should have just stopped before coming here.

As I passed by the mirror hanging on the wall, I stilled when I saw the girl staring back at me. *She's a sight for sore eyes*, I thought to myself. I frowned, looking closer at my appearance. My once long, beautifully red, curly hair was now dull and desperately needing a trim from all the split-ends and damage done to it over the years. At least my eyes were still their vivid bright green. I always though they were the only real pretty thing about me. My heart-shaped face had a defined widow's peak, and my body was rather thin. *A little too thin*, I thought. My face fell when I remembered why. Another reason I wanted nothing more to do with Peter.

I slowly reached up to touch the faint bruise on my neck. The yellowish-blue tint was the last noticeable signs left of Peter, and I couldn't wait to finally be rid of them. I tucked my hair behind my ears, noticing I needed new earrings at some point too. Mine were getting old and soon would be turning my lobes green if I wasn't careful. My daith was pierced as well as my helix and tragus. It was my one chance at rebelling growing up, but looking back on that, it was just silly. I still liked having them though.

I sighed heavily as I stepped away from the mirror. *I could be pretty someday*, I thought to myself, *just not right now*. Maybe now that I finally found some peace. Until then, I just looked dull and damaged.

I locked my front door as I left my beloved cabin and jumped in my truck to head back the way I came. I tried to focus on memorizing the roads I took, which thankfully was fairly simple heading back into town. I couldn't keep using this paper map.

My gas light flicked on as I came into town. *Another issue I needed to deal with*, I thought. Not tonight though. I decided to stop at the store first and the door chimed as I walked in. I grabbed toilet paper, toothpaste, and shampoo. I went ahead and grabbed paper plates and silverware too, seeing how I would have to save up for real plates. I grabbed a couple of snacks that would keep in the truck and a case of water as well with some cleaning supplies. I bit my lower lip as I looked at my cart. In reality, I needed so much more. But it would have to do for now. I sighed. *I've been through worse*, I thought. But the total made me *cringe*. The town of Diablo was expensive.

My stomach grumbled again as I placed the bags inside my truck. I looked across the road and noticed a bar across the street. It seemed to be the only place still opened, so I made my way over hoping they sold food too. Otherwise, it was potato chips for me tonight.

The Den, as it was called, seemed to fit its name. The dimly lit bar was small but cozy and not to mention extremely crowded. *Must be the place to be in this town*, I thought, trying to see past the crowd of people. I spotted an empty bar stool in the far back corner and made my way over. A loud mouth slammed into me and I barely caught myself in time to keep from face-planting.

"Sorry, miss," he grumbled, his eyes narrowing as he took a deep breath. He reeked of sweat and something else, so I tried breathing through my mouth instead.

CHAPTER 1

"It's fine," I replied as I brushed myself off and moved past him. You'd think it wouldn't be too difficult to just look down where you're moving but most here seemed to just look right over my head.

I crinkled my nose as the many scents that filled my nose. I couldn't even separate the foul smells from one another, it was so overwhelming. Strong earthy smells clashed with the smell of girly perfume and nasty sweat. My sense of smell had never been this great before. I scrunched my nose up, debating whether or not to just leave, but my stomach took first place over my nose. I rather deal with a headache than hungry pains.

Trying not to breathe through my nose, I sat down and grabbed a menu off the counter. It showed typical finger foods you'd find at a bar, which was perfect because I wasn't a picky eater, and I was more so relieved to see the prices here weren't too bad. The last thing I wanted was a high-end restaurant.

"What can I get ya?"

The deep voice startled me and I dropped the menu to find a young, stocky man smiling at me. He seemed almost familiar, with his gorgeous smile and pretty soft blue eyes. His medium brown hair, that was tapered down the sides, with a decent size beard on his face gave this warmth about him that seemed pleasant and kind. The stranger cleared his throat, and my cheeks heat when I realized I had just been staring at him instead of answering like a normal person.

"Oh, I ah—" my voice trailed off as I quickly looked through the menu. "I'll take the cheeseburger with fries and a coke, please."

"Are you sure you don't want a beer or something? It is a bar after all," he replied with a chuckle as he punched in my order on a keypad.

"No, I'm good," I said, placing the menu back. "I honestly don't drink much. I'm just here because you seem to be the only place open right now."

"Ah yeah, that's a small town for ya. The weekends have more places that are opened later in the night, but on a Wednesday, it's just us. My name's Caleb."

"Shanely," I replied as I shook his hand. He cocked his head to the side.

"Shanely?" he said slowly. "Now, that's a unique name."

"Yeah, I get that a lot," I replied, chuckling.

"Well Shanely, are you just passing through or are you staying?" he asked, leaning on the counter. I relaxed in my seat.

"I actually just moved here," I answered truthfully. "My grandmother left me her cabin, so I'm here to stay."

"Really?" he asked as his brows furrowed. "Who's your grandmother?"

"Her name was Willow McCoy. She owned the cabin about 15-20 minutes from here," I answered. His eyes widened the minute I said her name, and my stomach did a little flip. *Is he part of my family?* I thought anxiously.

"Willow McCoy?? You're her granddaughter?" he asked in disbelief.

"I guess," I replied cautiously. *Maybe I made a mistake*, I thought to myself. "I never knew Willow until I got a call from her lawyer. Did you know her very well?"

Caleb looked a little uneasy as he rubbed the back of his head, his lips pursed together as if he didn't know how to answer me. He half turned away from me, his gaze roaming the bar like he'd rather be anywhere other than here right now, and I was confused by the sudden change. *Did I offend him or something?*

"You could say that," he muttered quietly. "The McCoy family owns half the town and most of the surrounding woods. Everyone knew Willow honestly."

"What?"

My eyes nearly bulged out of my face, and I slumped in my seat. *My family was loaded?* I thought as I tried to process this new tidbit. She didn't leave any money, and the lawyers never said anything about her heritage or owning half the town! My anger rose as a single question took over my entire head space. Why did they give me away then?

My gaze drifted to the counter of the bar. I couldn't pry my eyes away. I couldn't even begin to ask Caleb where my family was because it was clear he knew. *Do I even want to meet them?* My stomach twisted into tight knots as I debated what to do.

"Yeah... You should stop by the McCoy's compound. I'm sure they would love to meet you! They have a huge family, which I guess means now so do

CHAPTER 1

you," he replied with a sad smile.

"I don't know about that. They may not want me around," I muttered, twiddling my thumbs together. *They have the resources to care for me. They must not have wanted me for a reason*, I thought. *But what about the cabin?*

"I wouldn't assume that," Caleb said, grabbing a glass to clean. "The McCoy's treat their own well."

"They gave me away," I said with a clipped tone. His eyes widened and guilt crept in. I took a deep breath before asking, "and do they not treat others well?"

"I didn't say that," he stammered, rubbing the back of his head again. The device on his hip buzzed. "They, uh, well— they just aren't super *cozy* with others outside their family is all."

My eyes narrowed. *Were they just some snooty rich folks who looked down on everyone or something?* I thought, leaning forward on the counter.

"You don't like the McCoys," I said, watching his every expression, "do you?"

"Oh no," he stammered, looking around nervously, "it's not like that."

His eyes darted back and forth across the room, and I turned around to see who he kept looking at, but no one stood out to me. The patrons here all seemed preoccupied with their own lives, so I turned back to Caleb.

He sighed. "My family and the McCoys just don't seem to get along very well is all. We tend to just keep to our own sides and don't really mix. You just didn't look like a McCoy, and being new, it threw me. You must take after your dad, I guess."

"I wouldn't know," I said, shrugging solemnly. "I didn't know either of my parents."

He frowned, giving me a sad look. "Well, if your grandmother was Willow, then your mother was her only child, Mercedes."

My eyes widened as I sat up in my seat abruptly. "You knew my mother?"

"Well, I knew *of* her. She left the mountains years ago, but that's about it. Like I said, we're not exactly cozy with the McCoys, but they never said why she left," he replied. The device on his hip buzzed again.

I slumped back in my chair, repeating her name over and over in my head. I knew my mother's name. I finally *knew* her name. My mother was Mercedes McCoy.

The door to the back kitchen flung open, and a waitress with short sandy-blond hair that just barely touched her shoulders came over with my food. She pushed it my way, glaring at Caleb.

"You can flirt later, Caleb. It's busy tonight, and we've got four people waiting for drinks, and that's not including all those people in the back who still need their order taken. Plus, the band is late and…" her voice trailed off when she laid her brown eyes on me. She took a deep breath, scowling and I slowly looked down at myself.

Did I smell bad?

"Octavia, this is Shanely. She's Willow McCoy's granddaughter," Caleb said, giving her a pointed look.

Octavia's eyes practically bugged out of her head as she looked at me. I gave a sheepish smile and waved. She didn't return it.

"Willow didn't have a granddaughter," she replied coldly.

"The lawyers would disagree," I said chuckling, trying to lighten this dark mood she brought with her. "I never knew her, but she left me a cabin not far from here. I just moved in today. It's nice to meet you, Octavia."

I extended my hand out to her, but she just stared at it. Her small nose scrunched as if disgusted with me, and I slowly lowered my hand. *Wow— I was off to a great start making friends here.*

"Welcome to Diablo," she finally said. "Get back to work, Caleb."

I blinked as she stormed into the back room. She *hated* me— and I didn't understand why.

Caleb sighed. A hint of pink appeared just below his eyes. *He's embarrassed*, I thought to myself.

"Ignore her," he said. "She just takes forever to accept new people, but it was really nice to meet you, Shanely. I have to get back to work, but you're welcome here anytime. Don't let anyone tell you otherwise, okay? If you have any problems getting in here, just let me know, and I'll fix it."

"Yeah, sure. Good to meet you too," I said quietly. I pursed my lips together as I realized what he said. *Who would tell me I wasn't allowed at*

CHAPTER 1

the bar? I mean this wasn't an exclusive place or anything. Was this a part of the whole feud thing they have going on between the families? I may be a McCoy by blood, but that didn't mean I was about to join in. I wasn't apart of this fight. I just wanted to make friends and learn about where I came from. Not join whatever was going on between everyone.

Caleb gave me a small nod and disappeared in the back as I mulled over the entire interaction. I ate my burger as my mind raced. Music played in the background, but I couldn't focus on it, let alone even understand the words. One of the speakers must be blown because it sounded strange, but the patrons didn't seem to mind. Lots of people had already started dancing in this too tiny bar. It was a sight to see, but I had no desire to join in. I had two left feet, but even if I was an amazing dancer, I just couldn't bring myself to try. My mind just felt muddled with everything, and learning more about my long lost family weighed on me. I had always dreamed of getting a chance to meet them, but my stomach twisted in knots whenever I thought about it. I had too many questions, and what if I didn't like their answers? Nausea crept in, making my mouth water, and I set down what was left of my burger.

Suddenly, a tall man plopped down on the seat next to mine with a smile on his face. He extended his legs out behind my stool, cornering me in, and my eyebrow rose slightly.

"Hi, I'm Patrick. You're new around here," he said with cheesy smile, "aren't you gorgeous?"

I nodded my head. *Is he a long-lost family member?* I wondered as I studied him closely.

He had a military haircut, but he didn't look quite like a soldier. His sandy-blonde hair and steel colored eyes seemed to blend in with the masses here. No beard, unlike most of the men in this bar, but the way he sat screamed some kind of service. I recognized the stance he took. The way he casually leaned back in his seat to keep an eye on the room while he focused on me. It was just giving me flashbacks of memories I didn't want to think about.

"Got a name?" he asked, grinning wide. His gaze went up and down my body, sending goosebumps up my arm. Warning bells were going off, and I shoved my basket of food away.

"Shanely," I replied with a quiet voice. Anxiety swelled in my chest. Soon, I wouldn't be able to breathe if I didn't remove myself from situation quickly. I could feel it already. The shortness of breath, the pain and stress— it was time to leave for the night.

"That's a pretty name," he said, scooting closer. My gaze dropped to his leg, which was getting awfully close to mine now. "Where are you staying?"

"Not far," I replied as I dug in my pocket for cash, "just the other side of town."

I hope Caleb didn't mind I paid this way, but he wasn't coming out of the back, and I *needed* to go. I wasn't looking for another relationship, and my stomach twisted as a sly smile crept up this guy's face.

"Interesting. Well, welcome to Diablo! Can I buy you a drink before you head out?" he asked casually. The hair on the back of my neck stood.

"I don't drink actually," I replied firmly. My heart pounded in my chest, "but thanks anyways."

Patrick frowned, and I shoved my stool away from the counter. He moved, but not enough for me to pass.

"I should go," I said. His legs were still blocking my path.

"Already? I was hoping to get to know one another," he pleaded with me. Anxiety filled my chest when I noticed the badge on his hip. *Not again.*

"No, thank you. I really should be—"

Patrick grabbed my hand and panic rippled through me. My eyes widened when he gently rubbed my hand with his thumb. "Come on, sweetheart. It's just one drink."

"Let go. I don't want to have a drink right now," I replied, pulling my hand back rather firmly. He frowned again when I stepped over his legs and made my way towards the door. I stumbled on my footing as the room spun slightly. My anxiety grew, and I forced one foot in front of the other.

"You know most girls *like* dating an officer," he hollered. I could hear his heavy steps chasing after me.

I snorted as I left the bar and started towards my truck. *Yeah, that was the wrong thing to say to me buddy*, I thought to myself. The sun had fully set

CHAPTER 1

now, but the breeze was still warm. I scurried to the crosswalk.

"Seriously? You won't let me buy you one drink?" he asked loudly. The few standing outside for a smoke turned to watch the two of us now.

I gritted my teeth as my eyes rolled. He was *still* asking to buy me a drink. I crossed my arms and turned, waiting for the light to turn so I could leave.

"C'mon! What's the worst that could happen?" he asked as the light flashed.

I lifted my leg to move but stilled. This was *my* fresh start. The old Shanely would have run. She wouldn't say a word out of fear of upsetting him and causing a bigger problem, but I was a new person here in Diablo, and I needed to *act* like it.

Patrick looked annoyed when I turned to face him. "Look Patrick, you're right—"

Surprise flashed across his face, and that wicked grin returned. His cocky arrogance returned in full force when he interrupted, "I'm glad you're reconsidering—"

I put my hand up to stop him. "No, you *misunderstand*. You are right when you said most girls probably liked dating an officer. However, I am not like most girls, and I will never date another cop again. In fact, I don't plan on dating anyone! I'm perfectly happy spending the rest of my life *entirely* alone, so please just accept my answer for what it is."

I looked both ways and quickly crossed the street instead of waiting for the crosswalk. Pride filled my chest and a slow grin appeared on my face.

I hopped in the driver's seat and pulled out of the parking space. Officer Patrick stared at me as I drove away, but I ignored him, feeling rather empowered and bold.

That smile widened the further I drove. I liked this new Shanely.

I think I'm going to keep her.

Chapter 2

The town's main road slowly disappeared in my rear-view mirror, and I was back in the safety of the woods. My confidence cracked just a little when I realized I left my map at home. *Crap—*

I flicked on my brights, lighting up the dark and somewhat menacing looking woods. The roads looked so different now that it was dark. *God, I was going to get lost*, I thought as my anxiety came back.

Pain slowly began to build behind my eyes, and I wiped a layer of sweat from my brow. *Eww*, I thought as I rolled the window down. A nice breeze cooled my skin, and I rolled my shoulders trying to get my body to loosen up, when a chilling howl filled the air. My foot hit the brake. *That sounded really loud and really close*, I thought as I scanned the road ahead. It made sense that there were wolves in these mountains, but knowing they were so close was a little unnerving.

I pushed the gas when my head began to pound. Trying to rub my temples to ease the pain, I blinked as I looked at the road. Everything suddenly looked blurry. I blinked furiously, trying to clear my vision but nothing helped. The pain in my head intensified. *God, I was going to throw up*, I thought as my mouth watered.

I hit the brake again and clutched the side of my head as sharp pain pierced my skull. My heart began to pound in my chest. I *had* to stop. I shouldn't drive—

Suddenly, a large brown blur flew across the road in front of my truck, and I swerved hard to miss it. I screamed as I flew forward, my seat belt saving me from flying through my windshield, when the truck hit something large

CHAPTER 2

on the ground before finally skidding to a stop. I groaned as my body laid against the window.

Silence filled the woods once more, and I began to breathe in and out slowly. My jittery limbs regained control before I finally opened my eyes to assess the damage. I turned the truck off, my eyes widening when I saw the white smoke coming from the hood. *That can't be good*, I thought.

The dizziness subsided, and my vision slowly returned to normal. I rubbed my head, grateful the pain seemed to have stopped too and checked the rest of me. Other than some bruises, I looked okay. A small cut on my forehead but nothing major. I leaned my head back against the seat and took a deep breath. *I cannot believe my first night here, I crashed my truck.*

The blur that ran out in front of me came to mind then. *Did I actually hit it?* I wondered. Guilt twisted my stomach, and I unbuckled my seat belt.

I slid out of my truck and made my way to the front. Thankfully, there wasn't a dead animal but I cringed when I saw my front end. A nasty looking dent was on my front bumper, and my passenger tire was completely flat. The rim was bent too, along with whatever I broke inside the engine bay. There was *no way* I was going to get my truck home tonight, and I groaned loudly.

I kicked the tire, frustrated with how my first night was going. I didn't have the money to fix something like this. *How was I supposed to work and live here if I couldn't drive myself around?* It wasn't like home was near—anywhere. Anger coursed through my veins as I glared at my broken truck. I clenched my fists together. My fresh start was *not* getting ruined.

Another howl sounded, and I looked around. Fixing my truck would have to wait. I had more pressing matters to deal with like how was I getting home tonight. I scanned the road, sighing when not a single pair of headlights appeared.

I leaned against the truck, contemplating my options. I was nearly home, so walking all the way back to town wasn't appealing. Caleb said most places were closed after 8, so I doubt there was anyone around to help tow my truck anyways. I just needed to make it home and figure out the rest in the morning.

Leaves rustled behind me, and I slowly turned my head, trying to see into the thick foliage. I couldn't see much of anything with how dark everything was and then a twig snapped. The hair on the back of my neck stood up, and I got the feeling I wasn't alone anymore.

Nope, I'm done, I thought to myself. My heart started to race when I yanked my door open and grabbed my keys. Logic was trying to convince me I was hearing things, but I couldn't shake the feeling I was being watched. Another howl sounded far in the distance, and I moved my feet faster.

Reaching into my glove box, I grabbed my flashlight. It came right to life, and I sagged in relief. *At least I won't being stumbling my way home*, I thought as I scribbled a message on an old receipt.

Hopping out of my truck, I locked the doors and slapped the note to the windshield. I wrote my address down with my name and briefly explained what happened. I planned to come back in the morning to retrieve my truck, and I begged them not to fine it. I couldn't afford the ticket if they did.

I straightened my jacket before clicking on the light. *Here we go*, I thought and started the long walk back home. I hustled my feet along the pavement, eager to put more and more distance from myself to whatever was out there. My mind wandered to the strange events of the night. I've had plenty of headaches before, but never something like that. I seemed fine now. Not a drop of pain.

Time passed slowly, and other than an occasional howl, it was quiet. My body relaxed too, which I just chalked up to being a nervous ninny. I rolled my eyes. I was just jumpy and gun shy from before. *Nothing was out there. Nothing was chasing me.*

A twig snapped, and I stilled. I turned the flashlight behind me, scanning the treeline carefully. A low growl filled the air, making the hairs on my neck stand. I held my breath, listening as I searched the woods. I took a step back.

Leaves crunched again, but I couldn't figure out where the sound was coming from. It echoed through the air, and I turned in a circle as my heart raced. *Something was out there—*

I wasn't alone.

CHAPTER 2

Forget this, I thought anxiously. *I'll sleep in my truck.*

I took off down the road, when suddenly a large brown wolf stepped out of the shadows. My eyes widened as I skidded to a stop. It held my terrified gaze as it barred its teeth at me.

This wolf was *big*. I never thought they were this massive in real life, but it was nearly eye level with me. I always just pictured the size of a dog, but he was *way* bigger. *I must have stumbled into his territory*, I thought as I carefully took a step back. It snapped its jaws, saliva dripping from its teeth, and I stilled.

The flashlight in my hand shook as we stared at one another. The only option I had was losing him in the woods. He was blocking the path to my truck, and despite the odds of me surviving, it was better than nothing.

The wolf snarled, and I bolted into the woods as his paws hit the pavement. I shot through the brush and ran faster than I had ever gone before. My heart raced with every step, and I could feel him directly behind me. Every snap of its jaw sounded like it was breaking its own teeth. I didn't want to think about what those teeth would do wrapped around my neck. I didn't know exactly how wolves hunted, but I knew they always went for the throat.

"Help!" I shouted, hoping there were more homes up this mountain. "Someone help me!"

The wolf snarled again, the sound deafening being so close, and I sucked in a breath to keep from screaming.

I slid in the grass as I turned and landed on my right hip. The wolf shot over me, slamming into the tree. It didn't seem to faze the wolf though as he bounded back on his paws and charged towards me again. I scurried to my feet and ran through the thick brush, getting scratched by the thorns along the way. My legs were jello by the time I splashed through the creek.

Another howl pierced the air, and my heart dropped. It sounded so close, despite my heart pounding in my ears. More than one howl filled the air then, and I knew the rest of the pack had found me. It was why this wolf toyed with me. It was pushing me towards its pack.

My foot slipped, and I tumbled to the creek bed. My hands shot out to catch myself, but I wasn't quick enough. My head slammed against a large boulder, and everything went dark after that.

Chapter 3

Something touched my leg.

I sucked in a deep breath as I slowly came too. My head pounded so badly, I felt like I was going to throw up. I groaned as I slowly tried to sit up, wincing when I put pressure on my left shoulder. *Well that hurts*, I thought to myself, and I rolled the other way.

What happened?

My head spun, and I didn't dare open my eyes just yet. I was mortified that I had somehow gotten myself into this position in the first place, and now I probably had a concussion to top off everything else. This whole evening was nothing but one mistake after another.

Something furry brushed against my legs again, pulling me from my thoughts. *The wolf...* I stilled as it rubbed against my arm. My chest heaved, and I forced myself to open one eye, seeing nothing but darkness. I blinked. *Why aren't I dead?* I thought as my heart began to race.

I lifted my good arm and touched my head, wincing when I touched a painful spot and saw bright red on my fingers when I pulled my hand away.

"Great," I muttered, "just great."

I groaned and used my right arm to slowly sit up. My left just didn't want to work. *Must be broken or dislocated*, I thought. My head spun as I straightened, and I slowly breathed in and out through my mouth until the world righted itself.

"Definitely have a concussion," I muttered. *God, the freaking hospital bill I was going to get from this.*

The forest was still, and the cool water from the creek drifted by like nothing happened. *It was still very dark out,* I thought to myself as I looked at the night sky, wondering how long I was actually unconscious for. Another question in the endless ones I had over tonight. *But the biggest question was; where was the wolf?*

It chased me through the woods, hunted me in the night, only to give up when I slipped and fell unconscious? I was no wildlife expert, but even I knew that made zero sense.

I took a deep breath, grateful for my miracle at least. A breeze swept by, and I shivered. *This wasn't good*, I thought as I looked down at my clothes. I was soaking wet and freezing. *And lost,* I thought as I pursed my lips together. *Can't forget I have no idea where I am, nor do I know idea how to get out of these woods.*

I spat out a laugh, clutching my head when I did. I knew the cabin and escaping my old life was too good to be true. *This...* I laughed again as I took in my situation. *This was more like it!* The universe was clearly balancing the scales since it gave me such a win earlier.

Suddenly, movement flashed from the corner of my eye and fear gripped my heart again. I wasn't alone like I thought. My eyes strained against the darkness as I scanned the tree line for movement again. My right hand slowly reaching down to grab a rock.

And then I saw eyes.

Three large wolves stepped out from the brush. They were *massive* wolves. Definitely bigger than the first wolf that chased me and none had that dark brown coat either. I held my breath and sat in utter silence, waiting for what I could only assume would come next. Death was imminent, that much was clear, and it was going to be a painful one at that. *They must have smelled the blood on me*, I thought.

The wolves slowly began to circle me as blood continued to trickle down my face. I didn't dare move to wipe away the blood. I was terrified to move *period*. They weren't snarling at me, and I didn't want to startle them or piss them off in any way. Warm blood hit the ground next to me, and the wolf on my left looked down to it. He scented the air, his lip curling slightly.

My heart thundered in my chest. I knew they could hear it and scent my fear, but they kept a good distance between us for some reason. They continued to look at one another, making odd sounds to each other like they were communicating. My eyes narrowed. *These three were as cautious as I am.*

The two sandy brown wolves stepped into the moonlight. My eyes darted between them. *They were nearly identical,* I thought to myself, and my eyes widened. *And they were coming closer.* I raised my hand, exposing the rock in my palm.

"Stay away!" I hollered, and the wolves froze. I blinked. *Did they really just listen to me?*

The jet black wolf in the middle moved now. *This wolf was beautifully dark,* I thought. In fact, it blended almost seamlessly into the shadows around it. I kept my eyes wide open, afraid if I closed my eyes even just to blink, I'd lose it in the dark.

One thing I realized, the brown wolf who tried to eat me was *nowhere* to be found.

The sandy brown wolf on my right yipped to the others, but they just continued to watch me. *Why weren't they attacking me?* I thought as I tried to scooch away down the creek bank. I swored, tucking my bad arm as close to me as I could, and used my right hand.

The sandy brown wolf on my left ran around to block my retreat, and I stilled. We were eye level with each other, and he was mere feet away. Close enough that if he lunged, I'd be a dead girl. He barred his teeth, giving no sound, but it was menacing even without the snarl. My heart thundered in my chest as I threw the rock.

"Go away!" I yelled, and he darted to the side. The rock splashed on the edge of the embankment. I grabbed another rock and held it high. Ready to throw it if either one took a step towards me.

Being loud and abrasive worked on scaring black bears. *Maybe it would work on wolves too?* The black wolf yipped.

My eyes widened when suddenly all three laid down in front of me. I dropped the rock in my hand, startled by their behavior. *They are not typical wolves*, I thought to myself. *Unless they're just used to people?* I took a deep breath, feeling every ounce of pain in my body when I did.

The jet-black wolf stood slowly and took a step towards me. My breath caught in my chest when the other wolf gave a low growl. But he wasn't looking at me, I realized. No... He was looking at the black wolf on its paws. Like he was *frustrated* with her.

The black wolf bared its teeth as she passed by the other wolf still laying on the ground. She softened when she turned back to me.

What in the world?

Adrenaline shot through my veins, and I struggled to control my breathing. My body swayed as the wolf drew closer. I couldn't take my eyes off her as she cautiously scented my feet. Her snout touched my legs, and I held my breath. I expected her to sink her teeth in my leg, but what I did not expect was for bones to crunch.

But they weren't *my* bones.

The black wolf's body slowly cracked and twisted around, moving her body into a different shape. Her jet black fur receded beneath pale skin, and when the wolf stood on its *human* legs, my heart stopped. The dark wolf turned into an older woman with long flowy hair, and my jaw dropped.

She opened her mouth to speak, but my eyes rolled to the back of my head, and I fell into darkness.

* * *

I wiggled my nose as something gently tickled my nostrils and moved my hand to shove it away. It was hot in here, and I rolled to my side. I was buried under a warm, fur blanket that covered my entire body. *No wonder I'm so warm*, I thought to myself as I gradually woke myself up. I chuckled to myself as I thought about the dream I had last night. *It was so freaking crazy.* I nearly died at the hands of freaking *werewolves* of all things. My wild imagination was running amuck again, and a slow smile curved on my face. I always loved my crazy dreams growing up. It usually was always fun, and frankly a better place than my reality, but this dream— it seemed so real.

I slowly rose my arms above my head, stretching my back that was currently in a kink. As my eyes fluttered open, my smile fell. The dry clothes that I currently wore didn't belong to me, and my eyes slowly drifted around the room. This plain room had a fire crackling to my left and other than a few closed doors and the couch I was currently laying on, there was nothing else here. I didn't recognize this place. *This wasn't my cabin—*

The werewolf. *Oh, God—*

"Welcome back."

I jumped, my heart leaping out of my chest as I tossed the blanket aside and shot to my feet. The older woman crossed the room with her hands gently raised, and my eyes widened when I recognized her. *The black werewolf.*

It was real, I thought as my heart thudded in my chest. *My dream was freaking real!* My chest heaved but no air would fill my lungs. My frantic heart scurried to catch up to the rest of me as my mind raced with a thousand different questions. *Those things shouldn't exist right?!* I thought anxiously, but I couldn't deny what I saw. *How? How is this even possible?!*

My eyes darted around the room, looking for a way out. I don't know why she kidnapped me, but I wasn't going down without a fight. I rolled my shoulders, stilling when I realized my body was miraculously healed. *How?* I thought as I scrambled to make sense of anything. *I should tell someone. I should alert the authorities and tell them— and tell them what?* A heaviness hit my chest when I realized no one would believe me. No matter what I'd say, they wouldn't believe it. Because werewolves shouldn't exist.

The woman took another small step towards me as I gently lifted my hand to my head. *No wound, no blood. No pain in my shoulder.* She took another step, and I clenched my fists together. Concern knitted her brow, and she frowned deeply.

I should be yelling. I should scream until my voice gave out for someone to come help me, but every time I opened my mouth, the words just wouldn't come out. It didn't help that she didn't say anything either. Her eyes would just gloss over every so often like she was high or something, and the waiting in silence was just killing me. *What did she even want? Was she going to kill me now that I knew her secret? Maybe that's what she's doing with her eyes. Maybe she's calling for backup.*

"Calm down, child," the woman finally said. "Just breathe. Everything will be explained for what you saw tonight, but you're safe here."

Her voice was kinder than I imagined. My brows furrowed as I watched her slowly make her way to the other end of the couch. I held my breath as she sat down, patting the couch beside her.

The door isn't blocked—

I bolted for it when a deep growl filled the room. I skidded to a stop, my heart pounding as I looked for another werewolf. *God, we're not alone—*

The strange woman was faster than I expected though. While my attention was on where the freaking growl came from, she suddenly gripped my hand tightly. When our skin touched, my anxiety and fear drained away. My eyelids furiously blinked, trying to make sense of what was happening as my body relaxed with her touch. *She didn't seem so scaring now.*

She pulled me back to the couch, and I let go of the breath I had been holding. My eyes sluggishly drifted from her to our hands intertwined. Her touch seemed to *soothe* me somehow. I felt *good. Better than I had in years actually.*

When I looked back to her, I realized her once soft, blue eyes were now a bright, gold color. Solid gold. It should freak me out, yet in this moment, I didn't care. *They were pretty.*

"There," she said with a grin. "Are you feeling better?"

I simply nodded; my voice unable to work. *Am I high? Is this what it feels like to be high?*

"Good," she said, pulling me from my thoughts. "Now, can you tell me why we found you in the middle of the woods like that?"

I slumped back in my seat. "I don't know."

The lady frowned again.

"Let me start over. My name is Cassia, and those two over there are my older twin brothers, Ash and Aspen. They were with me when I found you in the woods."

CHAPTER 3

My head drifted to the right, and sure enough, two older males sat in the dark at the table in the back corner. *I didn't even see them before.* They blended in with the shadows so well, but now I knew where the growl came from.

The brothers looked a lot like Cassia. All with dark brown hair, and they looked to be in their 50's if I had to guess. The men were nearly identical, but some of their features were different. The one on the left was broader in the shoulders while the one on the right was taller. It was the only major difference I could see from here. The hair on their head was short and both had short clean beards. Cassia had long, beautiful, straight hair and seemed to be aging well. She was taller than me but looked to be about about average height and wore simple clothes.

"What's your name?"

I looked back to Cassia. "Shanely. Shanely Thomas. You're a werewolf, aren't you?"

The taller brother sighed. "Cassia, I told you not to shift in front of her. It's against the rules. How are we going to fix this?"

She glared at him. "She was passing out and was going to hit her head again. I wasn't going to let her come to anymore harm. Not after she had clearly gone through something, which I don't need to remind you both that it happened on our land."

Anger spread across his face, and I held my breath. *Would they be mad that I trespassed? I didn't mean to*, I thought to myself, and I suddenly wondered if the wolf that was after me before was a werewolf or not. *Maybe that's why he was after me— because I trespassed into its territory.* My mind ran amuck then. I began to question everything in my life because this was the stuff of fairy tales. *What other humans have I met that wore sheep's clothing too?* As I felt myself start to panic again, the racing heart and jittery nerves were suddenly pulled away from me once more. I slowly looked back at the strange woman. *What was she doing to me?!*

"Plus, you can't deny the pull towards her. She doesn't smell like a human anyways." Cassia turned back to me, and I nearly dropped my jaw. *I'm not a freaking werewolf!*

"No, I am not a werewolf," Cassia said as another wave of calm washed over me.

"But I saw you turn from a wolf to a person! I know I wasn't seeing things!" I practically shouted, letting my fear come through my voice. Every time my heart began to race, her eyes glowed gold, and it was suddenly gone. *She was doing something to me!* I thought as I tried to pull my hand away. She held on tightly, her eyes glowing brighter, and my body felt sluggish again. I was suddenly *exhausted*.

"I know, I know. You aren't seeing things, sweetie, but I'm not a werewolf. I'm a wolf shifter," she replied.

"Isn't that the same thing?" I asked, my eyes blinking slowly.

"Hardly! Werewolves are just made up stories invented from sightings of us long ago. People couldn't explain what they saw or felt threatened by us, so they created stories to justify destroying our kind. Very little truth is in those stories, and soon they became just that. Stories, and movies, and books, and none of it's true. It's all rather comical, if you ask me."

"What is true then?"

I refused to close my eyes. I was more curious than I should be honestly, but I wanted answers to what I saw. The stocky brother turned his head to the side as if studying me. He almost looked impressed, but by what I did not know. I was a nobody, and I just wanted to go home. *I just wasn't sure where that was anymore.*

"We are called shifters, and we are just a different race living among the humans. We were born with the gift or ability to transform into a wolf while very few shifters are changed. That takes a very special kind of bite though. The wolf must conscientiously trying to spread the wolf gene for it to work. It's like a poison that coats our teeth, and that's what changes the human's blood and DNA around. It makes room for a wolf to be present. Our pack does not change humans though as it is very dangerous—"

"You're getting off topic now," the stocky man said, and Cassia sighed.

"We belong to a fairly large pack in these mountains, and we keep our distance from humans as much as possible. It's safer that way for us, but there is no truth to the moon being what draws out our wolves or silver being able to harm us. We are simply different, Shanely."

I stayed quiet for some time, processing all she just dumped on me. The twins shifted in their seats uncomfortably, and I understood how they felt. No one seemed to know really what to do with each other it seemed. I reached for my necklace and rubbed the pendant as I thought. *This all just felt unreal to me.* Like I'd wake up any minute and laugh over my latest wild dream, but no matter what I did, I wouldn't wake up.

This was real.

"Now that I've answered some questions for you, I need you to answer some of mine. Can you tell me what happened to you?"

Tears slowly filled my eyes as I thought back to earlier. "I don't know. I moved into my grandmother's cabin and needed food, so I went to the bar called the Den. When I left, I just felt super sick and dizzy, and then something big and brown bolted in front of my truck, causing me to swerve, and I crashed. I destroyed my truck's front end, so I tried walking home, but that wolf chased me into the woods before I could find my driveway. I slipped on a rock and woke up to all of you."

"A wolf? You sure you were chased by a wolf and not a bear or something?" the tall twin asked as he marched across the room.

"No, it was a wolf. I'm sure of it," I replied, and they both looked at each other.

"Can you tell me what it looked like?" he asked.

"I don't know. It was dark, and he was just large. Maybe dark brown colored, but why? What does that matter?" I asked.

"Crap, Cassia. That's like more than half the wolves in our pack. How are we supposed to deal with this?" the taller twin asked. "Unless it's a rogue, but then that creates a whole different set of problems."

"What's she doing on our land anyways?" the other asked, his voice gruff and surly.

"It doesn't matter what she was doing, Ash. What matters is who tried to harm her. We'll need to speak to the Alpha before deciding how to proceed," Cassia responded.

"Who's the Alpha?" I asked, curiosity getting the better of me again.

She smiled. "My mate, or husband, in human's eyes. He's our leader while I act as second in command, so to speak. Our entire pack listens to him, and he decides our laws and solves issues that come up. We need to discuss what happened to you, but I also want to talk to him about you in general. There's something about you I just can't figure out, but I promise you the wolf that attacked you will not get away with this. We do not harm others whether they are pack or human."

"Wait, what's wrong with me?!" I asked in a panicked voice.

Her eyes flashed gold, and my anxiety left as she said, "Oh child, nothing's wrong. Let's just meet with Cain and see what he thinks first. I'll explain everything then."

"How are you doing that?" I asked, watching her gold eyes return to blue.

"Some shifters have abilities, Shanely. Unique abilities to themselves alone. My ability is healing, whether it is emotional or physical. I healed your injuries when Ash brought you here, but right now I'm just helping you remain calm. I can feel you've been through a lot, and that's not including what happened tonight."

Shame filled my face, and I looked away. Thankfully, she didn't pry, and I managed to push aside my guilt and humiliation. *I didn't realize my trauma was written so clearly on my face.*

I turned to look at who I thought was Ash and narrowed my eyes. She didn't exactly clarify who was who, but I wanted to thank him for carrying me here at least. The taller twin snorted and must have guessed my dilemma. "Close sweetie, but I'm actually Aspen."

"Just remember the taller twin is Aspen. He's also the twin that talks the most," Cassia said with a laugh.

A small smirk slowly spread across Ash's face before it quickly disappeared. It seemed like he didn't give those out too often which made me smile in return. I watched Aspen roll his eyes and smile. *They seemed to genuinely care about one another, and they seemed to care what happened to me,* I thought as I studied them. Maybe I had finally snapped and gone crazy, but I was more intrigued than anything at this point.

"Well, thank you all for helping me tonight," I said quietly, and Cassia

CHAPTER 3

smiled.

Ash spoke up. "You mentioned moving into your grandmother's cabin. Can I ask who she was?"

"Willow McCoy," I replied, dropping my legs to the side of the couch nonchalantly. All three dropped their jaws, looking at me like they were dumbfounded by what I just said.

"What?" I asked nervously. *Did I say something wrong?*

"You said your name was Thomas though," Aspen said. He looked pale and his gaze darted between his siblings, who were still in shock.

"My last name was given to me by the state. The note that was left with me only had my first name or so I've been told. Did you know Willow?" I asked, trying to figure out what was going on.

"This can't be right Cassia," Ash said in disbelief.

"Wait, you're Willow's granddaughter? Cassia asked.

"That's what the lawyer said when I had to come in to sign for everything. He said it took some time to find me since my grandmother only knew my name and the place that took me in. I actually just learned my mother's name from someone at the bar. They said my mother's name was Mercedes."

"How did we not know, Cassia?!" Ash boomed, causing me to jump. My eyes widened as I pulled my legs toward me.

She stood angrily and shouted, "I don't know! She never told me about a granddaughter."

They started arguing then.

"Guys, we're scaring her," Aspen said in a calmer tone. He pursed his lips together, watching me panic as I tried to put air in my lungs again.

Fear crept in that they would turn into their scary wolves again. *They knew my mother*, I thought as anxiety crept in. *They knew my mother and my grandmother—* A bad feeling suddenly twisted my stomach.

Cassia sat back on the couch and offered her hand. When I didn't take it, she sighed saying, "I'm sorry, Shanely. Willow McCoy was our big sister. She died not that long ago, and this news just startled us. But it's besides the point because if Willow truly left her cabin to you because you are her granddaughter, then that makes you family. Our family."

"Our niece," Aspen said.

My eyes went big as I pushed myself further into the couch. *My family saved me tonight,* I thought as panic surged through my veins, *and they were wolf shifters.* My grandmother was a wolf, which meant it was in my blood too. *But I didn't feel anything inside me!* There was no way I had a wolf too. I had gone my entire life never *ever* turning into a wolf, and I wasn't about to start now!

"Which means that wolf attacked the McCoy family. They attacked the rightful—" Ash started.

"You need to call the Alpha now," Aspen interrupted, giving his brother a look.

"I already did," Cassia stated firmly. "He called for an emergency pack meeting at the lodge."

She stood promptly and held her hand out to me.

"Can you stand Shanely? We need to move you to our main lodge. I promise you are safe with us. We're just all in shock because no one knew Mercedes had a child," Cassia said sadly.

"I honestly feel okay physically which I think is because of you," I replied as I slowly took her hand. I had to know though. I had to ask the one question that's been rolling around my head since I was small. "Cassia? What happened to my mother?"

"Honestly," she said with a sigh, "we don't know. Mercedes left the mountains a long time ago, and no one has ever seen her again. I'm so sorry, Shanely. I wish I knew more, but you are with your family now. You'll never feel alone again."

She stared at me with such love in her eyes, and my lips puckered as I kept the tears at bay. I should have expected it. I had no answers about my parents for my entire life, and I've gotten by just fine without them. I don't know why it hurt like it did right now. Nothing's changed on that front, so I pushed my thoughts and feelings aside, focusing on another far more concerning matter.

"Does that mean I'm a wolf shifter too?" I whispered softly.

CHAPTER 3

"I don't know that either, Shanely," Cassia replied. "Your mother and grandmother both were strong wolves, but you don't smell wholly like a wolf. You also don't smell like a human either, which is why I'm so puzzled. There's something different with you, and I want Cain to meet you. I'm sure my mate will know what's going on. He's anxious to meet you."

"Wait, how does he even know about me? No one has used a phone since we've been talking," I asked.

"We can communicate with our minds between the pack. It works with any other shifter whether they are a part of the pack or not. We just need to be close for them to get the message. We're not far from the lodge, so Ash was able to reach Cain and explain what was going on," Aspen replied.

I slowly nodded, processing everything that has happened in the last 24 hours. I felt like I was living some fantasy book right now. None of this seemed real, but no matter how many times I pinched myself, I wouldn't wake up.

"We'll answer more questions later, child. If you're strong enough to walk, we will guide you to the lodge," Cassia said with a forced smile. "It isn't far from here."

I gave her a small nod and slowly made my way to the door. Thankfully, I was dressed in simple black sweatpants and a gray t-shirt, and it was modestly hiding everything I wanted covered. All the scars no one needed to see.

Aspen opened the door and extended out his hand. He patiently waited for me to accept it. I looked to the three of them standing before me, realizing the moment I took his hand and left with them, I was making a choice. A choice I didn't know how to feel about.

This wasn't exactly my life plan, but this was my family, I thought to myself. I had spent my whole life searching for my mother and wondering why she left me. This may be my only chance to learn, and despite everything that had happened tonight, I couldn't bring myself to walk away.

Not knowing where it was going to lead me but curiosity getting the better of me, I accepted his hand and followed them to the door.

Chapter 4

I was kind of surprised to be feeling as calm as I was walking next to three wolf shifters, but something inside just felt at home with these people. It was also nice knowing these wolves weren't trying to kill me and would probably shred anything that even came close to me. Ash kept his head on a swivel, scenting the air and listening for any threatening sound. Every sound that I heard made me jump, but he seemed to handle things okay.

"So, is everyone I'm about to meet a wolf?" I asked, breaking the silence as Aspen helped me over a fallen tree.

"Everyone you will meet tonight will be a wolf shifter, but you might meet other kinds in town," he answered. "That's neutral territory whereas these woods primarily belong to the wolves."

"Wait, other kinds?"

I was oddly curious about this world, but I felt like my head and heart were playing too different games. On one hand, I was excited to learn about my mother and the family I never knew, but on the other, I was scared. Worried about the dangers that could come with these people. *A life with shifters doesn't seem like the quiet and safe world I had envisioned when I moved out here. It hadn't even spent one full day in this place, and already I nearly died.* That thought made me hesitant to stay. I had enough peril living with Peter. *Would it be safer to leave and just live somewhere else?*

"We're not the only shifters out there, Shanely," Aspen replied, pulling me out of my own head. "There are shifters of any kind of animal you can think of all over the world."

Well, there goes that plan, I thought to myself.

"Each group has its own laws and deals primarily with their own kind. There are only two laws that are universal between shifter kind. One being; You cannot kill or harm a human. It was made a long time ago to maintain peace and order with a few selected humans. They helped us go back into hiding, and we became myths and legends while we promised not to harm them. If word gets out that humans are dying by animal attacks, then the Division *will* be sent out to investigate. They aren't always quick to get the truth of everything before dishing out punishment, making it a delicate thing to deal with," Cassia went on.

"So, does me being attacked mean the Division will come?" I asked.

"Well, it's complicated, Shanely. We can scent you're not human, but you've also grown up as a human your whole life. Unless we can prove you're a shifter, it could potentially be a problem," Aspen responded, and I felt sick to my stomach. *I didn't want to bring harm to anyone here,* I thought. *I just wanted to know my family.*

"I wouldn't worry about that, Shanely. No one will call the Division, and I can't see how they'd discover any of this. What happened tonight will be handled quietly amongst ourselves," Cassia replied.

"What about that wolf? Do you think he will come back?" I asked nervously.

Aspen gave me a sorrowful look but didn't reply. I turned to Cassia, who started to answer, but was interrupted.

"We're here," Ash said as he passed by us.

He pushed back the thick branch blocking the way, and when I stepped through, I saw the lodge. My jaw dropped when I entered the clearing. *No wonder they called it that,* I thought. It was a massive 3-story log building, with a wraparound porch. Like my cabin, it had wolves carved throughout in some form or another. I could see the long drive going back down the mountain on my left and lots of different trails heading off to the different parts of the woods. It was still dark outside, but the lights were all on, and I could see a few people coming in from the trails.

I dug my heels in, afraid to step any closer, but Aspen held my hand tightly and pulled me towards the front door anyways. It opened as I reluctantly made it to the top step, where a large man stepped out to greet us. He hugged Cassia before shaking Ash and Aspen's hand, and then he turned to me as I shifted back and forth on my feet. *This must be Cain,* I thought as my palms began to sweat. Cain had speckled brown and gray hair with a thick beard and was the largest man I had ever seen. As tall as Aspen and as thick as Ash, he towered over me.

"You must be my niece, Shanely," he finally said, his voice deep and powerful.

I nodded and extended out my hand to greet him. He suddenly barreled past my hand and pulled me into a bear hug. My whole body recoiled, and I scrambled to settle my heart. And surprisingly, my heart did calm down. I just felt safe in his arms like deep down I knew he would never hurt me. I was safe somehow— and insanely warm. *This man radiated heat like nobody's business!*

Cain finally released me as Cassia said, "Honey, don't scare her. She's been through a lot tonight."

Regret filled his eyes, and I felt bad. I didn't want him or anyone to feel like that around me, and I gave them a warm smile, hoping to ease their guilt.

"No, it's okay," I said. "I appreciate the welcome, just not used to hugs, I guess."

He hesitated, giving me a sad look then, and I frowned. *I don't know why I just said that,* I thought to myself. *I didn't mean to upset anyone, and I certainly didn't mean to admit anything personal about me.*

Cain simply nodded and opened the door without saying anything more. I followed my great uncle inside with my aunt behind me. My eyes widened as I took a look around. The inside was just as pretty and magnificent as the outside. A beautiful staircase was dead center in the comfortable living room, with a massive stone fireplace to the left and couches in front of it. You could see the open kitchen and dining room behind the staircase and a hallway leading down on the right.

I followed Alpha Cain down the hallway to the second room on the right. I noticed there were a few other people already sitting at the long table and

CHAPTER 4

a few younger guys standing against the walls and by the doors.

"Please, everyone sit. Shanely, I'd like you to sit by my mate and I at the end," Alpha Cain said.

I nodded and followed him to the other end of the room. I took the chair on Cain's left with my back facing the windows, while my aunt took the seat across from me. Uncle Ash stood behind me, and Uncle Aspen sat on my left. I had no idea if they even wanted me to call them Aunt or Uncle, but I figured what they didn't know wouldn't hurt them. *At least for now.*

Next to my aunt sat a woman who looked younger than the others sitting at the table. Two middle aged men took a seat next to her, and they all looked at me. They all seemed to wrinkle their noses and muttered quietly to themselves. I quickly looked away then, trying not to blush from their intense stare. I noticed a few men dressed in what looked like gear used in the military. They wore the same outfits that were in dark camouflage colors and stood near the doors and windows behind me. Their harsh glares were an intimidating presence, which I guess was the point.

As I turned back around in my seat, two more guys came into the room, and my eyes widened. *I didn't know men could look this good.* I struggled to breathe as I watched them enter the room. They were both tall, heavily muscled, and commanded the room as they walked past. I watched as the other guards lowered their eyes in respect of these two when they passed by, and I didn't know if my blatant stares were disrespectful, but it was hard to look away from them. Both were breathtaking, but my eyes were *glued* to the one in front.

My eyes shifted to the clothes I wore. Panic surged again as I realized I probably didn't have any makeup on anymore, and I was wearing freaking sweat pants in front of them. *I didn't even think about checking what my hair looked like after being attacked in the woods,* I thought, gritting my teeth. *I probably looked awful right now!* I wanted to melt away from embarrassment. Far, far away from the gorgeous guys standing five feet away from me now.

They took their stance behind my uncle Cain at the end of the table, and I bravely stole a peek in their direction. With this angle, I got a better look at their faces, and the one on the left made my heart *stop*.

God, he was beautiful. So utterly beautiful.

Staring was rude, but it was so hard to look away. He had the bluest eyes I had *ever* seen, and nerves rattled my bones. I was in awe at these two. These two guards, or whoever they were in this pack, didn't seem to even notice me.

As I continued to blatantly stare, I realized these guys had to be brothers. They looked nearly identical to each other, other than a few minor differences. Both had short fades with messy hair on top like they just rolled out of bed and neatly trimmed beards. Their hair color seemed to be the only real difference I could tell. The man who made my heart skitter uncontrollably had darker hair and features than his brother, and my eyes roamed over his body, soaking up every detail I could take in. They both looked somewhat near my age, if I had to guess. *Maybe a little older.*

They both looked forward, unmoving in their spot behind my uncle. *Clearly, they took their jobs very seriously.*

Suddenly, a bald gentleman quickly ran into the room, taking the seat next to Aspen. His huffin' and puffin' pulled my attention briefly, and I peeked around my uncle to find this man sweaty and out of breath. He refused to look my way, which was weird because the rest sitting at the table couldn't keep their eyes off me. They kept staring and muttering to themselves, but this one seemed like he wanted nothing to do with me.

I turned my attention back to the two gorgeous guys, trying to figure them out instead of the sweaty man. *They must be Cain's bodyguards or some kind of security around here,* I wondered. *What else went on around here to require security like this though?*

I didn't realize how long I'd been staring until the one on the right finally made eye contact with me. He winked at me, and I wanted to crawl in a hole and die. My cheeks heated, and I quickly dropped my gaze. Thankfully, no one else seemed to catch the encounter, but I refused to raise my head to check.

"I'm calling this emergency meeting to order. I thank each and everyone of you for coming in so late and on such short notice. We have a few things we need to discuss, but first everyone here needs to understand that what's

CHAPTER 4

about to be said *will* stay within these walls. Some very serious problems have come up, and this is not news for the pack or anyone else until we know how to handle this. Understood?" Cain asked sternly.

Everyone shook their heads in agreement, eagerly waiting to hear what he had to say. I noticed everyone sniffing the air again as they eyed me funny. *Did I smell bad?*

"Good. First things first, I would like to introduce my long-lost niece, Shanely. This is Mercedes's daughter and Willow's granddaughter. She now knows about shifters."

Everyone notably gasped and looked completely shocked. *I can't blame them*, I thought, leaning back in my chair. *I'm sure I looked the same way when I found out they were freaking wolves.* My body stilled as I felt sexy's eyes settled on me. His ragged breaths had me freaking out inside as he stared with such scrutiny at me, but I kept my head down, avoiding looking him in the eye.

"Willow didn't have any grandchildren."

"How can that be?"

"Are you sure? She doesn't smell like a full wolf."

Everyone started talking at once but was immediately silenced when Cain raised his hand.

"We know she doesn't smell fully like a wolf. While we don't understand why that's the case, we all can admit she does smell *somewhat* like a wolf. She is also in Willow's private will. We sent off the sealed original right after Willow passed away to the lawyer who had it drawn up, but it's been months. We hadn't heard anything, so I just assumed it was left to the family like it was always talked about. I checked the copy he sent me when Ash called in the incident, and sure enough, her name is on it."

"How did we miss this?" someone asked.

"The only thing the lawyer told me was that he would handle all the affairs for us and just send us copies of everything. With everything we've had going on lately with the Medvedev clan, I haven't had the chance to open it until tonight. The lawyer must have contacted Shanely here about the cabin and set the whole thing in motion. Willow left her cabin and the land to Shanely," Cain continued on. I continued to stare at my feet. "I know this will come as a disappointment to you, Derek. The land will not be sold to you anymore, and I am sorry about that. I shouldn't have started that whole process until I knew for sure what her will stated, but I had no idea there was an heir. Willow knew by law the land stays within the family."

"Unless it is agreed upon by the entire family," Aspen chimed in.

"Which can only mean Shanely is her next of kin," Cassia said, and I slowly looked to my aunt.

It took a minute for the words to sink in. *She thought my mother was dead too.* I pushed it to the back of my mind and folded my hands in my lap. *I already knew she was dead. I grew up without her, and I'll be just fine on my own.* It shouldn't come as a surprise to me, but for the first time in a very long time, I felt the pain of not having her. I had buried it for so long that I forgot what it felt like, and for a moment, it was crippling. I stayed quiet in my seat, waiting for the meeting to get going already. I didn't want to talk about my mother's death right now, especially amid all these strangers.

Cain hesitated before continuing, "I don't understand why she only smells faintly of a wolf, but there are only two possibilities. Shanely either doesn't smell like a wolf because her wolf's been dormant for so long or it's because her father wasn't a wolf."

The entire room erupted into an argument, and Cain let them go this time. Everyone seemed quite upset at this revelation, but I was lost. *Why would it matter if my dad wasn't a wolf?*

Cassia interrupted the group this time. "We know Mercedes was a wolf shifter, but she left so suddenly and told no one why. It makes sense if she was pregnant by another shifter."

"But that would mean she broke our second law!" Baldy or Derek shouted. *Baldy seemed more fitting,* I thought to myself. He was fuming mad and completely red in the face. Even his bald head looked red, which was kind of funny to look at. I narrowed my eyes to him, picking up on a hint of disgust, and he glared back at me. *He definitely doesn't like me one bit.*

"Wait, what is the second law?" I asked, finally speaking up.

CHAPTER 4

Cain leaned forward on the table. "We only have two universal laws between the shifter nations. One is with the Division; we are not allowed to harm humans or interfere with them, meaning we don't marry humans or deal with any issues with them ourselves. The other law came about after the Shifter Wars though. When humans discovered shifters, and the whole werewolf term came about, wolves were the only known shifter kind to humans. We were the primary target and were hunted at great lengths by people. This was all happening world-wide Shanely, and it was an awful period in our pack's history. Our pack was greatly affected, and the Alpha back then fought hard to rectify what happened. During that time other shifter kinds, specifically the bear clan neighboring us, decided to take advantage of the situation with the humans, and they attacked our pack, taking over the land in these mountains."

"They stole them, you mean," one of the men sitting at the table said. Cain simply nodded and continued on.

"The Alpha turned the tides and told the newly created Division that we weren't alone. Wolf shifters are the dominant shifters in the world because we have far more numbers than any other kind, and while wolves managed to hold their own against the humans, other shifters did not. They didn't have the numbers to protect themselves and many died because of the human's fear. Eventually, we struck a deal with the Division. We had one leader from each known shifter kind meet with the Division team at their headquarters. They wanted us to disappear and never interfere with humans again. To become forgotten, and the best way to do that was to keep us a secret and hidden in plain sight."

"They helped rid the world of our memory and kept tabs on all of us, making sure we followed the rules, but the second law came about after the Division's leader left," Aunt Cassia said.

"We had too much trust broken and way too much blood spilled that no one wanted to mix our kinds together anymore," Cain continued. "We separated all of shifter kind and started a rule that you do not marry or mate with other shifters. Shifters keep to their own kind. We separated after that and took the large portion of land back from the bears that they stole during the wars. The Alpha of our pack and the leader of the bear clan divided the town and created the neutral lines, and we haven't mixed since."

"Enough with the history lesson. She's an abomination and shouldn't be here!" Derek shouted again.

Cain slammed his hand down on the table, making it shake violently. I jumped out of my seat as my heart pounded out of my chest, but Uncle Ash put his hand firmly on my shoulder. As if he was either trying to reassure me or maybe make sure I didn't run. *It was tempting though.*

"Derek, you will show me, *your Alpha,* some respect. Do not speak to me or Shanely this way again," Cain growled, "is that clear?"

And I literally mean *growled*. His wolf looked just below the surface, and my eyes widened. I was *terrified* to meet him. *Cassia's* wolf was scary. I couldn't imagine what Cain's looked like.

Derek's face twisted into a crimson rage, but he dropped his tone saying, "Yes, Alpha."

"Now, *no one* will call my niece an abomination again. We don't know anything concrete anyways, so there is no point flinging accusations. We may never know exactly why Mercedes left, but my heart breaks to know she didn't trust any of us to stay and deal with whatever was going on. This pack is a family first, and we are all going to start acting like it despite the rule. Shanely is here, and I will not lose another family member. Whatever Shanely is, we will deal with it within our pack, understand?"

"Alpha?" the small woman with long blonde hair spoke up. Uncle Cain nodded at her to continue. "The thing is she will have to be a secret. If the other shifters find out, it could start another war. Who knows how they will twist this? You can't trust them, especially the bear clan."

"For now, we know there is some wolf DNA in her. We stick to that; no we will insist on it. She grew up human, so we'll say she doesn't smell like a wolf completely because she's dormant. Everything else will remain private. We don't give the other shifters any reason to attack. We control this area because of our numbers and the size of our territory, but we will prepare just in case," Cain replied confidently.

"*We* can scent she's different. Keeping her a secret will be almost

CHAPTER 4

impossible, I fear," she countered, and they all started talking at once again.

Derek rolled his eyes, but kept his mouth shut, for which I was thankful. My head already felt like exploding. *Everything was just a mess*, I thought to myself. *I didn't want to see them all fighting again, especially over me.* I laid my head on my hand as I let my mind run.

My whole life I never even knew my mother's name, and now I find out she left her entire life because of me. *Was I the reason she died? Did someone kill her because they found out she had me? Was she protecting me? Was she ashamed of me? Is my genetics why she left me all alone?*

Anger coursed through my veins, and I clenched the chair's arms tightly. No matter what, the answers to my questions didn't change the outcome. None of the answers would make me happy. I closed my eyes as the room spun again. *I just want this night to be over*, I thought. *I wanted to go home, but where was that even?* By the way everyone argued, I wasn't sure I should stay here after all.

"This is not the only issue we have to deal with," Cain said loudly, silencing the group. "Shanely was attacked tonight in McCoy territory."

My eyes opened slowly. The bodyguard standing behind Cain gritted his teeth and stared hard at me. I refused to look his way though. He was a whole other issue I didn't want to even think about. I couldn't deal with everything tonight *and* the way he made me feel. The butterflies that filled my stomach just looking at him from the corner of my eye was overwhelming. It wasn't logical, but I couldn't help but wonder why he even cared?

"What?" the woman asked dumbfounded.

"What do you mean attacked?" the other man, sitting across from Derek, asked.

"Shanely was chased into our lands tonight by a wolf. She was in bad shape when we found her, and I healed her enough to come here," Cassia stated matter of factly.

"She said something bolted out in front of her, causing her to crash, which forced her to walk the rest of the way home. Ash and I went back to check her truck while she was unconscious, and it was a mess. She's lucky she had her seat belt on when she crashed, Alpha," Aspen added in. My eyes widened as my mouth pulled down into a frown. *Glad I did too.*

"We found wolf tracks near her truck, Cain," Ash continued.

"Was it a shifter?" a gruff voice asked.

That voice rattled my bones. I bravely stole a glance in the bodyguards direction. In *his* direction.

The one on the right looked at me with such sadness and anger. It was pity on his face, but my eyes finally drifted to his brother. He emitted pure rage as he watched me carefully. Our eyes finally met, and the moment we connected, I felt my breath escape me. A strange sensation went through my body, almost like a shiver, but my chest instantly felt warm instead of cold. He seemed to struggle too, and my heart thundered in my chest. *What in the world was that?!* I thought frantically. But soon the feeling died within, and I was left feeling empty inside. Again.

Cain seemed to notice the brief interaction between us, and I realized he wasn't the only one. Heat flooded my cheeks as I dropped my head.

"We don't know" Cain replied, "but by the way everything looked tonight, we are assuming a rogue went after Shanely."

Everyone snapped.

The entire room was on their feet all shouting at once, and I scooted my chair back some. My eyes snapped to the gorgeous man again. He was pacing the floor now, and his eyes were no longer blue but solid gold. *Was he going to shift?* I didn't understand what a rogue even was, but the room was quickly becoming suffocating. It felt too small for all these loud voices, and I could *barely* handle the intense stare of one person in particular. His eyes were glued on me, and I wished more than anything the ground would open up and swallow me whole.

Suddenly, my aunt silenced the group when she stood abruptly from her seat, glaring at everyone.

"Everyone! Please settle down and remember that this is all new for her. She had no idea about our kind before tonight. Now, I know we haven't had a rogue in our territory since my father ran this pack, but what we need to figure out is how he got in undetected. Not lose our heads over the fact

CHAPTER 4

that one is here! This wolf managed to crash her truck and chase her deep into our territory without *any* of us knowing. That's a huge problem! My brothers and I only found her because she lost a decent amount of blood," Cassia bellowed, and everyone dropped their heads.

No one dared to look at her, and I wondered if this was a wolf thing. *It seems eye contact is a huge thing amongst shifters.*

Derek suddenly threw his hands up. "So your so-called niece just shows up and lures a rogue into our land? She's brought danger to the whole pack by attracting one here! It probably followed her from wherever she came from, and how do we even know she's telling the truth? This girl could be lying about who she is, and then by right that cabin should still be mine! *Everyone* here knows this girl isn't worth sacrificing the safety of actual wolves—"

The moment the words left Derek's mouth, the gorgeous man that had captivated me since walking in here, had launched himself over the table, grabbing Derek in the process. He slammed him against the wall behind me, and his hands went straight to Derek's throat. He moved so fast, I couldn't even follow him. I blinked, and suddenly he was squeezing the life from Derek's eyes. The room erupted, and I bolted from my chair, accidentally knocking it over. My chest heaved, watching Derek turn a deep shade of purple, and no matter how hard Derek pulled against his hands, they were unmoving. This man was firm in his grip, and his voice was rough when he snarled, "Don't you *ever* speak about her that way again."

"Bastian, let him go! That's an order!" Cain shouted.

The mystery man, who now had a name, snarled in Derek's face one last time before finally releasing him. Derek fell to the ground, gasping for air.

"Do you need to take a walk Bastian?" Cain asked sternly.

Bastian's gold eyes glared back at Cain. He shook his head no saying, "I'm not leaving this room."

Bastian slowly looked my way. Ash and Aspen stepped in front of me, putting a wall between me and him. I didn't understand this. I didn't understand *any* of it because for some reason the idea of him leaving made my anxiety rise sky-high. I had feelings that didn't feel natural or even my own going on within me, and all I wanted was to go home because it was *scaring* me to death. Even more than getting chased by the rogue.

I wrapped my arms around my waist and looked to my feet. *I couldn't do another relationship, and this guy was a beast in his* human form. He was way bigger than Peter was, and he is a shifter. Fear gripped my heart as I tried to picture his wolf. *I can't do this,* I thought to myself. I forcefully pushed aside the *intense* feelings I was having about a guy I barely knew.

Guilt ate at me as I noticed everyone watching me with worried expressions. *This wasn't over,* I thought. *Not after what just happened with Derek and Bastian. It was me.* I scared them for some reason, but I didn't want to be a burden to anyone here. I just stumbled into their life, and I wasn't going to disrupt anything further. *They didn't need to protect me or worry about me,* I thought, feeling resolved in my decision. I wasn't going to talk to anyone. I'd keep their secret because I just wanted to be left alone.

"Then control your temper. Do not make me regret allowing you to stay. Return to your post," my uncle's booming voice rattled the room.

I couldn't take it anymore. I stole a peek around Aspen's shoulders, finding Bastian still watching me. His face had softened some, and his eyes returned to his breathtaking blue when they met mine. Without a word, he made his way to his post, and I froze when he passed by me. He was so close I actually had to *stop* myself from reaching out to him. I wanted him. I wanted to know what it felt like to touch him. To lay in his arms and feel his lips against mine.

I dug my nails in my palms. *Stop acting like a silly girl,* I scolded myself. Bastian crossed his arms before glaring at Derek, who picked himself off the floor. Derek, still rubbing his neck, sat back down at the table in a huff, like someone didn't try to kill him just now.

"Don't mistake my calmness for acceptance, Derek. This is the second time you have disrespected my family tonight. I will throw you off this council and out of this pack if you do this again," Cain said, glaring at him, and a power I had never felt before filled the room.

Everyone must have felt it because they lowered their heads in submission, while I narrowed my eyes. *They seemed to be in pain almost,* I thought to myself as I watched on. *Everyone* but my aunt and I submitted to some invisible force.

My aunt looked at me with such curiosity before she nudged Cain. He glanced my way briefly, and then just like that the power was gone. Everyone else returned to their seats like nothing happened, but I stood there wide-eyed, trying to make sense of it all. I slowly took a step away from the group, and Bastian *noticed*. His eyes shot straight to mine, clear agitation knitting his brow. *Was he mad at me now? Or was he still just mad at Derek?*

Ash picked up my chair and gestured for me to sit again, but I was hesitant. I wasn't sure I wanted to sit down again. He seemed to understand and let it go but kept the chair open for me. He simply stood next to me then, accepting my decision to stay further away from everyone else.

Bastian continued to watch me, but I tried not to look over at him anymore. The more our eyes met, the stronger the feelings became. *It was better this way*, I kept telling myself.

"Since we have no way to figure out where the rogue went, we will just have to double up the patrols and maybe set up other security measures. Shanely will need extra protection too, seeing how she managed to get away. She's marked now," Cassia said.

"No, I won't," I snapped back. *No one even asked what I wanted yet or how I felt about this all*, I thought to myself, feeling rather annoyed now. *I didn't ask for any of this, and it was clear coming to Diablo was a mistake. For everyone.*

The council turned to look at me now. I stood nervously under everyone's gaze again, but I was done having them all decide for me what was going to happen. *I'm sick of everyone fighting, and I don't want to put anyone in danger because of me. Clearly, I was a huge problem to this pack, and I didn't want to be where I wasn't welcome.*

My aunt looked worried when I took another step away from everyone "Shanely dear," she said in a soft tone, "you can't shift right now. We need to make sure you're safe."

"No. From this meeting alone, I can see I'm nothing but a problem to you all. An *inconvenience* and a threat, and I refuse to cause you all harm or be a burden in any way. Look, I needed this escape, but I can move on just as well. If you allow me to stay in the cabin for a little while until I can save up enough to leave, I would appreciate it. You don't need to worry about protecting me. I'll do just fine on my own," I countered.

For the first time in my life, someone looked crushed that I was going to leave. My aunt opened her mouth, but before she could say anything another fierce growl echoed through the room. I turned to face Bastian, and he looked pissed off with me as well. I narrowed my eyes. *Why?* I thought to myself. *Why would he care what I did?*

Bastian stared intensely at me, but this time I stared right back. No one dared to speak as they watched the two of us glare at one another, and I refused to drop my gaze as everyone else did. I wasn't a wolf so I wasn't going to drop my gaze, but my confidence shook just a tad when my chest warmed again. A burning sensation traveled through the blood in my veins, and I tried not to let my voice waver as I ignored whatever was happening between us.

"Just leave me alone, and I'll be gone before you know it. The pack can return to normal then," I said quietly, my eyes never leaving his.

His face hardened by my words, but I refused to cave. My uncle Aspen stepped into my view, pulling my attention from the broody man in the back.

"Shanely, you're family. What happened to you is inexcusable, and you deserve to live here with your family and your own kind," Aspen said as he put his hand on my shoulder. Bile rose to the back of my throat as I fought against this feeling inside. My stomach churned as I tried to shove away these overwhelming thoughts, and I forcefully pulled away from him.

"No! You all barely know me, alright!? I'm not a wolf. I'm not a shifter. Look, I won't say anything about you guys, but I don't want to be a burden either, and I certainly don't want anyone to get hurt because of me. If the rogue is coming back for me then it's better I be alone anyways," I said as my eyes settled on Bastian, "and away from all of you."

The room erupted once more, but I couldn't look away from Bastian. His eyes widened, flashing red briefly as fury covered his face. I held my breath, taking another step away. *It was too much*, I thought. *He was too much for me.* I don't know what was going on between us or why I felt the way I did when I looked at him, but I can't go down this path again. I can't be in another relationship that scares me. Bastian *scared* me, and I needed space from him and everyone else in this room.

I put my hand up and everyone quieted down. "You have no idea how badly I have wanted to know my family and where I came from, but it's clear my mother ran away because of me. Maybe she was ashamed of who I was? I don't know, but she made it clear she didn't want me here. I'm not worth all of this fighting, trust me."

"So you're giving up just like that?" Bastian growled out, and I turned to him. "No one can even try to find this rogue or offer to protect you. You're just going to *leave* and never come back? All because of one fool in this room that doesn't think you belong here. Do you seriously think so little of yourself that you're willing to risk meeting this rogue again all on your own? Because we all know how well that turned out the first time, now don't we!"

My eyes widened, and I staggered backwards. He practically *screamed* the last sentence at me, scaring me and breaking my heart at the same time. I didn't understand why it hurt me so bad or why I hated seeing him like this. Utterly lost and feeling emotional, I took another step away from everyone.

"I can't do this anymore," I said softly as tears formed in my eyes.

Bastian's face suddenly softened when he realized how badly he hurt me. He started towards me before his brother got in his way, blocking his path.

That was the last thing I saw before I bolted from the room. I ran before anyone else could stop me, hearing them shout my name and begging for me to stop.

I ran as fast as I could out of the lodge and down the lane. I wasn't afraid of meeting the rogue anymore. I just didn't have it in me to care anymore. Not after tonight. Not after meeting him. *Let him come*, I thought to myself as tears fell down my face.

Nothing mattered anyways.

Chapter 5

It was a long, cold walk back towards town. I took the long way back home, not trusting myself not to get lost on the trails, and shivered the entire way to my drive. All I was wearing was the sweats and t-shirt my aunt gave me, and the night was surprisingly cold. Morning finally came, but it was still fairly early out by the time I saw my drive. I had spent the whole night between the woods and lodge, and I was just exhausted. My body was beat, and all I wanted to do was crawl into bed and never get up again.

I was halfway up my drive when realized I never passed my truck. *It should have been somewhere along the road, but it wasn't there*, I thought to myself. *Great—* I sighed heavily, knowing it had either been towed or stolen. *Just what I needed though. Another setback to keep me here longer.* But as I made my way passed the final curve in my drive, I noticed my truck was sitting there already.

I stopped dead in my tracks.

How did it get here? The right tire was still damaged, but there was tools left next to it to fix it. I watched and waited awhile to see if anyone was around, but no one came forward. Nothing but the sounds of birds waking with the sun kept me company. Everything seemed quiet around my cabin, so I slowly made my way forward. *I must have just missed whoever did this,* I thought as I strolled around the front side. There was a note on the windshield of my truck, and I carefully grabbed it.

Shanely,

I noticed your truck broke down on my way to work. I had my trailer with me

CHAPTER 5

today, so I just towed it back to the cabin for ya. I'm assuming you're okay since you weren't in the truck, but I can help you take a look at the front end, if you'd like? If you're looking for work we have a position opening up at the Den. Just give me a call when you can, and we can get together.

–Caleb.

He left his number on the bottom of the note, and I smiled. *Caleb seemed like a really sweet guy to do all this for a stranger,* I thought to myself. The job sounded promising though, and it would help me save up enough to leave this place faster if I needed to. I didn't have a phone anymore, so I'd have to walk back into town to meet him. Might take me a while to get there, but it could be worth it. *Maybe he could even give me a ride back to the cabin afterwards, and I wouldn't have to walk back and forth in the dark again.*

I wondered if Caleb was a shifter too. *He said his family didn't like the McCoy family, but is that just a family thing or a shifter thing?* I was curious about everything now and wondered how many shifters I had already met in my life.

I made my way to my front door and tried to open it. It was locked, and I rolled my eyes. *My aunt must have my keys back at her place,* I thought when I realized my pockets were empty. After everything last night, I didn't even think about getting my stuff back, and I couldn't go asking for it now. Not after I stormed out like that.

I quickly checked the windows on the porch, but they were locked too. I made my way around the back, and thankfully the kitchen window was unlocked. I shimmied myself inside and shut the window, locking it behind me. *I'll get my keys back another time, but at least I was inside.* I didn't want to think anymore. My mind was a muddled mess, and I just wanted to shut my brain off for awhile and sleep.

I didn't want to think about the rogue or the fact that I was no longer entirely human, and especially not about Bastian. I made my way to my room and locked my bedroom door behind me. I double checked all the windows here before I crashed on the bed. I made it all of thirty seconds before tears filled my eyes and a sob escaped my lips. I fell asleep shortly after that.

*　*　*

I awoke to full sun blasting me in the face. I rubbed my eyes, annoyed with the fact the window had no blinds or curtains on them. *I wonder if that store had any,* I thought to myself, but then again that really wasn't a necessity. *Curtains were going to have to wait. A lot of things were going to have to wait, especially if I was going to leave.*

I groaned again as I slowly pulled my feet to the end of the bed. *Weird,* I thought as I looked to the clock. *The clock says 7:30, which was odd because I know it was early morning when I got into bed in the first place.* I felt pretty good though, so maybe the clock wasn't working? Another thing to replace in this cabin that I honestly couldn't afford. I seriously missed my phone, but knowing Peter had no way to find me was a relief I wouldn't trade for anything. I'll just have to check prices when I get to town.

I stared at the floor as last nights events replayed in my mind. Finding out I wasn't human was going to take some getting used to. I didn't *feel* any different, at least now that I was away from Bastian. He seemed to be the only thing that made me feel anything new, with the rush of emotions like that. I had no idea what any of this meant for me either or why I seemed human for all my life. *Did this mean one day I'd just change into a furry animal? Or would leaving here mean I was giving up that part of me forever?* That thought surprisingly scared me. My whole life I had never felt a wolf inside. I was always just a lonely girl without a home to call my own, but I was a girl. *Human.* If I left my roots, if I left these mountains, would the dormant wolf inside disappear forever? *Did I even want it to?*

My whole life, I had nothing but this necklace to remind me of my parents. Now that I've discovered all this, the thought of giving it up angered me. *It wasn't fair. I deserved a family and a sense of belonging,* I thought as I gripped the sides of my bed. *Why was everything always so complicated for me? Why couldn't I have a happy life too?*

CHAPTER 5

If I had grown up around here with all of them, would I be a different person? Would I be brave or strong like them? I knew my past. I knew I pathetic and weak, letting bad things happen to me because I was too afraid to stop them. As scared as I was when I first saw their wolves, I had to admit they were strong and powerful. I *wanted* that. I wanted to be strong enough to protect myself like they were able to. I wanted to be something different, someone unique. My mother gave me that, but I've been separated from that part of myself since I was a baby. Pain twisted my heart. I didn't want to lose another piece of her, and I felt like if I left then I'd be doing just that. I didn't want to leave these mountains and her home. I didn't want to give up *anything* connected to my mother ever again.

But what about the rogue? What about Bastian?

My heart seemed to make up its mind, but my head was warring with everything still. I didn't want anyone to get hurt because of me either. I didn't want to be a burden, and deep down, I didn't want to owe anyone either. And that's what would happen. I'd owe these people *everything* if they had to change their lives just to accommodate me being here.

Plus, what if I caused issues with the other shifters or the humans who kept everyone in line? I wondered. Everyone looked human to me, and I couldn't tell by looking at them if they were shifter or not. According to those at that meeting, I'd be discovered immediately. My uncle didn't know what was wrong with me, and how could they honestly keep me a secret from everyone else? *What if I caused a war between everyone and ruined what good the pack had going for it?*

I groaned, rubbing my eyes as I tried to think this through a bit more. Staying had its pros and cons but if I left; where would I honestly go? I didn't have much money left. I was only making it work here because the cabin was free as I owned it outright, but I needed a job badly. Unless I sold the cabin, but I didn't like that idea. According to my uncle, it legally has to stay within the family. It was being sold to Derek *by* the family, but now that I'm here I don't think I could convince my family to sell it again. They are determined to have me stay, so this cabin will just continue to sit here, and I'd have to leave it behind. I ran my fingers through my hair. *None of this mattered until I could afford to fix my truck,* I thought. *I was grounded no matter what I decided.*

I hated this dilemma and forced my way to the bathroom. I was drowning and needed to do something other than think about this mess. I wasn't going to leave my bed today if I didn't make myself move. Anger filled my chest as I turned the water on the shower. *I finally find something good, and feel like I actually belong somewhere, and then this happens.* I found a place I want to call home, and now I don't know what to do. Life shouldn't be this complicated or messy, but it seemed to be my never-ending story. Now that I was in these woods and at my mother's old home, I couldn't stomach the idea of leaving. I had never felt this way before, but something pulled at me to stay.

I forced the thoughts from my mind and jumped in the shower, scrubbing my skin raw as I tried to focus on anything other than this. Bastian's eyes kept creeping up in the back of my mind though. Those beautiful, oceanic eyes that I couldn't help but get lost in. Every time I thought about him, my chest swelled and something deep inside felt like it was stirring. Fear crept in when that burning sensation returned. I wasn't sure if it was safe, but I didn't know if I could stop thinking about him either.

The man was gorgeous, I thought to myself, *so maybe it was just an attraction. A very strong attraction. But the shifters here seemed more emotional than most. Maybe this is normal to them?* I thought to myself, trying to rationalize what was happening in my head. No one really gave me a run down on how being a shifter works. *Maybe this is all just normal, and I didn't need to freak out over it.* It just felt so strange that whatever was going on inside was pushing me towards him. Not just this place but *him.*

I had never met someone that gorgeous either. My heart fluttered every time I pictured him. Peter was never someone that turned heads. He used his badge to get what he wanted normally, and with me it was the fact that I was homeless and needed a safe place to stay. One stupid night in a diner and everything progressed from there. Peter started off so kind and helpful, and I fell right for it. It didn't matter that I wasn't head over heels for the guy. He was kind, and I needed that. I fell. Hook, line, and sinker. I thought

CHAPTER 5

I had found something good in my life, and when he asked me out, I was excited. *Who better to feel safe with than a police officer, right?*

Wrong. So utterly wrong. I scrubbed my body harder as the memories came back. He insisted I move in with him, just until I saved enough to get back on my feet. He had an extra bedroom, and while I didn't want to rush in with anything, I also knew I didn't have much of a choice. Winter was coming, and I couldn't live in my truck forever. I moved in, and he made sure I could never leave.

Sweet and caring quickly turned sour, and I lost sight of myself. He just kept chipping away at who I was, replacing it with a mild and meek Shanely who obeyed his every word. I owed him for everything, and that was the excuse he gave when I tried to stop the abuse. When I tried to leave.

I should have left a long time ago, but I was scared and stupid, and then eventually broken. I never wanted to be in a situation like that again, and my mind drifted to Bastian. *Was Bastian like Peter?* I mean he was *really* angry last night, but the most he did to me was yell. I frowned slightly. *I yelled so does that make me just as bad?* I went over the events of last night once more. He was clearly strong by how he handled Derek, but I knew too little of their kind. *Was that just how shifters dealt with one another or was this just him? Would I be like that with my own emotions?*

Eventually, I made myself leave the shower. I wasn't getting any answers in there, and the last thing I needed was to waste hot water. I got dressed and added what little make-up I did own to my face, hoping to cover some of the awfulness up. It was the one thing that stuck with me from one of my foster homes. *Don't ever let them see you break.* One of the other kids told me that after the beating we received for breaking the TV remote. Crying was a form of breaking, and I should never let others see they've won against me. I never cried in front of Peter no matter how bad it got, and I wasn't about to look vulnerable to anyone at this pack. Not when they were so strong and courageous.

I started unpacking my bags and cleaning up the room. I hadn't got much done before everything happened yesterday, so I tried to clean the cobwebs and dirt just laying around. I threw the bedding into the washing machine, appalled I had slept on it in the first place. I was too tired to care then, but now I was contemplating another shower. There was a lot of dust and dirt in this place.

I opened the windows and let the morning breeze in to air out the room. Once I filled the dresser with my belongings, the last thing in my suitcase was my blanket. I threw it on the bed just as a striking smell filled my room. A thick, woodsy smell mixed with some kind of musk filled *every* space in my bedroom. It was intoxicating. I looked outside to find the source, but I saw nothing there. *I don't remember scenting this before, but maybe things were changing within me,* I thought as I watched the forest outside my window. Whatever it was smelled amazing, and I stayed there by the window just taking it all in.

My stomach growled something fierce, so I forced myself to leave. I left the window open, hoping the smell would fill my room and coat everything, and made my way down the hall.

No one from the pack had contacted me since I left, and I wasn't sure if that was a good thing or a bad thing. While I needed space to process everything, I wasn't sure if they were just done with me too. That brought on a whole new fear, which only made my head spin worse. I was suddenly afraid the pack would change their minds about me and not want me around anymore. I didn't want them to risk themselves trying to protect me, but I also didn't want them to reject me either. Frustrated, I needed to decide what I wanted first and foremost. *I couldn't keep going back and forth like this,* I thought. *It was ridiculous so— what do I want?*

I realized what I wanted most was my mother. She was everywhere here, and I didn't want to leave her home. As the morning went on, and I cleaned more of her cabin, I felt confident in my choice. I was staying, but now I just needed to figure out the best way to accomplish this without putting anyone in harm's way. And I needed to sort out this issue with that broody, *intoxicating,* man.

I opened all the cabinets and fridge, exploring the kitchen and dining room, all while thinking about Bastian. The man was so intense, and he was stuck in my head. I couldn't *stop* thinking about him. No matter what I did,

CHAPTER 5

I always circled back to him. He was gorgeous, any girl could see that, but it felt deeper than that, and that part scared me. I had never felt so drawn or connected to someone like I did with Bastian, and I only met the man last night!

This feeling I couldn't explain kept pulling on me, almost like the clarity was just out of reach. It didn't matter how I felt though because he would *never* want to be with someone like me. *Not with the past I have,* I thought as dread filled my core. *He'd find out eventually. There really wasn't a way to hide the trauma I went through. Not forever.*

It would never work anyways. Bastian was a wolf shifter, and I was an abomination that shouldn't even exist. I would never be good enough, and I needed to just accept that fact before I got myself so attached to him. While it was easier to walk away.

I decided to take a break from cleaning to sit on my porch. There was no food here anyways and nothing else to do at the moment. At some point I needed to make my way into town, but I just didn't have it in me to make that long walk right now. I *needed* to buy food soon though but skipping a meal or two wouldn't kill me. *I've done it before, so I can do it again.*

The morning breeze felt great as I sat down on the porch swing. Two rocking chairs sat on the far side, but I chose this massive swing, smiling that I had it all to myself. My smile fell when I realized I needed more security out here. It was quiet and very secluded. I had no real way to protect myself out here or know if the rogue was back. *That could be something worth mentioning to my uncle, but then again the cost would probably be astronomical,* I thought sighing. I'd have to figure out something else in the meantime.

I gritted my teeth, pushing the swing a little harder. *I survived Peter, so I could figure out how to deal with this rogue too,* I thought as my temper flared, but the reality of that was slim. I was living in a world I didn't fully understand, which means I needed to learn from my family about how rogues operated typically. *I don't want them to babysit me, but maybe I could set up some alarms or cameras around the cabin. Then I could at least hear the rogue coming,* I thought to myself. *If they could just teach me what to look for, then they wouldn't have to constantly watch over me.*

I had to speak with my aunt and uncle soon, I realized. I frowned again because that meant apologizing for running out on everyone. I sighed and pushed the swing again, rocking back and forth, trying to clear my head once more. I was giving myself a headache thinking about everything, even with the small game plan I had going for me.

Movement across the creek caught my eye, and I jumped hard in my seat. I scanned the woods as I slowly stood up, hair standing on the back of my neck. My heart pounded in my chest. *Was this the rogue?* I wondered as I searched for any sign of movement. My eyes drifted to my back door. *I just need to make it inside, and I can lock the door behind me.* I bolted, rushing to the large double doors when I finally saw what was out there.

A smoky grayish-black wolf appeared in the treeline, making my eyes widen. *This wasn't the rogue,* I thought, releasing the breath I was holding. But I also had no idea who stood in front of me. *It wasn't my aunt or uncles either.* I remembered their wolves, and I watched this wolf carefully. It seemed to watch me too. Neither one of us seemed able to move like we were both hesitant with the other.

The wolf stayed across the creek before sitting on its back legs. It was massive, and a little unnerving seeing a shifter so close to me again, but there was something about him I couldn't place. I wasn't frightened like I thought I would be, seeing one of the pack members in their wolf form again.

The wolf made himself known to me but didn't move any closer. I studied him for a moment, taking a good look at this wolf. I liked how dark his fur was, and then the spots that were more of a smokey gray color made this wolf so unique and beautiful. I was curious who it was though, but the pack was large so it could be anyone honestly. We watched each for a while before I finally recognized those eyes. They were a bright blue like the ocean and I sucked in a breath when I finally figured it out.

I knew those eyes.

This was Bastian's wolf.

Chapter 6

Bastian's wolf stayed right on the edge of the creek, and you could see he was anxious about something. He stood again before turning in a circle and sitting down once more. Agitation knitted his brow, but he never once stepped across the creek. I realized he was waiting for permission to cross. Bastian looked frustrated but didn't move any closer towards me.

I wasn't sure I was ready to face him though, and I couldn't help but frown. He seemed so upset with me last night, and I didn't want to be yelled at again. I know he doesn't know my past, and the reasons why I feel the way I do, but his reaction was still a trigger for me. *And why was he so upset with me in the first place?* I wondered. You'd think he'd be relieved I wasn't asking for help, but he was livid with me, and I didn't understand why he cared so much about it in the first place. I didn't want to speak to him and feel his frustration all over again.

I didn't want to argue with him.

But if I was being honest, I didn't want to speak to him because he scared me. I couldn't stop how I was feeling about him, and that freaked me out. Call me a coward, but I couldn't deal with it.

I started to go back inside when I heard him howl. I stopped with my hand on the door. *He sounded almost in pain,* I thought to myself, not liking the idea of him hurting either. My chest felt warm again when I turned around to check on him. He was laying down with both paws covering his face.

Was he apologizing?

I was curious by his behavior. It's not like I had any experiences with wolves before, but he seemed almost distraught. I closed the door, and he moved his paws. If it was even possible, his wolf looked surprised as he cocked his head to the side. Bastian sat up but remained where he was. His eyes were still a bright blue, and they just watched me, almost pleading with me. I caved then, and I decided to let him come over.

I slowly sat back down on the swing. "I'm assuming your wolfy ears can hear me, but you can come over."

He bolted over and past the creek faster than I would have expected but stopped abruptly at the stairs. He was hesitant, and I wasn't sure what was going on in his head. Now that his wolf was closer, I could get a better look at him. His wolf was fascinating and stunningly beautiful. It was exciting to think that one day I'd get to be a wolf too. I wondered what I'd look like.

Bastian briefly looked at me, while I simply waited for him to decide whether or not he was actually coming up. He slowly climbed the porch steps as if he was afraid to scare me by moving too quickly. *Or maybe I scared him too?* I wondered, smiling softly at the absurd idea. I didn't know, but at least I wasn't the only one who wasn't sure how to act with the other.

I patted the bench swing next to me as he got closer. "You can sit with me, but I don't want to talk. You can be here though if that's what you want."

I surprisingly wasn't as afraid as I thought I'd be around a large wolf, especially after last night. He approached the swing, and my eyes widened. Bastian's wolf stood taller than me sitting on the swing. *It was incredible how big he was as a wolf, and I wondered where he'd come up on me if I was standing.* But I was comfortable being this close to him, and it honestly made me feel safe, like no one could get to me with him here. It was his human form that scared me more. Bastian, *the man,* terrified me, and I was going crazy with my emotions as it is.

I shouldn't be so drawn to him, not this fast at least. I was nervous of actually talking to him when he switched back. I know I'd start babbling nonsense, and I had no idea how he'd even take it, but I seemed okay with his wolf being here with me instead. I don't know if he was conscientiously in there or if his wolf has taken over completely. All the silly books I've read each had their own version of this stuff. *Although, maybe fantasy books weren't exactly what I should use as a reference for shifters,* I thought, stifling

CHAPTER 6

a chuckle.

Bastian suddenly surprised me when he hopped up on the bench and plopped down. I shrieked as the swing shook and moved with his weight. It was an oversize swing, but he made it seem so tiny when he jumped up.

"I didn't mean literally next to me! Can the swing even hold your wolf?!"

He made a sound almost like a laugh. I've noticed even in their wolf forms a lot of their human side seemed to come through.

Bastian jerked his head up, and I followed his line of sight. The swing was held up by some heavy bolts. *Of course, this was a shifter's house,* I thought to myself, feeling a little stupid. *I guess that answered my question.* It also seemed to tell me how much Bastian was aware in this form.

He respected my feelings though and never returned to his human form. Bastian just laid there in his wolf next to me. *Well, half next to me and half on me,* I thought smiling. *He could barely fit on the swing!* It was sweet though. Bastian was trying hard to stay to his side of the swing, but with his size, he couldn't quite fit without leaning into mine. I grinned wider, watching him try to keep to his side and balance on the swing without touching me.

Without thinking, I patted my leg and said, "It's okay. You can rest your head here, otherwise I think you'll fall off."

My face turned red the second the words left my mouth. *I don't know why I offered that,* I thought as embarrassment crept in. I just offered him to lay his head *on my leg,* which was more intimate than I ever wanted to go. Embarrassment flooded my cheeks as I looked anywhere but him.

Bastian tilted his head to the side, studying me. Nerves took over my entire system, afraid he took it as weird as I'm sure it sounded. I immediately regretted opening my mouth. It was like my mouth ran away with itself before my mind could catch up. Like it had my entire life.

He stared at me for what felt like forever, and my heart started to race in anticipation. *Maybe my offer made him uncomfortable? Why in the world did I even say anything in the first place!? I didn't want to speak to him yet here I am babbling away!*

Before panic could set in more, Bastian readjusted himself and laid his head on my leg. He stayed close to my knee, completely respectful with me, and didn't move again. His fur was ungoldly soft, and a slow smile crept up my lips. I pushed the swing again, and we stayed quiet together.

Now that Bastian was so close, I could smell him. It was that same smell as before in my bedroom. The intoxicating one that I couldn't figure out. *Was this just because he was a shifter? Or was it because I was a shifter, and now I was finally able to smell things clearly?* There was no way I was going to ask him about it though. I was embarrassed enough as it was, and I didn't want him to also know that I thought he smelled amazing.

I noticed as we swung that Bastian *radiated* warmth like my uncle did. *Must be a shifter thing,* I thought to myself, but I was really cozy sitting next to him. It was honestly peaceful, and I found myself absentmindedly petting him as my thoughts ran in every direction. My face heated, turning blood red when I realized what I was doing. I don't even know how long I had been petting him for, and I quickly moved my hand away.

"I'm sorry!" I stammered. "I was zoning out and I—"

I didn't know how to even finish that sentence. *I was petting him?! What in the world is the matter with me?* I thought, wishing the ground would open up and swallow me whole.

To my surprise, he whined and moved his head back under my hand. Bastian kept pushing against it, and I didn't know what to say.

"You *want* me to pet you?" I asked nervously.

Bastian pushed against my hand again and finally relaxed when I scratched behind his ears. He laid his head back on my leg as I ran my fingers through his fur. A heaviness I didn't even realize was there lifted suddenly, and I felt like I could breathe again.

Bastian closed his eyes, giving myself a chance to calm down and stop blushing. I'm not sure how long we stayed like this, but long enough the sun was high in the sky, and my stomach growled.

I prayed he didn't hear that just now, and I looked back at Bastian. I'm sure he could feel me watching him, but he never let on. He just stayed still against me, and I had never felt so relaxed in my life. I couldn't help but wonder why he was so calming for me? *Why was I so comfortable with this man or wolf even though I haven't even known him a full 24 hours? And why was he spending his whole day with me?* He didn't know me either, and I'm sure he had better things to do than sit here on the swing with me.

Suddenly, Bastian's ears perked up. They twitched around towards a sound I could not hear. I scanned the woods, my breathing picking up slightly. I didn't hear or see anything but remained quiet anyways. I didn't want to distract him by asking questions he couldn't answer even if he wanted to.

Bastian looked at me with sadness in his eyes, and I worried about what was out there. I didn't understand what was going on, but he licked my cheek before slowly leaving the swing. My heart tugged at me, watching him walk away so sad like that, and I missed his warmth and presence. But something out there was making him leave the swing, and that made me nervous. I stood, ready to follow him, before my mind could even catch up to what I was doing.

I made it to my railing as more wolves poured out of the woods. I froze briefly until I saw my aunt Cassia and two uncles come closer. I relaxed then. *Not the rogue,* I thought to myself.

Bastian stopped at the end of my porch and waited for the wolves to reach the other side of the creek. They shifted, and I was in awe. The first time I was so out of it, I didn't catch how it all happened. It looked painful yet completely natural.

Cain stood first, and thankfully was fully clothed. Cassia shifted next followed by my uncles, Ash and Aspen. The last to shift was the one who looked just like Bastian. I never got the chance to learn his name during the meeting, but the other three wolves stayed behind in their wolf form, and Bastian didn't move or shift. He looked at me before turning his attention back to my uncle Cain.

"Bastian, shift now," Cain demanded. *He seemed angry,* I thought to myself. *Like really angry.*

Bastian shifted abruptly then, but this time it looked painful, like it wasn't voluntary. He was in new clothes since I last saw him, wearing more casual clothing than before. He wore dark jeans and a simple dark blue shirt instead of all that heavy looking gear.

Seeing him in his human form again took my breath away. Bastian was *gorgeous*, and I couldn't help but stare. His arms and back were solid muscle like his shirt would burst if he twisted the wrong way. I also noticed a tattoo peeking out of his left arm sleeve and neck. I couldn't tell exactly what it was, but I was dying to know now. His hair was messy like he hadn't had much time to style it this morning, but the messy bed-head worked for him. I couldn't *stop* staring at him and blushed hard when I realized my aunt was watching me.

Cassia smirked, while I turned beat red, and I was grateful to be standing slightly behind Bastian to his left. He seemed to have no idea of our little interaction as he stared straight ahead at my uncle.

"You realize you disobeyed an Alpha order, right?" Cain asked gruffly.

Bastian shook his head yes before dropping it as Cain frowned.

"I ordered you to keep your distance from my niece. You pushed the line with her that night, and we were *all* giving her space. You also skipped out on your job and responsibilities to the pack. Have you been here this entire time?"

Bastian lifted his head high this time, answering Cain with confidence. "I have been, Alpha, but I didn't cross the creek line until this morning."

I was shocked. "Wait, how long have you been here? How long was I asleep for?"

Bastian slowly looked back at me. "You slept sound for nearly 24 hours. I stayed close enough to keep an eye on you but far enough to not be seen or heard. I couldn't leave you alone out here. Not after everything."

Bastian looked down at his feet, and I didn't know what to think. On one hand, I was relieved to know I was never truly alone, but I was a little unnerved by it too. *I had no idea he was outside my house this whole time. If he could sneak up on me then so could the rogue,* I thought as my anxiety rose slightly.

Bastian seemed to draw me back from my unraveling thoughts, and I studied him carefully as he stuck his hands in his pockets. He knew I was watching him, but he didn't say anything. I couldn't figure him out though. *Why did he even bother with me? Why would he break his Alpha's command? I*

CHAPTER 6

mean my uncle was pissed, and he had to know he was going to be caught. I summoned the courage to just ask.

"Why?"

Bastian looked up curious now. "Why what?"

"Why risk whatever punishment Cain's going to give you to watch me? You don't even know me."

"My wolf does, and what happened to you is inexcusable," he replied. "Wolf shifters don't attack people, and if I can't kill the shifter responsible then I'll make sure he never comes close to you again. You don't need to leave your home because of a rogue, and I'm going to make sure you're safe. That's my ultimatum, and I refuse to budge on that."

My heart practically leapt out of my chest. No one has *ever* spoken to me like this before. He was firm but not harsh like Peter, and he was demanding to stay and protect me. *No one had ever stuck their neck out for me like this before*, I thought. *Peter was nothing but abusive. He was only ever kind or attentive when we were around company, but Bastian was here watching out for me, and I had no idea.*

He wasn't asking for anything in return either, which was surprising. Everything came with a price usually, but he didn't ask for one, and I wasn't sure how to take it. He seemed honest and true, and I was *captivated* by him. But I scolded myself when I remembered he can't be anything with me because of their laws. I needed to rein in my emotions before they ran away from me.

"Regardless of why you did what you did, you broke an Alpha command," Cain bellowed.

"Shouldn't that be impossible?" Aspen quietly said to Cassia. She merely shushed him and looked back towards Cain.

"Cain? Or Uncle Cain? Or Alpha? I'm sorry, I really don't know what to call you," I stammered nervously. I wasn't sure if I was overstepping, but I just felt like I needed to say something. If I could get him out of trouble then it would at least be some form of payback for what he did for me.

Cain's face softened as he turned to me. "You are the only person that can call me Uncle Cain instead of Alpha and get away with it. These two don't seem to be having kids anytime soon."

Ash snorted, and Aspen rolled his eyes saying, "Yeah, well not everyone is lucky enough to find their mate at 13."

"Anyways Shanely, you haven't officially joined the pack even though I have vocally claimed you as one of my own. Technically, you aren't even required to call me Alpha yet."

"Even when that's the case, we will always be your aunt and uncle first," Aunt Cassia chimed in.

"Well then, Uncle Cain, I understand what Bastian did was wrong, but can you give him a warning or something this time?" I asked, clasping my hands together.

Bastian's head shot to mine. He looked at me with a puzzled expression, and he opened his mouth to speak but snapped it shut instead.

Actually, *everyone* was giving me an odd look now, and I wondered if I did something wrong. Bastian's intense gaze flustered me, and I started talking nervously and way too fast. *I hated when I babble.*

"It's just that it was really kind that he stayed with me this whole time. No one's ever done something like this for me before, and I think it's probably why I was able to rest for so long, even if I didn't know one of your pack members was there. I was safe here at least. I— uh— I don't know," I stammered. "I just feel bad about him getting in trouble over me. I'm not trying to overstep, but I just wondered, and technically I did invite him to the house, so he really did give me some space."

My uncle looked amused as he glanced to my aunt. My aunt just beamed at me for some reason, and I got nothing from Ash or Aspen. I don't know if I crossed the line and interfered where I shouldn't, but I just couldn't say nothing. Not when he did all that for me. Someone he barely knew.

I'd feel better if maybe I could get him off with a warning instead of whatever punishment was coming his way. I hated the thought of him doing something for me, even if I didn't ask, and then being punished for it. Besides, whether I wanted to admit it or not, something was pulling me towards him, and I felt the need to defend him.

"I appreciate the request, but Bastian broke a big rule. He's not allowed to go against an Alpha command. He will still receive punishment just like everyone else," Cain replied, and my face fell, but he continued on. "However, due to the circumstances, I do appreciate him looking out for you and at least *waiting* to be invited in. I'll make the punishment fit the crime."

Bastian wouldn't take his eyes off me as Cain spoke. It made me feel unsure about myself, like maybe he didn't want me to speak up or something. I tried not to look at him anymore, but it was so incredibly difficult.

"So, what happens now?" I asked.

"Bastian," Cain said firmly. I felt that strange power again, like I felt the other night, but it didn't seem to affect me like it did Bastian. He winced but stood tall, waiting for his punishment. "For disobeying an Alpha order, you will be relieved of your responsibilities as an Enforcer for the next two weeks. You will not be allowed in the High Council's meetings nor will you be my personal Enforcer. Once your two weeks are up, you will be allowed in again."

The power snapped back to Cain, and Bastian took a deep breath. He merely nodded once towards Cain as my uncle continued speaking, "Now, seeing you'll have some free time on your hands, I'd like you to watch over my niece. That is if she is comfortable with that?"

"I really don't need a babysitter, Uncle," I said firmly. "I'm sure Bastian would rather do anything else with his time—"

"I'd be happy to," he replied, cutting me off.

"Shanely," Cain said, pulling my attention away from the broody man, "the Council and I all agree that you deserve to remain *here* with your family. We are actively hunting the rogue, and I promise you I will find him, but we want you to stay with us as part of the pack. Your scent is changing, Shanely, and you smell like a wolf. Even from the first night I met you, your scent is stronger, which makes you a target because you're not human. Until you shift though, you *will* be defenseless. You'll scent like a shifter without the abilities you need to protect yourself. Other shifters will be able to scent you out now, and you would be far safer attached to a large pack.

Hiding you amongst the pack would be the safest way to blend you in until we get more answers. Keep your cabin, your grandmother wanted you to have it, and no one feels right taking it back from you. We have some terms though we'd like you to agree on."

"What are you all thinking?" I asked, curious as to what they thought was best to do. *I was still struggling with it myself.*

"The Council and I discussed it at length, and we came up with three things we'd like to start today. One; you do not go into town alone. Even though it is neutral ground, the rogue may be blending in, and it would be easy to snatch you there. Bastian is an Enforcer, which is our pack's security, so he can escort you or one of us will. Two; we would like you to train with us. You can learn to defend yourself and try to awaken your own wolf. We all feel her, so it's only a matter of time before you do too. The goal is to get you to shift, so you can protect yourself. No matter where you are in this world you will be safe, and you won't be such an easy target for the rogue then."

I winced slightly at that word as he continued on. No one seemed to notice except Bastian as his eyes flashed in my direction, and he crossed his arms. I ignored him the best I could.

"And lastly; you will need to officially join my pack. That way we can always be able to reach one another if something were to come up. Technically, right now you are unclaimed, which might be why the rogue chose you in the first place. The rogue would be able to sense you are now a pack member, and that comes with protection. He would be less likely to come after you now that you are no longer alone," Uncle Cain replied.

I debated everything he said, and they patiently waited for me to weigh in. *The idea of learning to defend myself was really appealing,* I thought to myself. I was sick of always being so weak, and I'd like to be able to hold my own. I really wanted to meet my own wolf too, and truth be told, I had no idea how to be a shifter. Not a single clue on how to shift at all even if I were to try on my own. The only thing I didn't want was to owe anyone. I didn't want everyone to drop their lives just to take care of me.

"Alright deal," I finally answered, and Bastian's shoulders relaxed, "but I

CHAPTER 6

also don't want everyone to change their lives trying to keep me safe. I love the idea of training and unlocking my wolf, but I don't need a babysitter. I don't *want* one. I won't be a burden, Uncle."

My uncle grinned at me. "You will never be a burden, Shanely. This is what it means to be part of a pack, part of a family. Now Bastian, I'm trusting you to keep her safe. She is in your care now. Bring her to the lodge tonight at 7."

"But Uncle Cain—"

Cain ignored my protests and shifted back to his reddish-brown wolf. The others followed suit before taking off into the woods. My aunt winked at me before leaving too, and I blushed again. *I was going to have to speak to her soon about what she thinks she saw,* I thought to myself. I cannot have her or my uncle thinking *anything* like that. Bastian and I can't be anything anyways according to their laws, so I was going to get space between us. I didn't want anyone getting the wrong idea.

Soon, it was just Bastian and I with his lookalike.

Bastian stuck his hands in his pockets. *At least I wasn't the only one that seemed nervous.*

"Shanely," he said softly, "meet my brother Cade."

Hearing him say my name out loud for the first time gave me butterflies. Cade crossed the creek to meet me at the steps. Up close, they looked nearly identical, and I studied him more closely. Cade's beard was shorter , and his hair was lighter than Bastian's overall. More brownish than black, and Cade wasn't as defined as Bastian was. He was leaner than his brother but still strong, I'm sure. *He'd make any girl swoon, especially with that smile,* I thought. *Honestly, I bet they were both favorites among the girls here.* Cade seemed sweet though, and he definitely more outgoing than Bastian.

"Nice to officially meet you, Shanely," he said as he stuck his hand out, and I shook it. He had a strong grip, and I could feel calluses on his hand as they wrapped around mine. *He must do a lot of physical work for them to get that way.*

"Hi, Cade. Nice to meet you too."

He smiled crookedly, turning to Bastian then. "I covered as long as I could, brother. Cain seems to sniff out trouble quick, and once they realized I wasn't you, the gig was up. He knew *exactly* where you'd be."

"It's okay. I appreciate your help. It gave me a bit more time," Bastian replied, rubbing the back of his head.

"You guys swapped places?" I asked, curiosity getting the better of me. I had planned to tell them they were not responsible for me, and that they didn't need to stay. But I couldn't deny they were intriguing. I was curious about how they managed to hide Bastian, and *why* he wanted to hide in the first place.

"Once in a while, when it's really important," Cade replied, with this twinkle in his eye.

Great— So the brothers were not only gorgeous, they were mischievous too, I thought as butterflies filled my stomach. *Just what I needed. They were going to be the death of me, I just knew it.* I sighed, knowing full well I was pissing off a whole lot of girls by having them both with me.

I watched the two brothers converse with one another over something, but I wasn't paying much attention. I was stuck on how much they looked alike. I kept looking back and forth at them because they really were so similar. *They just had to be twins.*

"Are you guys twins?" I finally asked, interrupting Cade. Heat filled my cheeks when they both grinned wide.

Cade laughed. "Triplets actually. Though I'm the youngest and best-looking brother."

Bastian smirked and playfully shoved Cade, who just laughed it off. The whole interaction made me giggle. They seemed to be pretty close, and I was mesmerized watching them. *So, this is what having a true sibling was like.*

"I'm only older by four minutes!" Bastian cried out. "Our middle brother will be around later today. His name is Elijah."

"Yeah, we thought we'd come hang out with you today," Cade chimed in, moving towards the door, "if that's okay?"

My eyes widened in surprise. *They were really taking my uncle's request seriously,* I thought. I clasp my hands together nervously as I said, "Listen,

CHAPTER 6

I know my uncle asked you to watch me, but please don't worry about me. I'll get some sort of security out here soon, but I'm sure you have other pack responsibilities to handle."

"Nah, I want to spend my day with you. Besides Alpha Cain gave Elijah and I the week off too, so we have nothing going on," Cade replied.

"He did?"

"Well—" Cade chuckled, "in a way he did."

Bastian snorted. "They both got suspended for assisting me. Just for half the time."

My shoulders fell. I felt *terrible*. "Cade, I'm so sorry. I didn't mean to get you guys in trouble!"

He gave me a puzzled expression saying, "Why are you apologizing? You didn't even know, Baby Girl! It's this fool that always ropes me into his shenanigans! He's the one to blame!"

Cade started laughing as Bastian glared at him, and I couldn't help but smile. *Cade seemed great,* I thought to myself. He was a good filler with conversation, which was something we desperately needed. The thought of being alone with Bastian sent my nerves through the roof. Cade was way more playful and goofy than his older brother, and it filled in the awkward moments. Complete opposites despite looking so similar.

"If I recall, Elijah and I have pretended to be you too on more than one occasion," Bastian countered, and Cade bumped him. He winked at me, and the corners of my mouth rose.

"Well, look at that, Bastian. I think she's gotta have the best smile I've ever seen!" Cade said as he beamed down at me.

I scoffed, but Bastian agreed. He crossed his arms, smiling as he said, "She does, Cade. I'd like to see that smile more often."

I turned, dropping my head to keep them from seeing my now rosy cheeks. *I was right,* I thought as I grinned harder. *Their shameless flattery was going to be the death of me.* I bravely stole a peek at Bastian. *Yeah— I might be dead already.*

Cade headed for the door. "C'mon, let's see what there is to do for fun in here."

Bastian rubbed the back of his head before smiling bashfully. "Sorry, he's very— outgoing. After you."

I grinned again. *It was cute seeing him blush,* I thought to myself. He extended his hand out towards the door, and I followed Cade inside, with Bastian right on my heels.

Chapter 7

Cade was already in the hall closet looking around.

"Cade, you're being nosy," Bastian hissed. "Get out of there!"

Cade popped his head out with a sheepish smile. He simply shrugged and stepped out of the closet with his arms full of games and puzzles.

"No, it's fine really. You guys are welcome to go wherever. Most of the stuff here isn't mine. I was just trying to organize and clean up. It's kind of a mess really. I'm sorry about that," I replied as Cade set the games down on the table.

"Well, how about we help you fix the place up then? We can play these when we're done," Cade offered.

"Oh no, guys. It's okay—"

Bastian touched my arm, causing the words to feel stuck in my mouth. "Please, Shanely. Let us help out."

I nodded, giving him a small smile because I didn't trust my mouth not to fumble my words. If it were even possible, his voice had dropped into a low, gritty tone, making me weak in the knees. *How could I say no then? And if he kept looking at me like that, I was going to become a puddle on the floor.*

Bastian dropped his hand as he smiled back at me, and I instantly missed his touch. *God, my insides just melted away with that one wicked smile.* I felt completely out of place with him. My head and heart were not on the same page, and I didn't know what to do or say around him.

Thankfully, the two started goofing off with one another as they got to work, leaving me to gather myself together. I didn't realize how badly I needed the company until I was laughing so hard my sides hurt. I just felt terrible they were now stuck cleaning the place up with me. I didn't have very many cleaners or supplies, but I did manage to find a vacuum and a mop in the closet with some dusters. We made quick work of it then, and it felt *so* much nicer than before. Like how a real home should feel. All the windows were opened up, airing out the cabin, and the breeze felt amazing as it swept through the room, making my hair flutter.

Having the fresh air helped because every time Bastian walked by, I got a whiff of his amazing scent. It was becoming harder to not to let on that I even noticed it. It wasn't as strong as it was when he was a wolf, but it was still there. Just lingering in the air and pulling me in like a moth to a flame.

I noticed Cade had a slightly similar smell of the woods to him too, but it wasn't the same as Bastian's. It wasn't addicting nor did it compel me to leap across the room and plant my lips on his. *Nah— only Bastian's scent did that.*

And I was clearly a freak because this wasn't normal!

I ignored his scent as much as possible while we cleaned, and Bastian and Cade told me stories about themselves growing up on pack lands. I loved hearing every one, wishing more than anything I could somehow be apart. After the house was clean, we played board games at the table much to Cade's delight. I continued to pepper them with questions, but then they tried asking me about my childhood. That was not a conversation I wanted to get into, and I gave pretty vague answers to their questions. I pretended not to see their frowns or disappointment and moved the conversation right along. I was used to those kinds of looks, but I didn't want to give them anything personal right now. None of my stories were like theirs.

The clock in the kitchen chimed, and I noticed we had played the afternoon away. *Everyone must be getting hungry,* I thought, pursing my lips together. I was starving, and I couldn't imagine how they must be feeling. *We skipped lunch,* I thought as I looked to my perfectly clean kitchen. I wasn't able to head into town today so the house was empty, and I felt awful. Embarrassment crept in that I didn't have anything for them. Cade's stomach roared loudly, making me feel worse.

"Cade, your stomach sounds like a vicious animal," I said as I laughed,

CHAPTER 7

taking a seat next to him on the couch.

"Baby Girl, you have no idea. Agh, I could eat a bear right now."

"Not an actual bear though, right?" I asked, my brow rising slightly.

His loud laugh filled the room. "You're hilarious, you know that?"

I blushed and dipped my head low. *I don't think anyone has ever said I was funny,* I thought to myself. Bastian walked over and practically sat on top of Cade, making him scoot away from me.

"Geez, Bastian! You could have just said to scooch over," Cade cried out, pulling his leg out from underneath his brother.

"Huh, I didn't see you, Cade. I was too busy ordering everyone dinner."

Cade's ears perked up, and he completely forgot about the minor inconvenience of getting sat on. I chuckled to myself.

"Really?" Cade asked. "Whatcha get?"

"Elijah's bringing a couple pizzas. Calm down," he replied.

"I feel bad, you guys. You got suspended because of me, then you spent your whole day cleaning and organizing my cabin, and now you're buying me food? You don't have to do that!"

"Baby Girl, we need to feed you. Do you see how skinny you are? You clearly aren't eating enough, and we're going to fix that. Besides, you have literally nothing to eat in this cabin. I checked," Cade replied, beaming over at me.

My smile fell as I wrapped my arms around my waist. It was the first time someone had ever said I was *too* thin. I wasn't sure how to feel about that.

"Wait, there's no food here?" Bastian asked, his eyes furrowing in my direction.

"Nope. It's totally empty, brother. Didn't you notice when we cleaned the kitchen?" Cade asked.

"No, I wasn't being nosy like you," he replied sarcastically.

"What? I had the munchies," Cade said nonchalantly.

"Did you eat anything this morning then?" Bastian asked me, and I began to sweat under his intense gaze again.

"Bastian, I'm fine," I said, forcing a smile to my lips, "really."

He frowned at me. I didn't like where his mind was going as he sat up straighter in his seat.

"If you didn't eat earlier then the last meal you had was before the rogue attacked you, wasn't it?"

I gave him a look, hoping he'd just drop it. "It's not that big of a deal. I'll eat when I can get back into town. You really don't have to buy dinner for me."

"Oh no, I'm getting dinner. I'll tell Elijah to bring groceries too so you have stuff here. You can't go without food, Shanely," Bastian replied, taking out his phone again. My eyes widened when I saw the text drag on in length, and I quickly placed my hand over the screen.

"Bastian, don't do that," I said, giving him a firm look. "You don't have to spend money like that on me. I doubt my uncle expected *this* when he asked you to stay here with me today."

Bastian narrowed his eyes. His face suddenly filled with confliction before he took my hand off the phone and pushed send. I was taken back, and pulled my hand away, but he held firm, refusing to let me go. Instead, he simply said, "Come with me for a minute."

My heart began skipping beats as I zeroed in on his hand wrapped around mine. My hand fit perfectly against his, and it was hard to focus on the fact he just sent his brother to the store for me. I couldn't afford to stock up. I couldn't afford to pay him back for everything, and I just needed to the basics until I could get a steady income. I forced myself to pull back, and he released my hand. But he motioned to my backdoor, and I reluctantly followed. *I rather have this conversation alone anyways*, I thought. I hated talking money.

We walked back to the back porch, and he shut the door behind us. Unease crept in now that I was alone with him again. With his wolf, it cut off the chance to really communicate. We simply just got to be with one another, which I thoroughly enjoyed, but now he was standing right in front of me, looking all gorgeous and perfect. My stomach twisted in knots, but my eyes widened slightly when he shifted on his feet like he was *nervous* too. *I made him nervous—*

"Look, I really wanted to say this when I first got here, but you weren't ready to talk, and that was okay," he stammered, and I blinked. *He babbled too.* "I can be patient," he said, sticking his hands in his pockets. "Well, with you I can be patient."

I wasn't sure what to say. I had never had a guy act nervous with me before. Half my mouth rose ever so slightly as he continued to babble.

"I am sorry for my reaction the night we met. I let my temper get the better of me with Derek, even though everyone knows he doesn't do anything unless it benefits himself, and then I snapped at you. I'm *most* sorry about that. I was upset hearing what had happened in the first place, and then when you said you were going to just leave the mountains, I just—"

Bastian's voice trailed off like he wasn't sure what to say. He seemed hesitant to tell me more and studied me as if trying to get a read on me over what he just said. I folded my arms across my chest, debating what to even say back, but I appreciated the apology nonetheless. It warmed my heart knowing he was willing to admit when he was wrong. It wasn't something I heard too often, and it made me fall a little more for him.

But we couldn't be anything to one another. We *both* knew that. A small part of me wondered if maybe that's why he's been so hesitant with me. I was becoming part of his pack now; he will defend that without question as an enforcer, but we don't know what I am. *If my dad's not a wolf then what does that make me? I could be nothing more than a threat to everyone around me.*

Bastian sighed and butterflies filled my stomach again. He had this look of pity on his face that was getting hard to stomach. I felt like such a silly girl for getting wrapped up in him in the first place. *He was just apologizing for his outburst,* I thought. *Nothing more.*

I pulled my hair to side, needing something to fiddle with as I said, "Thank you for your apology, and for everything else you've done for me, but I really don't want you to worry about me. I'm not your responsibility nor do you have to spend all this money. I know my uncle asked you to watch over me, but I'll be okay on my own too. Joining the pack will help keep me safe, and I'm sure my uncle will find the rogue quickly. I'd like to be friends, but I don't want you to feel responsible for me. I'm sure your girlfriend or family will need you at some point, if the pack doesn't already."

Bastian frowned again, looking ever so puzzled with me. "I don't have a girlfriend, Shanely," he said quietly, "and my family is back home in Denmark other than my brothers. Besides, I'm right where I want to be."

My heart thundered in my chest as he stepped closer to me. I held my breath as his eyes dropped to my lips. *Bastian was making this incredibly difficult to keep my emotions at bay*, I thought as he took another step. *I could already see it happening. My heart breaking.*

"Bastian, I—"

Suddenly, his eyes dropped lower, and he emitted a low growl, closing the distance between us.

"Who did that to you?!"

Anger flashed in his eyes as he pointed to my neck. I had been playing with my hair, and it gave a perfect view of the yellowish-blue bruise that was there from my last encounter with Peter. I had completely forgotten about it and quickly pulled my hair back over to cover it up.

He wasn't having it though and pushed my hair aside again. I stilled as his hands gently touch the bruise, inspecting my neck for anymore. He had no idea how it made me feel, but I tried to act like I was unaffected. *If he didn't move his hand soon, I wouldn't be able to keep up the charade.*

"Bastian, it's nothing."

I tried to step back to get some much needed space, but he followed until my back was pressed up against the wall of the cabin. "It's not nothing," he said gruffly. "It looks like a *handprint*. Who did this, Shanely?"

"It's just a bruise, alright? I'm fine, I promise."

"Shanely, did this happen before you came to Diablo or was this from someone in town?"

"It wasn't anyone in town," I replied as I looked to the floor. Heat filled my cheeks as I prayed he would just drop this. Anger rose in my veins for letting him see it in the first place. I had dropped my guard with them and made a very big mistake.

"Then who did this to you?" he asked, waiting for a response I wouldn't give. He sighed then. "Please just talk to me, Shanely."

Panic surged through my body, and I clenched my hands tightly. *I do not want to talk about Peter,* I snarled in my head.

"Bastian, we barely know each other," I snapped. "I don't feel like airing out all my problems to someone I barely know, okay? This is just a bruise, and it will heal so *please* drop it."

Regret washed over me the moment the words left my lips. Bastian's eyes widened, and he stepped away from me like I struck him. He stuck his hands back in his pockets, and I instantly missed their warmth. My skin felt like it was crawling as he retreated further from me, and I couldn't take it anymore. I went to him instead.

"I'm sorry. That was harsh, and I didn't mean for it to come out that way," I apologized, and it seemed to soften the hurt.

Bastian simply nodded in return saying, "I didn't mean to pry. I just want to keep you safe, and it looks bad."

"I know my uncle asked you to watch me, but this isn't something you need to worry about. I don't mean that harshly either, but *no one* here needs to worry about it because it's in my past now."

"Will this be a problem in your future though?"

"Bastian, really don't—"

"Shanely, please just answer that for now," he said, giving me a firm look. "Will it be an issue I need to watch out for in the future?"

I sighed, caving for him. "No, he won't be."

Bastian gritted his teeth but nodded and said, "Thank you for telling me, Shanely."

I nodded back, pushing the hair over the bruise and hiding it once more. Awkward silence filled the space around us, nearly eating me alive because things still didn't feel right between us. I felt awful for snapping, but there was really nothing I should do to fix it. The two of us needed space, and the closer we became, the harder it would be for me to walk away. And I *had* to walk away. I have never felt so out of control of my emotions before. I wasn't sure I could be *just* friends with this guy.

"You know at some point I won't be your responsibility, right?"

The words left my lips before I talked myself out of saying anything at all. He frowned, narrowing his eyes towards me and making my heart race all over again.

I stammered, "I don't know if this is a pack thing or what, but I'm sure my uncle will be putting you back on your normal responsibilities after your suspension. You aren't required to waste your time trying to keep me safe, and *none* of that requires you to buy food for me. Let me pay for it, please? I'd like to be friends and not just a job."

I extended my hand to him, trying to get some sort of an understanding between us. *Friends. We could be friends.* I wasn't sure I was capable of being only his friend, but I wanted to try. The idea of walking away entirely killed me, but this was a decent compromise. At least one my head and heart were both accepting. Soon, they'd find the rogue, and we'd go our separate ways, and that would be that. I needed some boundaries up because I'm sure at some point he'd find a girl that was a full-blooded wolf and not a half-blood like I was. I didn't want to be hung up on him when he did, so I was going to figure out this whole friend thing.

Bastian stared intensely at my hand before slowly drawing his eyes back to mine. That one broody look did me in. *I couldn't help it,* I thought. *No matter what I tried to tell myself, all of it was lies.* I was completely in over my head with this guy, and there was nothing I could do about it.

I needed a new bodyguard.

Suddenly, he grabbed my hand and pulled me close. I yipped in surprise by his abruptness, but his large arms wrapped around me tight, holding me firmly against him. I felt incredibly small against his large frame, but it made me feel so safe. All the stress and anxiety I've been carrying melted away instantly, and I wondered if he had a similar ability like my aunt.

Bastian whispered, "I'd do anything for you."

I froze. Unable to stop replaying those words in my head. My heart ached. It desperately wanted to stay here in Bastian's arms, but my head knew this wasn't wise. It was just making everything so difficult. I fit perfectly in his arms, but I panicked because this was the opposite of what I needed. I tried to pull away, but he held firm.

CHAPTER 7

"Please stay. Just stay, Shanely," he said quietly, his voice laced with emotion.

That one request has me caving to his every whim. I'd do anything for him if he asked me like this again. With that tone and sincerity. I leaned in to give him a real hug back, when suddenly a sharp pain hit my chest. It knocked the wind out of me, and I couldn't breathe as my chest burned in agony. *What in the world is happening?!* I thought as my heart started to race.

Bastian pulled back, concern in his eyes as he asked, "What's wrong?"

I couldn't speak. I just shook my head and tried to catch my breath. The sharp burning pain turned into a throbbing ache, and I saw Bastian wince in pain too. *Did I do something to him?* I thought as panic took over. *Is this because I'm not a full-wolf shifter?* The ache slowly traveled down my veins throughout my body, making my muscles pulse and throb.

Bastian immediately started rubbing my back as I collapsed against his chest. For some reason the closer I was to *him*, the easier the pain was to handle, and I inhaled deeply.

Cade flew through the doors, looking alarmed when he saw me in his brothers arms. The two spoke to one another, but I couldn't hear what they was saying. The pounding in my ears muted everything, and I struggled to stand on my own two feet. *This was no panic attack*, I thought as the pain surged again.

Slowly, the pain subsided until it was nothing more than a dull ache in my chest. I leaned heavily against Bastian, feeling every ab under his shirt, and trying not to blush over it.

"Are you okay Shanely?" Cade asked. I slowly nodded, feeling too overwhelmed to say anything at the moment.

"What happened? You gasped, and then my wolf felt your pain," Bastian stammered nervously.

"What?" Cade asked, narrowing his brow.

"I don't know Cade, but I could feel that burn, and so did my wolf. It was coming from her. He was pushing me hard to shift because something happened with Shanely."

"Guys, I don't know. It was just painful." I said, rubbing my chest again.

Suddenly, they both looked to me, and the corners of their mouth rose ever so slightly, until the grin spread across their face.

"Do you feel that, Bastian?" Cade asked as he put his hand to his own chest.

"Yeah, I do. I can sense your wolf, Shanely, and it's strong. I think she's waking up on her own."

My eyes widened in surprise. *I actually had a wolf?!* I thought as my smile widened. I searched inside my head for anything out of the ordinary but didn't really notice a difference about me, and I frowned slightly. I still seemed like the same old Shanely. They seemed pretty excited though, and I didn't see why they'd lie about it. There was no point in doing something like that. *I guess I'd have to trust them for now.*

As scary as it was, if I actually had my own wolf then I could protect myself from this rogue or *anyone* on my own. I wouldn't be useless anymore. *I wouldn't be an easy target,* I thought to myself. That thought had me beaming from ear to ear. Even though the thought of physically turning into a furry creature freaked me out, the possibility that I could be strong enough and *brave enough* to fight my own battles far outweighed everything else.

"Bastian, I can—"

"I know, Cade," Bastian said, giving him a firm look. "I know."

There was commotion coming from inside the house as another deep voice shouted, "Guys! I bring pizza!"

Cade flew back through the doors excitedly. "Food! Thank the lord you're here, Elijah! I honest to God though I was going to wither away from starvation."

Bastian smiled, listening to Cade continue to whine before turning back to me. "Are you sure you're okay?"

I nodded my head, not really sure how to even answer that question. He seemed to understand.

"I'll talk to Cain about this," he said, sticking his hands back in his pockets. "Everyone's wolf is different, but we've never had someone like

CHAPTER 7

you before. I'm not sure what to even tell you, but I'd watch out for signs of your wolf emerging. Your hearing and sight should start to improve too and even your speed and stamina should perk up. Those all improve with being a wolf shifter. Just tell me if something more happens or if that burning feeling comes back. We'll help you with this, Shanely. I promise, my brothers and I got your back. You're more than just a job, okay?"

I smiled at him but didn't respond. It was weird having someone stand in your corner just because they wanted to. I spent so long caring for Peter and not really having anyone be there for me. I realized then that my grandmother didn't just leave me a cabin; she left me a family.

We headed back inside, and Cade had nearly finished an entire pizza by himself already. Elijah laughed when he saw my face. "Don't worry, I brought a lot of pizza. We're all used to Cade's stomach by now, but we'll feed you too little one. I'm Elijah by the way."

He pulled me into a bear hug before I could even say hello. Elijah had lighter hair than Bastian's and was the shortest amongst the brothers. He and Cade looked closer in looks together, with Bastian being the odd one out with his darker features. Now that the three of them were together, I could see the differences.

Elijah had a slightly bigger build than his brothers and leaned more towards being clean shaven then a full beard. The differences were subtle though. The one main feature that all the brothers seemed to share was their eyes. Each one had a slight variation to their bright blue eyes, but all three were gorgeous. Bastian's was the brightest, resembling waves of the ocean, while Cade had a grayish tint to his, making it look more like denim than the water. Elijah's had a slightly tealish hue to his color. They were enough to make any girl drool.

As Elijah pulled away, rubbing his chest slightly as he looked to his brother, I noticed he had a similar scent like Bastian's too. I could smell water for some reason and cocked my head to side as I studied the triplets.

"So I brought what you asked. It's on the counter over there," Elijah said, pulling me from my thoughts as he pointed to bags of groceries. My eyes widened. *They covered the entire counter,* I thought as guilt crept inside. *It must have been expensive.*

"You really didn't need to buy me anything, guys! I should be taking care of you since you guys spent the whole day cleaning and are stuck keeping an eye on me. I can pay for those, Bastian. Just tell me what it cost, please," I stammered.

Elijah eyed Bastian, and my heart sank. *Please let it be under $200,* I thought. *That was nearly all I had left.*

Bastian gave me a sad look, and I saw his eyes drop to my neck. I frowned, tugging at my hair to make sure it was covered as Cade turned to Bastian. *They seemed to wait on him to answer,* I thought as I waited for anyone to answer me. They just looked at me with pity, like I was a charity case they needed to fix. My feet moved, and I started rummaging through the bags for the receipt. I had barely pulled it from the bag, when Elijah yanked it from my fingers.

"Oh no," he said, pocketing the slip of paper, "you're not paying me for those, Shanely. We're taking care of you, *little one,* and besides Cade will be apart of the security team that's getting set up to watch you while we hunt this rogue. We need to make sure there's enough to feed him *and* you. We take care of one of our own."

"One of your own?" I asked as my brows knitted in confusion. Suddenly, it dawned on me. "Oh, because I'm about to be part of the pack?"

The three slowly looked to one another, and I frowned again. *They kept having these silent conversations between themselves,* I thought to myself. *And giving me half-truths like they were afraid to tell me everything.* I knew becoming a shifter was going to have some weird aspects to it, but I *liked* having information. I wasn't going to freak out or run from it, and I wished they'd just let me in on their little inner circle. But then again that meant becoming closer to Bastian.

Which wasn't smart for me.

Elijah just winked at me saying, "Yeah, sure. Because you're pack."

Bastian pushed him forward abruptly, giving him a death glare. Cade laughed, grabbing another slice of pizza, while I stood there utterly lost. I opened one of the bags then. My eyes widened when I saw what they brought. Milk, eggs, bread, and cheese. Frozen waffles and pizzas. Plenty of frozen meat, veggies and fruit, and ingredients to make quick meals like spaghetti and cheeseburgers. There was so much here. Even a bag of full of toiletries and kitchen essentials. *This was too much*, I thought, worrying that the total price was more than what I had. I remembered the prices at that store. But Bastian promptly pushed a plate of pizza in my hands before taking over in the kitchen. Not letting me fuss over the items anymore.

My eyes widened when I sat at my table. He had stacked the plate with four slices piled high and a bread stick on top. *There's no way I could eat all that!* I thought to myself, but when I opened my mouth to protest, he gave me a firm look that shut me right up. *Was there something wrong with me that I was attracted to that bossy no nonsense look he owned so well?*

I didn't know how to answer that, but my pantry and fridge were full for the first time in my entire life. Little did they know the gift they just gave me.

Once the groceries were put away, we ate pizza at my table and fell into a good rhythm with one another like we've known each other for years. The time creeping ever so closely to 7, and I tried not to focus on the clock. Officially joining the McCoy pack made me nervous but listening to the boys tell stories helped distract me. Elijah and Cade were hilarious, especially when they started teasing Bastian. The broody man just shook his head, unable to contradict anything they said, and I loved every second of it. My face hurt from smiling so much, and I loved seeing Bastian's eyes light up whenever he was amused with his brothers. He was quiet for the most part, letting everyone else talk around him, but every so often that devilish grin would make its appearance, and my heart skipped a beat whenever I saw it.

They spoke about their home in Denmark with fond memories of their mother and the land the pack lived on. The woods they described sounded gorgeous, but all three insisted these mountains were way better. Their father's pack was a lot smaller than the one here, but it was also more secluded. They didn't have any neighboring packs or clans like the McCoy pack had, which helped tremendously with security, I guess.

I learned they were here for training, but they were meant to take over their own pack back in Denmark when the time was right. Bastian was to be the next Alpha with either Elijah or Cade as Beta. I frowned while Elijah explained how the hierarchy worked in a wolf pack. A heavy feeling rested on my shoulders at the thought of the triplets leaving one day, and no matter what I tried to do, I couldn't shake it. Bastian didn't seem too thrilled with the idea of being Alpha and quickly changed the topic of conversation. I didn't pry and let him change the subject, more than ready to stop talking about it anyways.

We all crashed in the living room, relaxing before it was time to leave for the lodge. I beyond stuffed from pizza and anxious to get tonight over with. I pulled one of the quilts my grandmother had and snuggled on the couch.

But then, Elijah came out of the back of the cabin and didn't seem to be in a good mood anymore. His brows knitted as he twirled something in his hands and started to frown. Then he turned to me.

"Shanely," he said quietly. "Who's Caleb?"

Bastian and Cade stopped talking and looked to Elijah before turning to me. My eyes narrowed on the middle brother.

"Just someone I met at the Den the night I was attacked," I answered truthfully. "He was super nice, and he towed my truck home for me. Why?"

They all looked at me like I committed some grave error. Bastian's gaze looked downright feral, and he quickly looked to the floor. *What in the world did I do?* I wondered.

"You mean the bar in town?" Cade asked. "We don't really go there, Shanely."

Bastian fists clenched tightly at his side, but he wouldn't look at me. They all just seemed so angry with me for going to that bar in the first place, but I was lost as to why it mattered?

"Wait— Caleb Medvedev?" Elijah asked, frowning again. "He works at the Den, Bastian."

"I'm not sure," I replied cautiously. "I never got his last name. I met his cousin Octavia too, although she wasn't too thrilled to meet me."

"I'll bet," Cade said gruffly. His angry gaze turned to Bastian. *What in the world is going on?* I thought as I blinked, scrambling to make sense of

CHAPTER 7

anything. *Their open hostility towards Caleb was a bit much*, I thought, when it suddenly dawned on me. Our conversation that night came to mind. *Caleb warned me about this. The McCoy's and his family don't like one another—does this mean Caleb is a shifter too?*

"He left his number Bastian, hoping to meet up later, and he offered her a job at the Den," Elijah said as he passed him the note before crossing his arms. He stared rather sternly at me now, and my brows knitted in confusion. *This wasn't fair.* Irritation slowly coursed through my veins as I stared right back.

Bastian grabbed the note, glaring at it as he stood up to ask me, "Were you going to call him?"

My mouth dropped as the triplets hovered over me, waiting for my answer. I tossed the blanket aside and stood. *Everyone seemed angry with me, but I hadn't done anything!* I thought to myself. *I didn't even ask Caleb to tow my truck home! But he did, and frankly it was my choice on who I decided to be friends with. Not theirs!*

"I can't even if I wanted to. I had to ditch my phone when I came here, so I don't even have a way to contact him," I snapped, and Bastian's eyes flickered with doubt. Anger rippled through me again for getting too close to a topic I didn't want to talk about. I clenched my fists saying, "Caleb was *nice* to me. He was kind enough to bring my truck back for me, and he's offering me a job, which I desperately need right now. What's your guy's problem?! Why don't you like him?"

"Wait, ditch your phone?" Elijah asked but was quickly drowned out by his brother.

"He was nice?" Bastian shouted, rubbing his face. "Shanely, Caleb's a bear shifter! They aren't nice, and you cannot trust him! You're staying away from him *and* Octavia. You cannot work there."

"She's right though, Bastian. Her truck's outside with tools around it. I saw it when I came in earlier, but I just assumed someone from the pack towed it back. I didn't smell Caleb when I came in," Elijah mentioned.

Bastian's eyes flashed red as he stormed over and looked out my front bay window. He snarled angrily before turning to me. For the first time in my life, I felt brave enough to say something. Maybe it was my wolf awakening or maybe I had finally had enough confrontation like this, but I wasn't going to cower and back down. *Not this time*, I thought as my chest burned in agreement. I squared up to Bastian, taking him by surprise, and he staggered back as I jabbed my finger in his chest.

"You don't get to decide who I spend my time with Bastian. I'm not your girlfriend or even your family. Caleb didn't treat me badly. He was a complete gentleman, and he even told me about the McCoys. He's the one who told me my mother's name, and he didn't spew so much hate like you all are doing either! I *need* his help, Bastian. I have less than $300 dollars to my name, and I won't last the month without this job!"

Tears welled in my eyes, but it wasn't because I was sad. I was angry. Absolutely livid for some reason, but I hated getting teary-eyed when I got upset like this.

"Shanely—" Bastian's voice broke, and he slowly reached out to touch me. He seemed to lose whatever fight was in him at that moment, but I moved away, not ready to let go of my anger just yet. His look of pity was becoming unbearable, and I pursed my lips together as I wiped away my tears. *This is why I didn't want to tell anyone.*

"You're going to put yourself in harm's way by getting involved with someone like Caleb," Cade snapped angrily, and I moved my attention off the eldest brother. Cade stormed over to me, and I shifted nervously on my feet.

"Caleb won't hurt me," I said as the youngest brother towered over me.

"How do you know that Caleb isn't planning something behind your back because I can promise you, he could scent what you are," Cade asked matter of factly, "and what better way to get back at the McCoy Pack then with *you*. You're making yourself an easy target by getting involved with him, especially since he knows you're a direct heir to the throne now."

"Cade," Bastian hissed, and Elijah glared at him.

An easy target.

Those words struck me, and it didn't take much to hear Peter's voice in my head again. He used to tease me relentlessly, especially right before I

CHAPTER 7

left. *It was true though,* I thought as sadness washed over me. *I was an easy target with Peter, but I was trying to change.* I wanted to be different when I came to this place. This was my fresh start. To be the Shanely I wanted to be, but I guess I hadn't changed very much at all if that's how Cade saw me. And if Cade saw nothing but an easy target, Bastian and Elijah probably did too.

"Wow, Cade— it's good to know how you really think of me. Don't stop now," I said sarcastically, "go ahead and tell me how stupid I really am for believing he was a nice guy. Let me know I'm nothing but an idiot who can't do anything right."

Peter's words rolled easily off my tongue. Cade's eyes narrowed, and I knew I pissed him off by putting those words in his mouth, but I already knew they were coming. It was the next step in belittling my every move, so why not beat him to the punch? *Maybe then it won't hurt so bad when I hear it?*

"I don't think you're dumb, but how can you seriously trust Caleb? You don't know him like we do, and you are weaker right now without your wolf. You couldn't *even* handle the rogue, so how do you expect to deal with a grizzly? He's probably plotting against the McCoy pack right now, and he'll use you to do it!"

"Cade!" Bastian bellowed. "That's enough."

Cade's words stung. *That's what they thought? That I'd be dumb enough to put the pack in danger?* I thought as tears filled my eyes. I don't know why what they thought of me hurt so badly, but it did. Peter had said far worse, but these brothers affected me so much more. I *cared* what they thought of me, and Cade just thought I was dumb and weak. Bastian looked at me with pity like I was some charity case that needed rescuing, while Elijah looked like he couldn't believe I was even *considering* working for a bear shifter. My heart hurt, feeling as pathetic as I'm sure I looked. I covered my chest with my arms and looked to my feet.

"Get out."

Cade sighed, running his hands through his beard as he stammered, "No, Baby Girl. I didn't mean it like that. You're just new to all this and still human in most ways—"

"Get out! All of you!" I shouted, startling them all. I gritted my teeth, forcing the tears aside because I refused to let them see me break. I *refused* to cry in front of them.

"Shanely," Bastian said quietly, "please—"

"All of you out now!" I shouted again, side-stepping past Bastian's outreached hand. "I would never do anything to hurt my family or this pack, but if you think so little of me then leave and don't come back! I am not weak nor am I some charity case for you to fix. I do not need *any* of you to buy me anything. I'll figure it out on my own!"

I grabbed my entire savings that I had secretly stuffed inside one of the figurines my grandmother left and forcefully put it in Bastian's hand.

He looked distraught as I stepped away, but I refused to let him give it back. I know I was officially broke now, but I was so angry, I didn't care what it would mean for me later on. My chest burned in satisfaction as I glared at them. *I didn't owe them a dime now, and that was something I needed more than anything. Freedom.* My hair shifted off my shoulders, showing the bruise on my neck, and Cade zeroed in on it.

"What's that then?" Cade snapped, pointing at my bruise.

"Leave it, Cade," I replied back, losing some of my confidence now. I quickly pulled my hair over to cover it again.

"That's a handprint," Elijah said sternly, but Cade stepped closer to me, and my eyes widened.

"So someone else managed to harm you already. God forbid what happens if the rogue catches you or Caleb and his filthy clan steals you out from under our noses. See this is what I was trying to say! You don't understand what you're doing in the shifter world, and you're going to get hurt if you don't listen to us!" Cade bellowed.

Suddenly, Bastian stood in front of me, blocking me from Cade's view. His hand gently touched my shoulder as he snarled, "Cade, shut up!"

The triplets began to argue, but I stopped hearing anything they said. Because all I could hear was Peter screaming at me again. Screaming at me because I screwed something up yet again. I felt stuck in a loop, hearing nothing but how I couldn't do anything right, and that warm burning sensation grew cold. *Maybe they were right? Maybe I wasn't capable of handling myself or keeping the pack safe. Maybe this was just a mistake coming here.*

Elijah hovered over me, waving in front of my face, but I couldn't focus on him. I was falling down the rabbit hole of self-loathing and doubt. A place I was all too familiar with.

Bastian pushed Elijah aside, and I blinked when his hands started rubbing my shoulders. He looked worried as Cade ran his hand through his hair. Soon more arguing started up again, but I was struggling to keep the tears from falling. Memories with Peter flooded my head as they continued shouting at one another, and I truly felt small. *I always hated when he yelled.* I hated how freaked out I got whenever someone shouted.

Everything that I had pushed aside in my mind came flooding back to the forefront like a dam being broken. A tear slid down my cheek as my chest tightened, and I forced myself to do what I always did, which was count my blessings.

But what were my blessings even? I thought, feeling sorry for myself all over again. I may be alive but this wasn't living. My mother and most of my family was dead and gone. I didn't know who my father was, and the one man who has ever claimed my heart was looking at me like I was a broken doll and not someone worth loving.

I blinked again as Bastian gently pulled my chin up to look in my eyes. *His beautiful, oceanic eyes,* I thought to myself. *They need to leave. They all need to just leave.* I pulled away and walked calmly to the door, and the brothers all stopped talking as I opened the back door.

"You're right, Cade. I am pathetic and weak, especially these last two years. I have been abused in every possible way before escaping here. He told me I was an easy target too, and if you both are saying it, then it must be true. I let myself stay with someone who treated me horribly because I believed him when he said I couldn't do any better than him. That I *owed* him for everything he's done for me. From giving me a place to stay when I lived in my truck, to feeding me because I was starving and had no money.

I stayed trapped in that relationship for a long time because of how he made me feel. Because I couldn't see that I deserved better. When I finally gathered the courage to try and leave, this is what I got in return," I said as I lifted my shirt to show the 3 inch scar on my stomach. I shifted my hair, exposing the bruise on my neck. "Or this when I didn't listen and obey what he demanded of me."

They all looked at me horrified, but I didn't stop. It was like I couldn't turn my mouth off now that I started spilling the dark secrets I never wanted to share. Bastian's eyes had gone red, and I turned away from him.

"You want a list of injuries I've had from him, Cade? Do you want to hear all the stories from living in the foster system? All the awful homes I've shared with dozens of other kids all struggling with their own problems. Shall I continue on?" I snapped as another tear rolled down my cheek. "I told myself that I'd be different here. That I deserved better because I wasn't what he always said I was. I wasn't dumb or helpless or an *easy-target*. But thank you, Cade, for reminding me he was right. Thank you all for making me speak about something I never wanted to discuss again. For making me feel so bad about doing something for myself like becoming friends with Caleb or getting a job. Now please, all of you leave, and don't come back."

I left them standing in the living room, storming towards my bedroom and slamming the door behind me.

Chapter 8

I laid on my bed, feeling horrible, and unable to stop replaying what happened over and over in my head. Thankfully, no one was around to see me cry. The triplets didn't try to come and talk to me, and as much as I wanted them to just go and leave me alone, a small part wished they tried. I didn't want people to know about my past, but now the brothers know everything, and I'm sure it won't be long before the entire pack does too.

I groaned as I turned over and looked at the clock. It said 6:15 pm, and I sighed. I was supposed to be at the main lodge around 7 pm, which meant getting out of bed and into nicer clothes. *Sweats and a t-shirt probably wasn't an acceptable outfit choice,* I thought as I forced myself towards the bathroom. My face was splotchy red from crying, and my hair was matted on one side. My lip curled in disgust just looking in the mirror. *How in the world am I going to fix this?*

I started washing my face, hoping it would ease my puffy eyes and help my color return. I ran my wet fingers through my hair, knowing the water would reset my curls and be good as new in a moment. I applied more make-up, going heavier than I normally did just to cover more blemishes and redness up. I turned in the mirror, inspecting myself when I was finally done, and feeling like I actually didn't look half-bad. *At least you can't tell I've been crying,* I thought as I went to my dresser.

I scurried along, wanting to leave before Bastian came back to escort me to the lodge. My uncle commanded him to watch me, but I really didn't want to see *any* of the brothers after spilling so many secrets. Most of all, I didn't want to see Bastian. Heat flooded my cheeks as the horrified look

Bastian gave earlier came to mind. *They probably want nothing more to do with me after this afternoon,* I thought as I slid on my sneakers. Sadness overwhelmed me at the thought, and I tried to shake the feeling aside. *This was for the best,* I scolded myself. *I didn't need a bodyguard anyways. I'll join the pack like I agreed to, but then I'll get distance from everyone for a while then.*

According to my uncle, belonging to a pack is protection in itself, and maybe another enforcer could keep watch over the cabin instead of the triplets trailing me everywhere I went. It sounded like a good idea, but I couldn't get my heart to want it. I sighed as I looked back at my bed. All I wanted was to climb under the covers and ignore everyone and everything.

Cain will come find you, I thought as I debated doing just that. *Just join and then head straight back to the cabin.* I didn't think it would take too long to join the pack, and my uncle would understand that I was exhausted and overwhelmed already. Adding more people to the mix would just make everything worse, and I had a long walk ahead of me in the morning anyways.

Satisfied with my escape plan, I went to my door and tried to open it, but it wouldn't budge. I pushed harder this time and still nothing. *Was I locked in?! Did Bastian lock me in my room?* I thought to myself as my heart began to race. I knelt down and peeked under the door, only to find a large shadow lying in front of it.

Something was blocking my door! I thought as panic surged through me. Memories of when Peter locked me in the closet came flooding back, and I pushed even harder. My shoulder hit the wood, and the door budged just a bit. Something *grunted*, and the door flung open as I attempted to burst through. I yelped as I stumbled forward, and two sturdy hands caught my waist before I face planted on the hardwood floor. I looked up to find Bastian hovering over me.

He gently put me back on my feet as he mumbled, "Sorry."

"It's fine," I answered softly. The two of us stood there awkwardly then. Unsure what to do or even say. Heat crept up my cheeks again, and I turned on my heels to flee like the coward I truly was.

CHAPTER 8

"Wait," Bastian said, grabbing my hand. "Please, Shanely."

I couldn't look back at him. I bit my lower lip, trying to stop the tears from forming in my eyes and feeling so silly for being so emotional in the first place. My chest warmed as I forced myself to get a grip and quickly wiped my eyes. I stilled when he stepped closer, closing the gap between us and feeling his breath on the back of my neck. Nerves rattled my core as he gently pulled my chin to face him.

"We're sorry, Shanely," he whispered softly, "all of us. We care about you, but we seriously overreacted. You are *not* an easy target nor do any of us think you're stupid. We just don't want to see you get hurt again, and those marks on you aren't easy to look at. Our wolves see everything in black and white, and it's hard to control sometimes. Plus, knowing a rogue had marked you *scares* us all, but Cade was harsh, and he feels horrible for it. We had no idea about your past, but it's no excuse. Please, forgive us."

"It doesn't matter, Bastian," I muttered as I pulled away from him, retreating to my room once more. *Looks like I was skipping tonight after all,* I thought to myself. My eyes widened when Bastian blocked me from shutting the door on him and followed me inside.

"Shanely, it matters to me and my brothers. It kills me that I've hurt you when I swore I never would."

I scoffed, tucking my arms around my waist. "I don't remember you swearing anything like that, and you barely know me, Bastian. You don't owe me anything."

The breath caught in my chest as he stepped closer. His eyes darkened as he leaned in and whispered, "I'd give you *everything*, Shanely."

My heart skipped a beat as his words sunk in. *The way he looked at me right now—* I shook myself from those thoughts. *He and I can't be* anything. *You're going to get yourself hurt if you don't stop this.*

"You can't, Bastian," I stammered, pulling further away. "I was at that meeting too, alright? I'm not even supposed to be alive according to the shifter laws. Honestly, just being a pack mate is illegal, and you don't want someone like me."

The words barely left my lips, and I wasn't sure if he could even hear me.

I struggled to say the rest, but it *needed* to be said.

"I come with baggage, Bastian," I whispered softly, "and a past. We are two totally different people, and it just isn't going to work."

"What else has happened to you?"

Bastian's voice was low, almost like a growl, and his eyes had turned gold again. I held my breath, realizing how safe I truly felt with him. Those gold eyes meant his wolf was close, but the thought of seeing his wolf felt almost like a comfort rather than fear. *I don't think I would ever be afraid of Bastian or his wolf,* I thought to myself. The fact that he didn't scare me in the areas he should, but terrified me in other ways, only proves my head and heart did not agree when it came to Bastian.

I shook my head, ignoring his question altogether. "Never mind, Bastian. Please, just give me space."

He wasn't having it and took another step closer. "Shanely, how many people have hurt you?"

"Bastian, leave it—"

"No," he cut me off before I could finish. "My wolf wont rest, Shanely! You've been marked by a rogue that we can't find, and now this with your past. My wolf knows there is someone alive in this world who did horrible things to you, and he is *not* happy about that. I'm pissed that I can't kill him right now. I'm pissed I can't find the rogue. I'm pissed because I need to keep you safe and happy, but I'm failing miserably! If you don't want to give me the details, fine. Just tell me if this is something I need to look out for too. I can't protect you if I don't know."

I watched Bastian's eyes glow brighter and brighter and wondered how close he was to shifting. *He wasn't kidding when he said it was hard to control,* I thought to myself as I studied him. *His wolf was protective, and for some reason he wanted to protect me.* The corners of my mouth rose slightly as my chest warmed again. This giddy, High school, dorky girl meets the football jock feeling washed over me, and I ducked my head to keep him from seeing me blush like that.

And just like that, I caved. I put my own fears and issues aside to calm his wolf.

CHAPTER 8

"No," I replied, "there is no one else you need to watch for. I left Peter when I came here, and there is no way he will ever find me. It's why I ditched my phone, but I don't want to talk about him anymore, and I don't want to discuss my childhood either. I've already said more than I ever wanted to, and I need him and everything else to stay in the past. I'm already ruined, but I'm trying to be a different person, and I can't do that with everything hanging over me so please— just let that be enough."

Bastian's eyes returned to his normal piercing blue, and he gently touched the side of my cheek. "Shanely, you're not ruined. There isn't anything you could tell me that will change what I think of you. You're beautiful."

My eyes widened, and my heart fluttered inside my chest. That warmth I felt earlier came rushing back as he took another step towards me. I couldn't believe what was happening, and when his gaze dropped to my lips, my heart began to race again. *Was he going to kiss me now?*

"Bastian—"

A howl rattled the woods outside, interrupting us, and I nearly jumped out of my skin. It sounded just like the rogue, and I practically jumped into Bastian as the howl sounded again. *Please be friendly— please be friendly,* I thought as my heart pounded in my chest. But when Bastian wrapped his arms around me to hold me, I realized what I had done and quickly stepped back. My cheeks reddened slightly, and I crossed my arms over my chest as I about *died* from embarrassment.

"It's okay," he said, dropping his arms to his side. "It's just Cade. I made him leave after everything happened, but he won't leave the perimeter. His wolf has been pacing back and forth, waiting for you to wake up, and he must be close enough to hear us talking."

"I'm not sure I have much to say to him," I answered, looking to my feet.

"Just give him a chance to apologize, please. He and his wolf are in agony over it. Cade means well but sometimes his mouth messes everything up. He has a difficult time explaining himself, and when he gets riled over something, he can come across sort of harsh. Cade cares about you, Shanely. We all do."

It was the please that did me in, and I gave him a small nod, allowing

Bastian to lead me outside. I was mad at Cade, but I also hated that he was so upset. I didn't like all this tension between us, and surprisingly all I wanted to do was fix it. Just like with Bastian, I wanted to calm Cade's wolf and make it right again. I couldn't understand why I felt so strongly about the triplets. *Maybe it was the fact my wolf was slowly waking up?* I wondered, frowning slightly. *Every other shifter here acted emotionally so maybe it was just a wolf thing.*

I slowly peeked over to the broody man walking on my right. My heart skittered in my chest as I studied him. *He was breathtakingly gorgeous,* I thought as my eyes roamed over his defined jaw and full lips. He was tall too, nearing 6' 4 if I had to guess. My head came to the top of his shoulders as we walked, and all I could think about was shoving him against the wall and kissing him. My cheeks heated at the thought, and I forced myself to look away. *Nothing about the way I felt for this guy was normal. Not normal in the slightest.*

The sun was just beginning to set as we stepped out onto the porch, making my part of the woods absolutely beautiful. I didn't get to take it in before two large, dark gray wolves appeared from the trees. They reminded me so much of Bastian's wolf that I just knew it was Cade and Elijah, but being nearly identical in size and color, it was hard to tell them apart from each other.

One bolted forward, jumping across the creek and bounded the steps to us. He sat behind me and pushed his snout between my legs. He rested his head against my feet, and I looked to Bastian for help. The broody man said nothing though as he watched the two of us together, and I pursed my lips into a tight line. I was about to ask him outright who this was when I looked down and noticed the wolf had covered his snout with his paw. *Just as Bastian had earlier,* I thought to myself. The wolf stole a peek up at me before covering his face again and waiting. I leaned down and gently scratch behind his ears. *This must be Elijah. It seemed all three brothers wanted to apologize.* I stroked his fur, letting him know we were okay, and he nestled his head to lay on my feet. I smiled softly as he got cozy, but my smile fell when I looked back to the creek and found the last brother just sitting on

CHAPTER 8

the far side.

Cade.

He just waited across the creek for me, and I frowned, unsure what to do. Cade looked as sad as Bastian had this morning, but he continued to stay put on that side of the creek. *Bastian did the same thing this morning*, I thought to myself. *Is Cade waiting for me to invite him in?* I looked to Bastian, and he gave me a swift nod.

"He's waiting for permission," he said, crossing his arms. "The creek is the line and crossing it means coming into your personal space. He won't move until you tell him to."

I turned back to Cade, who waited with his head down. Sighing, I whispered, "You can come in, Cade."

Cade slowly crossed the creek. He could have easily jumped across and not gotten wet, but he walked through it, soaking himself with each step. I'm sure the water was cold by now, but he didn't seem to even notice. He stopped at the stairs before shifting in front of me.

"Shanely," he said as he finally looked at me, "I am so sorry. I completely screwed up earlier and said things that were cruel. I didn't mean it the way it came out. I just don't want to see anything happen to you because you're like—" He paused, glancing at Bastian before frowning slightly. I looked to the eldest brother, not understanding what was happening. "You're like my sister," Cade said, pulling me from my thoughts. "I'm here to protect you, Baby Girl. Always. And I'm so sorry I was the one to hurt you. I let my wolf get in the way, and it was wrong. It isn't always black and white like my wolf tends to see it. Will you please forgive me?"

My chest warmed again, and I held my breath. It felt *alive* and seemed to be pulling towards Cade and Elijah. Towards Bastian. *Was this my wolf?* I thought as the burning sensation traveled down my body. *Is she the one trying to tell me something?*

I smiled softly as another wave traveled across my chest. I realized for the first time in my life I wasn't alone. *She* was there. Albeit barely, but my wolf was there in some way, and she was helping me. No matter what happens, I'd never be without her. My chest warmed again, and I slowly looked to the brothers. They were the closest thing I had to friends, and I couldn't deny the pull I had towards Bastian. As wrong as it was, I wanted him. Smiling, I decided to just trust my wolf, and I sauntered down the steps and wrapped my arms around Cade. I didn't care about the fight anymore. I just wanted friends. I wanted to be *their* friend.

Cade tensed slightly as I hugged him, but soon I felt his arms wrap around me and squeeze tightly.

"Cade— I can't breathe," I choked out.

He released me, grinning like a banshee at me. "Oh, sorry! I forgot you're not a full wolf yet."

I laughed, getting a deep breath in before replying, "Yeah— working on that."

"I really am sorry, Shanely."

"It's fine," I said softly. "I've forgiven far worse, and this was the least of my problems. My gut is telling me you're not lying, so I'd like to just forget it ever happened, if that works for you?"

I leaned into his embrace again, noticing his frown. His eyes glossed over before his attention snapped back to me, and he smiled. "I would like nothing more, Baby Girl."

Cade kissed my forehead before letting me go. *Something happened just now*, I thought to myself as my gaze shifted back to Bastian. His tight lipped smile looked forced as he walked down the stairs to meet us.

My mouth opened, but before I could ask what was wrong, Elijah bounded into view and shifted next to me. He tossed an arm around my shoulder saying, "C'mon, Shanely. You can walk with me to the lodge."

I frowned as he pulled me away from his brothers, and I quickly looked to Bastian again. *He and Cade were talking quietly amongst themselves, and Elijah was clearly the distraction,* I thought to myself. *But why? What was so bad they couldn't say it in front of me?*

Elijah walked so fast, it was hard to keep up with his long strides. It took me three steps to his one, and soon my lungs ached as I huffed and puffed with every step. He seemed to finally catch on to my dilemma and slowed down for me. The others had quickly caught up, and I wondered how long

CHAPTER 8

it would take before I was able to run like they could.

Bastian smiled at me as they caught up to me and Elijah, and I decided to 'poke the wolf,' so to speak, and ask the question I'm sure they were hoping I'd avoid.

"So— are you guys going to be okay if I thank Caleb for bringing my truck back?" I asked quietly.

I noticed the look they gave each other, but I kept quiet about it. *They were allowed to have their feelings too,* I thought. Just because I didn't have issues with Caleb or his family doesn't mean the triplets weren't justified with theirs. I just didn't want any part of this feud.

"We don't trust bears, Shanely," Bastian answered, pulling me from my thoughts, "but if you insist on seeing him then at least let one of us take you. Can you agree to that?"

Wow, I thought, eyes widening. *I expected more of a fight with this.* The friends I chose *was* my decision, but I understood belonging to a pack changed certain things, and they grew up in this world, while I didn't. The feud may seem normal to them, but I just didn't feel that way. I didn't get a bad vibe from Caleb. Other than the triplets and my family, he was one I felt oddly comfortable with. Like I knew him for years somehow. I wanted to figure out why I felt so comfortable with him, but the triplets seemed to be trying with me, and it was sweet.

"A compromise. Sure, I can be okay with that, but I really don't think you have anything to worry about. I didn't get any bad vibes from him at all."

"We'll see," Elijah muttered.

A small smirk crept up my lips, and I shook my head.

"It will have to be in town though. That's the only neutral area we have around here," Cade chimed in, giving me a small smile.

"Why can't Caleb come to my cabin?" I asked. "It's my place, and if I'm inviting him then it should be allowed. Right?"

They slowly glanced at one other again, and I saw their eyes gloss over. *Just like earlier with Cade— are they talking to each other?*

"That actually might just work out. Technically, if they are formally invited then there isn't an issue with the land laws, but you have to get the

Alpha's approval for that one. However, your cabin is half in neutral lands anyways. That one road, the cabin, and your front yard is the very start of neutral lands. Your grandmother insisted on building her cabin right there on the line, I guess," Elijah answered.

"Is that why everyone stops across the creek?" I asked.

Bastian nodded his head. "The creek and your land towards the road are yours in neutral land. The 5 acres behind the creek that you own are in McCoy territory. Your property is literally right on the border."

"Ah," I said as everything these last few days made sense, "well when I can I'd like to say thank you at least. The number's useless right now since I don't have a phone, but I'd like to say something. He saved me a lot of trouble towing my truck back here."

"Speaking of phones," Cade said, handing me a box. "Here you go."

I raised a brow but opened the box to find a sleek, brand-new phone inside. *It was the newest model in touch screen phones,* I realized, and my eyes widened.

"Cade, I can't accept this. It's too much."

He backed far away from me with his hands up. "Oh no, you need a phone. None of us like you without one. You can't mind link us if there's a problem until you get your wolf anyways. Plus, I was a jerk earlier, and it's the least I could do."

"Cade—" I protested, handing him back the phone. "I already accepted your apology. You didn't have to buy me a phone."

"We were planning to anyways when we heard yours was gone. You need to be able to call *anyone* of us in the pack. Until you're a shifting wolf, this is the safest thing for you," Bastian said as his hand wrapped around mine, and he pushed the phone back to me.

My arm tingled everywhere his hand went, and I missed his touch the moment he dropped his hand back to his side. I looked at the rose-gold phone with multiple cameras on it. *I had never had a phone like this before,* I thought as a small smile curved on my lips. It was really cool, and I needed a new phone badly. *Plus, this number Peter wouldn't have or ever find. That was a huge selling point.*

CHAPTER 8

"Well, thank you," I said gratefully. "Just please no more. I don't like getting gifts, okay? I'll pay you for this when I can get a job."

"Absolutely not, Baby Girl. This is a no-strings attached phone, OK? Don't look at it as a gift. Just a bit more security for you while we look for the rogue," Cade said, giving me a pointed look.

Bastian held out his hand and helped me over a fallen log in our path. Butterflies filled my stomach, noticing he let his hand linger a moment longer before letting me go.

"Thank you," I said softly. "All of you really. I appreciate you watching over me with the rogue, and I really appreciate the phone. It would have taken me a while to save for one."

Cade wrapped his arm around me saying, "Anytime, Baby Girl."

Bastian pushed his arm off and glared at him, while Elijah just laugh. Cade grinned, winking at me.

"Cade programmed our numbers in the phone already along with the Alpha's and Cassia's. You can add the rest of your family's numbers tonight," Bastian said, turning his attention back to me.

"I added Caleb's number too. Although, I was seriously hoping you wouldn't want it," Cade said.

"I appreciate it. I'd like to at least say thank you. I don't know if he will want to stay friends now that I know I'm a wolf. I bet the job will be off the table now too," I replied with a sigh.

"Well, he must have smelled something different about you. He didn't run then, so who knows," Elijah chimed in as the lodge came into view.

"You really don't need to get a job though, Shanely. The pack takes care of its own, and you always have us," Bastian commented. He stepped closer to me, and I noticed every time his arm touched mine. *God, I had it bad—*

"I'd really like to do something," I said, getting space. "I don't want the pack or you three paying for everything. I don't like to owe people, and I can work. Will the pack or you guys be okay if he offers me a job still?"

I could see the despair on all three of their faces, but Bastian softened first. He sighed when he turned to face me.

"Let's just handle tonight first, okay? I want to make sure Caleb understands the deal with you before you decide what you want to do. And I need to make sure it will even be safe for you to work there because honestly, we really aren't welcome. We can also show you the places that wolf shifters own for safer job options than the bar, if you'd like. For now, let's just get you part of the pack officially. Are you okay with that?" Bastian asked.

A heaviness fell on me, and I didn't know why. I was excited to work at the Den for some reason, but I nodded my head anyways. *He was trying to meet me halfway,* I thought to myself. *I could see that.* I know I technically didn't need their permission on what job I took or the friends I made, but I also knew I needed to learn more about shifter life before deciding. *I needed to be smart about this, and nothing would happen tonight anyways.*

Bastian seemed relieved, and he pulled back the branch that was covering the pathway, exposing the lodge. Seeing it again made my anxiety rise, especially when a large crowd had already gathered. My feet felt like lead, and I quickly dropped behind the boys as nerves ate me alive. Bastian slowed down his walk to match mine.

"Hey, I can feel your panic. It's going to be okay," he said softly, "you know that, right?"

"What can't you wolves do?" I asked, barking out a laugh and hoping to change the subject. *Must be an animal thing like being able to smell fear,* I thought, but Bastian just grinned before shrugging.

"There isn't much I can't do when it comes to you," he whispered in my ear. His breath warmed my neck, and suddenly I was nervous about a whole different thing.

I'm sure his brothers heard with their wolfy ears, but they gave no indication that they did. *Thankfully.* My face was already as red as a tomato.

Bastian suddenly grabbed my hand saying, "Come on. I promise, I'll stay by your side the whole time."

"Thank you, Bastian," I replied, and he squeezed my hand reassuringly.

I smiled and let him lead me to the front porch where my aunt and uncle stood. The large crowd parted for us, whispering as I passed by. Some had tears in their eyes, which was odd, but I noticed a few looked downright angry. Derek was standing in the middle of that group next to a young blond

CHAPTER 8

girl, who was outright glaring at me.

Figures.

Bastian and his brothers didn't miss a beat and emitted a low growl in their direction. They quickly turned and changed the look on their face, giving me the fakest smiles now. Well, everyone but the young girl. She just stared back at Bastian and I. At our hands intertwined. *Maybe this was his ex?*

Great— I thought to myself. *Now I get to worry about her too.* We weren't together, but a small part of me loved the fact that she thought that.

Bastian squeezed my hand again, tearing me away from my thoughts. I looked up to see my aunt and uncle coming down the stairs to meet us. They smiled before they both gave me big hugs and then greeted the brothers.

"Looks like you have your very own enforcers, Shanely," Aunt Cassia said, chuckling.

A blush stained my cheeks, and I ran my hand through my hair nervously. "They've been taking good care of me, but I wouldn't call them mine."

Cade bit his bottom lip as he dropped his head. He shifted on his feet, and my uncle Cain noticed. *I wasn't trying to throw him in the hot seat*, I thought, but thankfully Cain merely gave him an odd look before moving on.

"I do like knowing you have my best enforcers protecting you. I might just keep it this way while we hunt the rogue, if you're okay with it, Shanely," Cain asked, taking his eyes off a nervous Cade.

"I'm sure they're going to have better things to do than watch over me, Uncle Cain."

Bastian gave me a pointed look before responding, "We'd be honored, Alpha Cain. We enjoy spending time with Shanely, and we will protect her with our lives."

"We'd be honored, Alpha," Elijah and Cade said in unison as they gave my uncle and I a bow.

My eyes widened, and I stepped back a little. *My uncle may be the Alpha, but that didn't make me anything special.* Once I had my wolf, I really didn't need protecting anyways, but my uncle spoke before I could object any further.

"Good. It's settled then. You three will be assigned to protect Shanely from here on out and are not allowed to leave her side," Cain commanded with that power again. This time it was quick, and the triplets merely took in a sharp breath. No pained look. No hum in the air. Just one charge, and it was over.

I whispered to my aunt, "What was that?"

She leaned over as my uncle talked to the triplets. "That's the Alpha's power. Cain's able to command everyone in our pack when he uses it. Any shifter really. Your uncle gave the brothers an Alpha Command, which basically binds them to whatever he tells them to do. They physically cannot go against it now. It's painful to resist, and he can also force a shift by using his power as he did with Bastian earlier today. We have sort of a hierarchy just like natural wolves. Kind of like a chain of command. An Alpha's eyes are the only ones to ever turn red. I am Alpha female, so my eyes turn gold or red, depending on which power I use, but my power isn't as strong as my mate's. It's why we were so surprised when Bastian was able to disobey before."

"How did he do that?"

The corners of her mouth rose. "I have some theories, but for now let's get this show on the road!"

Bile rose to the back of my throat as she drug me up the stairs. The triplets stood behind me to the side, while my uncle Cain stood in front. Ash and Aspen stepped forward and hugged me before standing to my left next to my aunt. All I could see was a plethora of faces.

So *many* faces.

"Everyone! Thank you for coming to a very special ceremony tonight. Tonight, we welcome our long-lost niece into our pack!"

Everyone cheered and clapped their hands. I *was* excited, and desperately trying to show it because all I wanted to do was throw up. *God, I felt like I was standing on a stage with every pair of eyes settled on me. Just me.*

I wanted to run.

"Everyone knows how this will go, but I'll explain it to Shanely as she is new to this. Shanely, our pack has been around for a long time. We've

CHAPTER 8

moved all over this earth before our ancestors settled on this land. We've grown and changed over time, but we still keep our traditions. Each shifter race has a special song we sing to announce important events. Our song calls to our wolf and has been said to have been sung when the first wolf shifters appeared long ago in a land far from here."

The pack started stomping and clapping to a beat I had never heard before. It sounded intimidating as well as familiar and beautiful. I looked back to Cain who smiled at me.

"This, Shanely, is the most important event to us."

And then he started singing.

My mother told me someday I would buy
Galleys with long oars
Sail to distant shores
Stand up on the prow
Noble barque I steer
Steady course to the Haven
Hew many foe-man
Hew many foe-man

Everyone joined in, and the voices rose in harmony. My eyes widened. *It was a sight to see.* I looked back at Bastian as he smiled and sang along with the rest of them. His deep, gritty voice sounding utterly perfect, and my chest warmed again.

My uncle took my hands in his, pulling me from the man who had stolen my heart. Because I guess I could admit that now. A warmth came from my uncle, traveling up my arms to my center core. I held my breath, feeling it wrap around my heart, and then suddenly it locked in place, and I could feel everyone's wolf around me.

I gasped, breathing hard as the pack bonds connected to me. Every single wolf here was connected to me. My senses burst to life as my heart pounded in my chest. I could smell them, hear them, and see things so clearly. Pain burst through my chest, and my uncle Cain's eyes went wide. He stared at me in stunned silence as that warmth turn to a burn inside of me. My whole body felt hot like a fire rippled through my core.

And then I felt her. *My wolf.*

She was yanked from my center and pushed through so forcefully, I gasped for air. I felt everything from the softness of her fur to her steady, strong heartbeat all *within* me. No more wondering if she was actually here. There was no denying her presence, and my knees shook. *This is impossible!* I thought as her eyes opened.

Everything surged again, and I dropped to the floor and into the dark.

Chapter 9

I woke up inside a room I did not recognize and was laying on a rather comfortable bed. *I must be inside the lodge,* I thought to myself, trying to get ahead of the anxiety this time. The room I was in was dark yet cozy. A simple bedroom with a hand-carved, log bedframe, and a fireplace across from it. There was no fire lit, but it didn't matter as I was plenty warm, and soon I realized why.

Bastian was in his wolf form, laying across my legs, fast asleep. I tried to think back on what happened before I dropped like a sack of potatoes. I remembered the burning sensation hitting me like a truck, and then I got connected to the pack. I remembered the pack bonds, which looked almost like ribbons that wove between us as my wolf appeared.

I could feel her right now nestled inside me. *Well, this will take some getting used to,* I thought as a small smile grew on my face. My wolf was here. I was an, honest to God, shifter. My small smile turned wide. *I was like my mother after all—*

All this time I was so much more than what I ever realized. I focused internally again and blew out a puff of air. She wouldn't budge when I tried to wake her, and I frowned. I could feel her and sense her there, but that was it. She wasn't communicating or reaching out at all. Not even to shift, which was odd because it seemed like everyone struggled to stop their wolves from shifting. Bastian always talked like he knew what his wolf thought and felt at all times, but mine was quiet. Like the necklace that hung around my neck, she was just there. I sighed and decided to leave it alone for now. She was here, and that's all that mattered. I gently scratched behind Bastian's ears, waking him up.

"Hey."

Bastian stirred briefly before perking his head up. He was fully awake now and let out a soft whine before scooching closer to lay his head on my chest. His presence was comforting, and I rubbed the top of his head.

"What happened, Bastian?"

Before he could answer, my aunt and uncle entered the room. Bastian emitted a low growl but softened when the light came on.

"You're alright," my aunt said with a sigh of relief. *Why wouldn't I be alright?* I wondered nervously.

"What happened, Aunt Cassia?" I asked, needing answers. By the look on her face right now, I don't think blacking out was a common thing when joining a pack.

Cain looked solemn when he turned to the wolf lying next to me. "Bastian, can you give us a minute alone?"

Bastian emitted a low growl and didn't budge. *He clearly did not want to leave,* I thought as I shimmed up in the bed. Bastian placed one of his paws on my leg as if warning me not to move any further, and I turned to my family, unsure what to do. I had seen this look before. They had bad news and were trying to give me privacy to spare my feelings. My stomach churned as I thought about what they possibly had to say. *Were they changing their minds about keeping me a secret? Was something wrong with my wolf?*

Cain sighed. "Bastian, I'm going to forgive that one but not again. Are we clear? She's my niece, and she's safe. You and your wolf need to head out for a little bit. Go and get Shanely food. She's probably starving by now."

Bastian looked to me, eyes full of concern, like he hadn't thought about me possibly being hungry. Like he was kicking himself for not planning ahead. It was sweet, but he really didn't need to do this. *It's not like I was his girlfriend,* I thought. *Just the girl he's been ordered to watch.* He still wasn't budging, and my uncle glared.

"Go ahead," I said, scratching the back of his ears and giving him a tight lipped smile. "I'll stay here until you come back with food, okay?"

CHAPTER 9

Bastian seemed to accept this and slowly trotted out the door. Uncle Cain closed it behind him.

"Okay, out with the bad news," I said as I sat up fully in bed. "It's why you made him leave, right? Am I losing my wolf or something? I know I feel her, but I can't wake her up or shift or anything. I'm losing her, aren't I? That's what's wrong—"

"No, no, sweetie," Cassia stammered, placing her hand on mine, "you didn't lose her. Joining our pack seemed to wake her up, but she's being dormant for now. We aren't sure as to why that is, but we do need to discuss something."

I frowned. *If it wasn't my wolf then what was wrong?*

"Have you been feeling sick at all? Any noticeable changes?" Uncle Cain asked me, and I gave him an odd look.

"Some," I answered truthfully. "I'm assuming it's because of everything that's happened though and the changes with my wolf."

I was taking my feelings for Bastian to my grave, but when my uncle looked at my aunt grimly, I tucked my knees to my chest as my stomach twisted. *Something was really wrong,* I thought as Cain leaned against the bed frame.

"Shanely," he said softly, "did you know that wolf shifters are pretty similar to regular wolves?"

I shook my head no, frowning as I waited for him to get to the point.

"Like wolves, we carry children for a shorter time than humans do. Around 5-6 months is normal for a shifter to carry to full term. We tend to have more than one at a time too, just like wolves in the wild do. We have one major difference though, and it's the ability to notice when a wolf is carrying."

I froze in fear and slowly pulled my hand away from my aunt. *No—* I thought as my heart thundered in my chest. *They can't mean—*

"As Alpha, I am able to tell when someone in my pack is carrying a pup. Even at the very beginning before the mother even knows. It's a safety thing, so we can guard that wolf more carefully because at the halfway mark, they can't shift until they give birth. I'm the only one with the ability."

My shoulders fell as I stared blankly at my uncle. He sighed, sitting down on my right side, saying, "Shanely, when you joined my pack, your wolf woke up. When the bond snapped in place, officially making you part of the McCoy Pack, my ability was now able to work with you. Shanely, did you know that you're pregnant?"

The second the words left his mouth, my whole world came *crashing* down. Panic surged through my veins as I scrambled far away from them both, instantly having a hard time breathing. *This can't be happening,* I thought to myself as I paced the room. My body shook hard, and it was all I could do to remember to breathe. *I was pregnant. I was pregnant, and Peter was the father.*

Oh God, Peter was the father.

A sob escaped my lips as those words repeated themselves over and over in my head. I gasped for air as I sobbed even harder. *I couldn't be pregnant—I just—*

My aunt and uncle rushed over, but I was lost. I was so lost to my own desperate and horrifying thoughts that I barely even saw them.

I was pregnant by a monster—

Anger surged through my veins, and my chest burned again. I shook my head. *Not just anger,* I thought to myself. I was *livid.*

I had fought so hard to flee that man, and now a piece of him would always be with me. *There was no escaping him,* I realized. *Oh God— what if he ever finds out?*

I screamed in agony, gripping my hair as I crumbled to the ground in tears. My aunt wrapped her arms around me, holding me as my uncle knelt down looking terrified. I could scent their fear as they spoke low to one another, but I couldn't stop crying to even explain.

"Please, tell us what's wrong?" Cain demanded, but I shook my head. I couldn't get my mouth to work right as fear rippled through me.

My aunt tried to console me as I sobbed on the ground. They didn't know what to do, and how could they? The only people who knew about Peter were Bastian and his brothers. *Oh God, Bastian! He can't find out about this! What would he think of me then?*

CHAPTER 9

I fell onto my aunt's shoulder, completely lost in my own anger and fear. I thought I was free of that man. I thought I had a new chance at life, but now I was forever tied to him. I didn't know what I was going to do. *I'm too young to be a mom*, I thought to myself. *I never even had one; how would I know how to raise a baby?*

The door slammed open, and Bastian ran inside, dropping my food at the door.

"What happened? What did you do to her?!" he demanded as he crossed the room to me. His eyes settled on mine, and another sob escaped my lips. I buried my head in my aunt's embrace, unable to look at him anymore.

Bastian is never going to want me now, I thought as my chest burned in agony. Even my wolf seemed angry, making everything that much harder to deal with. *Being not a sole wolf was bad enough, but this? This was too much to ask him to be okay with.*

My wolf howled inside, and it felt like my chest split wide open from the heartbreak. *I should have never let myself get attached to him.* Some pack members already thought I was an abomination. *What would they think of this child?* This child that would be *half-human*. If the Division found out, we could all be dead before I've even given birth.

The weight of everything felt too much, and I couldn't stop my mind from racing. More footsteps sounded as others had come in to see the latest spectacle. *I just wish everyone would go away*, I thought as I wrapped my arms around my waist. *This was humiliating enough as it was.*

Shouting ensued, and then a scuffle, but I couldn't bring myself to look. I had curled into the fetal position, wishing the floor would open and swallow me up forever. I've never had a panic attack this bad before. I had never felt this angry before, and that's when I felt her.

My aunt.

She was using her ability, pulling my fear, sadness, and panic from me, while screaming at everyone else. My eyes suddenly dried up, and they widened when I finally looked to everyone.

My uncle's nose was bleeding, and boy did he look pissed off. Bastian's face was red with marks on him as well, with Elijah and Cade holding him back from advancing Cain again. And by the look of it, he *wanted* to.

"Everyone needs to stop right—"

I tugged on Cassia's arm, halting her from spilling my secret, and she turned to me with wide eyes.

I whispered, "Don't tell them."

Then I passed out because she pulled too much.

Chapter 10

The morning light shown on my face, and my eyes fluttered as I rolled to my side to get away from it. Suddenly, I sat up.

Morning, I thought to myself. *It was morning.*

My heart raced inside my chest as I looked around the room. I was alone and let out the breath I had been holding. *They were gone— it's for the best anyways.* Tears filled my eyes, and I cautiously let my hand drift to my stomach. *There was a baby in there,* I thought as my stomach churned. *A little person that would count on me to love and protect it from harm. Me— of all people.*

Bile rose to the back of my throat, filling my mouth with saliva as the weight of it all hit me like a ton of bricks again. I ran into the small bathroom attached to the room and heaved into the toilet. I couldn't stop, and my eyes watered as I lost what little was in my stomach. Soon, I was just dry-heaving as there was nothing left inside. I leaned against the tub when it finally subsided, and just let myself be for a moment.

If Bastian didn't think I was ruined before, I thought to myself, *he will when he finds out now.* He will never look at me the same way again. No one will, for that matter, and my heart broke again. There were moments between us I felt like maybe one day Bastian could look past everything and accept me. The real me. It was a long shot as it was, with me not being a full wolf, but the things he'd say, and the way he made me feel gave me *hope.*

Even Cade and Elijah were becoming fast friends, which wasn't an easy thing for me. But now, everyone will only see the baby bump, and the danger it would bring to the pack. I can never fully put Peter in my past now. I felt the tears run down my face as I pulled my knees up to my chest.

What am I supposed to do now?

My first night at the lodge came to mind. It wasn't safe to stay here anymore. That much was clear. The pack barely wanted me as it was. They won't want this kid here too. The only way to keep us both safe was to leave.

But how was I supposed to be a mother anyhow? I wondered as I turned around and leaned my back against the tub. I didn't have a mother growing up. All the foster moms either didn't care or were too tired from working to even do anything motherly towards me. I once was in a *home* with 8 other children. We all shared two small rooms. One for the boys, and the other for the girls. The kids were mean and selfish, and we barely had enough to eat. The man, who played the role of foster dad, spent most of the household's income on alcohol and lottery tickets. It was horrible, and someone eventually reported the family for gross negligence. Honestly, I think it was because of the way we all looked and probably smelled heading into school.

I shuddered, thinking about that place and how horrible it was for me. That was my life with a family. *That* was my experience. Except now I was the one responsible. I was the one who had to raise this child and provide for it somehow with my nonexistent job— *I was going to screw this up somehow.* I just knew it.

Oh, God.

My eyes widened when I realized I would have to give *birth*. The horrible school video from my child development class came to mind, and my stomach twisted as bad as it did when I first saw it. Panic surged through my veins again as I tried to push it out of my mind, but the screaming from the video played over and over again in my head. It wouldn't stop. Just the agonizing pain of a baby, the size of a *football*, getting shoved through that tiny space.

I was going to die.

Terrified, I forced myself to move. To leave the bathroom and that awful thought behind. It was the only thing I could think of to keep myself from plummeting down the rabbit hole again. I needed to go, and I couldn't

CHAPTER 10

get stuck in my depression and grief. I grabbed my phone, thankful the brothers got me one now, and saw many messages from all three brothers, demanding that I call them when I woke up. I could read the worry and panic from Bastian's texts, and for a moment, my fingers hovered over the keys to write back.

```
"Shanely, please call me as soon as you wake up!"
"I'm sorry. I didn't mean to lose my temper in front of you
again. I just don't understand. What did Cain say to you?"
"God. This is all my fault. Please let me in so I can apologize
in person."
"Shanely, please tell me why Cain threw me out and won't let me
back in."
"Please don't push me away. Just let me in, and we can figure
whatever's going on together. I promise."
```

I pulled out of his texting feed then. I couldn't read anymore. Bastian was worried I pushed him away because of the fight, and that made me feel even worse somehow. *He is so far from the truth.*

I let a tear fall down my cheek, admitting to myself that I wanted Bastian. I wanted Bastian more than anything. He made me feel so much better, and I needed him, but I couldn't tell him that now. I was too afraid to see the reaction I knew was coming when he found out about the baby. Watching him pull away from me, *reject me*, was something I really didn't think I could handle. So it was better to just not even go there. It was better to just leave before anyone else found out about the baby.

I noticed I had one text message from my aunt, and I reluctantly opened it.

```
"Shanely, don't worry about any of this. You and your little
one will be safe here, I promise you. This doesn't change how
Cain and I feel about you, and I need you to know that
nothing's going to change, sweetie. We have a doctor in our
pack that I want you to see as soon as you wake up. We'll sort
this out. I promise."
```

But everything's going to change, I thought as I gripped the phone tighter in my hand. If the Division found out about this baby; would they try to kill it? Would the pack kill my baby to keep anyone from ever finding out? Those horrific thoughts flooded my brain, and I put my hand on my belly. I looked down, gently rubbing my thumb back and forth, realizing it was *my job* to make sure this little one had a real chance at life. And the only thing that would guarantee this baby's safety would be if I left the town of Diablo and never looked back.

Suddenly, the thought of my mother flashed before me. *What if this was the reason she left all those years ago? What if she did it to protect me?*

I quickly wiped the tears from my eyes before they could fall. *If my mother could leave this place for me, then I could leave for my little one too.* I stood, shoving the phone in my pocket and paced the room back and forth, trying to decide my next move. *I needed to leave the lodge quietly,* I thought as anxiety swelled within me. *Get back to my cabin and use what little money I had saved to leave.* My eyes widened as I ground to a halt. *My money!* I had completely forgotten I gave everything to Bastian when I got mad at them, and my shoulders fell. *What should I do now?*

Anger flooded my veins for making everything so much harder because of my pride. I clenched my fists together tightly as I shoved the issue aside. I'll figure it out later. Right now, I just needed to get out of here without anyone noticing. My heart hurt, knowing this was my final goodbye before leaving my family for good, but this was the only way. *My mother left after spending her life here,* I thought to myself. *I could do this after only spending a few days.*

I went to the door but froze, remembering last time. I quickly checked under the door, and sure enough, a wolf lay in front of it. My heart dropped, knowing it was Bastian. I recognized the dark fur from the crack under the door, and I scurried away before he could hear me. He'd stop me and demand to know what happened. And I didn't have it in me to tell him the truth.

I left the door alone and went to the window instead. Thankfully, I was on the first floor, and I unlocked it and dropped a few feet to the ground.

CHAPTER 10

As quietly as I could, I fled into the woods. No one seemed to be around, but it didn't stop my heart from thundering so loudly in my chest. I couldn't hear *anything* but that, and I ran even faster. *The further away I was from the lodge the less likely they'd find me,* I thought as I followed the drive. *Right?*

It didn't take long before I ground to a stop and doubled over. *God, I was out of shape,* I thought as I looked around. *I need help.* My head was still a little woozy from joining the pack alliance, and this running wasn't helping any. My eyes widened. *The pack bonds!*

Because I joined the pack, I could sense *exactly* where my pack mates were. I sucked in a deep breath as I scanned my surrounding area. I found clusters of wolves nearby, but they weren't coming after me. *Maybe my uncle did something to shield me? Or maybe no one really cares what I do?* Either way, I didn't want to be found and started down the road again. I watched their ribbons closely, when I realized my grave error. *If I could see them like this— then they'd be able to see me too.* Panic flooded my system again, but I gripped my head, trying to slow my breathing enough to focus. *There had to be a way to shut this off—*

Everything seemed mental when it came to shifters, so I tried focusing on the many ribbons I could feel and shoved them inside a box inside my mind. My wolf said nothing as I shoved more and more, frowning when I realized how large the McCoy pack was. Eventually, I was completely alone again. *Well, other than my wolf.*

I walked quietly down the road towards my drive, recognizing where I was for once. I just wanted to get home before anyone knew I was missing. Every howl I heard startled my heart, and I scurried along, wishing I brought a jacket with me. But I stopped dead in my tracks when I realized my truck still had a messed up tire. *I never got to call Caleb yesterday to fix it!* I thought angrily as I dug in my back pocket for my phone. I quickly dialed the only person I could think of that might help. It rang a few times before he finally answered.

"Hello?"

"Caleb? This is Shanely."

"Oh, hey!" he replied in a friendly tone. "Sorry, I didn't recognize the number. How are you? I was hoping to see you around the Den."

"Yeah— some stuff came up, and I haven't been back to town, but I was wondering if you could do me a favor?"

"Sure, what's up?"

I blew out a deep breath saying, "I need a ride. I wasn't able to get anyone to fix my truck, and I feel horrible for not calling sooner. I really appreciate you towing it back for me, but I need a ride this morning, and I'm a ways from my cabin still. Do you think you could pick me up?"

I expected a flat no. Caleb barely knew me, and I'd be hesitant to get involved with a stranger like this, but I had no choice. To my surprise, he agreed.

"Sure, I can do that. Where are you?"

I rattled off the road I was on, and silence filled the empty space. So much so that I thought maybe he hung up.

"Are you sure that's where you are, Shanely?" he finally asked, and I sighed heavily.

"I am," I said, running my hand through my hair, "but I formally invite you to enter McCoy's land to escort me to my house."

More silence.

"So, you finally know?"

"I do," I answered. "Well, I know enough."

"Okay," he said softly. "Well, I'll take it. I'll see you soon."

The call ended, and I shoved my phone back in my pocket and continued my slow walk home. It was surprisingly chilly outside, but other than the occasional howl, I was alone. With every step on the pavement, my mind ran amuck. *Once I'm home, where would I go? Do I even try to explain myself or should I just disappear and make this easier for everyone?* A thousand different questions ran through my mind, and each one only made me feel worse.

The wind shifted then, and the hairs on the back of my neck stood. I slowed to a stop, looking around carefully. *Had the pack found me already?*

I narrowed my eyes, trying to focus on the forest around me, but everything seemed normal. Anxiety rolled in my stomach as I looked to my wolf for answers. She just seemed quiet, and I wondered why my senses

CHAPTER 10

weren't as clear as they were when I joined the pack. I felt more human than shifter right now, and I didn't like it. I couldn't shake this feeling that I was being watched, and I quickened my pace, taking off down the road, and hoping Caleb would get here soon.

My anxiety rose with every rustle in the trees, and I moved my feet faster. Suddenly, my phone went off, startling me and my already racing heart. Bastian's name appeared on the screen, and I stilled. *He must have realized I wasn't at the lodge anymore,* I thought. I clicked ignore but barely had a chance to put my phone back in my pocket before another call came through. Each of the brother's names appeared on my phone and then my aunt. I bit my lower lip as I ignored her call too. *They didn't need this burden,* I told myself as I shoved my phone back in my pocket. *They didn't need to deal with me and my issues.* Multiple howls filled the air, and I sucked in a breath. *I had to get home.*

A branch snapped behind me, and I whipped around to look. Nothing was there, but my anxiety rolled even more as I stared at the empty woods. *Cade was right,* I thought as I stood a step back. *I was stupid. So consumed by the pregnancy that I didn't even once think about the fact I was still marked.*

Movement rustled in the woods again, and I turned on my heels and ran. My heart thundered in my chest, when a brown blur moved out of the corner of my eye. *The rogue—* I turned to face the demon hunting me, but nothing was there. *But I saw—* More howls sounded off in the distance, and I ran even harder, ignoring my burning lungs and aching legs.

Suddenly, a loud diesel sounded down the road, and I prayed it was Caleb. I was winded already, and if the rogue truly was out there, I was about to be dead.

A red pick-up truck appeared over the hill, coming down the road towards me, and I saw his familiar friendly face. I slowed my jog, grateful to see Caleb waving as he pulled up next to me. Bile sat at the back of my throat, and I tried to steady my breath. Last thing I needed was to tip him off something was wrong. He smiled as he rolled down the window.

"There you are!" he said, grinning. "You caught me just in time as I was on my way to work. Hop in, I really don't want to be chased by any wolves today."

I nearly sagged in relief as I hopped in the truck.

"Thanks," I huffed out, locking the door before grabbing my seat belt. I scanned the forest, but a wolf never appeared. *Maybe I was seeing things?* I thought as I turned towards Caleb. I frowned when I caught him staring.

"Everything okay, Caleb?" I asked, my brows raising.

He inhaled deeply, frowning as he studied me. *He looked almost— angry,* I thought to myself. *Was the triplets right to be wary?*

Finally, he gave me a simple nod and popped the truck in gear. My stomach twisted as he turned the truck around and headed towards my cabin. *The brothers warned me about their relationship with Caleb and his family, but I honestly thought Caleb wouldn't be that way with me,* I thought as I scrambled to come up with what I had done to upset him. *He knew I was a wolf on some level, and he decided to come despite that— so why was he so angry now?*

Caleb didn't say much of anything. No matter how much small talk I tried to start. Eventually, I gave up and stared out the window.

My phone went off a few times during the ride, and I silenced every call. I didn't have it in me to deal with anyone, especially in front of Caleb. I kept one eye on the treeline the entire drive, wondering if I'd see Bastian's wolf appear. I missed his wolf. I really wasn't sure I'd be able to do the right thing if he found me.

Caleb pulled into the drive, and I bit my lower lip nervously as we rounded the last curve, revealing my cabin. I half expected to see one of the triplets here already, but no one was here. Not a wolf in sight, and I sagged in relief. I turned to thank Caleb and found him watching me closely. I forced a small smile to my lips and opened my door.

"Thank you for picking me up again. I really appreciate the help. It would have been a long walk—"

My eyes widened when Caleb got out of the truck with me. He scented the air, and my brows knitted as I watched him. *What was he doing?* I wondered, making my way to my front door. He followed, and I let him inside. *Was he staying? Maybe he could give me a ride to the bus station once I've grabbed some of my things?*

"Do you want something to drink?" I asked as I made my way into the kitchen. "I have water, juice, milk—."

Caleb didn't respond right away, so I turned, finding him standing in my living room with his arms crossed, glaring at me. My heart slowly started racing, and I closed the fridge. There was a pull towards him too. An undeniable pull, but the way he was glaring had the hairs on the back of my neck rising. *The brothers said he was a grizzly,* I thought as I shifted on my feet. *A 900 lb grizzly who I just happened to have pissed off.*

"What's wrong?" I asked quietly. I carefully eyed the clock on the wall. *I needed to hurry if I wanted to leave before they found me.*

"Shanely, why did you call me?" Caleb asked, and I frowned. His voice had changed. It sounded gruff and gritty almost. *I had never heard his voice like this before,* I thought as I rubbed the goosebumps running up my arm.

"I just needed a ride, Caleb. Actually, I need another ride if you don't mind?" I asked.

"Another ride?"

I slowly nodded my head. "To the nearest bus stop. Please?"

"Bus stop?" he asked, frowning. "Planning on leaving already?"

"I just need—" My voice trailed off as I scrambled to answer such a simple question as why. I sighed. *The less he knew the better.* "I just think it's best that I move on," I said, crossing my arms over my chest. "Can you help me? If you can't, that's okay. I'll figure it out on my own."

His eyes flashed gold, and I sucked in a breath. *Was he going to shift?* I thought to myself.

Caleb put his hands on his hips saying, "You admitted that you know about me and the shifter laws. I can *smell* you're a wolf, but there's something else with you that's off. You were running all alone away from McCoy's lodge, and yes, I know what's up the mountain on this side. You seem upset and afraid, and yet you're running away from your pack and not towards it."

I held my breath as he stepped closer.

"The pack, which is supposed to have your back and protect you from anything and everything. Am I right? And now you're carrying a pup?! Which you definitely were not when we met a few days ago. I knew you couldn't trust any McCoys, but this has to take the cake! This is supposed to be *your* pack and family, but you seem like you're running away from them. Did they hurt you somehow, Shanely? Is that why you called me instead of another wolf?"

My entire world came tumbling down as he glared at me. *How did he know? I thought Cain was the only one with that ability—* My terrified gaze dropped to the floor as the words barely escaped my lips.

"How did you know I was pregnant?"

"What? What does that have to do with anything?! Are you in trouble, Shanely?!" he yelled again.

"HOW DID YOU KNOW?" I shouted right back. He staggered back a step, his eyes widening, and I asked again, "How did you know?"

Caleb regained his composure and tossed his hands in the air. "I can smell the pup on you! It's one of bear shifter's talents, alright? Now, answer my question. Who did this to you? You look terrified!"

Suddenly, my back door burst open, and Bastian stormed inside. He had kicked it clean off the hinges, and I stumbled back in surprise.

"Back off, Caleb!" Bastian shouted loudly. "You stay away from her!"

He promptly put himself between me and Caleb, glancing my way only once before snarling at the bear shifter.

I stood frozen in place. *He had found me,* I thought. *He found me and leaving was going to be near impossible now. He would find out about the baby. There was no way I'd keep my secret, and now he was standing here, trying to protect me from something he didn't need to. Caleb wasn't hurting me. Oh God— what had I done?*

Elijah and Cade barreled in seconds behind their brother, and I staggered on my feet, breathing hard.

"Baby Girl! Thank God, you're alright!" Cade said as he hugged me tightly.

Caleb growled loudly, and Cade pulled away as Bastian snarled right back.

"I should have known the Fenrir brothers were involved with this! Back

CHAPTER 10

off, Cade! Don't touch her again!"

The room grew loud as they snarled and growled at one another. *This was getting out of hand*, I thought as I struggled to catch my breath. My stomach churned again as I watched my mistake play out. Caleb and Bastian were about in each other's faces already, and I didn't know what to do. Elijah stood beside Bastian, while Cade blocked me from advancing.

"Guys, please stop! You don't understand!" I shouted, but no one paid me any mind.

"Shanely, we're leaving now. I'm not leaving you with these wolves any longer! Whatever's going on, you can tell me in the safety of my clan's land."

Caleb jerked around Bastian to reach for me, but Bastian snapped. My hand rushed to cover my mouth as he threw Caleb back against my front door. *Like it was nothing.*

"Don't touch her!" Bastian snarled at him. My eyes widened when black hair slowly appeared on his arm. *He was barely holding back the shift, and it was all my fault.*

Caleb stood up shaking himself off. "You won't hurt her ever again, Bastian. She doesn't belong to you, and I'll make sure you never see her again."

Bastian charged then, and the two crashed through the front door towards my truck. The door landed loudly on my front porch, and Elijah and Cade bolted towards them with me right on their heels. *I needed to stop this now!*

A full blown fight ensued on my front lawn, and I dug my hands into my hair. *They're going to kill each other because of me,* I thought as my heart thundered in my chest. Bastian had Caleb pinned as he wailed on him, and I cursed myself for being so stupid and calling Caleb in the first place

I bolted off the porch steps, but Cade caught me before my feet could touch the ground. I struggled against him as Caleb decked Bastian. My heart stopped when he toppled off, and Caleb swiftly got to his feet. Bastian had barely anytime to get to his own before Caleb tackled him to the ground. Neither one was giving up and both were quickly turning bloody.

Cade twisted back, planting me back on the porch steps. "No, Baby Girl.

Not this time."

"Cade, you don't understand! This isn't what it—"

A loud snapping sound cut me off as Caleb shifted in my driveway. In his place stood a monstrous, brown grizzly bear. My eyes grew wide seeing the size of Caleb. *My guess earlier was accurate.* He was massive and downright scary looking as he roared loudly. Bastian didn't hesitate and quickly shifted to his wolf form.

"Oh, crap," Elijah muttered before shifting next to his brother.

Cade ran his hands threw his hair, agitated now. My eyes were glued to the brutal fight before me, and Cade gripped my chin harshly, forcing me to look him in the eye.

"Shanely, do not leave this porch!" he demanded. "You understand me!? I need to be there for my brothers, and I *need* you to listen to me!"

I blinked as he let go of my chin and ran towards the fight. Cade jumped, shifting mid-air, and colliding against Caleb. They all charged towards each other, and I couldn't keep up. I didn't know where to look as Caleb took a swipe at Bastian, who barely got out of the way in time. Elijah was swift in distracting Caleb for Cade to come through and bite down on his arm.

My wolf stirred when I scented blood, and I felt like screaming at her to shift and fix this. But she watched from the safety of my mind as the brutal fight continued.

My eyes were glued to Bastian's wolf and every hit he seemed to take. My feet left the porch, and I jumped, shrieking when Caleb struck him. He bounded on his feet again, and I let out a sigh of relief. Only to get squashed when Caleb roared in pain from a slice from Elijah's claw.

"This can't be happening!" I thought, gripping the sides of my head as my chest warmed.

Caleb turned abruptly to face me, and my eyes widened. He stopped everything to just watch me, and my eyes narrowed. *What was he doing?*

Bastian took the momentary distraction and clamped down his back leg, causing Caleb to fall. Bastian pulled hard, dragging the massive grizzly further from me, and my eyes widened. *He was going to tear it off*

CHAPTER 10

completely—

Cade leapt on his back, while Elijah went for his front paw. Caleb shoved Bastian off, barely able to get his footing, but the brothers were relentless. He lost the upper hand by looking at me, and he was paying for it now. I scented more blood in the air, and my heart thundered in my chest. *I didn't want to see him hurt either.* My wolf growled low in my mind as fear gripped my heart. *He only was here because I called him, and this wasn't fair.* It was three wolves against one very large bear. Even though Caleb's bear was stronger than their wolves alone, with them working together, Caleb didn't stand a chance. *Would the brothers even stop before killing him?*

I screamed, "STOP!"

The brothers continued to snarl as they charged Caleb again, and I took another terrifying step towards them. And then I heard it.

This voice inside my head that didn't belong to me.

"Shanely, stop! I'm okay."

I froze.

My eyes widened as Caleb tossed Cade to the ground. He looked at me next, and my jaw dropped. *That voice sounded like Caleb. But how? Why could I hear him inside my head?!*

Bastian moved to check Cade, who stood slowly. Caleb nodded once to me before roaring back at Bastian again.

Elijah circled back, waiting for Bastian to give the go ahead once more, and I took the momentary pause to bolt. My chest warmed again as I stopped dead center with my hands raised. I glanced back and forth between them, begging them to stop.

"Bastian, please stop" I stammered. "This is all a misunderstanding."

Bastian softened as I stepped in his view but continued to pace back and forth. I knew he calmed himself enough as his eyes turned blue again, but he was still so angry. He didn't like that I was standing between them and a large grizzly. I knew he didn't because he tried to grab my shirt with his snout. He just wanted to deal with what he thought was the problem, but little did he know the only problem here was *me*. Caleb roared again and moved closer to me.

"Don't let him touch you again, Shanely!" Caleb shouted in my head. *"I'm fine, just step aside."*

Bastian snapped his jaws angrily at Caleb, who was roaring again. I was so stunned at hearing Caleb's voice in my head though. I didn't understand how this was happening, but I knew this fight needed to stop right now. I decided to try something not knowing if it would work. I pushed a thought to Caleb.

"Caleb, stand down," I said, and he stilled. *"Please. Bastian won't hurt me, and I can explain. Shift back. You're safe, I promise.*

"Please," I whispered, feeling Bastian tug on my shirt again. I pulled away from him, and his wolf growled low.

Caleb stared at me. The gold faded from his eyes as we watched one another. A heartbeat passed, and I wasn't sure if he'd listen.

Warm fur touched my hand as I whispered, "Please, shift back."

To my surprise, Caleb shifted. He looked awful, and I gasped, looking at his wounds. He was bleeding from his right ear and by his eyebrow. A lot of blood came from that wound on his face, and I was worried about how deep it went. The sight sickened me, and it was all *my* fault.

Bastian shifted immediately, and I felt his hands around my waist. I tore my gaze from Caleb only to be startled by him. He was bloody too, and my heart hurt even worse. With his thick fur, he didn't look as injured, but Caleb did a number on him as well. His chest seemed to be the worst as three large gashes stretched across his chest where his heart was. He pulled me further away, but I shoved off him, needing space to say what I needed.

"No, Bastian! I need you both to look at me when I explain this."

The brothers shifted then, and they were haggard, wounded, and breathing heavy. My lips puckered slightly as tears filled my eyes. I quickly wiped them away, taking a deep breath to gain my composure. *No amount of running was getting me out of this now.*

I turned to Caleb first. "The triplets never hurt me Caleb, nor did anyone else from the pack. Someone did hurt me, but it wasn't them. I did run away from them, but not for the reasons you think. What I'm about to say, I need you to promise me you will keep my secret because I don't want my pack to be hurt. Do we have an understanding?"

Caleb's brows furrowed, but he nodded anyways.

Bastian stepped closer. "Shanely, you don't have to explain anything to him. You can't trust him anyways."

Caleb growled again. "I wouldn't hurt Shanely!"

"Yeah? And we're just supposed to trust you, Medvedev? You've never had a problem hurting wolves before!" Cade shouted back.

"Shanely's different," he growled. "I don't understand what's going on, but I feel protective of her! My bear would never allow me to even *think* about hurting her, and this fight goes both ways, and you know it!"

They started shouting again, and I felt Bastian's hand on my wrist. I pulled away, raising my hands up and shouting, "Stop! I have the floor right now! You will all be quiet until I am done speaking. After you hear what I have to say, I'm sure you'll realize that I'm not worth all this trouble. The only problem here is— me."

"Shanely—" Bastian said, his eyes full of hurt, and he reached for me again. My heart split in two as I stepped back again.

"No! Let me just get this out, otherwise I don't know if I'll be able to. I can't stand seeing you all fight, especially over me. I'm not worth this!"

I stepped further away from Bastian, afraid that if I allowed him to touch me again, I'd lose my confidence and be unable to speak. I needed to do this alone and let go of my need for him.

He started to reach for me again, and I shouted before he could stop me. "Bastian, I'm pregnant!"

Bastian ground to a halt. His entire body froze, and a single tear fell down my cheek. His brothers swore behind him, looking at me with what I was sure could only be disgust.

"Bears apparently can smell pregnancy," I stammered, looking solely to the man who fought so fiercely to protect me. "I didn't know that when I asked him to take me home, and he thought someone from the pack hurt me because I wasn't pregnant when we met, or at least not far enough along for him to notice. Caleb, no one would ever hurt me from the McCoy pack. I needed to escape someone back home in Indiana where I'm from. I'm carrying his child."

Caleb's eyes widened as he ran his hands through his hair. I slowly turned back to Bastian, who looked stuck in a trance. *This was it,* I thought as I looked to the floor. *This was the moment before he fled for good. And I didn't blame him.*

"I was afraid if anyone saw me with a half-human child then the Division would wipe out the McCoy pack, and I didn't want that kind of blood on my hands. Some in the pack already think I'm an abomination because no one knows what I am exactly, and I didn't know how they would take this child."

My chest heaved as I held back a sob. I turned to Bastian again, looking at his shoes instead of that gorgeous face of his.

"I ran from you most of all. I didn't know how you would take news like this, and the idea of you rejecting me was too much. We aren't anything, I know that, but I'm drawn to you for some reason. It's stupid and silly because we've barely just met, but I feel like I'm falling for you. I was afraid you'd see me as nothing but ruined if you found out about the baby. I was afraid I'd be more trouble for you and your brothers, and I didn't want *any* of you to be hurt by me."

Silence filled the woods then, and my heart hurt more than I could bear. *This is what I was afraid of,* I thought, waiting to hear the sounds of footsteps leaving me. But no one made a sound. No one spoke, and my cheeks heated as embarrassment swept through me. I turned to run, when two arms wrapped around me, halting me from escaping. I closed my eyes as tears welled inside and pulled further away from him. I didn't want to see his disgust or worse, *pity* because the feelings I had were one-sided.

"If you think this baby will drive me away then you are completely wrong," Bastian said softly, and my eyes shot open. I turned, finding his piercing blue eyes looking into mine as he smiled. He smiled so wide, I didn't know what to make of it. Bastian's hand gently tucked a fly-away strand of hair behind my ear, and I leaned into his touch ever so slightly, unable to stop myself. My chest warmed as his grinned again.

"Shanely—" he said softly, and I looked into his eyes as he sighed. "I feel

CHAPTER 10

like you're my mate. I was afraid to tell you too soon and scare you away, but my wolf and I are drawn to you too. I feel lost and frantic when I can't find you, and my wolf and I *both* feel like our life finally has purpose now. Like the missing piece is *finally* in place, and I know exactly where I want to be. I'm falling in love with you too, Shanely. I couldn't possibly leave you, baby and all."

Bastian kissed me hard then. His lips found mine and fit perfectly against my own. His fingers gripped my waist, keeping me firmly rooted in my spot next to him. My heart soared, and my wolf beamed inside. It was the most awake I felt her be since unlocking her, and this chord snapped in place between Bastian and I. Just like when I joined the pack, but this bond was different. Despite feeling faint, there was no denying what it was. *A mate bond*, I thought as he kissed me again. *Bastian was my mate.*

Just like how I knew I was a girl, I *knew* Bastian was mine. His wolf and his heart belonged to me, and no one could ever take that away.

Bastian finally broke our kiss and rested his head against mine. I couldn't contain the grin forming on my cheeks, and when Cade started whistling in the background, I blushed hard. Suddenly, I felt direct lines snap to both Cade and Elijah too, and I cocked my head to the side. We were connected in a much stronger way than before. *Even more than the rest of the pack.*

And a faint line pointed to the bear shifter standing behind me.

"So, I guess we were right in why we felt a pull towards her?" Elijah asked, rubbing his chest.

Bastian smiled at me, never breaking his loving gaze. He chuckled when I gave him a look.

"Siblings feel a different sort of bond between one another. It's a pull or connection that's different from pack and mates. It's only between siblings or in this case the mate's siblings."

"Like the faint line I feel for you right now?" I asked as he gently touched my cheek. *God, he felt like heaven.*

Bastian nodded his head. "Sight usually connects mates for wolves, but you grew up a human. The bond must not be as strong because you haven't shifted. You'll be able to find me and my brothers always with that link once you shift. My brothers felt the bond form with us, and they will do whatever they need to protect you. We'll feel it when they find their mates too."

I chuckled softly as my eyes glistened for like the millionth time today. It made sense and nice not to feel like I was going crazy anymore. *All my feelings and emotions that have been all over the place*, I thought. *Why I was so drawn to him before. It was because my wolf was waking up slowly, so the bond was gradual.* My wolf was just trying to tell me something.

"So eye contact is all it takes?" I asked quietly, and Bastian nodded.

"Most wolf mates feel their mate's presence before even seeing them. Their scent is intoxicating, so they know they are close. Once their eyes lock together, the bond snaps into place. It must be slow with us because your wolf woke up in stages," Bastian replied, kissing my forehead softly. I melted in his embrace, wishing he never had to let me go.

"I wondered why I loved your smell. I noticed the first day we spent together," I said, leaning further into him, "but it was stronger when you were in your wolf form."

He grinned playfully at me. "You were able to scent me then?"

I nodded. "I first noticed it when I opened my windows that morning. It was amazing and smelled so strongly of the woods."

Bastian kissed my forehead again. "I wondered what you were doing at that window."

I smiled back at him. "What do I smell like, Bastian?"

"You smell sweet," he said softly, and I swear I saw his wolf's canines sharpen. "Almost like honey."

I blinked, and his teeth returned to normal. I shook my head, not caring in the slightly over what I saw and rested my head against him, processing all this new information. It was a lot to take in. I didn't even know it was a thing until I felt it myself. This unbelievable joy pouring out of my soul was enough to tell me this was a good thing. Bastian was someone that wouldn't hurt me like Peter did. For the first time in my life, I knew what home was.

"So, you're my mate?" I asked quietly.

CHAPTER 10

"I am," he answered. "I belong to you, just like you belong to me, Shanely. And what a lucky guy I am."

"Are you sure you're okay with this?" I asked quietly. "It's a lot to ask of you being my mate and all."

Bastian pulled back, placing both hands on my face as he looked me in the eye. "Of course," he answered, giving me a firm look. "We were chosen for each other. Mate bonds are never wrong, Shanely, but let me make this clear. This will be *my* baby. No one, especially this child, will know anything different. Alright? This is what we tell the pack, and the Division if it would ever get to that point."

"Bastian—"

I covered my mouth as tears fell down my face. Grateful wasn't enough to describe how I felt, but guilt was slowly creeping in. *"He was giving so much, and I had nothing to give him."* Bastian was saving me and our pack by claiming the both of us like this, and he was willing to raise a child that wasn't his. *"I can't imagine how difficult that must be,"* I thought he gently wiped a tear away. *"Most wouldn't do this— it must be the mate bond forcing him too."*

"Stop," Bastian said as he pulled my chin up to look him in the eye. "I'm not giving too much, and you are my everything, love. Just being in my life is a gift enough, trust me. Not everyone finds their mate, and no one will have a mate like I do. I'm the luckiest guy in the world, Shanely, and I'm not accepting your child simply because of the mate bond. Remember our bond isn't even fully formed. I want to protect you and this little one, okay? He or she is apart of you, which makes them special. You're mine, so they will be mine too. I wanted kids anyways. It's just happening sooner than I expected is all."

I frowned, startled because I was *positive* I didn't say all that out loud.

Bastian laughed, pulling me from my thoughts. "Your wolf is there, Shanely. She's stronger now, and it's open enough to allow the mind link, remember?"

I turned beat red. "I'll have to remember not to share everything then."

"Share everything with me, babe. At least now I can always find you."

"I thought you could since I joined the pack," I said, feeling slightly confused. *I had seen where everyone was. Shouldn't that mean they could see me?*

"No, we can use the mind-link when we're close to each other, but I can't locate everyone. No wolf can except mates, siblings, and the Alpha. Alphas can mind-link anywhere, and they can always see the bond to whomever is a part of their pack. Siblings have the same bond locator too, but the further away you get, the harder it can be to read though. Once our bond is fully connected, I can find you anywhere and everywhere, but right now I can't. Everyone else is like a regular wolf. You have to track someone to find them."

"But I can see everyone," I replied, and he looked at me funny.

"You see the entire pack?" he asked.

I nodded. "Yeah, it's how I avoided everyone when I left. I just assumed they all could see me too, so I turned it off— somehow. Wait, how did you find me then?"

"When we realized you were gone, and no one could get ahold of you, we started looking on foot. Even your uncle couldn't see where you were, so everyone was starting to think the worst. We were nervous that the rogue somehow found you, and I was pissed because Cade had the location services turned off on your phone by accident. He didn't realize he had to turn it on manually, so we decided to just try your cabin after searching the surrounding lodge first. Elijah smelled Caleb as we came up on the creek in the back," he said.

Why couldn't he see me? I wondered to myself. None of that made any sense, but suddenly my eyes widened, and I turned to the quiet shifter currently watching everything.

Caleb watched me closely, and I felt bad for forgetting him, even momentarily. Cade walked over and extended out his hand. Elijah followed closely behind, but Caleb just looked at the two brothers before turning back to me. Bastian's words suddenly rattled my mind.

"I'm sorry, man. Thank you for defending our sister," Cade said rather nicely and waited patiently for Caleb to accept.

CHAPTER 10

Caleb's eyes narrowed before he carefully shook Cade's hand and then Elijah's. Even I was surprised after what we just went through.

"I'll call our pack healer, Caleb. You don't deserve to deal with that on your own," Elijah said, phone in hand.

"Yeah, I don't want to either," Cade chimed in as he hobbled towards me now.

"Thank you, Elijah Fenrir," Caleb replied before turning back to me. His sharp gaze boring into my soul. *Don't look at me buddy,* I thought. *I don't know what to do either.*

"So, Fenrir huh?"

Bastian looked down, his brows furrowing. "What?"

"Nothing. I just realized I never knew your last name."

He laughed and pulled me close again. "It wasn't important until now, I guess, and I believe you mean *our* last name."

I blushed as Caleb interrupted our conversation. "Shanely?"

Bastian didn't growl or snarl as Caleb slowly approached. I cocked my head to the side, realizing I could *feel* Bastian's emotions through our bond ever so slightly. Like our bond itself, I could feel what he felt, and he was just content and happy. Even as he watched Caleb, there was no hate or anger coming from him anymore. *This was probably the most civil the brothers had ever been with a bear shifter before, especially with Caleb in particular,* I thought to myself. Once the bond formed for me and Bastian, it was like all the anger and tension just left. Instantly.

"Shanely," Caleb said through the link, *"do you know what this means?"*

I looked at him, his own eyes searching mine, and I gave him a small nod. I had an idea at least, but it posed a whole new set of problems. This faint bond between us explained why I felt like he was so familiar. Caleb, was somehow the family I had always wanted, and had just fought three wolves to protect me before he even knew who I was. He felt it too. I don't know how I'm going to make this all work, but I knew I didn't want to give him up. Somehow, he was my own flesh and blood.

"Do you want me to stay quiet?" he asked. *"We can keep this a secret between us. No one needs to know. I don't want to make anything worse for you."*

"No Caleb, I don't want to keep you a secret. I've never had a family before, and now that I found you, I don't want to lose you. I want to know where I came from and this somehow includes you. Besides, Bastian deserves to know."

Caleb carefully looked back at Bastian, who was distracted talking to Cade now. The Alphas were on their way.

"Bastian hates bear shifters. Me in particular. There's no going back if we do."

"I know, but he's about to raise a baby that isn't his. I think he can handle this, plus it will mean learning more about who I am. I want to know my parents, Caleb."

"We will need to proceed with caution, Shanely. This won't be easy nor is this legal."

"Your aunt and uncle are close, baby. They have been worried since you left the lodge," Bastian whispered in my ear, interrupting Caleb and I.

"Are they mad at me?" I asked anxiously.

"No, but I wouldn't pull that again. You gave us all heart attacks."

"I'm sorry. I was panicking over everything, and I couldn't face you guys yet. I thought I'd just slip out before anyone found me."

"I know, but we're in this together from now on. Deal?"

I hesitated before answering him. "You promise? We're together no matter what?"

His brows furrowed again as he studied me, and I pursed my lips together. *Yeah — sneaking anything by him was going to be tricky*, I thought to myself.

"Of course," he finally said. "Nothing will make me want to leave you, Shanely."

Before I could answer further, multiple wolves shot around the backside of the house. My aunt and all 3 of my uncles shifted and stared immediately at Caleb before turning to the broken front half of my house. Ash snarled.

Caleb immediately dropped his head, stepping away from me slightly. He was uptight now, taking in all these wolves before him. My face fell. *This wasn't right, nor was it fair.*

"Caleb Medvedev. I didn't expect to see you here so close to our lands," Uncle Cain said firmly. He was nothing but Alpha now, and I could feel

CHAPTER 10

some of his power leaking from him.

Caleb took another step back from all of us, saying nothing. He gave me an anxious look.

"It will be okay, Caleb."

"I don't know, Shanely. He's well within his rights to beat the snot out of me for destroying McCoy property, let alone what I just did to the Fenrir brothers. There are rules here, Shanely. With severe consequences, and I just broke them."

"Care to explain yourselves, boys?" my aunt asked sternly, interrupting the two of us.

I felt awful as Caleb tucked his hands in his pockets. I didn't realize all that I put Caleb through today, and he was extremely quiet right now, waiting to see what would happen. I squared my shoulders, ready to take the blame because this was *my* fault. I had hurt Caleb enough as it was.

I stepped forward, but the second my foot hit the ground, all four boys stepped in front of me and started talking at once. No one would let me pass or even see Uncle Cain standing before us. I rolled my eyes and tried to pass by Bastian. I barely got a glimpse before he tucked me behind him again. The only one who looked amused was Uncle Aspen.

"Enough! One at a time, and do I need to call your clan leader, Caleb? Because from what I'm gathering by the looks of the house and all four of you, there was *another* brawl," Cain shouted angrily.

Caleb ran his fingers through his beard under his chin nervously. He eyed me, unsure what to say, but I could see that *this* is what he was talking about. Bastian opened his mouth to speak again, but I cut him off and finally pushed past him.

"Listen," I said firmly. "This was all my fault, Uncle Cain."

Bastian grabbed my wrist and pulled me back against him, but I yanked my hand free and shot him a look. His eyes widened, and I turned on my heels, straightening my shirt.

"I didn't handle—"

"It's my fault, Alpha. I charged in and didn't let her explain anything. I'm the one that lost my temper *again* and started the fight. I swung first," Bastian cut me off, and I glared at him.

My uncle and Caleb both looked surprised, but I wasn't going to let him take the blame. No matter how sweet he was being.

"I accused you of hurting her in the first place, Bastian. This is just as much my fault as yours," Caleb countered, putting his hands on his hips.

Shock covered the Alpha's faces as the boys slowly explained what happened. Both sides were trying to take the blame for a brawl instead of throwing the other under the bus. While I was proud of the fellas, no one would let me get a word in edge wise. No one should take the blame but me.

"Can you heal Caleb, Cassia? We did a number on him," Cade asked sheepishly.

She nodded. "I'll heal you all, even though you were all acting like fools! I swear, starting brawls like this! And why in the world are you even here, Caleb? How did you get dragged into all this?"

Caleb looked at me, refusing to answer. Bastian noticed the looks between us and nudged me.

"Shanely, what is going on? I assumed you called him because he wasn't a wolf. Is there another reason you called Caleb?"

I blew out a hot breath before speaking, "There is another development you should all know about. While I did call Caleb because he was the only non-wolf I knew, there is more than just that. I was just afraid to be honest with you before, but when I met Caleb, he felt familiar and— safe almost. I couldn't figure it out why then, and apparently Caleb felt the same way."

Bastian cocked his head to the side, frowning.

"Wait, what are we talking about?" Elijah asked.

I gestured to Caleb. "I figured out why today. Caleb and I can use the mind-link with each other."

Cain turned to Caleb. "You have a bond with him?"

"A mate bond?" Aspen asked, bewildered.

Both Bastian and Caleb shouted, "No!"

"Shanely is my mate, but this isn't possible. I would have felt their bond like she did with my brothers," Bastian said loudly. His voice unraveling slightly as he looked from me to Caleb.

"He heard my thoughts during the fight, and we've been able to commu-

CHAPTER 10

nicate ever since. When *our* bond connected, my wolf felt more awake and alive than ever before, and I have the faintest bond with Caleb now too. I don't know, but I assume the reason for that is because we're blood related," I said softly, pursing my lips together and trying to read my mate's mind. Bastian's eyes widened, and he briefly looked like he bit off more than he could chew when he bonded to me.

"Oh, my. This is a problem, Cain," Aunt Cassia said. She rested her hand on my uncle's arm.

My other uncles looked frightened almost. *Was it really so bad that he was related to me somehow?* I wondered. I know it was against their laws, but maybe some laws shouldn't be in effect. Caleb didn't seem like a bad person, and it just felt silly that *this* would cause such a fuss.

"I closed your mind-link to the pack when you fainted. I was afraid it would be too much for you to handle after everything, but you can mind-link Bastian and his brothers because of the mate bond, correct?" Uncle Cain asked.

I looked at the boys standing behind me and shrugged. "We haven't tried it, but Bastian was able to hear me."

All of a sudden Elijah and Cade's voices boomed through my head, and I covered my ears, as if that could help.

"Guys, not at the same time!" Bastian yelled as he smacked Cade, who smacked Elijah.

"Yeah, Elijah," Cade shouted. "Wait your turn!"

Cain didn't laugh however and moved past them to me. "Yet, you can hear Caleb?"

I nodded again. "Does that mean Caleb is my—"

"Brother," Caleb finished.

"Which means I'm half—"

"Bear, Shanely. You're half-bear," Caleb answered again.

Chapter 11

No one spoke for a few minutes. Time stood still as everyone processed this new information, and I stood awkwardly rocking on the back of my heels while they caught up. Cain finally snapped out of his trance as he looked around worriedly. I scanned the forest too. Everything seemed normal, but he seemed more uptight than usual when he ushered everyone inside.

"This *must* remain a secret everyone. There are some in the pack who aren't as welcoming to Shanely as it is. She's also pregnant, and that's going to raise enough questions," Cain said as we all sat down on the couch.

My aunt went straight to Caleb, who leaned against the wall as far away from everyone as he could. She placed her hands on his arm, and I watched as the scratches and bite marks slowly began to stitch themselves together again.

"No, it won't. That baby is mine, end of story. No one needs to know anything else," Bastian exclaimed, pulling me closer to him. I grinned wide.

Cassia dropped her hands, startled by his words, and gave him a smile before returning to her work.

"You would do that for my niece?" Ash asked him.

I blinked. *I think I have only ever heard him speak once, and that was the night they found me,* I thought as the corners of my mouth rose. Hearing him call me his niece made me feel good.

Bastian looked straight ahead to my uncle Ash. "I'd do anything for my mate. This baby is apart of her, so I want it to be mine. I want *everything* to do with Shanely."

CHAPTER 11

Uncle Aspen clapped Bastian's shoulder proudly as Uncle Cain reached out to shake his hand. They all seemed really proud of Bastian and a trickle of warmth seeped through our bond. I smiled, falling more and more in love with the man. I rested my head on his shoulder, and he smiled down at me before patting my leg affectionately.

"Well, that issue aside, we already have some in the pack that don't like Shanely's presence," Cain said. "Finding out about her heritage won't go over well."

"Like Derek," Aspen interrupted, giving Cain a pointed look.

Cain sighed. "Yes, like Derek. I'm afraid of what he will do when he finds out she's a mixer. He's been looking for a change in leadership for some time."

"What is a mixer exactly?" I asked.

"Just a term we use to call someone who has more than one animal to shift into. It's extremely rare, but it happened more often back in the day," my aunt answered.

"My father deserves to know. My clan can stay in the dark for all I care. I don't want to draw too much attention to Shanely either, but he deserves to know his daughter," Caleb stated firmly. My heart stopped.

"Wait. My dad is alive!?" I asked as I sat forward.

Caleb nodded his head yes. "My mother died in childbirth with me, but she wasn't his mate. They were dating prior to the age when mates are made known to bear shifters, and when they both turned 18, the bond didn't form. They were shocked because they were so sure they would be mates, but she was already pregnant with me, so they decided to stay together anyways. Finding your mate is difficult for bear shifters."

"That would mean Mercedes was his mate, Cain. It's the only thing that makes sense. How is that possible?" Aunt Cassia asked.

"It's never been impossible. Just extremely rare," he answered, half zoning out on his thoughts.

"It's the only logical explanation. Mercedes would never do anything that wasn't good for the pack, but the mate bond is stronger than the pack's bond. They wouldn't be able to stay away if they tried," Uncle Aspen said.

"Did Willow know?" Ash asked, but Aunt Cassia just shook her head.

"I have no idea what she knew. At some point she must have because she put Shanely in her will."

"What happened to your mother, Shanely?" Caleb asked, and I slowly dragged my eyes to him. "I was told Mercedes left pack lands long ago, but we never knew why, and my father certainly never even hinted he knew anything about it."

"I don't know. I was told she died when I was young, but the case worker also told me my father died too. I grew up in the system and didn't even know about this place until a lawyer contacted me about my grandmother's cabin," I answered, feeling down about the whole thing.

"Mercedes was under a tremendous amount of stress and work from her father. One day, she was just gone, and no amount of tracking could find her. I always thought it was because of Jack though. Everyone was distraught over the whole ordeal except her dad, but he was an arrogant prick so no one really expected him to care that she was gone," Cain replied, rubbing his face with his hands.

"How did she even meet Daniel? Jack had the pack locked down tight back then, and she was always in some sort of training exercise," Aspen asked.

"They must have met in the neutral zone, and then saw each other here. On the border," Bastian suggested. My eyes widened. *Was that why my grandmother insisted on building her cabin on the border?*

"Maybe. We won't know until Shanely meets with Daniel," Uncle Cain said.

"Daniel. Daniel Medvedev and Mercedes McCoy," I said, saying my parents name out loud for the first time together. *I spent years daydreaming what their names were, and now I finally knew.* It may be silly, but it meant something to me.

"It explains the pull I had when we first met that night at the bar," Caleb said, pulling me from my thoughts.

I smiled, thinking back to that night. "You felt familiar too."

He smiled at that, shaking his head as he chuckled softly. "I can't believe

CHAPTER 11

I have a wolf for a sister."

Caleb walked over, tussling my hair as he plopped down on the couch next to me, and I batted him away. He seemed way more relaxed than when we first walked in, and I liked seeing us altogether. *It was nice to see him loosen up.*

"And I apparently have an annoying big bear of a brother."

Everyone chuckled, and I leaned against my mate, feeling happy and content. Truly happy for the first time in my life. I had a family and someone who loves me despite my past and all the troubles I bring.

"How old are you anyways?" I asked. I was curious about my new brother, and I tried to look for any similarities I could find between us.

"Same age as triplets here," he answered. "We all turned 21 last month. How old are you?"

"19. I'll be 20 in a few months," I replied, smiling. Soon, my smile fell as I leaned forward on my knees. "Caleb— are you sure your dad never mentioned anything about me or my mom?"

He shook his head no. "*Our* dad, but no. At least not to me. I mean maybe he confided in my uncle, but I kind of doubt that. Uncle Thomas would do anything for family, but he doesn't like wolves at all. He wouldn't trust any of you, so it's hard to say if my father said anything to him."

"He probably knows war would happen if he did, especially since Mercedes disappeared like that and then shortly after Jack was killed," Aspen said.

"Wait, my grandfather was killed?" I asked, frowning. "How?"

Cain nodded his head slowly. "It's a long story, Shanely, but those were really rocky times for the wolves in our pack. I imagine Daniel kept quiet about his involvement with Mercedes."

I slumped back in my seat, knowing Uncle Cain wasn't going into more details about it. *It must have been a really bad time if he didn't want to even tell me,* I thought to myself.

"What I want to know is since Shanely is half-bear; will she have *both* animals to shift into or not?" Uncle Ash asked, crossing his arms as he leaned against the wall.

They all turned to me, and my eyes widened.

"Don't look at me," I cried out. "I have no idea!"

Bastian laughed. "We know she has a wolf for sure. Shanely and I can both feel her."

But would I get a bear from my father now too? Part of was thrilled at the idea. A chance to have something special from my dad, but the other half was terrified. *How in the world would I be able to handle two animals when one was weird enough?*

"For now, this needs to remain quiet. No one breathes a word of this to *anyone*. We will meet here if we need to discuss anything because the cabin's at the border, and it's farther away from where most of the pack homes are. We will have a mating announcement for Shanely and Bastian as soon as we head back to the lodge. We'll just say the pup came early, and no one needs to know the details. In the meantime, Caleb, you are allowed to tell your father and only him. Once you tell him, we can arrange a time here for everyone to meet. We will see if we can get some answers from him yet," Uncle Cain told us, and we all nodded in agreement.

"On that note, we will leave you all. Caleb, I managed to heal what I could but still no more brawling, boys. You are all family now," Aunt Cassia said, and all the boys slowly looked at one another.

A lifetime of hate was being forced out the window, all in a blink of an eye. I was the one that connected everyone now, and I grinned, watching the four of them awkwardly sit there, not knowing how to deal with each other. While I didn't want to cause unnecessary stress, I also wanted everyone in my family to get along. I couldn't shove Caleb to the side, no more than I could shove Cade or Elijah.

"One last thing, Alpha," Bastian said as the group stood. "I know you closed Shanely's mind-link with the pack, but did you do anything else to her?"

My uncle's brows rose. "No, why?"

"Shanely can feel bonds with the whole pack. It's how she managed to leave the lodge without running into anyone," Bastian answered.

"Interesting," my aunt said.

CHAPTER 11

"Huh. As far as I know only Alphas can do this. Everyone else only has the ability with their mate and siblings. She must have a strong wolf. That explains how she was able to hide from me earlier then," Cain said.

"She said she was afraid if she could see us then we'd see her too. She was able to close the bonds, and everyone's connections disappeared. Is that something you can do?" Bastian asked, leaning forward in his seat.

"I can. It doesn't ever truly turn off, but I can close my mind to just focus on one wolf or none at all if I'm tired and need a break. It takes a toll constantly being connected to one another, but it doesn't ever hide me from anyone. It just gives my mind a break."

"How is the even possible, Cain? You're still Alpha with Cassia being the Alpha Female. Why is Shanely gaining that ability?" Aspen asked.

"And what other abilities will she get?" Ash countered.

Silence filled the air. *I am an anomaly,* I thought to myself, taking a deep breath and leaning against Bastian's shoulder.

"Let us look into it," Cain said, breaking the silence. "We'll try to figure out what's going on, but this is completely new territory for us. I can't even ask other packs for fear of bringing attention to Shanely, but I'll check my study tonight. I have a great many books on our history before the laws. Maybe something in there will help us."

"We'll be doing the perimeter run ourselves around Shanely's house from now on. No one will know you all are here," Uncle Aspen stated, and Ash nodded in agreement. The two older brothers left without another word, shifting as they disappeared into the forest. Cain held his hand out for my aunt, who fell in a step behind him.

He turned to the brothers one last time before leaving. "Elijah, Cade, and Bastian fix this door, and *all* of you, watch my niece. That's an order."

With that, the Alphas left, leaving us alone with one another. Cade flipped open his phone the second the door closed behind them, dialing a number before putting his phone to his ear.

Elijah gave him a weird look. "Who are you calling?"

"Pizza, duh. Caleb, what do you like on a pizza?" he said as he rolled his eyes. Bastian and I giggled as Caleb shifted uncomfortably.

"You don't need to worry about me, guys. Really, it's fine," he turned to me, "I can help fix the door though."

Cade walked over and slapped him on the back. "Didn't you hear the Alphas? We're family now, and we're all in this together. Plus, look at Shanely. She's so small! She needs to eat, especially now that she's eating for two. She needs pizza!"

Bastian laughed hard saying, "You mean you need pizza! Quit using my mate as an excuse to order food! Just pick something, Caleb. He won't stop."

Caleb looked at me for direction, and I shrugged. "I'm still getting used to them too."

A small smirk appeared on my brother's face, and he shook his head saying, "Okay. Well, thanks man. I'll pitch in, and nothing but meat for me."

"My man! That's my favorite as well. Who knew I'd have so much in common with a bear?"

Elijah pushed him forward as we laughed again. Cade smiled and pushed right back before rattling off the large order for pick up. The two waved goodbye as they went to grab lunch and supplies to fix my door. Or doors, as the backdoor was broken too.

Once the brothers were gone, Bastian reached across me and extended his hand to Caleb. "I am sorry, Caleb. I jumped to conclusions, and I hurt you. That wasn't okay. If we're going to make this work, we need a fresh start, so I am *sorry* for everything my brothers and I have done to you and your clan since we arrived in these mountains."

My chest warmed as I carefully watched the two. Pride filled my heart seeing Bastian own his part in their feud. My wolf watched him too and seemed pleased with our mate. *At least, I think.*

"I appreciate it. Not exactly like I was totally innocent either," Caleb said, shaking his hand, "but let's be honest, Bastian. Your wolf is probably going crazy with me being here, isn't he?"

Bastian didn't answer, and my heart sunk. *I thought we were making progress.*

Caleb nodded his head slowly and clicked his tongue. "It's okay. My grizzly isn't happy sitting with wolves either, but he's content around her," he said, pointing to me. "She's the key with us. Our animal halves won't get through this quickly, but I think they can with her at the center of all this."

"I agree. My wolf does feel better knowing you're her brother and not just a bear," he said, smirking at me. I rolled my eyes.

Caleb laughed. "Yeah, never once felt *that* kind of pull with her."

"Just eww," I chimed in. My nose scrunched in disgust, and the two laughed at me.

Bastian planted a kiss on my forehead saying, "Well, that was my wolf's first thought when Caleb was trying to take you away. It's why we shifted so quickly."

I chuckled, leaning into Bastian's embrace. "So, how do we make this work?"

Caleb sighed. "Start small? I'd like to get to know you, Shanely. Bastian and I will slowly warm up to each other the more we see one another, but I think we need to establish a few ground rules."

Bastian raised his brow. "What are you thinking?"

"First off, if we see each other outside this house, we need to be civil. It's too confusing for my other side," Caleb said, and I pursed my lips together. *Made sense,* I thought.

"I think we can manage without our normal— interaction," Caleb went on, giving Bastian a pointed look.

Bastian seemed to maul it over as I asked, "What is your normal interaction?"

"It's never been good. It's why we usually avoid one another," Caleb answered truthfully, and I frowned.

"Done," Bastian agreed. "My brothers and I will be on board. I can't speak for the pack though, seeing how no one else will know."

Caleb nodded his head. "As long as you understand the same for my clan."

"What else then?" Bastian asked.

"The next one is for Shanely. I would like to know about your past. I'm not trying to push or be nosy, but I can see the marks on you. At first, I assumed they were from the pack, but now that I know differently, I'd like to know what happened. Who is he, and will he ever be able to come here?"

I blew out a deep breath, feeling nothing but dread over discussing Peter. Again. "Do we have to?"

Caleb frowned and looked to my mate. Suddenly, Bastian scooped me up and placed me on his lap. He nuzzled against my neck, and it seemed to center me. The dread I felt seemed to ease, and I realized it was because of him. In fact, I felt stronger and a whole lot more confident than I ever used to be. Touch seemed to help too, and I snuggled against my mate, feeling like for the first time in my life, I could talk about this.

"My last foster family was in northern Indiana. Long story short, things weren't working out between us, so I made a deal with my foster mom. She'd let me leave and make my own choices, while she'd continue to cash the checks given to her. I wouldn't say *anything* to anyone about it, and she helped me get my truck. I lived in my truck my senior year of high school, but it was hard to find steady work that paid well, and it was getting colder. I met Peter at the diner I worked at late one night, and he seemed nice. He graduated the year before me and was new to the police force. He helped me get back on my feet when we started dating, and when he found out I was living in my truck, he insisted I'd move into the spare room. Once I did, everything slowly started to change."

Bastian stayed silent as he listened to me go into more detail than I ever thought I would with anyone. Our bond just made everything seem possible though. I wrapped his arm around my waist, hoping my touch eased him too.

"At first, it started with him becoming verbally abusive with me. Then I noticed every time I started to leave something would happen, and I needed him again. Something would break in my truck, or I lost my job for a bit, and I couldn't leave him. I couldn't afford to. Stuff would go wrong in the house and needed fixing, and he'd use my savings to pay for it. Looking back on it all, it was just lies, but I felt so stuck. During that time, he worked

CHAPTER 11

hard to make things right with me, and then one day we argued over money, and he backhanded me across the face."

Bastian tightened his hold on me. I don't even think he realized he was nearly squeezing the life out of me, and I stroke my thumb over his to calm his wolf.

"Why didn't you leave then?" Caleb asked quietly.

I sighed. "I did try," I answered softly. "I tried to leave that night, but I didn't make it out of town before he found me. I couldn't walk for a week after that, and I never tried to leave again. Being a cop, Peter threatened to spin the story however he needed to if I ever told anyone, and I believed him. I had nowhere to go, and I was too afraid to try again."

Bastian buried his nose in the crook of my neck, inhaling deeply. Caleb looked sick to his stomach as he stared at the floor, but for the first time I didn't feel shame talking about it. It was like a weight was finally lifted, and I was ready to rebuild the person I wanted to be. I ran my fingers through Bastian's hair.

"How did you manage to leave?" Caleb asked, his voice deepening slightly. *His bear was close to the surface,* I realized, picking up more of the shifter side than before.

"The lawyer called me one day and explained everything. He asked if I could come into the office to sign the papers for the cabin, and I told Peter I was heading into work for a double shift just as he was called away to an emergency," I said, trying to wrap up the story before my mate exploded. "I will forever be grateful to that lawyer. He took one look at me and pulled his wallet out. I signed the papers, and he filled my truck up for me. He told me to go and never look back. I raced home, filled a bag as quickly as I could, and left shortly after that. Peter had no idea that I was even gone until after his shift, and I ditched my phone with all the records of the lawyer's call. I drove through the night and didn't stop until I got here."

"My love—" Bastian said, pulling back and kissing my cheek. His lips lingered on my skin, and I smiled softly.

"It's okay. I'm okay, but I had a panic attack when I found out about the baby. I never wanted anything more to do with the man, and now I'm forever tied to him."

"Can we kill him now, Bastian?" Caleb asked, and I chuckled. My laughter died when I saw how serious he was.

"Hang on there. You guys can't go looking for him," I said.

"I'm starting to think Caleb's got a good idea. We could be back within the day if we flew," Bastian countered, shifting me off his lap to stand. My eyes widened.

"Absolutely not! He's a cop, guys! You aren't going anywhere near him. Plus, he's human, and you can't go after him."

Bastian shrugged as he pulled out his phone. "No one will know it's us, Shanely."

He was dead serious, I thought as my heart stammered in my chest. *He was actually going to kill Peter.* I shot to my feet and tugged on his arm.

"I don't want him to *ever* find me. I'm invisible right now. Understand? *Invisible*. Please, let me stay like this" I pleaded, clinging to Bastian's arm.

"Shanely, I can't just sit by knowing that man is still walking around after what he did to you," Bastian replied firmly as his eyes shifted gold. His wolf was close, but I didn't care. I wasn't going to back down either.

"You figure out a way to calm your wolf because you can't leave me. I'm pregnant and still marked, remember?"

Bastion muttered a curse under his breath, and Caleb promptly stood. "Marked? What's this now?"

"We have a rogue in the area. He targeted Shanely her first night here, but she managed to get away. Rogue's don't normally give up their hunt, so she's been marked. We're looking for him now," Bastian replied as he pocketed his phone. A smirk crept up my face.

"Good Lord," Caleb replied, "What is it with you and danger, Shanely?"

I shrugged playfully. "It's not like I go searching for it, but I think the rogue's still somewhat nearby, so you can't leave me."

Bastian's blue eyes narrowed on me then. "What makes you say that? Patrols haven't picked up on anything."

"When I was waiting for Caleb this morning, I felt like I was being watched. Just something shifted in the air, and I didn't feel alone anymore. I couldn't

CHAPTER 11

see anything, but I could hear something moving through the trees. It was the same as the first night. That's why I was running when you found me, Caleb."

"Why didn't you say anything?!" Bastian said as he bolted to the windows. He scanned the woods before grabbing his phone to text.

"We've been a little busy Bastian! It wasn't on purpose," I replied, putting my hands on my hips.

"Do you need help finding him?" Caleb asked.

"I sent a mind-link out to Ash and Aspen now, and I texted some of the enforcers. They'll check the road to the cabin and see what they can find, but I won't say no to help, Caleb. Thank you."

"Of course. I'll keep an eye out in my land and in town when I work just in case he's hiding somewhere there. How is he getting past you guys though?" Caleb asked, crossing his arms. "These lands are usually locked down tight."

Bastian shrugged in frustration. "I have no idea. Rogues usually have a distinctive smell, and no one can pick it up. We'll keep looking though, but for now Shanely doesn't go anywhere alone. Right, babe?"

I rolled my eyes. "Right."

Caleb sighed as he sat back down. "I had a bad feeling in my gut that night. I was drawn to you, and I should have never left you alone. Octavia made sure I was too busy in the back instead of working the bar like normal. I think she could smell you were something different and freaked out. You were gone by the time I got back out."

"It's not like anyone could have anticipated that night, Caleb. I remember Octavia though. She's a bundle of joy, isn't she?" I asked, giving Caleb a look.

Bastian snorted saying, "Something like that."

Caleb gave him a pointed look. "She's had a rough life, alright? Deep down, she's a loyal friend and cousin, I might add."

"I'll believe that when I see it!" Bastian laughed, and soon Caleb joined in.

"Whoa, wait a minute! Cousin?" I asked excitedly.

Caleb nodded. "Our dad's younger brother, Thomas, is the leader of our clan. He has two girls, Octavia and Alana. He also has a son, but he's been training and working in Russia with the main clan for a long while now."

"I probably won't meet them. Will I?" I asked, slumping back on the couch.

"Probably not. Uncle Thomas has a lot of issues with wolves."

We grew silent with that comment, but soon Bastian and Caleb started to pick up the broken pieces of my cabin. Well, *our* cabin.

Caleb went out to his truck and pulled a tire out of the bed. I gave him a grateful look, and the three of us quickly jacked up my truck and changed the rim and tire. Well, I mostly watched, but they showed me how to do it in case I ever needed to again. There was some more damage with the tire that they needed parts for, but it all went over my head. The guys seemed to know what I needed though, and Bastian had the parts ordered within minutes. He'd pick it up sometime Monday, and they'd get it fixed in no time. At least that's what they claimed.

Bastian started to walk around my beat-up, old Dodge and started listing things in his phone to help *upgrade* the truck. Caleb quickly joined in, and soon they were discussing trucks and overlanding gear to add to it. They talked like they had been friends for years, and they were both really knowledgeable with vehicles. I, however, was not, but it was fun listening to them go on though.

The brothers got back with their massive pizza order, and I ate more than I usually did, surprisingly. Maybe it was because of the baby or maybe it was because my wolf was finally awake, but it tasted incredible, and it was hard to stop at just a single slice. It didn't escape my notice that *all* four boys kept sneaking food onto my plate either. Extra pepperoni or a chunk of sausage, and Bastian even added a whole extra slice. Like I wouldn't notice my plate was no longer empty. I eyed him funny after that one, but all he did was give me a sheepish smile. I collapsed on my couch feeling like I was going to burst after the fourth slice.

While the fellas all talked about truck projects and what to do about the rogue, I let my mind wander to my shifter abilities. My wolf had gone utterly

CHAPTER 11

still again, and I frowned. *Wouldn't I feel the need to shift sometime soon? Why was she alert in some moments but frozen in others?*

I had so many questions rattling in my head that I barely noticed a text on my phone.

```
Hey Shanely! I just wanted to let you know Dr. Malin is very
anxious to see you about the baby. I want you to see our pack
doctor right away to make sure things are going smoothly.
Things are different for shifter mothers. Call me in the
morning.
```

I took a deep breath. While I had accepted the fact I *was* pregnant, I wasn't ready to dive head first into motherhood just yet. Those school movies still haunted my mind.

```
Thank you, Aunt Cassia! I'll come in soon, but after everything
today, I just need a little time to adjust to the idea of
motherhood. Can I meet with her later?
```

Those three little dots bubbled on screen.

```
I understand, but sooner rather than later. Alright? This is
happening whether you're ready or not, and it's happening
faster than you think.
```

I frowned again and set down my phone. *I wasn't giving birth today so I didn't have to think about it now.*

In record time, the boys had fixed my doors and the little damage to my porch. Thankfully, my grandmother had a huge tool shed off to the side that helped everything along. I assumed it belonged to my grandfather, and I tried to push my curiosity aside. He wasn't a kind man, so I shouldn't waste energy on him, but it was hard not wondering who my family was. Like it or not, that man's blood was in my veins, and I wanted to know where I came from.

The day quickly left us, and Caleb soon had to leave for town. He had a late shift at the bar since bailing on work this morning. Octavia was pissed, but he simply shrugged when I tried to apologize. All I got in response was that *it was totally worth it,* and he'd call me when he talked to our dad.

After Caleb left, Cade and Elijah insisted on staying here instead of the bunkhouse for enforcers. Bastian wanted extra eyes on me since the issue this morning, but I didn't mind. They could stay as long as they wanted. One took the spare room, while the other grabbed the spare bedding for the couch, but when Bastian's gaze shifted from me to my bedroom, my heart began to quicken its pace. Nerves rattled my core as I led him down the hall.

"Are you cozy with this?" he asked.

His voice dropped an octave, sending a shiver down my spine, and I slowly turned to face him. Bastian looked between me and the bed, and when his eyes settled back on me, they were pure gold.

My wolf perked her head up, and I smirked playfully. "Easy there, wolf boy. You can sleep here, but nothing else."

"Wolf boy?" he asked as he slowly stalked towards me.

I gulped. My eyes widening as I slowly retreated further into my room. "Kinda cute, right?"

He chuffed. "You know I wouldn't keep backing away like that if I were you."

My back hit the wall, and before I knew it, he had used his increased speed to pin me there. Both his arms were on either side of my head, and he was so close I could feel his breath on me. I stilled. *There wasn't anywhere left to go,* I thought as my heart skittered in my chest. I narrowed my eyes as he just smirked wickedly at me like he won or something. *The arrogant man.*

Bastian's canines sharpened, and he leaned closer. I held my breath when his lips gently brushed against my ear as he whispered, "You know wolves like the hunt, right?"

His wolf had mixed with his voice, changing it to this gritty, almost husky, tone. It made my knees wobble, and all I wanted to do was leap into his arms and kiss him senseless. My chest warmed as his lips lowered to my neck and gently kissed towards my jaw line.

CHAPTER 11

"We're already married according to pack laws," he whispered again, "and I need you, Shanely."

I moaned softly at his touch, and that seemed to do him in. His lips suddenly met mine, and he pulled me close, gripping my waist hard enough to leave marks. I was breathless and excited as I tried to keep up, but he moved so fast. I had never felt this way before. So utterly complete and safe. I had never kissed a man that I was not only *so ungodly attracted to*, but one I was also head-over-heels in love with.

Bastian's sharp teeth grazed the sensitive spot where my neck met shoulder, and like a bucket of ice water, Cade's voice boomed through the door as he pounded against it.

"Oh, no! Absolutely no hanky panky while we are here, thank you very much! The walls are way too thin for this! C'mon dude! You know I can hear better than the rest of you!"

"Yeah, go to bed, newlyweds!" Elijah yelled from the couch.

Bastian groaned. "I swear to God, Cade. Go away!"

A soft chuckle escaped my lips as Bastian rolled his eyes. He rested his head on mine as we caught our breath, and I watched those gorgeous blue eyes return.

"I'm sorry about them," he whispered.

"It's okay," I chuckled. "It's honestly for the best. I'd like to be married according to human laws before anything more happens anyways."

Bastian gave me a puzzled look. "Human laws don't apply to shifters, my love. We're not the same kind, and marriage for us is when the bond forms. There's a party sometimes, but it's the bond that connects two shifters forever. No one fools around before the bond either. It's sacred, and it's for life."

"I know, but I've only been a shifter for a little bit. I've grown up a human most of my life, even if I wasn't really one and—"

I frowned as my voice trailed off. More aware of Cade and Elijah's ears, I whispered, "I didn't have a choice with Peter. I wanted to be married before anything ever happened, and that choice was taken from me. I want to do this differently, Bastian."

His face suddenly softened, and he quickly nodded. "I would never force you to do something you aren't ready for, Shanely. You are mine, my love, and I plan to shower you with love and affection and be the man *you* deserve. If a wedding is what you want, then a wedding is what you'll get."

My smile grew as I tossed my arms around my mate. I had no words to describe how grateful I was for the gift he just gave me. "Thank you, Bastian."

"You're welcome, baby."

He let me go and sauntered over to the bed. My eyes watched every step he took, when suddenly I realized what he said earlier.

"Wait. So, you've never—" My cheeks heated as my voice trailed off. Unable to finish that sentence.

Bastian smirked back at me and kicked off his shoes. "No, I haven't. It doesn't end well when you fool around before finding your mate. Most shifters in general wait, but not all."

"I guess that makes sense," I said as I dug in my drawer for clothes. "I'm going to change. We can head to bed then."

He nodded, and I felt his gaze as I practically ran to my bathroom. I collapsed against the closed door and sucked in a deep breath. *God, this was going to be harder than I thought.*

A wicked grin tugged the corners of my mouth, and I pushed off the door before my thoughts ran amuck. I quickly put my pj's on in the bathroom and brushed my teeth, hoping I didn't reek during my little make-out session a moment ago. I primped in the mirror, tossing my curly red hair to one side and wishing I had taken a shower earlier. The frizz was becoming unmanageable, and I needed a reset soon.

Bastian was already under the covers by the time I came out, and my face flushed when I saw him shirtless and his jeans tossed to one side. *Oh God— I don't think I am going to make it,* I thought as my eyes roamed across his bare chest.

Bastian was *built*, and I was a little lost staring at his sculpted torso. His defined abs and strong arms had me frozen in place. I couldn't stop staring at how utterly perfect this man was. My eyes shifted up to find Bastian

CHAPTER 11

smirking at my blatant staring. My cheeks heated, and I scurried into bed. I buried myself under all the blankets as embarrassment permeated *every ounce of my body.*

Bastian laughed as he snuggled up behind me. "Don't be embarrassed for enjoying what's yours, my love. I won't be when it's my turn."

Butterflies fluttered my belly, and I felt his warm lips touch my cheek before he settled in behind me. I muttered a goodnight and tried to fall asleep. I mean I *seriously* tried. But all I could think about was how a drop-dead gorgeous guy was currently sleeping with one arm tossed over me, *and one day soon*, I was going to have him do all sorts of wicked things to me.

Chapter 12

"Well, you're definitely pregnant," Malin, the pack doctor, said while checking the stupid pee stick.

I was up bright and early this morning to meet with her, and even though I trusted my uncle and his ability, I made her do the test again, just to be sure. It was still weird that it was just something he could sense, and I needed to see proof the human way, I guess. It's been a couple of weeks since Bastian and I discovered we were mates. I should be around 5 weeks pregnant now, but it was completely different for shifters. I didn't know where that put me.

I should have come in sooner, but every time the baby was mentioned, an overwhelming feeling overtook me, and it was all I could do to settle the anxiety building. Not to mention, I haven't been sleeping well.

Bastian and his brothers had basically moved into my cabin and have been renovating the spare room to be a baby's room. I tried to just offer it to them to share, but they shook their head and insisted on a nursery. Bastian just said *he'd figure it out* every time I asked about where his brothers should stay.

Caleb comes by nearly every day to help the brothers out and spend time with me, of course. He and Bastian managed to fix my truck as promised and have been slowly upgrading it for me. They've been fixing it on the sly, despite the many times I've insisted on them not buying me stuff. I can't pay *anyone* back, but I get the same speech every time I object to it.

"You need a reliable working vehicle, Shanely."

"I'm your mate, and it's my job to make sure you have everything you need."

CHAPTER 12

"What are brothers for? Just let me take care of it."

It's the same thing every time, and after awhile, I just gave up.

I was disappointed that I had yet to meet my father. Caleb explained he was away on clan business and had to go back to the main clan in Russia for a while, and he didn't want to explain any of this to our dad over the phone. It was disappointing to say the least. Until he returns, the two of us have just been getting to know one another.

We have the same favorite color, black. He also hates olives, and absolutely loves all Disney movies. Although, he made me promise not to mention that last one to anyone. I gave him a wicked grin, holding onto that piece of information to use at a later time.

Caleb said he'd keep the job at the Den open for me, but only after we found the rogue. No amount of protesting got them to budge. The four liked to gang up on me, which they did often when I wanted to do something they deemed *unsafe*.

The rogue had *completely* disappeared, and I didn't think it was coming back, but Bastian hasn't let me out of his sight. I was ready to get back to normal life again, but I was still grounded to pack lands for the moment.

In the meantime, Bastian paid for everything, and I hated the idea of borrowing money from him. He keeps reminding me that I'm his mate, so it was his responsibility to care for me, and while I loved having a partner in life, I felt like I was just taking from him constantly and never giving anything back. I couldn't even assist with pack responsibilities because I couldn't shift. The pregnancy seemed to throw everyone too. No one wanted me to lift a finger, and while it was very sweet, it also drove me crazy. I didn't want to be useless. Bastian tried to reassure me that I was the furthest thing from useless, but I couldn't change how I felt.

The only thing I secretly did was legally change my last name. Uncle Aspen was apparently a lawyer as well but did mostly work for environmental law firms. He helped me figure out the paperwork, and now I am officially Shanely McCoy instead of Shanely Thomas. I didn't want the state's given name anymore. I wanted to proudly have my mother's name as my own, even if it was only for a little while. Soon, I'd legally marry Bastian, and my name will change to his, but for a little while I wanted to be a McCoy.

My uncle was proud to help and said it might help me feel connected to her a bit more. That it will be good for me to feel rooted here in this town and with my family, and I think he was right. My wolf awoke when I joined my mother's pack and changing my name gave me a sense of belonging even more than the bonds. I smile every time I write out Shanely McCoy.

I had dragged my feet long enough though, and Bastian finally made the doctor appointment for me. So now, we sat in a small exam room attached to the lodge. Bastian stayed with me the whole time for the exam and tests Dr. Malin ran. All while my nerves ran amuck.

"Congratulations by the way. Alpha announced your mating some time ago."

I smiled softly. "Thank you, Dr. Malin."

She waved her hand. "Oh, just Malin. I'm not so formal with the title. Now, let's go over a few things. First things first, I know this isn't Bastian's pup."

I sucked in a breath as Bastian moved his hand to mine. He leaned forward somewhat blocking me from her view. *What happened to our secret?!* I thought to myself.

"Don't be alarmed!" she stammered. "Your secret is safe with me, but I needed to know in order to help you. I have some questions for you, if you don't mind."

Bastian didn't move, and Dr. Malin pursed her lips together.

"Is that alright, Bastian?" she asked, looking at my mate.

Bastian turned to me, giving me a look like he wanted my opinion first. The corners of my mouth rose, and I nodded once. He promptly sat back and motioned for Malin to start.

God, I love this man.

"I've heard briefly about the story with the biological father. We don't need to discuss that anymore, but I would like to know how you are doing with everything. How are you handling carrying his child?"

I shrugged my shoulders, staring at my feet. "I honestly try not to think about it. I'm content to just view this as Bastian's baby."

"Are you having any issues at all? You went through some serious trauma, and now are dealing with a pregnancy. Your hormones are all over the place, Shanely. Your life has turned upside down since finding out about shifters, and that's not to mention the rogue, who still hasn't been found. That's a lot of stress to be juggling," she asked, giving me a look of concern.

I knew she was only trying to help, but I wish she'd leave this alone.

My silence must have been answered enough as she spoke to me again, "Shanely, we need to deal with your stress, but I can't help you if you don't tell me what's going on. This isn't good for the baby, and I can tell you aren't sleeping well."

Bastian's head perked up. "She has nightmares, doctor."

I glared at him. "Bastian!"

"Shanely, did you hear her? This isn't good for you or the baby. I made you a promise to protect you and something is going on with you. You talk in your sleep sometimes. It's not easy to hear," he muttered that last part, his eyes flashing briefly with emotion.

"I didn't know I talked in my sleep," I replied, feeling a little guilty. "Why didn't you tell me?"

Bastian gave me a pointed look. "You have enough to deal with. I wasn't adding another thing on your plate to stress about."

I leaned my head back against the wall and closed my eyes. I didn't want to think about my nightmares, let alone tell her about them. No one but Bastian and his brothers knew that most nights I wake up screaming. I wake up in complete terror, unable to explain what even happened because it doesn't even make sense to me.

"How about you tell me about your nightmares? Are they about Peter?" Malin asked.

"No," I answered softly. "Peter has nothing to do with them."

Bastian narrowed his eyes.

Malin replied, "What happens during the nightmare then?"

"I don't even know why they're happening. I've never had dreams like this before. The setting may change, but what happens remains the same. I end up seeing Division men in full gear, armed to the teeth, and attacking the pack. When I look around, I see my family lying on the ground dead. Everyone close to me is dead, and there's blood everywhere. I shriek and hold onto—" my voice drifts as I look at Bastian. I sigh, choosing to move on instead. "I see Patrick stalking towards me then, and I wake up when he grabs me."

Malin frowned. "Patrick? Like the sheriff's kid?"

"I don't know," I said, shrugging. "I met Patrick briefly the night I met the rogue. He was clingy and pushy but harmless. That was the last I've seen of him. I don't know why he's in my dreams now."

"You've never mentioned Patrick before. He's the son of the Division's assigned Head for this area. We deal with his father all the time," Bastian chimed in, looking concerned now. "He talked to you? What did he want?"

"He wanted to buy me a drink," I said casually, "and he didn't like taking no for an answer, but I haven't seen him since. Why would he be in my dreams?"

"Are they all the same?" Malin asked, leaning forward in her chair. I narrowed my eyes, frowning.

"It has been since my wolf woke. It's always just a different danger with Patrick and the Division at the center," I answered.

"It sounds like your dreams may be an ability. Did anything happen after you spoke with Patrick that night?" she asked me.

I shook my head no. "No, nothing happened. I just—"

My voice trailed off as that night came to mind. That freakish wave of sickness that came and went so fast. *Was that because of him?*

Bastian interrupted my thoughts. "Shanely, what is it?"

"That night. I spoke to Patrick *right* before the rogue found me," I said, turning to face him. "I left Patrick at the bar, and by the time I had made it to the main road that goes up the mountains, I felt so sick. My vision blurred, and I was so dizzy, but everything went away after I crashed."

"It might have been the start of an ability, but I've never seen one tied to a human like that," Dr. Malin replied wearily. I frowned, seeing a hint of alarm on her face, but she quickly gave me a smile and patted my leg. "I think the pregnancy is bringing these abilities to the front a lot faster than they would normally. It's not the norm to be able to use your gifts before you shift, and most wolf mothers *do* experience a high volume of vivid dreams, terrible night sweats, and an extremely sensitive stomach. I wouldn't be alarmed normally, but your dreams are oddly specific."

Dr. Malin stood then, grabbing a couple of bottles from her cabinet and handed them to me. *Prenatals.*

"Take these, and I'd like you to have weekly chats with either myself or your aunt. She helps me out here at the clinic a lot, so she would be a good one to talk to as well," Malin said, and I frowned.

"Like therapy?" I asked uneasily, looking to Bastian for guidance.

"Exactly. It might help relieve some stress for you, and maybe the dreams will lessen on their own."

"If this is an ability; what could it be?" Bastian asked.

"Well, it's hard to say honestly. Because of the type of dreams she's having, it might be the seer ability. Seers in modern day movies don't exist, but it's a very rare ability in the shifter community. It lets the shifter see a possible future or outcome for themselves."

"Wait, I'm confused," I said, shaking my head. "What's the point if it's just a possibility?"

"The seer ability is more like a personal warning system. Usually, the more the dreams or warnings happen, then the higher the probability it *will* happen. It's just one possibility though. It doesn't mean it's set in stone. Our choices constantly change the future, and we can never fully know what lies ahead. It's just a warning system the seer has to try and make the future better if they can. Sometimes no matter what you do, your future will happen one way or another," Malin replied. "It's a taxing ability."

"Do you think I'm a seer?" I asked, fear creeping into my voice.

"I don't know, Shanely," she said, with a sigh. "You are a rare mixer, and you're pregnant. All of this could be completely normal or it could be the start of an ability. I'll tell the Alpha about it, and we can keep an eye on you for now."

"But if I *am* a seer then that would mean my dreams are warning me this is about to happen," I said, leaning forward as fear stabbed my heart.

"Everyone will die—"

"It's not something to fret about yet, Shanely," Malin said, cutting me off. I slumped in my seat. "We don't know that you even are a seer so don't view these dreams as warnings. I'm going to give you some sleep medicine though. It's safe for baby and should give you the rest you both need. Now, I do want to talk to you about this baby. Shifter pups are different from regular human births. Instead of the normal 9 months, shifters tend to give birth around 5-6 months."

My eyes bugged out of my head. "Excuse me?"

Bastian reassuringly grabbed my hand. "It will be okay, honey."

"You knew about this, and you didn't tell me?" I hollered, glaring at him. *God, I thought I had more time than this.*

His deep laugh filled the room. "Yes, I knew! It's just a detail I wasn't really thinking about. I've been a little preoccupied, Shanely."

I smacked him in the arm. "The baby coming possibly 4 months sooner than I was expecting is a big thing!"

It was Malin's turn to laugh now, and I sent her a glare. Their incessant laughs were only pissing me off more.

"Remember you're the one who blew me off," Malin said, grabbing the sleep medicine. I crossed my arms in annoyance. "I was told you needed space and were coming in as soon as you could. You're not very far along though, so you still have time to prepare, I promise. Don't be alarmed if the baby grows quickly. Some have even delivered sooner than 5 months to a healthy child, but I can't predict anything, and it's even more off now because this baby will be a mix of human, wolf, and bear."

I stilled. *Malin knew my other secret.*

Malin smirked, watching the two of us. "Another secret safe with me, but I needed to know. We have no idea what you've passed to the baby. This baby is half human, so it may not ever shift. It may be just a regular child or it may only have special abilities. This child could end up a shifter, but which one? Bear, wolf or both?"

My hands went to my belly as my stomach rolled. Breakfast threatened to reappear as I thought about the many possibilities for my kid.

CHAPTER 12

"Is it possible to have both animals?" I asked quietly.

She nodded her head. "It's very rare, but not impossible. Before the law came into play, mates were found from anywhere. It was uncommon for shifters to find their mates amongst a different shifter kind, but it still happened. Usually, the child would favor one side. Either their mom or their dad, but every so often, we'd see a child with both animals. They were stronger than most, and usually became the alpha or clan leader. They are what we call mixers." I gently rubbed my belly, lost in thought, and Malin continued, "We will keep a close watch on the baby once he or she arrives and take everything one day at a time. Now, the last bit before I let you go is a bit of fun news. Part of my healing ability allows me to be able to tell the gender of the baby well before it's even possible. Would you like to know now?"

My eyes widened, and I looked from her to Bastian. *I could know what I'm having right now?*

He whispered, "It's your call."

I pursed my lips as I looked back at my belly. *Did I even want to know what I was having? Was I ready to even start thinking of names or picturing what it would look like?* My stomach twisted in knots, and my shoulders fell as the anxiety built within me. This tidbit of news should be exciting, but I felt more scared than happy. I didn't know how to be a mom and finding out the gender just made everything feel too real.

"No, thank you," I answered, looking away from my stomach and the little bundle inside. "I'd like to wait."

Bastian squeezed my hand, kissing my forehead as Malin smiled. *He probably assumed I wanted to be surprise, but in reality, I was just a big fat chicken.* I slumped further in my seat then.

"No problem," Malin said. "Come find me anytime if you change your mind. I'll see you next week unless you meet with your aunt. It was great to finally meet you, Shanely."

We left the clinic in silence, and Bastian let me process everything on my own. He just held my hand, lacing his fingers within mine as we walked outside, giving me the space I needed to wrap my head around it all. I just wasn't sure how long it would take for me to come to terms with being a mom.

It was beautiful and sunny outside, and the lodge was busy with everyone having something to do. I inhaled deeply, enjoying the forest and the wonderful day we were having. *Everyday with Bastian was wonderful though*, I thought, smiling to myself.

"Hey!"

We turned, finding Cade and Elijah waving as they ran to greet us. Cade was shirtless and wearing basketball shorts, while Elijah had a gray sleeveless shirt with black shorts on, and by the looks of those two, I'd say they were just finishing up training for the day. Both continued to jog in place as they reached us.

"Well, how's my Baby Girl's baby girl?" Cade asked in between breaths.

I gave him a puzzling look. "How do you know it's a girl?"

"It's not a girl! She's carrying my nephew!" Elijah stammered as he jogged in a circle around us. He was already breathing hard, which means they had probably been running for a while.

"We don't know the gender yet," Bastian answered. "Shanely wanted to wait."

Cade rolled his eyes. "Oh, I know. Mark my words, it's a girl! But anyways, how is she?"

I chuckled to myself, feeling lighter than before. "The baby is fine. We're watching and seeing how he or she develops for now."

"Is she a wolf?" Cade asked us, raising his left brow.

"Don't know. The baby could be a wolf, bear, or have no shifting abilities at all," Bastian answered.

Both brothers stopped jogging and frowned.

"The baby could also have both," I said, rubbing my hands together.

"Both?" Elijah questioned, his frown turning to a crooked smile.

I nodded. "Yes, both. Bear and wolf. She said those mixers tend to be the strongest and usually the leader."

"Whoa. So, my niece is basically destined to be amazing!" Cade practically shouted, and I shushed him.

CHAPTER 12

"What if *she*," I said, drawing out the last word, "is human? With no abilities?"

"That would really suck," Elijah said quietly, and my face fell. *Would no one accept her if she was human?* I wondered, shrinking back ever so slightly. Bastian smacked him upside the head.

Elijah gave him an annoyed look before turning to me. "Sorry, that came out wrong, Shanely. *We* would love her no matter what, but Bastian is a full-blooded wolf and a strong one at that."

"Would anyone be able to disprove Bastian as the father?" Cade whispered quietly to us.

My heart sank. *I hadn't thought about that*, I thought as my stomach rolled again. *No one would believe a strong wolf like Bastian would have a child with no abilities or animals at all.* That just wasn't normal for shifters. Everyone would know something was up, which would put my baby at risk. A growl nearly escaped my lips as I thought about *anyone* trying to harm my baby. I put my hands to my mouth, startled by what just happened, but thankfully no one seemed to notice.

"This will always be *my* baby," Bastian said in a firm tone. "No one is disproving anything. If the kid has no abilities, then it will just be listed as an anomaly. A rare recessive gene or something like that. It's happened before."

Elijah looked at him. "When? I have never heard of that before."

"Elijah," Bastian warned, giving him a pointed look. Their eyes glossed over, and I knew they were talking about me. My mouth opened to say something, when a voice entered my mind.

"Shanely?"

"Aunt Cassia! How are you?" I asked, tuning the boys out.

"Doing just fine. How's the baby?"

"He or she is doing good. We got a lot of information today."

"I'm sure! Do you mind if your uncle and I talk with Dr. Malin about you and the baby? We had some questions of our own, but I'd like your permission to know before we go."

I smiled. *"Yeah, I don't mind. I was planning on informing you myself, but this works out too. What questions do you have?"*

"Oh, not much. Mostly just stuff on genetics and old legends. Our wolf heritage is full of them, and she would know if there is any truth to them," Cassia answered.

"Hmm. Maybe sometime we can meet, and you can tell me about them too? I'd love to know more about where we come from," I said.

"I would love that! Just let me know when you want to get together."

"Actually," I said, sighing in my mind, "I'm supposed to have regular therapy sessions with either you or Dr. Malin. Can I meet with you next week instead? I just thought it might be easier."

"Sure! I'm mostly here at the lodge, so just find me whenever you're free. I'll tell Dr. Malin of the change."

"Thanks, Aunt Cassia."

"No problem," she said in a cheerful tone. "Don't forget your uncle Ash wants to meet with you after the baby is born. He wants to give you a self-defense course, and he and Aspen are in charge of all that."

"Oh, sure," I said, my voice falling ever so slightly. "That would probably be a good thing since I can't shift."

My aunt could hear the trepidation in my voice. The fear that I may never shift pulling through.

"It will come, Shanely," she replied softly. "I'm sure of it, but this training won't happen until after the baby is here. I think he just wants to give you a crash course is all. He's been wound up since we found you."

"Okay, I'll talk to him about it soon."

"Good. Be safe, Shanely."

I felt my aunt leave my mind, and I focused back on the group. Everyone was staring at me with grins on their faces and heat crept up my cheeks.

"What?"

They all busted out laughing. Bastian wrapped his arms around me and tugged me close.

"We've been talking to you for the last five minutes! Did you hear anything, Baby Girl?" Cade asked.

I blushed more. "No! I was busy talking to my aunt."

CHAPTER 12

"It's okay, babe. The mind-link takes some getting used to," Bastian said as he kissed my forehead, and I buried my face in his chest.

"What were you guys asking?" I asked sheepishly, my voice muffled from being smushed against my mate's body.

"We *asked* when you wanted to go into town. You two have a wedding coming up, so we need to start grabbing the supplies. We would offer to just pick everything up for you, but we figured most girls would like to get their own wedding dress," Elijah said.

"Oh, right," I said as I perked up. I'd need a dress if I was going to walk down the aisle. Suddenly, my face fell when I realized I didn't have any money. *I didn't want to just assume Bastian would pay for it,* I thought, shifting on my feet. *He's already paid for enough.*

"You don't have to go. You can stay in the safety of the pack," Bastian said, rubbing my back reassuringly.

"No, it's not that. I just wasn't sure—" I replied, letting my sentence drop. Every time I brought up the discussion of money, Bastian seemed to get upset. He wanted to pay for everything for me, and he had been these past few weeks. I didn't want to hurt my mate's feelings, but it felt like I was taking advantage of him. I know we were a team, but I just felt— bad.

"Bastian?" I said through our link.

"Yes, my love?" he answered with a sly grin.

"Can we even afford to get a dress?" I asked, turning towards him. *"I don't have any money for one."*

"Shanely," he replied, giving me a firm look. *"Of course, we can get your dress. I have everything covered. You just need to pick one out, but like I've told you before, I've got you."*

"And I do appreciate it, Bastian. But I feel bad assuming you will cover everything constantly. I haven't even seen you guys work, other than training at the lodge or your enforcer work. I know I'm taking a toll on everyone's wallet, and this whole wedding is only happening because I want it."

Bastian's chuckle sounded in my head, and it was odd to see his mouth not moving with the sound. Amusement filled his eyes like I was just being silly over this whole matter, but I just felt guilty.

"First off, I have zero issues about marrying you. In fact, ever since you brought it up, it's become something I want too. I want to own you in every possible way, Shanely."

My breath caught in my chest. *God, why did that sound so sexy?* The one little word did me in, and all I wanted to do was kiss the man. His voice pulled me from my delicious thoughts.

"My brothers and I do have outside jobs, but we primarily work here at the lodge. Your uncle pays all of the enforcers, so it can be their primary job and focus. The McCoy family is loaded anyways as they all are either lawyers or in finance, plus my own family comes from old money, so we each have our own trust fund, and our father sends money to us every month to cover expenses. Believe me, we have more than enough."

My jaw dropped, and Bastian just winked at me. *My family was rich? His family was rich? A trust fund?!* Here I was fussing over what was colossal amounts of money *to me*, but it was just chump change to the rest of them. Heat filled my cheeks again. *I had no idea.*

"What do you guys even do?!"

Bastian opened his mouth to respond, but Cade interrupted.

"Now that you two are done talking about who's paying for the dress; do you want to go into town today?" Cade asked again, and I blushed again, sticking out my tongue at him. He grinned and reached out to snatch it. I yipped in response.

"I'm game if Shanely is," Bastian said, turning to me.

"You guys will both come with me, right?" I asked, feeling more nervous than I expect to feel.

"Of course, Baby girl!"

"You didn't think we'd send you on your own, did you?" Elijah asked, raising his eyebrow.

"No one is getting within 10 ft of you, babe," Bastian said reassuringly before giving orders to his brothers. "Cade, send a message out to Caleb and grab your truck. Let's make sure he's around today for an extra set of eyes. Elijah, reach out to the enforcers. Let's spread out where we can without being obvious. Have them keep an eye out for anyone that seems

CHAPTER 12

overly interested in Shanely. Maybe we can spot the rogue in town? Oh, and Elijah, see if we can pull a few guys to go with us as well. I'll tell the Alpha, and we'll leave before lunch."

The brothers nodded and took off in different directions without question.

"Wow, that was very Alpha-like," I commented, taking Bastian's hand as we walked back to the lodge in the direction of my uncle's office.

"It is in my blood," he answered with a sly grin, "especially when it pertains to you."

"What do you mean in your blood?"

"My father is an Alpha, which means I have that dominant trait too," he answered matter of factly.

"How does that all work with Uncle Cain then?" I asked.

"My dad sent my brothers and I here to learn and train with Cain, Ash, and Aspen as he has the largest pack in the world. My father's pack is one of the oldest though, and I come from a very old line of strong Alphas. Our last name means "Monstrous Wolf" in the old Norse mythology."

I snorted. "Seriously?"

Bastian laughed with me. "Personally, I think long ago when people started seeing our *other* form, they called us that as their own way of saying werewolf, and my family just changed the spelling a bit and made it our last name because it's funny. Now, we live hidden in plain sight, and no one is the wiser."

"What did they call you before they changed the wording for your name?"

"Fenrisulfr. Both mean wolf," he replied, giving me a wink.

"How come you and your brothers came here for training then?" I asked as we walked down the hall. "Wouldn't your father want to oversee your training himself?"

I had realized that in the weeks I'd spent with my mate, he rarely spoke of home. None of the brothers did. I didn't know much about his home life, and I was anxious to meet my future in-laws.

"The whole destined to be Alpha didn't sit well with me growing up, but Dad's very set on tradition," he answered, sighing. I frowned, seeing his brows knit together. "The Alpha title must be passed to the oldest child, the heir, who is normally the strongest wolf. I was unfortunate to be delivered first, so it fell to me. My wolf's size is abnormally large compared to most and even compared to my brothers, which Dad thinks is just another sign I should be Alpha."

Bastian slowed his steps as a bad feeling crept inside. *He doesn't seem happy*, I thought.

"My father reached out to your uncle in hopes it would inspire me to want the title. Shifters respect Cain, and his word means something amongst the wolves. He decided I was coming here when I was 15, and Cade and Elijah demanded to come too. My father thinks *this* will convince me to take my place, with Cade or Elijah taking the spot as Beta, but I've never wanted it. We trained hard here, and your uncles noticed. Soon, we became the Alpha's personal Enforcers. Cain's never pushed me to return home, and honestly, I'm happy to never go back. Especially now that I have you."

"You don't think you'll change your mind and want to go back though? That is your family after all," I asked as guilt ate at me. *What if he has to leave one day?* I thought. *What if he realizes he needs to go back, and I'll have to choose between my mate or my family?* Suddenly, I felt selfish. *How can I ask him to give up his own pack and family because I didn't want to give up mine?*

"Never. Honestly, I think this was all supposed to happen anyways. Most are desperate for the Alpha spot, but I could never shake this bad feeling I got whenever we talked about me taking over my father's pack," he said, tucking me into his side as we paused before my uncle's door. "I think I was meant to come here so I could find you, love. And I wouldn't ask you to leave your family when you've only just found them. Besides the thought of leaving these woods freaks me out anyways."

My mate knocked on the door loudly, leaving me a muddled muck. I traced his face for any sign he may be lying or saying what he thinks I want to hear. My mouth watered as bile rose to the back of my throat, feeling more guilty than ever. I don't think I could blame this on the baby. My uncle's voice boomed through the door, and Bastian led us inside.

"Bastian, Shanely! Glad you're here!" he practically shouted. "We have

CHAPTER 12

a lot to do before the wedding. How's the baby doing, little wolf?"

My smile didn't reach my eyes as I replied, "Baby's good. We're all doing okay."

Cain sat at the edge of his desk, while Bastian and I sat in the big comfy chairs in front of him. This was the first I had been in his private office, and I loved how cozy it felt. His office was decent size and full of books. Books were literally covering every shelf from floor to ceiling all around the room, and I wondered if he read them all. There was a large map of McCoy's land behind his desk, in between two tall windows that let in plenty of light. A thick line had been drawn on the map, and I wondered if that was the border.

"Good! That's what I want to hear. Well, the pack is a buzz talking about you two. This is the fastest mate bond to expecting their first pup this pack has ever seen. I mean don't get me wrong, *everything* moves quickly with wolves, but this is fast even for us. We haven't had a mate bond in awhile so be prepared for the gossip that's bound to happen," Cain said, wiggling his eyebrows at me.

"Really?" I asked, giving them both a look. *Who knew the pack even cared about me?*

Bastian groaned. "Bunch of old biddies that like to talk about everyone's business."

Cain laughed. "You know it's not going to be just them. Bastian is a favorite among our young women. Now that he's taken, you will become a target, Shanely. Wolves are jealous creatures after all."

And there it is, I thought.

"I thought this pack was extremely close?" I asked.

"We are. This pack runs very well and works great together, but that doesn't mean we're perfect. Every pack has that group that likes to stir the pot," my uncle replied, "and you can guess which family group is ours."

"Derek's," Bastian spat out angrily. *I had forgotten about that wolf.*

"Will Derek be a problem?" I asked, feeling a little nervous when it came to that wolf. He didn't seem to like me when we first met, but he's never said much else the few times I had seen him in the lodge.

"Derek won't touch you. I promise you that," Bastian stated confidently.

"Derek will keep to himself," Cain chimed in. "I'm not going to lie, he isn't your biggest fan right now, but I'm sure as he gets to know you that will change. I mean you are the heir after all."

"The pack isn't going to want someone they barely know to lead. I'm sure they will take a vote if you step down," I countered. I had no desire to run anything, and in reality, I couldn't even shift. There was no way I'd be Alpha *anything*.

"Shanely, the McCoy Pack is made up of multiple family groups and some of them are quite large. The right to lead has always stayed within the McCoy's line," Cain stated firmly, and I swallowed hard. "*Always*. There is no vote or decision. It goes to the next McCoy heir, and that should have been your mother. Your grandmother Willow was the Alpha female, along with her mate for some time. She was the first born of the siblings, so it fell to her—"

"What happened to my grandmother?" I asked, cutting him off. I knew very little about her.

Cain sighed. "A few years after your grandfather died, Willow fell sick with *something*. No matter how hard Cassia tried, she couldn't heal Willow. Mercedes was long gone, and it was like Willow had just given up. It seemed to be the end of her lineage, so I took over with your aunt Cassia when Willow couldn't handle the responsibilities anymore. I was an Alpha in my own right, but I gained new abilities since mating your aunt."

My heart felt heavy imagining how lonely my grandmother must have been. To not know what happened to your only child, and to lose your mate, even one as wicked as Jack sounded. It still must have hurt.

"Sharing abilities is a thing?" I asked, needing to move the conversation along. Bastian gave my hand a gentle squeeze.

My uncle chuckled. "Yeah, most mates share their abilities. It creates stronger wolves and adds another way to connect them again. I have your aunt's healing abilities. Although, I can heal a crowd, where she has to do it one at a time. But my ability is for basic ailments or wounds. I can't do anything complex like she can."

CHAPTER 12

"Bastian and I haven't seemed to share anything yet," I said, frowning again. *Why wasn't our bond like everyone else?*

"I wouldn't worry about it. You haven't even shifted yet. Your mate bond is there, but it doesn't seem fully completed yet. Just enough to establish that you are mates to each other and everyone else. All the rest comes later, I'm sure."

"Will I ever shift?" I asked quietly.

"You will, honey. I can feel your wolf, and sometimes I can see her. She's there," Bastian replied reassuringly.

"Wait, you can see her?" Uncle Cain asked.

Bastian nodded his head. "I have dreams sometimes too. I'm in my wolf form, and this beautiful, white wolf appears from the forest. My wolf is not only content and unthreatened by this new wolf, he's overjoyed. I didn't think much of it before, but it must be Shanely."

"I didn't know you were having dreams too," I said quietly. My uncle straightened. His playful expression gone.

"She's white?" he asked. "Like completely white?"

I shot Bastian a look. *What did it matter with the color of my wolf?*

Bastian slowly met his eyes, seeing the shift in mood. "Yeah, completely white. I've never seen a wolf like that before. I mean, I've heard bedtime stories about a white wolf, but they were always that, stories. Does it mean anything to you?"

Uncle Cain rubbed his chin. "I don't know for sure. I'll talk to your aunt; she'd know more than me, but for now keep that to yourselves. Alright?"

We both nodded and looked to one another briefly. I may be lost again, but it looked like Bastian had no idea as well.

"Why is my uncle so worried?" I asked privately to Bastian.

"Wolves have legends and old stories that deal with the color of wolves, but I doubt any of it is true. They were always just bedtime stories to us."

"What stories?"

Cain moved back to the chair behind his desk, disrupting our link. I couldn't get that question out of my mind. *Why did it matter what color my wolf was?* Bastian just shrugged so I let it go and moved on to another concerning issue. At least for me.

"Can I ask you a question?" I asked, leaning forward. "I want to know about Jack. No one really wants to talk about him though."

My uncle sighed, rubbing the bridge of his nose. "He really wasn't worth mentioning, Shanely. He was just an awful streak in this pack's history."

"What do you mean though?" I pressed further. "What did he do?"

"Your grandfather was not a nice man. He was extremely tough on your mother, grooming her to be the Alpha he wanted. Your grandmother had a hard time with him too. It's why she built the cabin. He stayed mostly at the lodge here, and she stayed with Mercedes at the cabin."

"He made connections to the Blackwood pack, didn't he?" Bastian asked. I wondered who they were.

My uncle nodded. "I permanently ended that treaty. They're another ruthless pack south of us."

Great—

"So, he wasn't a good man or Alpha then?" I asked, pushing for more.

"He did a few good things like establishing the Council within our pack. The pack doubled in size, and he needed help keeping everything running smoothly, so he assigned one person from each family to serve on the Council with him. They assisted him in making decisions for the good of the pack, but other than that he was just brutal. His punishments were way over the top, and he used his Alpha power a lot. Not just when necessary but simply when he entered a room. He wanted everyone to know their place beneath him. I hated living here on McCoy lands with him, but Cassia would never leave her family home. She stuck by Willow, and I stayed to protect her. Over time, I grew to feel defensive of the whole pack and tried to make it better around what Jack did," Uncle Cain said.

"What exactly happened to him?" I asked.

"He died, right? Like brutally," Bastian said, and my eyes widened.

"Shortly after Mercedes left, we found your grandfather far up the mountain. Someone or *something* shredded him to pieces. Your grandmother didn't want to look into his death. Just said we all needed to grieve and move on. Everyone was really relieved honestly that his brutality had ended, and I stepped up after Willow was unable to lead."

"So someone could have murdered him, and no one wanted to find out who?" I asked, my voice raising a few octaves. His killer just possibly hanging around was unnerving. *What if the one who killed my grandfather was the rogue after me?* I quickly shook my head from those thoughts. *I'm so ridiculous—*

"I checked the area. He was in many places, Shanely. There were all kinds of scents around too. Wolves, bears, foxes, and even a mountain lion. We'd never know if it was a shifter or just a wild animal. He was getting older and slower, so when your grandmother asked for it to be left alone, we just respected that decision. Because she was his mate, she made the choice. Mercedes was gone, so there was no one who could of even challenged Willow's choice, according to pack customs. I started working hard to improve the pack, and we pushed it far from our minds. We never had an attack like that again, so we assumed it must of been a wild animal or something," he replied.

I sat there and mulled it all over. *Maybe my grandfather was the reason my mom left?* I thought to myself. *If he was as brutal as Uncle Cain said, maybe he drove her away? Maybe it really wasn't because of me.*

"So if Bastian is having dreams, does that mean you are having dreams as well, Shanely?" my uncle asked.

I nodded slowly. "I consistently have the same nightmare. I told Dr. Malin all about them, and she was wondering if maybe I'm a seer."

My uncle frowned.

"What are they about?"

"All centered around the Division attacking us. I wake up when Patrick grabs me," I replied, not wanting to get into it again.

"That's it in a nutshell. She met him her first night here and got really sick right after she talked to him," Bastian added.

"Well, Patrick's father is our Division Head, so it makes sense if we were attacked that he'd be there," Cain went on. "The only way it would work for him to be involved is if his father was dead or unable to continue his duties. Only one may know about us at a time, and they handle everything for our area. It's odd he's so involved in your dreams."

"Why would I get sick though?" I asked. "I've never felt like that before."

"Your wolf was still dormant. If you are a seer, then *maybe* Patrick was a trigger and *maybe* a warning was trying to push through," Cain replied, and my nose scrunched in disgust. *This just all seemed ridiculous*, I thought.

"My thoughts exactly. If she is a seer, and this is our warning, then what do we do to stop this?" Bastian asked, crossing his arms.

"Until we know for sure she has that ability, let's just be cautious. I'm assuming the attack would be prompted by something happening to bring the Division in. Maybe the bear clan or even the pack finds out about your other side and a war starts. Or maybe something happens between Patrick and Shanely, causing all this to spiral out of control. We don't know, so we proceed with extreme caution. Stay far away from Patrick in the meantime. The less interactions they have the better, on the off chance he is a trigger for her," Cain stated, and Bastian nodded in agreement. *Great— someone else I needed to watch out for,* I thought to myself.

My uncle interrupted my thoughts. "Do you have any plans today?"

"We're going to venture into town today. Shanely and I are going to get everything we need for the wedding because I'd like it on the next full moon like my parent's mating ceremony was," Bastian stated.

"That's next Sunday. Short notice, don't you think?" Uncle Cain replied with a smirk.

Bastian just shrugged. "Shanely will start showing soon, and I want this to be perfect for her. I thought it would be a good gesture to my parents too, seeing how they are mad I didn't tell them I found my mate."

"You didn't tell them?!" I cried out, turning to give him a look. *They're probably mad at me too.*

"Well, Cain beat me to it!" he hollered back, and I began to rub my temples before the migraine started.

"Hey, that's still Alpha to you at least for the next week. I assumed you called them already," he replied, giving Bastian a pointed look. "They were shocked when I mentioned the wedding. You and I both know it changes things between the packs. Your father sent you here for training with the intention you were coming back."

"You and I both know that wasn't going to happen," Bastian replied firmly. Guilt swept over me again.

"I know," Cain said, "but he didn't. Apparently, someone hasn't talked to him in a while."

Bastian rolled his eyes. "I have, just not about that. He doesn't see much past his own wishes."

"Well, this is only going down a few ways. Your father will be here the night before the wedding to discuss everything. This permanently connects the packs," Cain said.

"Will Bastian be forced to return?" I asked quietly, and the two looked to me. I was genuinely concerned about their answer. I didn't want to cause any issues, but I hated the idea of him leaving. I couldn't leave my mother's pack, and I didn't know where that left us.

Cain sighed. "Pack politics are tricky, Shanely. Short answer no, but someone has to take over for his father. It could cause a battle for the throne, so to speak. Wolves are naturally dominating creatures, and I'm sure there are already some looking for a way in."

"It sounds brutal," I replied. His answer didn't make me feel better.

"It's going to be fine. One of my brothers or my sister can have it. She stayed back at home, but is old enough to be Alpha," Bastian explained as he gently rubbed my cheek. I leaned into his touch, when his words finally hit me.

"You have a sister?!" I cried out as I shot forward. *Why is this the first I've heard of this? What else do I not know?*

"I do," Bastian chuckled. "She was too young to leave home when we came here, but you'll like her. She's feisty for sure. If my brothers don't want to be Alpha, she can definitely do it."

"How old is Bay now?" Uncle Cain asked.

"She turns 18 soon," Bastian answered, "so close to your age, Shanely."

"I'll mention it to your father. It might be the simplest solution, but that is *if* he will even consider it. Your father is a very old fashioned Alpha, Bastian. I'll speak to your brothers privately first, and we will go from there.

For today though, stay away from Patrick, and keep an eye out for any wolf you don't recognize. That rogue is smart, which makes me think he's older and has been around the block, so to speak. He won't be easy to catch."

"Thank you, Alpha. Cade went to alert Caleb, so he will be another set of eyes for Shanely, and Elijah is grabbing enforcers as we speak."

"Does the Medvedev clan know about the rogue?" Cain asked, raising his eyebrow at my mate.

"No, they have no idea. Caleb's been learning how to run security for his clan, so he's working it to our favor. He's been helping keep an eye out on his land and parts of the neutral area. All new wolves get reported to his leader, and so far no one has seen anything."

Cain seemed happy with the answer before he turned to look at me. "Go. Have fun today, and try not to stress, Shanely."

I hugged him before we left. As soon as Bastian shut his door, my mind was all over the place. I was lost in thought as we made our way to Cade's SUV. My dreams, Bastian's father and what he thinks of me, the possibility my mate would have to return to Denmark, and the rouge were all problems that plagued my mind. My head hurt just thinking about it. I had no idea how painful things would be when I actually had to deal with them.

Bastian seemed to flip a switch the moment we left the office and was in full enforcer mode now. He was already scanning the area as he pulled me along, even though we haven't even left the lodge or pack lands. He looked confident as he walked down the path to where the trucks were parked like he wasn't worried about the dreams or the rogue. I didn't understand how he could do it because I was freaking out inside.

"Aren't you worried, Bastian?" I asked, tugging on his arm. "What if I really am a seer and this is our warning?"

"Babe, I *am* worried for you. It's why I handle things the way I have been. To make sure you are as safe as I can possibly make you, but I also know who I am, and I trust this pack. I know you, and even though you don't have your wolf yet, I know one day you will, and everyone will have a hard time trying to hurt you once that happens. I'm trusting in that more than my fear," he replied as he squeezed my hand.

CHAPTER 12

Bastian gave me space to process as his words hit home again. *I needed to see myself as they all did,* I realized. *I was a shifter just like them. No, I was more than that actually. I was a mixer, and once I could shift, I would be unstoppable.* Pushing the human mentality out was incredibly hard, especially when I was stuck in my human form. Without being able to shift and growing up solely as a human for so long, I still didn't view myself as one of them. I wanted to be somebody my mother would be proud of. She lost everything for me, and if she could see me now, I wouldn't want her to ever be disappointed.

Cade and Elijah were waiting in the Excursion already, completely changed and ready to go. My eyes widened when I saw his truck. It was lifted with massive tires and a swing away tire carrier on the back. There were a few boxes attached to the swing arm as well with a massive tent sitting on the top. *This truck was a freaking beast,* I thought to myself.

"We like overlanding," Bastian said, grinning. "This is Cade's big rig. It can go all over despite its size."

"Don't you just sleep in your wolf form when you're in the woods?" I asked.

"Well, yeah we do, but some of the places we've got to visit, we can't be in our wolf forms. Too many people around, so having the big ole tent up there makes it a lot nicer than sleeping on the ground. We drove to the Wolf Summit once and camped all the way to Canada where the world headquarters are stationed. It was pretty cool."

"The Summit?" I asked. "I've never heard of that."

"We go once a year, and it's like a week-long party. We actually just came back right before everyone found you. I'm sure you will see it soon though. All the packs go for a week full of different activities, but most just look for their mate. Just a fancy way for the World Council to show off their control and power really, but it's fun in moments," he replied, tugging me along. A small part of me thought more than likely I wouldn't get to see it.

"Hey, fellas. Thanks for joining us today," Bastian said as he waved to the wolves inside the SUV. There were two other enforcers in the back seat already. I didn't recognize them, but the brothers seemed to know them well. They looked around their age but with lighter hair and no beards.

"Shanely! Come meet some of our enforcer buddies!" Cade shouted through the window of the driver's side. Bastian had to help me inside the truck as the bottom of the SUV came up past my hips. Being 5' 1 made things difficult sometimes, but I hopped up and scooched over for Bastian to jump in, turning to address the new wolves.

"Hi. It's nice to meet you both. Thank you for joining us today," I said shyly. I noticed Bastian leaned forward to speak to Elijah and Cade privately. *Probably telling them about the possible issues with Patrick now,* I thought sarcastically.

The one to my left smiled and stuck out his hand. "It's an honor to be escorting Bastian's mate. I owe that man my life, so I'm happy to return any favor I can. The name's Ryder Thompson."

I shook his rough hand as I studied him. Ryder had slightly longer, blond hair with gorgeous, green eyes. Not as bright as mine, but more olivey than emerald. His hair fell just past his eyes a bit, so he was constantly pushing them to the side so he could see. He wasn't super muscular like Bastian was, but you could tell he took care of himself and worked out.

"I'm John McGee," said the other wolf, "but you can call me Johnny. It's a pleasure to meet you today, Shanely. Congratulations by the way."

Johnny stuck out his hand as well and was gentle when he shook mine. He was about the same height and build as Ryder but with sandy brown hair instead of pure blond. It was all spiky but not in any specific style. *Honestly, it looked like he just crawled out of bed,* I thought to myself, noting that the messy look worked for him too. His eyes were a light gray and both guys wore simple jeans and t-shirts. *Nothing about them screamed dangerous, but I'm sure their wolves were a sight to see if they were enforcers.*

The fellas started joking around with one another, and I simply watched with a smile. Ryder seemed goofy just like Cade, where Johnny was a lot more laid back. *I think I was going to get along with them just fine.*

"How long have you all known each other?" I asked as Cade started the big truck.

"We all joined the training program together back when we first arrived.

We were all what— 15 then?" Bastian asked. He wrapped his hand in mine, and I relaxed at his touch.

"Yup! We're only a few months apart," Cade answered as he backed the SUV around and headed into town. *The truck drove fairly smoothly despite its size*, I thought to myself. They must have done a lot to it because it wasn't a bumpy drive like I thought it would be.

"So how did you save his life? That sounds like an interesting story," I asked Bastian, who looked a little uncomfortable then.

"Oh, he's exaggerating that," Bastian said. "It wasn't a big deal really."

Ryder laughed, clapping his hands on Bastian's shoulders as he cried out, "Exaggerate, my butt! I've never seen a mountain lion that size that wasn't a shifter."

"A mountain lion?!"

"Yeah, it surprised me. The cat was massive and going for the kill. We were only like a week or two in the training program, learning to do our patrols, when he surprised me from behind. I didn't even scent the cat, which threw me because I'm pretty good at scenting. Anyways, I was alone, and it managed to catch me off guard. I thought I was done for when he scratched me across my chest the way he did," Ryder replied as he lifted his shirt, revealing a long thick scar that spread across his belly and over his heart. My eyes widened just looking at the mark.

"See? Even she can see the trouble I was in! Exaggeration—" he said, with playful annoyance as he shook his head, but Bastian just shrugged uncomfortably, and I twisted further around in my seat to hear more.

"Anyways, this dude flies out from God knows where and managed to kill the beast. He carried me all the way back to your aunt too. She did all she could, but the scar remains, which is fine. I kind of like it honestly."

"Wow. How did you manage to kill it?" I asked my mate, completely engrossed in this story now.

Bastian shrugged again. "It wasn't hard. I was bigger than it was. He just caught Ryder off guard, otherwise he would have been able to take'em too."

"That cat was a beast. I think I would have struggled on my own at least back then. I've completed training since then, so I'm better than before, but no wolf ever comes close to the Fenrir brothers. Well, other than the Alphas," Ryder said.

"I'm impressed, babe. It seems like you've been hiding all the exciting stories. Y'all are going to have to tell me more," I said to the four of them.

"No, no, no. *No* more stories about me," Bastian proclaimed but was quickly drowned out by the others. My poor mate dropped his head as the truck grew loud with excitement.

"Oh, we got you, little wolf! Don't you worry. We'll tell you everything, I promise!" Johnny said with the biggest smile. "Have they mentioned Emma yet?"

Bastian groaned and buried his head in his hands now. "Please don't tell my mate about her."

Well, that got my attention, I thought as my brows rose. Jealousy filled my veins, and I wondered what could have possibly happened to get *this* kind of reaction from my mate.

"Who's Emma?"

"Derek's daughter, Emma Ferguson. She has the hots for Bastian over here, and you would not believe the crazy stuff she's done to get his attention," Ryder said, laughing as he smacked Bastian's shoulder. Bastian just squirmed further in his seat, clearly irritated with his friends.

"What has she done?" I asked, more nervously than I meant to. A small part of me really wasn't sure I even wanted to know.

"What hasn't she done? She delivered food to the enforcer barracks once in nothing but her bikini. Came up with some excuse about going sunbathing after and thought it would be easier to deliver the food along the way. Your aunt scolded her for that one," Johnny replied.

"Yeah, and Derek and his mate didn't seem to understand what was so wrong with it," Elijah chimed in, chuckling.

"Everyone knows you three are Alpha material. Derek's been trying to get to the leadership position for a long time now," Ryder said.

"Well, nothing has ever worked. I've done nothing but ignore her. I promise, baby. She's repulsive," Bastian grunted out.

"Yeah, she's crazy that's for sure. You should have seen her when everyone was told of Bastian's *sudden* mating," Johnny said, laughing.

"Oh! I nearly forgot about that! She threw one of the wolf statues in the front part of the lodge before storming off. Alpha Cain sent her dad the bill," Ryder went on, laughing hard.

"Whoa— guess I'll need to keep an eye out for her," I said, internally groaning. *It just had to be Derek's own flesh and blood.*

"Don't you worry about her, Baby Girl. She's got nothing on you," Cade said as he winked at me through the mirror.

Bastian pulled me against him. "I've never once had a thing for her, I promise babe. Don't worry about her anyways. She's annoying but harmless."

"Eyes up, everyone. We're here," Elijah said firmly, switching over to his serious enforcer side.

I took a deep breath as Cade pulled into a parking space on Main Street.

Chapter 13

"You ready, Shanely?" Bastian said as he grabbed my hand and squeezed lightly.

I looked around the street, and everything seemed fairly normal. It was a beautiful sunny day, and Main Street looked peaceful. Everything was the same as the first time I came here. *Other than the bouncer now sitting in front of the Den.*

"Let's do this," I replied confidently. I was like Little Red surrounded by a bunch of scary wolves, except unlike the story, these wolves were here to protect me. *No rogue was going to try anything today,* I reassured myself.

We all filed out of the SUV, ready to go shopping. Well *the boys* filed out of the truck normally. I, on the other hand, slid all the way down on my butt until I could finally touch the ground. Elijah laughed at me as he watched me try to get out of the truck, and I stuck my tongue out at him.

Bastian smacked him upside the head saying, "Help her next time."

Elijah laughed even harder. "I'm sorry, but it was just so funny."

Bastian grabbed my hand and rolled his eyes at his brother. I giggled along with Elijah because I knew how ridiculous I must have looked. We started walking down the sidewalk to the dress store, and the boys immediately surrounded me. I couldn't even see past them or anything. Bastian held my hand and walked beside me, while Cade and Elijah stood directly in front. Ryder and Johnny brought up the rear, and I couldn't see anything but wolves. It was incredibly sweet, but I'm sure we were a sight to see. *We didn't look conspicuous at all,* I snickered to myself.

"Guys. While I appreciate the concern, I'm not royalty or anything. This isn't exactly keeping a low-profile either," I said. "Spread out or people are going to notice us."

They all looked at each other sheepishly before relaxing a little. I was finally able to see in front of me at least and couldn't help but smile at the boys.

"Sorry. Habit, I guess. We don't want anyone to be able to approach you," Elijah said, rubbing the back of his head.

"It's better to hide in plain sight. We need to seem like a normal group of friends. The less the Division knows the better so spread out," I said confidently.

"You sure she's not an Alpha too?" Johnny asked.

Bastian smiled. "That has yet to be determined, but it does look that way, doesn't it?"

A blush barely had time to fill my cheeks before Cade pushed me forward to lead the group.

"Okay, let's just get a move on. This is the dress store, but it's the only one in town, so I'm not sure what it will have. We can do this big task first in case we need to leave quickly. And no, before you give me that look, Baby Girl, it's *just* precaution. We can't change all our ways. Now let's do this, so we can eat!"

Elijah laughed. "Is that all you think about?"

Cade scoffed. "Not all the time, no."

He pushed me inside the small store before I could say anything more, but I smiled when I looked around. *It was super cute inside,* I thought to myself, knowing I'd find something to wear here. It had prom dresses on one side, bridal on another, and simple dress clothes in the middle. The store had this vintage vibe going for it, with hardwood floors and massive wooden beams spread through-out. Just the color blue thrown about to help with the heavy amounts of wood, but it tastefully done.

Johnny immediately perked up the second we walked in the store, which was a little odd when he started sniffing all over the place and slowly walking around, going up and down each aisle. I quickly eyed the store for any humans, who would surely start recording him for his weird behavior.

Bastian just shrugged his shoulders as a small voice came from the back.

"Hi! Welcome to the Dress Barn. How can I help you?"

A small petite woman with long dark hair and pretty, green eyes walked around the corner, and I cocked my head to the side. *They looked a lot like mine*, I thought to myself. *Actually, there were more similarities between us than I saw at first.* We had the same widow's peak, and our nose was near identical. Her scent was different too, and she seemed to think the same of us as she wrinkled her nose, frowning.

"Wolves," she said matter of factly. Her pleasant demeanor changed in an instant, and Bastian pulled me slightly behind him.

Bastian smiled before gesturing to me. "This is Shanely McCoy. Soon to be Shanely Fenrir. We're getting married this weekend, and she needs a dress."

She studied us all for a moment. "No trouble?"

"None. We'll all be angels, I promise," Elijah said, with a cheesy grin.

She looked back at me, narrowing her eyes, and I smiled at her. I felt a little bad. She clearly was uncomfortable with us being here, and my chest warmed at the idea of easing her mind. I *wanted* to make her feel cozy with us. *These guys wouldn't hurt a fly*, I thought. *Well, I mean they wouldn't hurt her.*

I shook my head and stepped forward. "I'm new to— well everything. Can we put aside grudges that I still don't know much about? This is neutral territory, right?"

I turned to Bastian because suddenly I didn't know where the boarders were. I didn't study that big map in my uncle's office closely enough.

He nodded at me, keeping his gaze on the small women. *I guess that interesting smell meant bear shifter.*

She pursed her lips before nodding. "Okay, but anything happens, and I'm calling for help. Understood?"

Bastian grinned as he spoke, "Understood. Feel free to call Caleb now, if you'd like. I wouldn't want you to feel uncomfortable around us."

I gave him a brief sideways glance. *Cheeky wolf.* He just gave me a devilish grin and waited for her response.

CHAPTER 13

She finally sighed and said, "Follow me. Guys, you can sit over there in the bridal section."

"We can't stay with her?" Bastian asked, frowning.

She gave him an odd look. "No men allowed in the back dressing rooms, plus you're not supposed to see your bride in her dress before the big day. Don't you know that?"

My mate gave her a frustrated look, and she jutted out a hip, waiting for him to throw a fit so she had an excuse to kick him out. I stepped between the two then.

"I'll be okay, Bastian," I said softly. "It's just the fitting room, and you all will be here by the main door."

"Just holler if you need me then," Bastian said as he reluctantly let me go.

I followed the small girl to the left side, where the bridal dresses were, and we made our way back to the fitting rooms. She was grabbing dresses left and right as we passed through the racks. Once we put some distance between us and the guys, she leaned back to say, "You like pack royalty or something? Got a lot of security with you."

I laughed, trying to figure out the best way to answer. "Nope, not royal or anything. Wolves are just protective, I guess."

"And bears aren't?"

Her abruptness took me by surprise. "Well, I um—"

Now she laughed, and my cheeks heated. "I'm just messing with you. Geez, you weren't lying when you said you were new to all this. Is this your first time speaking to a bear shifter or something?"

"No, I've talked to a bear shifter before. I just didn't grow up in the shifter world. I'm still learning the ropes," I replied. *Little did she know I was half-bear, and my brother was pretty high up in her clan's hierarchy,* I thought to myself.

"Wait," she stopped, and I about slammed into her, "but Bastian said you were a McCoy, like part of the *actual* Alpha's family. How do you not know all this?"

I shuffled nervously on my feet. "I didn't grow up around here. My mother left before I was born, and I only found out about my family recently."

She looked at me as it dawned on her who I really was. "So, you are wolf royalty. You're Mercedes' kid. Octavia mentioned seeing you around."

"No, I'm no one special. My mother was Mercedes, although I never knew her," I said as I looked at my feet.

"Everyone remembers when she left. It rocked the entire shifter community when she did because she just *disappeared*."

"You knew my mother?" I asked. *She didn't look that much older than me*, I thought, cocking my head to the side.

"Not personally, but I heard plenty about her. I just turned 19, so this was before I was born too. Apparently, she was the only wolf who was nice to us lowly bears," she replied sarcastically. I ignored the tone as any information was worth the snarky comments.

"What else do you know?" I pleaded with her.

She opened the curtain to my dressing room, and I followed her inside. "Not a whole lot, but she was the only wolf allowed in certain parts of bear territory. We don't admit that to anyone really, but the older bears remember her and always had nice words to say about Mercedes. She'd stand up for us too when in town and made sure her pack was on their best behavior. She looked out for us while most wolves avoided us at all costs or started trouble."

"Interesting."

"*What is?*" Bastian's voice filled my head. *I didn't realize I projected that thought.*

"*Everything okay with the bear?*"

"*She has a name, Bastian, but yes everything is fine. I'll tell you later.*"

I heard him snort before he disappeared. I blinked, realizing I never got her name.

She startled me as she unzipped one of the bags saying, "She was the only decent wolf my clan has ever met."

My wolf bristled inside, but I chose to ignore her. "I've heard about the shifter wars and the problems with the Division but—"

She scoffed, cutting me off. "I'm sure you didn't hear the full story.

CHAPTER 13

Wolves are stubborn and judgmental after all."

"Hey! We are not," I declared with my hands on my hip.

She gave me a pointed look. "I'll bet you know a very different story than I do."

"What's your story then?"

She sighed. "I only know because I'm one of the very few who has access to our old archives, but there was an issue over the land here. When humans got involved with the wolves, one of my relatives decided to use the war to his advantage and forced the wolves out of the land. Bears require more land to roam because we're more solitary than wolves are, and the clan was big enough that we didn't have enough room for everyone, so he took it," she said, pulling out a dress. She frowned when she saw the look on my face.

"It's not right, I agree," she went on, "but what the wolves did to us was way worse. We merely pushed them off the land, while they threw us up on a pedestal for the Division to slaughter. My grandfather *died* in those wars, and our clan was nearly cut in half. The wolves took control of most of the town and land in the mountain after the laws came into effect. *They* were the ones to create the borders between us, and it's been a feud ever since."

"You're right," I said softly. "That is a little different than what I was told."

She smirked. "See?"

"The real difference I've heard is the death toll," I went on, and she frowned. "My pack suffered too. If shifters had worked together instead of trying to steal for themselves, I doubt any of that would have happened, and that's the way it should be. Shifters should unite together against the Division, not annihilate themselves. I don't understand why we can't share the mountains up here."

The wheels in her mind were turning as she thought about what I said. *This feud has wrong on both sides,* I thought to myself. *But it was over a hundred years ago! We should find a way to get along instead of adding fuel to the fire.*

"You might be the only wolf who wants to share," she replied softly. She promptly turned her back to me, and I wondered if maybe I offended her somehow. *I really wasn't trying to do that,* I thought as she pulled dress after dress out of the bags. Her eyes narrowed on each one before turning to look me over. She tossed the first one, and the awkward silence began to eat me alive. I had to do something.

"You said you are one of the few allowed into the archives. Why isn't the whole clan invited to know?" I asked, placing my hands behind my back while I waited. "Maybe knowing the whole truth could help make amends?"

"Yeah—" she snorted, "like that would work. From what my father mentioned, his father tried to make amends once, and the Alpha before Cain wouldn't listen. My father said it's safer to keep the hate and separate the shifters, so he locked the archives instead."

"Your dad is the clan leader, isn't he?"

I was right. There is a reason she looks like me.

She turned, smirking at me. "I guess that makes us both royalty then. Here, try this one on. You don't have many options to choose from what's available. I can't order anything in time for your wedding date, but I think this one will be beautiful and hide your bump if you show early."

I stopped undressing when she said that. "Oh right, I forgot. You bears can smell pregnancy."

She eyed at me funny. "And I thought I'd surprise you with that one."

I chuckled. "Yeah, nope! Someone else already surprised me with it."

"Kinda quick after the mate bond to be having a kid. You wolves do everything fast, don't you?" she teased.

My cheeks heated, and I shot her a glare. "Very funny! It just sort of happened. I always wanted a wedding though, and I grew up as a human so Bastian's going along with it."

"What a trooper! Well, I give him props for that. Weddings do happen in the shifter world, but the mate bond is what makes you married. Bears can't find their mates until they turn 18 though. Mates are harder to find for us."

"What do you mean?" I asked as she shimmied the dress up and started tying the lace behind.

CHAPTER 13

"Wolves can find their mate at any given age. The bond doesn't form for the wolves until they're of marrying age though, but it still shows up the second they lock eyes. Bears have no indication until they are of age and usually need touch for the bond to spark. Makes it harder when there aren't many bear clans to begin with too. But mates are sacred and are always honored for bears. Even the Clan leader can't interfere," she replied.

"Huh. I didn't know that."

She laughed. "And why would you. Wolves don't keep up on other shifters."

I frowned. "Well, I like learning it all."

"You're different, aren't you?" she asked quietly. There was no sarcastic tone or malice in her words. Just genuine curiosity as she lifted my arms and slid these lacey bands halfway up them.

"You tell me," I replied, with a chuckle.

She smiled and turned me back around to face the mirror. "Here. What do you think?"

My jaw dropped. I had never worn anything so pretty. The bodice went up to almost my neck, and it was full of lace. I could see my skin ever so slightly through the lace as it covered my belly, with pearls and small gems woven throughout the bodice. I turned, and the back was opened in the shape of a diamond, with a string of pearls that fell right through the middle. A soft, flowy skirt completed the ensemble, and it was just breathtaking. My favorite part were the sleeve cuffs. They were matching lace flowers with pearls that hung down. They weren't attached to the main dress and stayed perfectly on my arm. It was a little long since I was such a short person, but I didn't care. *It was perfect!*

"It's beautiful," I said as I twirled around.

"It's perfect on you," she complimented. "I've had a few people try this on, but no one has ever been able to pull it off. Not like you."

I grinned wide, feeling Bastian hover in the back of my mind, desperate to send me a link.

"Thank you for helping me today," I said, taking her hands in mine, "and for telling me your side of things. I think you and I are going to end up friends."

She laughed, cocking a hip to the side. "Is that so?"

"It is! You can't stop it," I said, giggling as I spun around in my dress. I had never felt so pretty in my entire life. I couldn't contain my toothy grin.

"Here. Hold still, so we can get you out of it. I'll put it in a dark bag so lover wolf out there can't see it," she replied.

In the mirror I could see her smiling, and I managed to hold still enough for her to undo the back. I was sad to step out, but she did just like she promised and hid the dress from sight. A part of me wished I could just wear the dress all the time, but I knew that was a ridiculous notion.

We walked out to the fellas sprawled out on the waiting couch, looking utterly bored. Well, everyone but Johnny. He was pacing back and forth agitated over something, and I really hoped he'd quit already. He was scuffing the wood flooring.

Bastian shot to his feet when he saw me. It took him two long strides to cross the space between us, and he promptly pulled me into his arms. I melted into him, not realizing how much I missed him just now.

"That took too long. You can't leave me like that, Shanely," he said, scenting my hair and diving his nose in the crook of my neck.

"Geez, lover wolf. It was maybe twenty minutes. Get a grip!" she said, winking at me as she carried the dress to the counter.

Johnny shot towards her. "Need some help?"

Her brow rose slightly. "No, but thank you. I can manage."

Bastian looked annoyed by her comment but smiled when he turned back to me.

"Aw— I missed you too, big guy," I said.

His presence calmed me as much as I calmed him. He wrapped his arm around me, and we headed to the counter. Bastian paid for the dress, which I tried to put back after I saw the price. He put his foot down though, especially when the bear shifter chimed in that it was perfect for me.

"Trust me," she said as she ran his credit card. "No dress will ever compare to this one."

The corners of my mouth rose as another blush filled my cheeks. *She was*

CHAPTER 13

too sweet, I thought to myself. It was then I realized then I never got her name. She was my cousin, but I couldn't remember what Caleb said her name was.

"What's your name?" I asked abruptly.

"Huh," Elijah said, rubbing the back of his head. "Sorry, Shanely. I guess everyone basically knows one another. We introduced you, just not the other way around."

"I'm Alana," she answered with a smile. *Alana! That's right. She's my uncle Thomas's eldest daughter.*

"Here," I said as I dug in my bag and pulled out my phone. "Put your number in. We can keep in touch then."

She looked at the guys like she wasn't sure how to answer. "Are you sure you want—"

I cut her off. "I'd like to be friends. I don't have many friends—"

"Hey!" Cade interjected.

I rolled my eyes. "I meant girlfriends. I really don't have any right now, and you seem nice. I think we'd get along well."

She hesitated but punched her number in anyways. Excitement filled my soul as I made another connection to the blood running through my veins. I knew I was supposed to be careful with drawing attention to myself, but I just couldn't help myself.

Johnny hovered over her shoulder for some reason, and my brow rose when he caught me watching. His face reddened, and he promptly went to the door. *I didn't mean to embarrass him,* I thought as I watched him finally just step outside.

"Alright, well cool. It was nice to meet you," she said.

We said our goodbyes and left the store. Cade ran my dress back to the truck as we all talked about where to go next.

"Shanely's just breaking all kinds of barriers, isn't she?" Ryder asked.

"As far as I'm concerned, she can do anything she wants," Bastian said before whispering to me. "Just make sure I'm always with you when you do though."

I laughed and playfully pushed him aside. Since Cade insisted on food being the next stop, we hit the diner on the next block over. I felt at ease with our little group, and we all seemed to be having a good time.

I loved the restaurant they chose. It was a cute little diner just like you'd see in the movies. Lots of black and white tiles with red booths and a jukebox in the back corner. I sat in the middle of Bastian and Johnny with my back facing the door. I felt so small in the booth next to these guys. We all ordered burgers, fries and a variety of milkshakes. My favorite was Bastian's double chocolate Oreo, which he happily shared with me when my strawberry didn't make the cut. *I guess the baby preferred chocolate,* I thought with a grin.

"You sure you're full, babe? You didn't eat very much," Bastian asked, looking concerned. I spat out a laugh. I'd eaten more today than I had in my entire life.

"Yes, I'm good! If I eat anymore I will explode, I promise you," I said, leaning back in my chair. "So was that the first time you guys have been in that store?"

Ryder nodded saying, "I would have to say I think that was a first for all of us."

They laughed, while I blushed.

"Oh, right. Duh, it's a woman's store," I said, feeling a little silly. Bastian just playfully nudged me, and I continued, "Do you all know Alana well then?"

"I wouldn't say well. We've all seen her around here and there. I think this is the first time we've really talked to her though," Cade answered as he rocked his head back and forth like it would help him think better.

"It's the first time I've talked to her," Johnny said as he zoned out.

Elijah gave him a weird look. "Well, yeah. You two are usually stuck on patrols in the woods, while us three are following the Alpha. We aren't sent into town too often and never to that store."

Cade laughed at that. "When we see Alana and— what's her sister's name again?"

"Octavia," Bastian answered.

"Right, Octavia. Anyways, they're usually in the middle of the guys from their clan. We tend to deal with the fellas and leave the girls alone and vice versa."

"Well, it's nice to know you were never mean to the ladies," I replied back, and they looked mockingly offended.

"You really think us Fenrir brothers would ever be mean to a lady?" Cade asked condescendingly.

"Or us!" Ryder chimed in.

"You boys are complete gentlemen, I'm sure! But with the issues between everyone, I didn't know how things usually go down," I countered.

"Fair enough," Bastian answered. "We've done a lot of stupid stuff to the bears, and they've messed with us in return, but we've left the girls alone. I promise you."

He kissed my forehead before turning back to the onion rings.

The door chimed, and suddenly Elijah straightened and looked full on pissed off. Cade's eyes bolted forward, and he emitted a low growl before stopping himself. Bastian inhaled deeply and instinctively pushed me closer to Johnny, who looked utterly confused right now. By the way they reacted, I knew *exactly* who walked in behind me. Patrick.

"How do you want this to play out, Bastian?" Cade whispered, watching the officer from the corner of his eye.

"I don't know," Bastian snapped. "I honestly didn't think we'd see him around today."

"No one said anything either," Elijah growled as he checked his phone.

"What is going on with you? What's wrong with those guys?" Johnny asked as he glanced behind him.

I heard Patrick's voice booming in the background as he talked to the waitress behind the counter. I just shrunk further into my seat, ready to leave before anything else happened. If I was a seer, I didn't want to set off a warning and push us towards a nightmarish future.

"I shouldn't be around him, Bastian. What if this makes my warnings come true?" I asked quietly to my mate.

"You don't have to say a word to him. We're going to try to sneak you out, okay?" Bastian said softly. His lips gently touched my forehead, and I took a deep breath.

"What don't we know guys?" Ryder asked in a clipped tone.

"The Alpha asked us not to say anything, but we need to keep Patrick away from Shanely," Bastian replied.

"Yeah, that makes zero sense," Johnny said sarcastically.

"Just help me get her out unnoticed, alright?" Bastian snapped back.

"Yeah, I don't think that's going to work, brother. Heads up," Elijah whispered as a large shadow fell on our table.

"The Fenrir brothers left their little compound! Didn't think we'd ever see you guys come out of the mountains!" Patrick bellowed.

Elijah just nodded his head saying, "Yup, but we were just leaving."

It was then Patrick noticed me tucked behind Bastian.

"Hey, you're still in town? I haven't seen you around for a while, so I figured you were just passing through. Maybe now you'll let me buy you that drink?" he asked as he winked at me. My stomach twisted.

"Yeah, that's not going to happen," Bastian said, glaring at him.

Patrick narrowed his eyes from me to my mate, frowning as he said, "I think she can answer for herself, buddy."

Nausea crept in, and the burger I just ate sat at the back of my throat, ready to make an appearance the moment I opened my mouth. Malin's words about being a seer would not leave my head. *What if this interaction helped my nightmares to come true?* Patrick was part of the Division, and he was in *every* single dream I've had for the last few weeks. He was the only one to ever grab me. He was the only face I recognized other than the multitude of dead at my feet. *I should have never come out today.*

My gut was telling me to stay far away from this man, and my chest suddenly began to burn. I had gotten used to the warmth my wolf gave to guide me when she was awake and alert, but this *hurt*. My eyes widened when she barred her teeth, pushing against my skin like she wanted out. *I can't shift now*, I thought as panic crept in. I looked to Cade, my eyes flashing in warning that something was serious wrong, and he swore under his breath.

Suddenly, Bastian squeezed my thigh hard, and I sucked in a harsh breath.

My wolf relented some, and I forced myself to focus on my breathing to keep the anxiety from rolling in my stomach again. *In and out*, I thought. *In and out.*

Bastian gave a low chuckle, and *my God*, he sounded scary. "You misheard me, Patrick. My fiancé will not be going anywhere with you."

Patrick's eyes shot to Bastian. "Fiancé?"

"Yes, and it's time for us to leave. Have a nice day, officer," Bastian replied as he helped me out of the booth. "Pay the bill, Cade."

Patrick's gaze followed me up and down before glaring back towards Bastian. The guys seemed to be having a silent conversation between them before Bastian quickly blocked me from his view, pushing me towards the door. *What was it with men communicating like this?* I wondered to myself. *At least my wolf had settled within me.*

Patrick abruptly stepped back in my way, blocking my retreat. "I think it's a bit odd that you're suddenly engaged to a man you've just met. As I recall, you had just moved here what— a month ago? And now you're attached to this man?"

"What exactly is that supposed to mean?" Bastian snapped angrily.

"It means that it seems awfully fast for someone who wasn't ready to date anyone anytime soon. Right?"

"Things change when you meet the right person, I guess," I replied quietly.

Patrick squinted his eyes as he studied me. "Or maybe you're feeling pressured. The Fenrir brothers have been known to create mischief in this town. They may not be the best crowd for a pretty girl like yourself to be hanging out with."

I could feel Bastian's anger coming from behind me. His emotions poured into me like the blood traveling through my veins. It was such an odd feeling, and it surprisingly gave me a bit of confidence. But I was afraid to push him any further. He was already angry, and I didn't want Patrick to see something he couldn't unsee. *It was time to leave right now.*

Cade and Elijah seemed to be thinking the same thing and stood side-by-side with us, watching their brother closely.

Johnny went to pay the check instead, and Ryder squared up to Patrick's fellow officer. He just looked confused by the whole thing but stayed close just in case.

"Maybe you should come with us, Shanely?" Patrick offered. "My partner and I can drive you back to your cabin over on Hemingway Drive."

"Wait, how do you know where I live?"

Surprise flashed on my face, and Bastian tensed behind me. His fingers gripped the belt loops on my pants, holding me in place like he thought Patrick might snatch me and run.

"I didn't until now," Patrick replied smugly. "We heard someone moved into that abandoned cabin up the mountain, and I assumed it must be you since you're still here."

"I appreciate the offer, Officer, but Bastian can take me home. You have nothing to worry about, I promise you," I replied and tried to step around him.

Patrick held his hand up. "You come to me if you need anything, you hear me?"

"I promise you, I won't need to. The Fenrir brothers take great care of me, and I'm marrying Bastian because I want to. Have a good day, Officer Patrick," I said as Bastian pulled me away without another word.

I glanced back towards Patrick, and there was something on his face I couldn't quite figure out. *Anger? Confusion? Maybe envy?* He seemed puzzled by us, and I couldn't figure out why it would matter to him so much. He offered to buy me a drink, and I said no. There was nothing else between us. No connection, no history, but he seemed bothered that I was with Bastian.

We left the diner in a huff and made our way back to the truck in complete silence. Bastian was moving fast, pulling out his phone and hitting a button on speed dial.

"Caleb?" he said as we turned the block. "Hey, change of plans. We're heading home now. The boys will grab the rest of the supplies for us. No. The rogue didn't show, Patrick did. She's okay, but we got her out pretty quickly. I don't know honestly, but I can't imagine it would kick start

CHAPTER 13

anything. He's pretty fixated with her though, so we need to be careful. I'll talk to Cain when we get back. Yeah, sure. Thanks, man."

"Wait— Caleb from the Den? Why did you call a bear, Bastian?" Ryder asked angrily.

Cade's truck came into view, and I sighed in relief. My stomach was still in knots, and I just wanted to lie down for awhile. Bastian ignored his friend and helped me into the SUV instead.

"Everyone in," he commanded, and soon we were all piled in. Cade started the truck.

"Bastian, what do we not know? You called a bear, who already knows about Shanely's situation with the rogue and with Patrick. The enforcers know she was attacked and marked, but what's the deal with Patrick? I don't like being kept in the dark. You can trust us," Ryder snapped. My head started to pound, and I buried my face from the world around me.

"We're missing a key piece of information it seems, Ryder," Johnny chimed in sarcastically.

Bastian immediately buckled my seat belt before forcing my head up to inspect. *Scanning me like wounds would suddenly appear,* I thought but let him do his thing anyways. I still felt jittery from seeing Patrick, and I was completely aware my mate was ignoring his friends right now. Guilt ate me alive for lying to them, especially after they've been so nice to me.

Bastian gripped the sides of my face, forcing me to look him in the eye, as he asked, "Are you okay, Shanely?"

My mouth opened but something pierced my head sharply. My eyes rolled to the back of my head as I fell into darkness.

* * *

I walked down the hall in my cabin towards the kitchen. The storm came out of nowhere! I thought to myself. No one even knew we had one coming, but it was okay. We could still celebrate inside the lodge, and with this being our last celebration for God knows how long, I wanted it to be perfect. It needed to be perfect.

I hit the switch on the lights, but nothing turned on. The storm must have knocked out the power, I thought. I could still see fairly well with my wolf's sight, so I just tried to hurry along. Cade would mad that I left without him. I put my hand on my pregnant belly as I saw my reflection in the mirror. I blinked.

My hair was pure white, and I looked older. Different almost. A nagging feeling entered the back of my mind that something was off. The rain starting to pour outside and thunder shook the house. I shook myself from my thoughts and pulled the cakes out of the fridge. I was trying to figure out a way to stack them, when I heard something.

Footsteps outside pulled me back to reality. Did Bastian send Cade to follow me? No, I thought to myself. That couldn't be it. He was on his way to answer Brody's call. The hair rose on the back of my neck, and I quickly got to my feet.

The footsteps grew louder as I locked the door. Someone started jiggling the handle before slamming into the door hard. Fear gripped my heart, and I quickly linked my mate.

"Bastian!"

"Shanely? What's wrong?"

"Someone's at the cabin! They're trying to get inside!"

"What? Why are you there? Where's your Beta?!"

"I ran here alone, Bastian! I was just grabbing the cakes before the storm, but it moved in so fast!"

Whoever was outside ran around to the front, but I made sure to lock it as well. There was no other entrance into this place, and I clicked the dead bolt over when I felt them hit the door. They started slamming into that door harder and more frantic. I backed far away.

"Shanely, I'm all the way out by Brody's patrol near the river! I won't— oh, my God."

"What!? Are you okay?"

"There's blood everywhere, Shanely. Oh God, we were wrong! We were wrong!"

"What?!"

"I'm running back now! Alert the pack! Shanely, we are under attack!! Don't leave the house! I'm coming to you!"

CHAPTER 13

I could feel his adrenaline pulsing through our bond. Bastian was scared, I thought to myself He was almost never afraid of anything, but pure terror came through our bond, clouding my ability to think clearly. All I could feel was fear. His and my own.

I put my hands to my head, unsure what to do, when suddenly it got eerily quiet. I bolted to the bedroom on the main floor, hoping to sneak out the window there, but as I passed the kitchen, a loud crash of breaking glass startled me. Before I could stop myself, I collided into a tall figure. They wore a black hoodie, and they grabbed my wrists hard. I screamed as they threw me against the wall with my hands above my head. My heart raced, and I knew Bastian could feel it too. That's when I saw his face.

Patrick smiled down at me. "Don't worry, Shanely. I made a deal with my father for you. You won't be anywhere near the carnage tonight."

I tugged on my arms, trying to break free of his hold, but he was strong. I heard Bastian's voice in my head briefly before it was yanked away from me as Patrick clamped something down on my wrist. It was a thin metal bracelet, and it had a lock in the center.

"Best you forget about your mate, Shanely. You belong to me now."

Howls sounded into the night as Patrick hit me, forcing me into darkness.

* * *

Bastian shouted my name loudly, and my body shook as I was slowly coming to. It took a moment for my vision to clear, and I saw all five men staring at me, scared out of their minds.

"What happened?" Bastian hollered.

I rubbed my head and took a second before answering. Everything spun violently though, and the constant motion from the truck was making me sick.

Elijah reached around his seat and grabbed my wrist. "Her heart is racing, Bastian!"

"I know! I can feel it!" my mate shouted. "Shanely baby, please talk to me. You just passed out on me, and then you were screaming."

"I think we have our answer, Bastian. I'm a seer," I replied as I leaned against him. I felt awful, but I just couldn't answer him anymore. I couldn't talk or even begin to explain what I just saw. *This was one ability I did not like.*

Bastian sucked in a deep breath and started barking orders. "Cade, get us out of here now! Elijah, call the Alpha! We need to discuss everything with him."

"What is going on right now? A seer?! Why weren't we informed of anything?" Ryder demanded angrily.

"Not now, Ryder," Bastian snapped back. He rubbed my arm, trying to comfort me, and I fell harder against him. I was exhausted from my warning, and in no mood to answer anymore questions. I was in no mood to listen to everyone bicker either. I just wanted to go home.

Cade drove fast through the back roads, churning my stomach with every turn. But the fighting between the guys wouldn't stop, and I groaned as Johnny shouted again.

"No, Bastian! What in the world happened to her?!"

"And why does *that* bear get to know, and we don't? We're your best friends for Pete's sake!" Ryder cried out.

"Alpha Cain told the enforcers what they needed to know. There are other details that have been kept quiet for Shanely's safety, and for the safety of the pack. Some on the Council weren't happy with Shanely to begin with, which is why everyone's being kept in the dark. It wasn't my decision, Ryder, nor was it because of a lack of trust," Bastian bellowed.

Bile rose to the back of my throat as my mouth filled with saliva. *God, my head was killing me,* I thought as I rubbed my temples, trying to ease the head-splitting pain piercing my skull. *All their yelling wasn't helping things either.* Every turn Cade made just made my stomach feel worse. I wasn't sure if I was going to make it home.

"What details?! And what does *any* of this have to do with that cop, who by the way thinks we're all crazy because of your reaction back there!" Johnny snapped back angrily.

I didn't blame them for being angry. I'd be angry too, but I didn't know

CHAPTER 13

how to fix this without telling them. My stomach churned again.

"Do you two know what's going on?" Ryder demanded.

"Look guys, it wasn't our decision, alright? But yes because we live with Shanely. We've been apart of her life since she got here, and we are Bastian's brothers. We share everything, whether we want to or not," Cade stated matter of factly.

I stole a peek at my mate who pinched the bridge of his nose. *He was stressed*, I thought, and I hated it was all my fault. Cade weaved around the last curve to my cabin, and my stomach rolled, bringing that burger to the back of my throat. My hand shot to my mouth as the arguing continued.

"Wow— so, you all can know but not us. Got it, Bastian," Ryder said sarcastically.

"I can't tell you!" Bastian bellowed again. "I told you this wasn't my choice—"

I shot forward and tugged on Cade's arm. "Pull over!"

"Baby Girl, we need to go home—"

"No! Now!"

My lunch lurched forward, and I barely held back the gag that was coming. *If he didn't stop this car right now then I would not be responsible for what would happen!*

Cade seemed to finally understand my dilemma, and he carefully pulled us over into the trees. I shot out of the truck before it was even fully parked, stumbling on my feet when I forgot how high up we were, and Bastian was right on my heels. *God, I wish he was slower,* I thought to myself. *I did not want anyone to see this.*

"Shanely? What is going on?" he asked.

I didn't answer. Instead, I puked my entire lunch onto a pile of leaves on the ground. I heaved and heaved until I couldn't hold myself up and collapsed on my knees. I didn't even notice Bastian had grabbed my hair for me.

When I finally stopped, Elijah handed me a water bottle. I took a drink, spit it out, then took another drink, and this time swallowed it before I slowly turned around. All the guys looked at me with concern as they stood outside the truck.

Cade came up and hugged me. "Oh, Baby Girl. I'm so sorry. I didn't realize you were feeling sick."

I leaned into his embrace, feeling a little weak but infinitely better than before. I turned to the two that had been left in the dark, making a choice to trust them too. My chest warmed, and I smiled. *My wolf agreed.*

"It's okay. It was just too much seeing my warning and then between the arguing and the swerving in the truck, it just pushed me over the edge. I am so sorry you all had to see that, but I am most sorry to the two of you."

I looked at Johnny and Ryder, and they shifted on their feet clearly uncomfortable.

"No, we're sorry. We shouldn't have yelled at you guys. I was out of line, and I apologize. If it's not our business, then it's not our business," Ryder said as Johnny nodded.

"No, if you're on my protection team, you should at least know why," I countered. "I never meant to become a wedge between you all. You guys are such close friends, and I don't want to be in the way of all that."

"Shanely, we're not supposed to say anything," Bastian warned.

"You may not be able to, but Uncle Cain's Alpha powers don't work on me. Besides, I want them to know. It's my choice, Bastian, and my uncle will understand that."

I turned back to the fellas by the SUV. "The reason Caleb knows and is part of everything with me is because he's my brother. Well, my half-brother. My mother was a wolf, but my father is a bear. I'm a mixer."

Their jaws dropped before Bastian shot them a glare, making them shut them hard.

"You're a mixer?" Johnny asked dumbfounded.

"Derek called me an abomination and said I should be sent away from the pack, but my uncle and the rest of the Council disagreed. Everything is being kept quiet because we're afraid it could start a war amongst the pack or with the clan. It could cause all kinds of problems between us and the bear clan. If there are problems between us then the Division would get involved. Plus—" I said, hesitating with this next part, "this baby isn't

Bastian's biological child. It's part human, which is against shifter laws, even if I didn't know who I was then. If Patrick or his father were to get wind of this baby being half-human then the Division could come against us. We could all be annihilated. Mixing between shifters and humans is completely against the rules, even if it was a human's fault. My child's biological dad is extremely abusive and can *never* find out the baby."

"She's also been having dreams, or nightmares for awhile now, and Patrick is in every one," Bastian said, crossing his arms.

"Why?" Johnny asked, raising a brow.

"He's always after me for some reason, and Dr. Malin wondered if I was a seer," I answered. "We didn't know for sure, but we wanted to avoid Patrick just in case. Seeing him today triggered a different warning though, and it was more detailed than what I've ever seen before. This was also the first time I've ever had one when I was awake too. This warning— I need to tell the Alpha about, but at least now you know everything. You have to swear not to say anything to anyone though. Please?"

Ryder blew out a deep breath like he'd been holding it the entire time I talked. Johnny looked shocked as he fell against the truck, processing everything slowly.

"You must keep this from everyone else. All enforcers included because you are the only two, other than my brothers, on the team that know this. And this baby is mine and mine alone. Understand?" Bastian said firmly, his voice deep and commanding. Even his eyes glowed gold, and I thread my fingers in his. He slowly looked to me, sucking in a breath as his eyes returned to normal.

"Of course, man! It's just a lot to process," Ryder stated, giving Bastian a look.

"You have our word and our support. We'll still protect you just the same, even if you are half-bear," Johnny smirked. I walked forward and punched his arm.

"Ow! Good lord, she's got some power behind her," he said, rubbing his arm.

"Just be happy it was her and not me," Bastian said, with a smirk.

"We are sorry for pushing the two of you," Ryder said again. I gave him a hug, reassuring him everything was alright with us.

"Let's just head back to Shanely's cabin. We can discuss this on the way, but it isn't safe to stay here any longer," Elijah said as he scanned the area.

This time the ride was a lot smoother, and my stomach felt so much better. Within minutes, we were back at my place, where my aunt and uncle were waiting on the front porch. I sighed as I saw the group before me. I really didn't feel up to talking about it.

The four boys said their goodbyes after Bastian and I hopped out of the truck and went back into town to gather the rest of what was needed. *Cade was smart in getting the dress first,* I thought to myself. *I honestly didn't expect my afternoon to turn into this.*

Bastian talked to my uncle about Patrick, while I explained my warning. I told him how I seemed older in my warning, and that I was pregnant too. My stomach clenched at the idea that this could all happen in just a few months. *Or was I seeing a much further future?*

My uncle said he'd do some more research on the seer ability, but that we should be extra cautious from here on out. I didn't even feel like leaving my cabin.

Caleb called to check in too. Patrick disappeared, and no one had seen him since the diner, which was odd. He didn't return to his beat, which made me wonder if he met with his father instead. That was a little nerve-wracking, but at least he wasn't hanging around my cabin. I didn't like knowing he knew where I lived or that he played me into figuring it out. Caleb also said he got word our dad was flying in tomorrow morning. He was hoping to stop by sometime soon so we could finally meet, and I agreed. It was the good news I needed after today.

While I was beyond excited to meet one of my parents, I also was extremely nervous at finally putting a face to the image I conjured up in my head growing up. One question continued to gnaw at me. Did he even know about me?

And if he did— how come he never came to get me?

Chapter 14

I woke the next morning to an empty bed and the smell of bacon. I inhaled deeply, smiling as the delicious smell permeated my nose, when suddenly the smell morphed into something awful, and my stomach twisted. That fantastic smell quickly turned sour in my nose, and I covered my mouth with my hand. I barely made it inside the bathroom before dry-heaving into the toilet. My eyes watered as nothing but bile came out, and I groaned before heaving again.

Footsteps rushed down the hall, and I groaned again, hating the walls were so thin here.

"Shanely?" Bastian said from my left. "Babe, are you okay?"

That horrible stench filled the room, twisting and churning my stomach all over again, and I stole a peek at my mate. The poor guy brought the pan with him, and I shook my head. I could hear the bacon sizzling in the grease. *He must have just rushed in when he heard me getting sick.*

I gave him a pleading look and shook my head before I threw up again. Leaning my head against the rim, I ushered him away. "Take— the— pan— away."

His eyes widened as it dawned on him what was wrong, and he ran back to the kitchen. I hit the switch on the fan before laying back down on the floor. The cold tiles felt good, and I didn't want to move a muscle until I could guarantee I wouldn't puke again. A few minutes later, my mate returned and closed the door behind him.

"Bacon?"

I nodded my head.

"I'm sorry, honey. I didn't realize. Cade's eating it all as we speak, and Elijah's airing the kitchen out too."

"Thank you," I muttered as I stood up to brush my teeth.

"Whoa baby, look at your belly!" Bastian exclaimed excitedly.

My jaw dropped when I looked in the mirror. *Overnight*, my belly grew and stuck out in a small bump. It was actually noticeable, and I was very aware of this little one now. I could no longer pretend it wasn't happening or that I had time to wrap my head around it. This kid was just here now.

In my rush for the toilet, I didn't even notice my belly. Now, I couldn't stop looking at the bump and turned from side-to-side, looking at every possible angle. Bastian knelt down beside me and put his hands on my belly. His smile was infectious, and my heart melted when I realized what he was doing.

"Hi, little one," he whispered, kissing my belly. "It's your daddy."

My eyes filled with tears as he talked to the baby. *Our baby.* That thought has me smiling wide. *It wasn't Peter's*, I realized. *My ex would never know.* He would never have a say in how this kid is raised, nor would he be around to traumatize or influence them in anyway. It was Bastian's. My mate would be the *only* father they would ever know. They'd grow up wanting to be like *him*. Or like Cade and Elijah, who were just as incredible as my mate. Seeing such a soft side to Bastian had my heart melting, and just like that, I was excited to be a mom. I blinked away the tears that threatened to fall, and Bastian's face softened when he noticed.

"Hey, don't cry, my love," he whispered as he stood tall. His thumb gently wiped away the tears I lost control of, and I leaned into his touch even more.

"It's just that— you're amazing," I said softly. "You've never once had to think about raising this child, while I struggled to accept the fact that I was even pregnant. You just claimed him or her immediately, and I can't thank you enough. You could have walked away from me. I know this wasn't how you imagined your mate to be, and I just— I love you."

The second those words left my lips, Bastian kissed me. I felt our bond glow bright, pulsing between us, and then I felt her again. My wolf. She howled with excitement, and I felt my chest warm again. *It seemed like admitting my feelings to Bastian strengthened our bond,* I thought to myself. *I could not wait to be fully bonded to this man.*

Bastian broke our kiss, smiling wide. "I love you too, Shanely."

I returned his smile as he rested his head against mine. We stayed like that for a moment, and I inhaled his woodsy scent, smiling as it relaxed me to my bones.

"I can feel her," I whispered to him.

"So do I," he replied. "My wolf is begging me to shift, so he can meet her."

I laughed. "Get in line."

He laughed with me, pulling back to tuck a fly-away strand of hair aside. "Come on. I made pancakes too. You know, it seems like the closer we get as mates, the more we feel your wolf. The more we feel your wolf, the stronger our mate bond gets. It's exciting to be apart of helping you shift."

"You're the key, Bastian. I think she's only here now because of you."

Bastian smiled bashfully. "She's strong. With or without me, you were going to meet her one day. I just can't wait to see her."

We entered the kitchen, and thankfully the smell of bacon was mostly gone. A giant stack of pancakes were on the counter just waiting for me, and my stomach growled loudly. I blushed as I made my way to the plates.

"Well, look at you, Baby Girl! Already starting to show," Cade announced loudly as he pulled me into a hug.

"How's my niece?"

I rolled my eyes. "Or nephew."

"Nah. I know my girls. I can recognize her just like you," Cade replied.

I sighed. "Well, baby's good. Just doesn't like the smell of bacon."

Elijah gave me a weird look. "Kind of weird for a wolf or bear."

I shrugged, but Bastian commented, "Could just be normal pregnancy stuff. Mom was like that a lot when she was pregnant with Bay, don't you remember?"

Cade rolled his eyes. "No. We were young, and no one has the memory that you do."

Bastian scoffed. "Well, she did."

"Moving on. What's the game plan for today?" Elijah asked.

"I have a meeting with the Alpha this morning and then running over the last few details before the wedding. Can one of you stay here with Shanely?" Bastian asked.

"I'm okay home alone too," I pointed out.

All three paused to look at me.

"Or not," I muttered as I shoved another bite of pancake in my mouth. *God, this was good.*

"I have training later this afternoon, but I was planning on finishing painting the nursery first, so I'll stay today," Elijah offered.

"Thank you," replied Bastian.

"What are you up to today?" I asked Cade.

"I honestly don't know. Johnny asked me to join him on an errand but never really told me why."

"Huh. Well, let me know what's going on," Bastian said as he leaned in to give me a kiss. "I have to go now. Do you need a ride, Cade?"

"Nah, I need a run," he said, stretching his arms above his head. "My wolf's going crazy."

"Mine too," Elijah said.

"If you all need to run, you guys can go tonight. Caleb and my dad will be with me," I offered.

"No, we'll be there for that. I want to meet your dad," Bastian said.

"Can't get rid of us so easily, Baby Girl."

I laughed, my mouth full of pancakes. "I never want to get rid of you three. I just don't want your wolves locked up either because you all are too busy watching me. How about after the official meet? I'm sure Caleb will stay for a while so you can run."

"We might go then. My wolf actually feels better knowing two grizzlies would be around with you. Crazy, huh? I'll see you around 6," Bastian said, kissing my forehead again. He left, and Cade followed quickly behind. He shifted fast and ran across the creek. I heard my truck start up and slowly disappeared down the driveway.

CHAPTER 14

"Just you and me now," Elijah said. He stole a bite off my plate, grinning as he walked around the other side of the counter.

"Not a bad thing," I said, with a laugh. "So, what color is the room going to be?"

"Oh, no. This is a gift, and you cannot peek," Elijah countered, wagging his finger at me.

"Oh, come on. I'll still act surprised! No one will know, and I won't say anything," I pleaded, batting my eyelashes at him.

"Ha! No. Every expression or thought is written on your face. You don't lie very well. Cade and Bastian will know I told, and then they'll be pissed with me," he said as he backed up with his hands up.

"Fine! I'll just go outside for a while," I said, pouting. "Get some fresh air while you work then."

"Just don't go past the creek, please. My hearing isn't as good as my brothers."

I gave him a look. "Really? Why is that?"

Elijah answered, "We're triplets, so we each got a stronger skill than the others. Cade hears better than Bastian or myself. I can scent better, while Bastian has better vision."

"Interesting. I did not know that," I replied. *Wolves were so unique and just cool*, I thought to myself. *I could not wait to shift.* "Alright, I'm going to change, and I'll stay by the creek."

He nodded and entered the nursery. I leaned far off my stool, trying to sneak a peek while he had the door opened, but he was too fast. I heard music playing shortly after the door shut.

I hopped off the stool to change out of my pj's. I chose comfy black leggings with a gray tank top today. *I wasn't leaving the house at all so there was no need to get dolled up.* Not like I had many clothes to choose from. My belly looked cute in the shirt though, and it made me smile. I put my hand on my belly then.

"Hi, little one," I whispered softly. "Mama just wanted to say hi."

I smiled softly. I hoped my baby was big enough to hear me. I liked knowing that they could learn my voice and know how much I loved them.

How much their dad loved them too.

I pulled my hair back into a ponytail as I sauntered down the hall and stepped outside. I immediately took in a deep breath. *Outside was beautiful.* Everything smelled so fresh and clean, while the sun was nice and bright. *My wolf senses were kicking in more and more it seemed,* I thought to myself, noticing how crystal clear everything looked. Even my nose seemed to be working on overdrive. I could smell *all* sorts of things. Flowers, the creek, and what I was sure was some sort of animal. I wrinkled my nose. I wasn't honestly sure what that scent was, but I quickly shrugged it off. *Today was beautiful day, and I was going to enjoy it.*

"Still alive, Little Wolf?" Elijah teased me through the link, and I rolled my eyes.

"Yes, I'm alive, you goofball. I just walked outside, and it's clear. No big bad wolf coming to get me."

His deep chuckle filled my mind.

"Just checking. I've got music playing, and a patrol should be around, but I can still hear when you walk. Just holler when you need me, alright? I won't paint for long."

"Sounds good, Elijah. I'm just going to the creek for now. Nothing special."

"Okay, I'll check in soon then."

I felt him leave my mind as I made my way to the water. I sat down and ran my fingers through the creek. It was deep enough that small fish swam around but still easy enough to cross. It was a little chilly but crystal clear, and I bet it tasted amazing. I looked around, still not believing this was all mine. I lived here and not back in Indiana. I wasn't in some crappy lot in town. I was where I belonged, and I sent another thank you to my grandmother for bringing me here.

I noticed a patch of wildflowers just past the creek by the large oak tree then. I didn't recognize the bright pink and yellow flower, but I thought they'd look perfect in the kitchen. *This was just the sort of silly thing I wanted to do with my day today,* I thought to myself. *Decorate my cabin in wildflowers.* Rolling up my pant legs, I crossed the creek with no issues other than cold feet.

CHAPTER 14

After fixing my pants, I strolled casually to where the flowers were by the massive tree and picked the best ones. The cabin was still well within my sight, so I went about my business without a care in the world. I had never done something so trivial as picking wild flowers before, but it seriously made me happy. There were so many to choose from that I couldn't stop and quickly filled up my arms. The scent of wolves filled the air, and I smiled, knowing someone from the pack was nearby. Soon, the pack's song softly came from my lips. I had never been a fantastic singer, but I wanted to practice so I could join in with them the next time they sang it. It was so pretty when they all sang together, and I wanted to be apart of that. I didn't want to miss out on *anything* pack related anymore.

When I had picked every single flower because they were all so beautiful, I stood, ready to make my way back to the cabin. Suddenly, the hairs on the back of my neck stood. Warnings bells went off in my mind, and I froze nervously. My wolf's ear twitched inside me, and I turned to the direction I felt her looking. *Something was wrong,* I thought to myself. I wasn't sure what, but I *knew* better than to ignore this gut feeling. I was learning to trust it, or more specifically, I was learning to trust my wolf.

I inhaled deeply like I've seen the fellas do multiple times, but it was the same jumble of different scents. I couldn't tell what was a bad thing and what was just normal woods. My sense of smell had never been great prior to coming here so I didn't know how to tell them apart.

I slowly turned in a circle, but I didn't see anything. A branch snapped to my left, and I abruptly turned back, breathing heavy as I waited for something to happen. *Anything* to happen but nothing did. *I needed to go inside,* I thought anxiously to myself. *Just in case.* This could be nothing, but I didn't want to take any chances.

I slowly turned back to my cabin and made my way towards the creek again. I scanned the pack bonds, but other than Elijah, no one was around. I crinkled my nose. *I could have sworn I scented the pack,* I thought before shaking my head. My nose must seriously be off, and I made my feet move a little faster. I just needed to get back inside my cabin.

Suddenly, a massive grizzly bear walked past the tree directly in front of me. I skidded to a stop as he noticed me and sucked in a deep breath. This bear was large, and I had no idea what to do. *Was it a shifter or just a real animal?* I wondered as I took a small step back. *What were the special instructions to scare off a bear?*

My mind reeled as I tried to think of that silly children's song we learned as kids, when the bear started huffing. He stared right at me with its sharp black eyes, and I couldn't look away. He definitely seemed agitated as he pawed the ground before me, but I didn't know what to do. He stood up on his hind legs and sniffed the air, growling before slamming his front paws back down.

I dropped my flowers, stepping backwards as fear gripped my heart. "If it's white say goodnight. If it's brown— uh—"

Oh God, I couldn't remember!

He roared loudly, and my hands shot forward to cover my ears. His roar was near deafening, and my ears started ringing like the drums were about to burst. My chest burned like lava, and my body felt like my insides were trying to rearrange themselves. I sucked in a breath as pain rippled through me. *Was this how shifting felt?!* I thought as my heart pounded in my chest.

Suddenly, the bear charged towards me, and I stood there frozen in fear. The burning feeling subsided as my heart beat faster and faster. I didn't know what I was doing wrong or why I couldn't shift. Suddenly, she growled inside my head, and I snapped out of my trance and ran.

My vision blurred like the world around was too bright, and I squinted, trying to keep myself from face-planting. My ears rang again, and I covered them to block out the sound. *What was happening?* I shouted in my head. I couldn't get my lungs to work right, and every step was agony.

"Elijah!" I screamed as loud as I could. The bear was surprisingly fast, and I barely saw the swipe of its paw in time to duck. *I had to get space between us,* I thought as I ran around a large tree. *Or he was going to catch me.*

I bolted right but slid in the wet grass. I scrambled to my feet but not fast enough. The grizzly hit me on my side, causing me to fly to the left, and my body slammed hard into a fallen tree. I gasped for air. It knocked the

CHAPTER 14

wind out of me, and my hands went straight to my belly. My vision swayed again as a large shadow covered me.

"Elijah," I stammered as the bear roared again.

That burning sensation suddenly came back, and I clutched my chest in agony. My breath was taken by the intense pain, and I groaned as I rolled to my knees. *Get up, Shanely!* I scolded myself. My body shook as I tried to get to my feet, and my wolf snarled within my head, but I couldn't move with that fire in my veins.

The bear charged again, and my heart thundered in my chest. *This was it,* I thought to myself. *I was going to die.*

He reared up, when suddenly a large gray wolf leapt on his back. It shifted the bear from his path, forcing him away from me. I let go of the breath I'd been holding as they twisted around, and I nearly screamed when the bear almost stepped on me as they passed by. I flattened myself against the log, watching the two animals fight mere *feet* from me. The bear roared angrily, but the wolf wouldn't let go. He had bitten down on the grizzly's shoulder and clung for dear life. He was finally thrown to the side, and the wolf bolted right back in front of me.

It was Elijah! I thought as relief washed over me. *He found me!*

"Elijah! You're here!" I shouted.

My savior briefly looked in my direction just as the bear took another swipe. It struck him, and he shot across the ground with a sickening crack. I cringed, feeling horrible I distracted him. *Oh God—*

The bear charged towards him again, and I panicked. Terrified I was about to watch my brother-in-law be slaughtered before my eyes.

"Elijah! Look out!" I screamed.

He stood in time to dodge the next attack, but he was no longer using his right paw. It was twisted in a direction it was *not* supposed to be, and my heart broke. *The bear broke his leg, and it was all my fault!*

I scurried to my knees, seeing blood ooze out of the wound on my arm. I didn't even realize he got me with his claws, but it didn't matter. *Helping Elijah was the only thing that mattered!*

Elijah snarled at the grizzly, even though he was in no condition to keep fighting. There was no fear in his eyes when he tried to bite the bears paw. My heart hurt seeing Elijah stumbled around with that broken leg, and I had to do something. I searched around me for anything I could use as a weapon. *How am I in the freaking woods and I can't find a freaking stick!?*

Elijah suddenly howled in pain, and I turned, finding the bear with its teeth sunk in Elijah's spine. I screamed as he tossed him aside, and Elijah rolled in the dirt. My fingers dug around me, finding a rock half buried in the ground. *Thank God!* I thought as the bear charged again. I threw the rock, and it smacked the side of the bears head. It snarled when it turned to me.

"Elijah, you have to stand," I begged as the bear left Elijah. He roared at me, and I scurried to my feet. My eyes widened as he reared back again. *He was going to charge—*

Elijah whined loudly, and my eyes settled on him. He was struggling to move, and my heart broke watching him like this. *This was all my fault— but maybe I could help still.*

I knelt down and grabbed another rock. It smacked him in the eye, and he snarled again. I was just pissing him off, but I'd do anything to pull him away from Elijah.

"*Shanely!*" Elijah bellowed through the link. "*Run now! Don't look back, just run!*"

"*I won't leave you!*" I snarled.

Without warning the bear charged, and I stumbled back, tripping on a tree root before falling hard on my butt. Embarrassment flooded my cheeks, but it was quickly replaced with fear when the light disappeared above me. My eyes widened when the grizzly towered over me and roared in my face.

"RUN!"

Fear gripped my heart, and I froze again. Its teeth mere inches from my face, and I shut my eyes tight, trembling on the ground. The stench of its breath nearly gagged me, and I braced for the impact that was sure to come.

Except it didn't.

Suddenly, bright light covered my face, and I opened my eyes to find another wolf had entered the fight. I shook with relief. *It was Bastian! He*

CHAPTER 14

was here, and so was Cade. Bastian was already on the grizzly's back, when Cade flew through the brush.

Another large black wolf and a brown wolf appeared as well, and they rushed towards the grizzly. I recognized Cain as the dark wolf, and my eyes widened when I realized Bastian was nearly as big as he was. *He wasn't that big before,* I thought as I watched my mate sink his teeth in the bear's shoulder.

A black blur stole my attention, and I turned to see Cassia shifting back near Elijah. I scrambled to my feet and hobbled over, feeling every bruise I earned today.

"Thank God, you're okay!" she cried as she put her hands on Elijah. His eyes were closed.

"Is Elijah okay? This was all my fault! He's only hurt because he came to save me, and I couldn't help him," I rambled, letting the tears fall down my cheek. "I distracted him."

My body began to shake hard now that I knew we were safe. I didn't know how to stop it, and I had nowhere to put all this pent-up energy.

"Honey, try to calm down. He's okay! Elijah's alive, Shanely. He broke his arm, and part of his spine, which is why he couldn't move, but I got to him in time. I'm focusing on his spine right now, so he will have to wear a cast for his arm for a few days until his own shifter healing does its thing. I doubt he will mind, knowing he will still walk normally," she replied, and I watched her eyes glow gold again as she used her ability.

Relief washed over me again, but I still felt guilty. *None of this should have happened,* I thought, gritting my teeth together. *And it wouldn't have if I had grown up with my family.*

I shoved those thoughts aside, knowing they weren't doing me any good, and pulled Elijah's head in my lap. He cracked one eye open, and I chuckled softly. He snuggled his head against me, and I gently rubbed his fur, trying to give him some comfort.

"I'm so sorry, Elijah. I didn't think I went that far. The cabin was right there, and I couldn't sense anything was wrong until it was too late. I'm so sorry I got you hurt," I said quietly, and I heard him whine softly.

"Do not blame—"

A loud snap jerked our attention away, and I saw Bastian's jaw around the bear's neck. Its head finally slumped to the ground, and Bastian howled with the other wolves following suit. My eyes narrowed on my mate. I didn't notice before, but Bastian coat *was* a little darker now. He still had that smoky gray appearance like normal, but it was darker than before, especially when Cade stood next to him, but what really threw me off were his paws and chest. They were completely white. It even went up his legs just a little bit too, and the color spread over his chest. Bastian was always beautiful, but this was something else. His wolf was stunning.

Bastian leapt off the dead bear and came straight towards me. He nuzzled my head, sniffing me all over and looking for injuries. He focused awhile on my belly, which I'm assuming was his way of checking the baby before looking over his brother. I could see the pain in Bastian's eyes before he shifted. The others followed suit.

"Are you okay?" Bastian asked me, rubbing my cheek with his thumb. "I had barely made it to the lodge when Elijah called."

I sighed heavily. "I was just enjoying the fresh air outside when I saw these wildflowers. I didn't go very far, just to that large tree on the other side of the creek, and I didn't sense the bear until it was too late. My senses have been getting better lately, but I don't recognize all these different scents. It just all smelled like wildlife, but that doesn't really matter. It was all my fault. The grizzly blocked my way back to the house, so I bolted in the opposite direction. I didn't expect him to be so fast though, and it caught up to me. I tried to shift, but something stopped it from actually happening. Elijah rescued me before the bear could kill me, but I distracted him by accident. It's why his leg is broken and— I'm so sorry!"

"It struck you," he muttered as he looked down at my arm. Blood dripped down from two scratch marks, and a large bruise had already formed around it.

"That doesn't matter, Bastian. It's nothing compared to Elijah's injuries," I muttered as tears filled my eyes. Bastian gripped my chin.

"It matters, Shanely," he said, giving me a look.

CHAPTER 14

I shook my head. "No, it doesn't. I'm so sorry you guys. I put you all in danger—"

"Baby Girl," Cade interrupted, "this is not your fault. We live deep in the mountains surrounded by lots of different animals. *This* happens sometimes. Remember Ryder?"

Bastian nuzzled my neck and whispered, "It's not your fault, my love. I'm so glad you both are okay. My heart stopped today, and I don't think I can go through that again."

"Let's move Elijah back to the cabin now. I've put him to sleep to help with the pain, but he needs to rest comfortably. We need Malin to bring over a sling for him, Cain. I don't have enough strength to heal his spine and arm since working at the clinic already today. His spine was trickier than I thought it would be, but it will be fine now. Elijah's own natural healing will fix his arm in a few days," Aunt Cassia said as my uncle helped her to her feet.

Johnny, who came with Cade, ran back to the lodge in search of Dr. Malin, while Cain and Cade carefully picked Elijah up. It looked difficult as he hadn't shifted back and was still in his wolf form.

My heart hurt as his head left my lap. The overwhelming disappointment in myself hit me hard, and it was hard not to feel so useless. I watched as the two carried Elijah back towards my cabin.

Without asking, Bastian hauled me up into his arms and followed after them. I tried to protest, but one look from his golden eyes shut me right up. I knew not to push him right now, and I let him carry me back. We left the bear to the care of the forest. *At least it wasn't a shifter,* I thought to myself. That was the last thing we needed to deal with right now. *I couldn't even imagine trying to explain to the clan leader, who was my uncle, why we killed one of his men.* Guilt ate me up inside, and I couldn't help but feel stupid.

"It's not your fault, Shanely, and you are never stupid."

"Hmm?" I was so lost in thought and self-hate that I barely heard him.

"I can hear your thoughts. You're broadcasting them loudly," he whispered.

Embarrassed crept in my cheeks, and I buried my face in his chest. "I didn't mean to get Elijah hurt, Bastian. I just feel like I'm useless here. I couldn't do a single thing to help him, and he got hurt because of me."

"My brother's fine, and we live in the mountains, honey. We're not the only ones out here. This happens to the best of us, but we've grown up with all of our shifter abilities. We were taught how to avoid larger animals up here and how to fight them. Your abilities are spotty at best right now, and you don't have your wolf to rely on. Besides, I am *your* mate. It's my job to protect you and our kids, and I hate that I wasn't here. But I promise I will teach you how to recognize other animals so you're not caught off guard again."

"You're not mad then?" I asked, looking down as I played with the end of my shirt.

"No sweetie, and neither is he. We all swore to protect each other's mate like our own. Right now, that just means you, and I will always be grateful to my brothers for protecting you. I will return the favor when Elijah finds his mate," he replied, giving me a kind smile.

"How did you guys find us?"

"Elijah sent us a mind link once he knew something was wrong. The lodge is close enough to reach us, and Cade was just leaving for town with Johnny, so he caught the link in time too. Elijah said he stepped out front to the truck to get something, and when he came around the back to check on you, he noticed you were gone. Then he smelled the bear, so he followed the tracks until he heard you scream. That was the last link I got from him before finding you guys."

I groaned.

"Now, I feel worse. I forgot all about the mind link! I should have used the link when I first felt like something was wrong," I said, burying my head in his shirt again. *God, I was so stupid!* I thought to myself. He chuckled softly.

"You're not stupid! This is all still new to you. We grew up as shifters, while you haven't even shifted yet. Don't be so hard on yourself, babe," Bastian said, leaning down to kiss my forehead.

"I still feel dumb, and how come I can't shift? She's there, and I swear it felt like she was trying to shift earlier, but I could never get passed that initial pain. It was so annoying."

Bastian shrugged. "You are different from the rest of us, Shanely. It's hard to say what's even normal for you."

"Well, it would have been helpful if she had just show up!" I snarled, feeling my wolf's anger rise within. I pursed my lips together and moved the conversation on. I didn't want to piss her off anymore than I clearly already did. "Your wolf is bigger by the way."

Amusement flashed in his eyes, and he winked at me.

"I'm sure it just seems that way," he replied, but I shook my head.

"No, I swear. You're as big as Uncle Cain's wolf and definitely bigger than Elijah or Cade."

Bastian bit his bottom lip thinking. I noticed he did that a lot when he's really focusing on something. I grinned, watching him try to work out a reason as to why it would be happening.

"I don't know why that would be though," he finally responded.

"Maybe because of the mate bond? Didn't Uncle Cain say mates share abilities and stuff?"

He laughed. "Being larger isn't really an ability though, baby."

I sighed, leaning my head back as I said, "Yeah, that's true, I guess. Well, we should watch for more changes. It could give us an idea as to what I am at least. Your color has changed too."

My aunt fell behind to walk next to us, interrupting our conversation. Bastian seemed lost in thought now. Entirely distracted as he didn't even acknowledge Cassia joining us.

"Malin is on her way with the sling and to check everything with Elijah. I want her to examine Shanely too and make sure the baby's okay."

That snapped Bastian out of his thoughts, and he nodded in agreement. "Perfect. She will need to wrap her arm as well. It's still bleeding."

Cade shouted from ahead, "I can hear the baby's heartbeat! It's strong!"

Bastian chuckled, wiggling his brows. "Got to love those ears, right?"

"Thank you!" I shouted back as Cade turned his head and grinned. That made him trip on a root, causing the two to struggle with Elijah. Cain muttered something fowl to Cade, who laughed hysterically, and he turned back around and stayed facing forward. The three of us laughed at them.

"I'm sorry I couldn't heal your arm, Shanely," my aunt said as she regained her composure. "I can help with the scars once I regain some strength."

"Actually, don't worry about it. I kind of like the idea of scars," I said with a smile, thinking back to Ryder. "Besides, if you had any strength left you give it to Elijah. My hero deserves it."

Bastian chuffed. "And what about me? I mean, I'm the one who killed the bear so technically that makes me your hero too. Right?"

I laughed, wrapping my arms around his neck. "You're already my hero. You're the love of my life, Bastian."

I leaned up and kissed his cheek. Bastian's eyes momentarily flashed gold before going back to their normal stunning blue. He smiled and tightened his hold on me.

My aunt smiled at our interaction, but let us have our moment. We made it back to my property, and they laid Elijah on my bed. He was still unconscious so his wolf barely fit on the bed, but it worked, and soon Dr. Malin walked inside. She went straight to me and ignored my protests to check Elijah first. Bastian insisted that even Elijah would say check the baby first, so I caved and let her do her work. I trusted Cade though and just wanted to ease Elijah's pain.

She listened to the baby's heartbeat and double checked my vitals before giving my aunt supplies for my arm. She quickly went into the back room and closed the door behind her.

My aunt had just started pulling out the supplies to wrap my arm when the doorbell rang. Nobody moved. The bell rang again, and my eyes widened when I realized who it must be.

"Caleb! I forgot he was coming," I exclaimed as I rushed to get the door.

Bastian reached out to stop me but just missed my hand. I didn't make it to the door in time before it suddenly burst open, and Caleb bolted inside. He scrunched his nose, scenting the air deeply, when his eyes met mine.

"Is that blood?" he demanded.

CHAPTER 14

I ignored him and jumped in his arms, knocking him backwards a bit. "I'm so glad to see you!"

"Shanely, you're bleeding! What happened?" Caleb cried out as he set me down, but my whole body froze. My eyes widened as I watched a tall man step out of Caleb's truck.

I couldn't breathe.

Our eyes finally met, and he seemed stricken with the same affliction.

"Shanely," Caleb said softly, "meet our father."

Chapter 15

"Hi," I said quietly, giving the stranger a small wave.

My voice seemed to snap him out of his trance, and he quickly stepped up the porch steps. My eyes roamed over this man, taking in every detail I possibly could. There were such similarities between him and Caleb. His dark brown hair matched Caleb, but his was speckled with gray. He was a tall man, taller than most, I imagine, but he was more on the leaner side. Being a grizzly, I didn't doubt his strength, and he walked with enough confidence that made me feel like he earned the right to, but his eyes— they were just like mine. Those vivid green eyes, that had been my favorite feature my entire life, *came* from him.

My father seemed to scent the blood finally and zeroed in on my arm.

"What happened to your arm?" he asked quietly. The corners of my mouth rose slightly. *I had always imagined what my father's voice sounded like*, I thought to myself. *And now I was finally meeting the man.*

"It's a long story. Come on in and meet everyone," I said, gesturing to the living room.

My father hesitated but soon followed after me. I shut the front door as my father and Caleb took in the room. They both seemed nervous, and I had hoped our initial meeting would have gone better than this. My eyes were glued on my father, who seemed to be trying not to look at me. I frowned slightly. I couldn't read him very well, and I wasn't sure if I was making him uncomfortable. *Maybe he didn't want to meet me and I forced him too?* My shoulders fell at that thought, and I glanced towards Bastian.

He was already on his way to me, and I stepped into his embrace, trying to

CHAPTER 15

stop the overflow of thoughts happening right now. Caleb shifted nervously on his feet.

"I didn't know your Alpha would be present for this," Caleb whispered in my ear.

"We had an emergency, hence the arm, so they all came to my rescue," I explained, feeling guilty they were on the spot like this.

Bastian extended his hand to my father. "It's good to meet you, sir. I'm Bastian Fenrir, Shanely's mate."

My father shook his hand, and Bastian greeted Caleb with a clap on the back. I liked how cozy they both seemed with each other, and I quickly looked away so I wouldn't tip them off that I was spying on them. My father eyed Uncle Cain though, and then his eyes went to Aunt Cassia. *Would he bolt before I got a chance to get to know him?*

"We can get out of your guy's hair and give you some privacy. Malin just sent me a mind-link that Elijah has shifted back and is stable. She gave him some meds to knock him out for a while," Aunt Cassia said as she crossed the room and hugged Daniel. He stiffened but gave a light hug back. "Please, let us know when you come back. I'd like to get to know you too."

He nodded but remained quiet.

Uncle Cain extended his hand saying, "It's good to see you again, Daniel."

"You too, Cain. Been a long time," he replied. I frowned slightly. *This was not how I thought things would go.*

Cain nodded his head as Malin came out of the bedroom. She waved and smiled at Caleb and my father, who looked a little more at ease now, and then the three left us in peace.

"I guess that just leaves me then. I'm Bastian and Baby Girl's brother, Cade."

Daniel shook his hand and then stuck his hands back in his pockets. The silence was seriously awkward, but I had no idea how to fix it.

"Sorry, we're a little early. I got someone to cover my shift today, and we were anxious to get here," Caleb said, and Bastian waved him off.

"Don't worry about it. We're just glad it could work out. I told Cain I wasn't going to make it to the meeting after all, so we're free," my mate replied, and I gave him a look. He just gave me a wink instead.

"Yeah, I bailed on Johnny too," Cade chimed in, and I turned to give him a look now.

"Guys, you didn't have to bail on everything because of me!"

"Elijah's down and out now, and after everything today, I don't want to leave you anyways," Bastian continued before kissing my cheek.

"But—"

My mate gave me a look that told me to quit pushing him, so I sighed and turned back to my guests.

"Does anyone want anything to drink?"

They both shook their heads no and then things got quiet again. I don't think anyone really knew what to do with each other. Bastian gestured to the couch, and everyone sat down. My mate quickly pulled out the supplies and started wrapping my arm up in the bandage and whatever cream Malin left behind, while I watched my father study Bastian's every move. He seemed very curious about the two of us but didn't say anything.

My father's eyes looked sad, and I felt awful. *Maybe he wasn't ready to see me?* I opened my mouth to say something, but the words just wouldn't come out, and I snapped my jaw shut. *God, I was a chicken*, I thought to myself. *All the years I spent wishing I knew my dad, and the second I finally meet him, I can't figure out what to say.*

"*It might make things easier if you had some privacy,*" Bastian suggested through the link. He smiled softly when I glanced his way. "*You're broadcasting again. Do you want us to step out?*"

"*No,*" I replied. "*I'll see if he wants to step outside a moment. Maybe the fresh air will do us some good.*"

Bastian patted my leg, and I turned to my father.

"Dad? Or Daniel? I'm sorry, I'm not sure what you want me to call you, but do you want to sit out on the porch with me? I'm sure Bastian can fill Caleb in about our bear attack."

They both swung their heads to me in unison. "Bear attack? Was it a shifter?!" Caleb demanded.

"Nope, real. Just massive. Come on, we'll fill you in," Cade responded.

CHAPTER 15

"*Let me know if you need me. Keep the mind link open, alright?*"

I smiled and kissed my mate's cheek. I stood up, and my father followed me to the door.

"*Of course. We'll be on the porch.*"

"*Please stay on the porch. I'm too tired to fight another bear.*"

I smacked him as I passed by and could hear his deep laugh fill the room. *The nerve of the man to make a joke like that,* I thought to myself. Bastian playfully rubbed his arm as if I could actually hurt him. Cade looked at us funny before chuckling, but I didn't care. *He deserved it.* I led my father past our kitchen towards the back door.

I closed the door behind us and motioned to the set of rocking chairs on the other side of the deck. They were beautiful, hand-carved, rocking chairs that had an *extremely* comfy cushion tied to the bottom.

Daniel sat down slowly and rubbed the arms of the chair. "Haven't seen these in a long time."

"They were here when I moved in. My grandmother left me the cabin in her will," I replied.

Daniel seemed to mull over the information. "So, she knew about you then—" he muttered before quickly moving on. "I made these chairs. For your mother and I."

I sat back, admiring them a little closer now. *I never knew they were a piece of my father.* Imagining the two of them sitting out here like my mate and I had so many times made me smile.

"They're beautiful," I replied in awe. "I never knew you made them."

"Thank you. They ought to be. It's my trade after all," he said, giving me a small smile, which I eagerly returned.

"Did you come here often?" I asked, trying to get the conversation rolling.

He nodded, his eyes glazing over as the memories passed by. "All the time to see— your mother."

"If you're uncomfortable meeting me today, we can reschedule. I don't want to push you, Daniel. I can meet you somewhere else if you prefer," I said softly, trying not to let the pain in my voice show. "Or if you need time—" I let my voice trail off from that sentence. Fear crept in that maybe this was all too much, and my dad may not want to see me at all. I didn't realize the cabin would hold so many memories for him, and I felt bad suggesting we meet here in the first place. *I should have known though, seeing how my mother lived here,* I thought to myself.

"Dad," he said, and I blinked in surprised. "I'd prefer Dad, if you don't mind, and I'm alright here. I just never thought I'd see this place again, but it's safer here anyways." Silence filled the empty space between us again, and my father looked at me. His eyes flashed with such emotion as he said, "We have the same eyes."

I smiled as tears filled my own. "I noticed that too."

He sighed, rubbing his hands together. "Look, Shanely. I'll be honest—I'm not very good at this. I'm not a naturally outgoing person and being back here in this cabin is hard, especially when you look just like your mother."

The corners of my mouth rose. "I look like my mom?"

My father nodded slowly, and a tear ran down my cheek. *I had no idea I looked like my mom.* He suddenly looked so broken when he noticed the tear that fell. His hand lifted before hesitating and dropping back to his side. *Guess I know who I take after though,* I thought as I wiped my own cheek.

"I'm not good at this either. Until a few weeks ago, I never even had a family. Ever since I learned I'm a shifter, everything about my life has changed," I replied as I gestured to my belly.

He frowned before shaking his head. He gave a tight lip smile saying, "I noticed that. Caleb informed me of what happened, so you wouldn't have to go through explaining it again. Congratulations on finding your mate too. Is he up for all this?"

Dad pointed between the two of us.

"Thank you, and he says he is. Bastian jumped on the father train immediately, and he's been amazing during this whole process. Honestly, without him, I'm not sure how well *I'd* be handling everything. I'm told the bond will be fully formed when I finally shift, but who knows when that will be."

He seemed to consider that for a moment before leaning back in his chair.

It creaked loudly with his weight. "You might be warring internally with your animals."

My brows furrowed. "You think I have a bear as well?"

Dad shrugged. "I come from a very dominant bear line. We're big and powerful, so it wouldn't surprise me, seeing how your mother's wolf was the same way. Both might be fighting to emerge first."

"Do you have Alpha traits?"

He nodded.

"But you aren't the clan leader?" I asked, eyes narrowing.

My father sighed. "It was my birthright to lead the clan, but when I found your mother, I was too consumed by keeping her safe from all the fighting, and struggling to keep our relationship a secret from everyone. It took a lot of my focus away from the clan, and my father noticed. After he had tried to make amends with your grandfather, and it ended badly, he said he wanted nothing more to do with wolves. Anyways, my father gave my birthright to my younger brother Thomas, but the Alpha part of me is still there. And I guess now you. It's why I think you're struggling to shift. You have two strong shifters warring to show themselves first."

"I can't believe he did that to you," I said, shaking my head. *What was wrong with my grandfather? Or grandfathers.*

He shrugged again. "Thomas has been good for the clan. Your mother left shortly after that, and I never knew what happened to her. I've been a shell of a man ever since, Shanely. Not exactly good for leading anyone, I'm afraid."

I put my hand on his, and he stiffened. "I think she left because of me, Dad. I think Mom was afraid of her father finding out about her pregnancy, " I said, sighing heavily. "Or maybe he already had and forced her out."

"What do you mean?" Dad asked, straightening in his seat.

"Bears can sniff out a pregnancy early on, right?"

My dad nodded.

"Well to ensure the pregnant wolf has protection, the Alpha receives a special ability when he becomes the Alpha of a pack. He can see the pregnancy from the very beginning. There's no hiding it, even if you don't show or know yourself. I'm not sure how the details work, but if her Alpha or father was anywhere near her, then he'd be able to tell long before she started showing. It just makes sense to me that she ran instead of letting anyone else find out about me. It also makes sense that he found out and banished her too. I honestly don't know. We've just been speculating really, but somehow my grandmother knew or found out at some point. She amended her will, and they found me after she died."

His face hardened as he spoke, "I always hated her father."

"I've heard very little about him."

Dad snorted. "His name was Jack. He wasn't a kind wolf and led his pack brutally. Willow was *supposed* to lead with him, since it was through her line the Alpha position belonged too, but he never let her. I remember your mother in tears a lot because of the training course he put her through. There wasn't anything I could do about it either. It was extremely difficult to control my bear as I watched her work so hard. All I wanted to do was protect her, but if I did anything I knew I'd only make it worse," he replied, and my heart broke hearing the pain in his voice.

"I was told my grandmother insisted on building the cabin way out here on the border," I said softly. He slowly looked back at me. "For my mother and grandmother to have some peace, I guess."

He rubbed his chin. "I bet. Your grandmother was a kind woman. This cabin benefited your mother and I, being right on the line. I was able to sneak in and out without letting the pack know. Looking back on it now, I'm sure your grandmother knew about us. There's no way she wouldn't have known. Mercedes and I thought we were being careful, but I think her mother always knew."

"Didn't my grandfather ever stay here?"

"No. He preferred to stay at the lodge you guys have up the mountain. Jack was getting older and didn't like to venture too far away from his comforts. Although personally, I think he just liked to be at the center of everything all the time."

"Who's tools are here then?" I asked. "I always assumed they belonged to my grandfather."

CHAPTER 15

The corners of his mouth rose as happy memories flooded his head. "They're mine, well in a way. Your grandmother bought them all for the cabin and hired me to repair the roof and add on the deck. She gave them to me afterwards since she no longer had a use for them. The job was kept secret though from Jack. It was well known I had a successful construction company, so thinking back on it, I think it was your grandmother's way of giving me an excuse to be here if anyone were to see us together. I often wonder if she was prepping this cabin to be ours one day, but I guess I'll never know."

"What happened to my grandparents then? Uncle Cain told me Grandmother Willow got sick. That no one really knew how to help her, and it made her very weak before she finally died sometime earlier this year, right?"

"That's correct. I don't know the details though, being a bear and all," he said, looking at me with a smirk.

"And my grandfather?"

His face fell, turning into a grim look as he pursed his lips together. "They simply found him shredded far up the mountain. Whatever got him mangled him though. When Willow was too weak to lead, Cain and Cassia took over the pack, and they seemed to thrive with them. They permanently closed the doors though. No one gets in or out of their land without them knowing. My mate was gone, and I had no reason to ever come back. I heard Willow died not long ago, but I wasn't allowed to pay any respects," he said solemnly.

"You're always welcome here, Dad. This is my place, and I'm insisting on it. I know Uncle Cain wouldn't keep you from being apart of my life either."

"Shanely," he said softly, leaning forward in his seat. Pain gripped my heart as I saw the rejection coming. *Please— please don't leave me.* Dad took my hand in his and sighed. "As badly as I want this; are we sure this is safe? I can't imagine my brother Thomas will understand *any* of this. He's holding onto his hatred of wolves fiercely ever since our father passed away, and the strain has only gotten worse since then. *Your* mate has been a thorn in Thomas's side since he first arrived too. How am I supposed to explain this without starting a war? I don't want to put the only piece I have left of your mother in danger because I'm too selfish to let go."

"Dad—"

My heart broke, and Bastian hovered in the back of my mind. I leaned forward, hugging my father as my eyes filled with tears. *Doesn't he understand?* I thought as I scrambled to come up with someway to make him stay. *I can't lose him after finally finding him. My whole family was ripped away due to these stupid laws!* I could have grown up with both my parents and a brother if the hatred between the shifters wasn't a thing.

I thought of Bastian and my baby then. I tried to imagine spending my life alone, away from my baby and my mate, and I couldn't bear it. *Yet, this was the fate of my parents.*

I would *not* accept this for mine.

I will make sure that our family would stay together no matter what. We needed to mend the wounds between us because I would not accept my baby growing up the way I did. I clung to my dad as the warmth returned to my chest.

"I'm sick of the fighting between the shifters! They should unite and not be at each other's throats. The Division is the problem. Don't you see? We're stronger together than we are apart, and I am each of you. Wolf and bear. How am I to choose only one side? I refuse to let your grandchild grow up alone like I did."

He pulled back, and his eyes dropped to my belly. "Shanely— you're breaking my heart. Did you really grow up all alone?"

I nodded solemnly. "I was told you both died. I want to be a family, Dad."

My father sighed and reached for my hand. "I don't want to lose you either. I'll work on my brother. Maybe I can sway his mind? He used to see Mercedes in clan lands every once in a while before he became the leader. I will try, Shanely."

I smiled wide.

"I know Uncle Cain will help us too. He and Bastian have let go of their mistrust of bears somewhat. They've been working with Caleb a lot actually. Besides, he seems more concerned with the rogue, and Patrick right now

CHAPTER 15

than the clan."

"Patrick? Our Division Head's son? I knew about the rogue, but what's going on with him?"

I groaned slightly. "It seems I may be something of a seer. I've been seeing him in my dreams a lot lately."

He mulled that over. "Well, stay far away from him. We'll try to see how to undo your warning. It's not set in stone, you know?"

"I know, but I saw him yesterday, and it triggered a new warning. It seems my interactions with Patrick only made it closer to actually happening," I replied solemnly.

"It still can change. Just takes something big to counteract the warning," he said as he nudged me. That gave me something to think about. *I just needed something big.* I thought about my dreams so far, and I realized it was just the wolves who were involved. *Maybe that's what I needed to do?* I thought as the gears in my head started turning. *Maybe I just needed to merge the groups together somehow and stop the war from happening—*

"You will be careful, won't you?" he asked, interrupting my thoughts.

"I will. Just stay in my life, please. You are going to be a grandfather after all."

He smiled warmly at that. "Yeah, I guess I am."

Caleb peeked his head out. "I was just curious if you two were hungry? Bastian has steaks."

I internally gagged. "Please, no. Tell him I'll stay out here while he cooks those."

"You're a wolf and a bear, and you don't like meat?" Caleb jested.

"No, the baby doesn't seem to like meat," I said as I rubbed my belly.

He grinned. "I'm sure that will change. Bastian said he has you taken care of too. Is it okay to come visit now?"

"Please! I miss my Baby girl!" Cade shouted from behind him.

Caleb pushed him back. "Space, dude."

I laughed and nodded as I said, "Come on out, guys!"

Cade barreled past Caleb and settled down next to me, rubbing my belly. Caleb rolled his eyes towards Cade.

"Got to say hi to the little wolf."

Caleb settled next to his dad. "And what if she's a bear?"

"I'm sensing wolf," Cade replied back, wiggling his eyebrows to my brother, who rolled his eyes again. *They were going to get stuck like that if he weren't careful,* I thought, chuckling.

You could really see the resemblance between Caleb and our dad now that they sat together. *It was uncanny, and I looked like my mother.* That thought made me smile. I had long, curly, red hair, and I was very short. At only 5' 1, all the guys in my life towered over me. The only big difference between Caleb and my father were their eyes. *Caleb must have his mother's eyes, while I got our dad's.*

"Was my mother short?" I asked, interrupting the conversation. They all turned to look at me. "Oh, sorry. I was just lost in thought and blurted it out."

"It's fine, Baby Girl. We were just goofing off anyways."

"Your mother was only around 5' 2 maybe. If that honestly. She was fierce though. Not afraid of anyone or anything, and her wolf was huge too. Like bigger than most. It was the only thing her father seemed happy with," Dad said, gritting his teeth, "but it was funny to see such a tiny thing shift into something so big and strong."

"I met someone yesterday. She said she knew about my mother too, and that Mom was the only wolf allowed on Bear land," I said, thinking back to Alana.

My father smiled at the memories going through his mind again. "Aye, she was. Not everyone was keen on it, but there were a lot that loved her. She was allowed in certain parts of our territory. It was a secret, mind you. My father wouldn't have approved, so she'd visit when he was away on business, which was often. He went home to Russia quite a bit before your mother disappeared. My grandfather was dying, so he was with him a great deal of the time. My father came home frail with his own illness and passed the leadership soon after. Who told you this?"

"Alana. I met her at the Dress Barn yesterday. She's your niece, right?" I asked.

CHAPTER 15

Dad nodded his head, while Caleb piped in. "And our cousin."

"Any more family I should know about?"

"Thomas has a son, who is staying in Russia for now. His name is Noah. I doubt you'll see him anytime soon, but he's a little older than Caleb. His other daughter is Octavia, who is the baby in the family. Other than that, my brother's mate died a few years ago."

"I'm really sorry to hear that. I wish I had gotten the chance to meet her too. Octavia seems like she will be difficult to get to know, but I really liked Alana," I said as Bastian came out of the kitchen, handing me a bowl of fruit. In his other hand were a bunch of raw steaks, and I tried not to look at them.

"Alana? Oh, the bear we met at that dress shop?" my mate asked as he bounded down the steps to the grill.

"Yeah, apparently we're related!" I beamed back at him, my mouth already full. Amusement flashed over his face as I popped another piece of kiwi into my mouth.

"No kidding?" he said, laughing as he pulled the cover off the grill.

"What's so funny?" Cade asked.

He set the steaks down and leaned against the porch railing. "Do any of you feel the same annoyance or hatred of the other kind anymore? Or any other shifter for that matter."

My brows furrowed slightly. "Bastian, what are you asking?"

"I'm asking this. Caleb, do you hate me?"

"No, I don't hate you. Why?"

My brother shot me an odd look.

"See, I don't hate you either. Not anymore. Before Shanely, I couldn't even stand getting a whiff of a bear shifter, let alone be in the same room as them. Now, I'm making two bear shifters the best steaks I have in my freezer and not because I'm being forced to. I honestly *want* to. Caleb, the minute we discovered you were blood to Shanely, I felt the anger and disgust just fade away. Instantly. I'm not the only one, right? I mean what about you, Cade? Even without the bond fully in place to Shanely, the prejudice just slowly melted away, right?"

"Wow. I guess I didn't really think about it but yeah," Cade said, deep in thought.

"Me too. It's just gone," Caleb agreed.

"We're working together, trusting one another, and trusting others we barely know from each other's kind. That would have never happened without Shanely. I think you have a gift babe," Bastian said.

"A gift?"

"Yeah, maybe something similar to your aunt Cassia. She pulls people's emotions and helps them heal. I think you're unconsciously quelling our hate and mistrust. You're blending us together again."

I leaned back in my chair. "Interesting. I'm not doing anything on purpose."

"Your mother was special like this too, though she never did tell me what her extra ability was. She wanted to surprise me but never got the chance. This sounds a lot like her though, and she was the only shifter I had ever met that could blend everyone together. She always wanted to become Alpha and demolish the law separating the different shifters," my dad said.

"Really? I honestly would love that," I replied as Cade stole the bite off my fork. I punched his arm, but he just winked at me.

"Can you imagine a world where we didn't war with you guys? How many of our people never find their mates because we're separated," Caleb chimed in, resting his hands against the back of his head.

"It's a beautiful thought. If anyone can do it, can really unite us again, it would be you Shanely. The mixer, who's just too adorable to ever be angry with," Bastian said, smiling as he went back to the grill.

My dad leaned over and whispered, "I like him."

"Me too."

Chapter 16

Texting my dad nearly every day since we met has been surreal. I smile every time he sends a gif or just calls to check in and see how me and the baby are doing. He and Caleb try to visit when they can too, but Dad's been cautious about bringing up the issues with wolves to his brother, and I didn't blame him.

The wedding was tomorrow though, and everyone was running around finishing up any last-minute errands or taking care of things that needed done still. Bastian's parents flight was delayed, so they were getting in later this afternoon rather than this morning, but I was okay with the few extra hours I had before meeting the rest of his family. No matter what Bastian said, I wasn't sure how they'd take me being a mixer. At least my scent was mostly wolf.

Elijah's arm healed up nicely, and he was enjoying all the attention he received from the girls in the pack. I'd tease whenever they hovered around him, begging to see the tiny scar on his spine, and he'd scold me, telling me to hush whenever I opened my mouth. I owed him, so I let him have his fun without too much torment.

This morning, I waved goodbye to Bastian as he drove down the driveway. He was planning something special and told me to stay at the lodge while he ran to work and did whatever it was he was doing. I watched until his truck was long gone before turning on my heels in search of my uncle. I had my own plans to take care of.

Cade, however, followed me into the lodge too. I frowned, thinking I'd get a moment to myself, but he followed after me.

"Cade, you don't have to babysit me," I said, chuckling. "I'll be with my uncle anyways."

"Ha! Bored of me already?" he asked as he playfully nudged me.

"Never," I answered as he tossed an arm over my shoulder. "You're one of my best friends Cade, not to mention my brother. I just know I'll have plenty of bodyguards here, and it's okay if you need to get stuff done too. I mean your family will be arriving in a few hours."

Cade rocked his head back and forth, considering my offer. He pursed his lips together before answering, "You'll stay here then?"

"Yup. I have plans to talk with my uncle anyways. Might take a while, so go! Be free little birdie!" I exclaimed, waving my arms like a silly little bird.

Cade laughed and tousled my hair. "You goofball! Okay, I'm gone. Just don't do anything crazy while I'm gone and stay away from bears!"

I put my hands on my hips as my eyes narrowed, and he laughed even harder. "Shanely, you know what I mean!"

I laughed, letting him off the hook and watched him take off outside and hop in his SUV. Finally alone, I turned abruptly to head into Cain's office, when I ran into a girl I hadn't met before. We slammed into each other, and I accidentally knocked a bunch of papers from her hands.

"I am so sorry! I didn't even see you there!" I exclaimed, picking up the papers she dropped. She didn't bother to help me. She simply waited for me to finish before snatching them out of my hands rather rudely. My eyes narrowed on her.

This girl was taller than I was, with long, straight blonde hair that reached her waist and eyes as dark as fresh brewed coffee. *There really wasn't much shape to her though,* I thought. She looked more like a stick with clothes, but her round face was strikingly pretty, and I envied the light freckles on her nose.

"You really should watch where you're going," she said sarcastically.

"It was an accident," I replied before brushing off her rudeness and extending my hand. "I'm Shanely. I'm sorry, I'm still in the process of meeting everyone, but it's nice to meet you."

She didn't receive it. Her harsh gaze merely looked up and down, and I

CHAPTER 16

dropped my hand. "Oh, I know all about you, Shanely. You're that *mixer* that has Bastian all in a tizzy."

And there it was, I thought, gritting my teeth. *It all made sense now.* I thought she looked familiar, and I remembered the first night I saw her. She was standing next to Derek when I joined the pack. *This was his own flesh and blood. It just had to be.* The jealousy was literally oozing out of her pores, but I forced myself to be cordial.

I gave her a tight-lipped smile. "Emma, right?"

"Oh, so you've heard about me then?" she said, with a grin. "Has Bastian been talking about me again?"

"Actually, no. He's never once mentioned you, but the others have filled me in about you plenty. I'm sure not in the same way that you're thinking though. Now excuse me, I have a wedding to plan. You know with Bastian," I said sarcastically as I pushed past her.

Her face twisted in anger, but it was hard to feel bad for the girl. She was barking up the wrong tree if she thought she could push me away to take my mate.

"Whore," she muttered softly.

My wolf snarled within, and I turned around, clenching my fists tightly.

"Excuse me?!" I snapped angrily.

"Shanely!" Cain shouted from behind. "I've been looking all over for you!"

I glared at Emma, who simply walked down the steps like nothing had happened between us. My chest burned again, and I seriously wanted to follow after her and correct this little attitude problem right now, but I took a deep breath and let her go. *Now was not the time to start fights.*

"You wanted to see me, kiddo?"

I turn to face Cain and forced a smile to my lips. "Yes, actually. I wanted to ask your permission about something."

"Sure, whatcha need?"

"I'd like to invite my family to my wedding. My Medvedev family."

Cain's eyes widened, and he carefully look around, running his hand through his beard. He pulled me to the side and lowered his voice. "Kiddo,

I don't know about this. It's not that I have anything against them, but we still have a lot of issues with bear shifters. Most in the pack still don't like them, and we're supposed to be keeping a low profile, remember? No one knows about your dad yet."

"Uncle Cain, I can't choose between two halves of myself. I belong to the clan as much as I do this pack, and he's— my dad. He should be able to walk me down the aisle, but instead he's not even allowed to attend!" I scoffed, shaking my head. "I never even thought I'd have my dad at my wedding, and now that I know him, he can't go? My mother is gone, and no one will ever know what happened to her. She more than likely died alone because of this stupid feud, and I don't want *this*. Not for my baby, not for myself, or my pack. This is the best thing for us. I know it."

I straightened my shirt, feeling a little winded at the end of my rant, and Cain just smiled at me. That smile turned to a smirk, and he shook his head. "We'll start small, okay? They can formally be invited to our lands for the wedding only. I'm worried we will need to ease the pack into this, but regardless, I don't think your dad should walk you down the aisle. It's not safe for others to know that part right now. The pack just now seems to be somewhat accepting of the fact you're different. I don't want to push something too soon here. Do we have a deal?"

My face fell, but I nodded my head yes. *It was a win for now, and at least my dad can come,* I thought to myself. "Deal. Thank you, Uncle! I'll go invite them right now."

Cain frowned. "Oh no, you won't. You cannot go into their lands alone, Shanely. I'll send some enforcers with an invite or better yet, I'll give them a call."

"That will never work. Thomas will just burn the invite or ignore your call altogether. Someone needs to go in person, and who better than me? I'm kin," I replied matter of factly.

"But Thomas doesn't know that little detail right now, does he? It's not safe for you, Shanely. You just about died at the paws of a real bear. What do you honestly think will happen with a shifter?" he insisted.

"No one there will hurt me. I feel like this is what I'm supposed to do,

CHAPTER 16

Uncle Cain. You can trust me."

"Shanely, I do trust you, but I also can't risk you and the baby. Bastian would agree with me on this too. Until more shifters have accepted this new way of life, you shouldn't put yourself in the middle like this," he countered, crossing his arms.

"But I am the middle, Uncle Cain," I protested. "This needs to be done in person, especially with it being such short notice. I should have asked sooner, but I've been so wrapped up with everything with my dad, I just—."

Cain's phone rang interrupting us. He grabbed his phone and checked the screen. "I'm sorry Shanely, but this is a business call. We can discuss it later, alright?"

I nodded my head, knowing he'd send enforcers out before discussing it with me anymore. He quickly jogged back to his office and closed the door, leaving me with my thoughts. I was worried the bear clan would take the bulky enforcers showing up unannounced as a threat or straight up ignore my uncle's call altogether. *Cain's plan wasn't going to get us anywhere.* I glanced over and saw the pack's truck sitting unattended.

I looked back to the lodge, and no one was around. For once, it was fairly quiet, and I rocked back and forth on my heels, trying to weigh my options. My wolf stirred inside me, warming my chest as if saying *go. Go, and ask them yourself.*

My feet scurried down the steps. *This was the right thing to do,* I told myself as I opened the door and hopped inside. I grabbed the keys hidden against the above mirror and started the truck. I just hoped that no one would catch me before I got there.

The drive through the mountains was uneventful, and my phone stayed silent as I drove across the border, feeling rather proud of myself so far. Even my wolf seemed pleased, but I kept an eye on my surroundings just like the triplets taught me. I turned left onto a dirt road, and my stomach rolled. Large signs were posted by the road for my father's construction company, and I knew I found the place. Much like our side, the clan had bears carved into everything imaginable through-out the trail, and I drove slow to look at it all. *It was pretty incredible the talent people had,* I thought to myself. *I wondered if my dad did any of the carvings.*

With the window on the truck slightly cracked, I got a wonderful breeze as I drove down the long drive. Suddenly, I could smell them. The bear clan. I was getting better at identifying different smells, thanks to Caleb and Bastian, and I sat up further in my seat. *Scouts must be close, seeing how I hadn't made it to the main gates yet,* I thought to myself as my eyes drifted all around me. *Maybe I should have called Caleb first?* My eyes widened.

Caleb— I grit my teeth in frustration. *I didn't even think to check to see if he was here first.* I was going to need his support with this, and I chastised myself for not thinking everything through. I was so worried about getting here without the pack knowing that I didn't think about what I'd do once I *was* here. My wolf huffed inside my chest as the large wooden gates appeared.

I really hope I didn't just start a war right now.

I slowed the truck to a stop, and waited for the gates to open, but they never did. My stomach rolled as I looked around, noticing a camera at the top of the wall on the left side. I forced a smile to my lip, waving at whoever was watching me right now. *Please don't make this anymore awkward than it already is,* I thought to myself.

Suddenly, a small black bear appeared next to the truck and startled me. I jumped hard as it stuck its snout in the open crack of the widow and chuffed. My heart thundered in my chest as I glared at the bear shifter.

"That's not funny," I muttered, and I swear it sounded like he *laughed*. The bear stood on his back legs, sniffing all around my truck and peeking in the back seat. He abruptly pushed off my truck and made his way towards the gate. I slowly looked back to the camera, raising a brow. *Umm— okay?* The gates groaned, swinging open wide enough for me to pull the truck inside, and my eyes widened. The bear moseyed forward, but I waited before moving.

Am I supposed to follow?

He turned suddenly, stopping to give me a look.

"I guess so," I muttered, putting the truck in drive again and pulling forward. *There was no going back now.*

CHAPTER 16

The gates closed behind me, and I tried not to feel trapped here. I looked at the gates in the rear-view mirror. *Yeah, I don't think the truck could bust through them,* I thought as I turned the truck off. Quite a few people had come out to see the new arrival already, and they were watching me with such scrutiny that my nerves were starting to get the better of me. I was surprised to see children running around playing without a care in the world though. Some were playing in their bear form, which was adorable to watch, but they didn't seem frightened by my presence. That made me smile.

This place was so different than home, I thought to myself. I shook off my jacket and tossed my phone in the passenger seat as I looked around. The main village was quaint but beautiful. Less modern than the lodge, but I sort of liked the close-knit feel it had. Huge A-framed cabins surrounded a large community fire pit, with a large building in the center. Every building had some sort of carving built into them, connecting them together and making this the place to be here at clan land. *I wonder if this was all here when my parents were first together,* I thought to myself. *Did my mom spend any time here?*

I snapped out of my thoughts when my dad suddenly appeared in the door frame of the middle building. His eyes narrowed on mine, and I swallowed hard. *He didn't look too happy with me,* I thought as an even bigger man stepped out after him. *This was his* little *brother?!*

Thomas stood shorter than my dad, but what he lacked in height he made up for in size. His shoulders were broad, and every muscle seemed to be bursting out of his shirt. My family may hail from Russia, but my uncle looked like a straight up *Viking* with his long, braided hair and thick beard. But his eyes— they matched mine. *Must be the family's trademark,* I thought to myself.

I took a deep breath before slowly opening my door and sliding to the dirt. My uncle Thomas inhaled deeply, giving my father a puzzled look as the two started whispering to each other. My father's eyes never left mine. I watched my dad take a deep breath and his eyes widened too. I frowned. *Had my smell changed or something?* I wondered as I cautiously approached the Clan leader. My wolf snapped her jaws, and I shook my head. *I had a job to do, and how I smelled wasn't important right now.*

"I don't believe I gave you permission to come on my lands!" Thomas bellowed, and I skidded to a stop. The crowd around us stopped too, and the mothers pulled their children away. I frowned again.

Caleb, Alana, and Octavia filed out of the building on my right. *Oh, thank God, Caleb was here*, I thought to myself. All eyes widened when they saw me, and Caleb immediately pulled out his phone. I shook my head, knowing who he was calling. *If Bastian showed up right now this was going from bad to worse.* He gritted his teeth and started furiously typing away anyways.

"Caleb don't—"

My uncle interrupted my link.

"I said, I don't believe I gave you permission, wolf."

"I know!" I stammered, trying to find my voice. I held my hands up defensively. "I came alone and in peace. I simply wanted a moment to speak with you."

"I don't mingle with wolves," he replied dryly.

"Thomas," my father said, but Thomas held his hand up, silencing my father.

"If you were to just give me five minutes of your time—"

"Five minutes of my time?" he bellowed out. "That's asking a lot, wolf."

"Not really," I countered. "All I'm asking is for a mere conversation with you. It's free and—"

Thomas spat out a laugh. "And who are you to even ask this of me? The only person I deal with is Cain, and that's only when I have to."

"I'm Shanely McCoy," I said proudly. "The rightful heir to the throne. I do believe that gets me at least five minutes of your time, don't you?"

I smiled smugly at the fact that Thomas looked actually thrown by that tidbit of information.

"I had heard the child of Mercedes came back. You are as brave as her," he muttered softly, "I'll give you that."

My heart fluttered hearing him talk about my mother. I couldn't contain the smile that crept up my face just thinking I was anything like her, but Thomas seemed lost in thought while he studied me. He inhaled again and

CHAPTER 16

frowned.

"No wolf has ever driven up to my lands like this. They tend to stab in the back," Thomas went on.

"I'm not here to attack anyone or anything here! Well, maybe a candy bar if you have one, but that's mostly because of the baby, who is also pushing on my bladder. May I come inside, please? I really have to pee."

Octavia scoffed from the side, but I didn't care. If this baby could be my way in then I was going to take it. I refused to go home empty handed.

Cain would only insist he was right if I did.

Thomas seemed amused with me, and his tone of voice softened. "I do not like your wolf, little one, but my own mother raised me to care for our pregnant women and littles. You may come inside for five minutes, and then you will leave."

With that, he stalked back inside, leaving me to catch up. My entire family looked surprised, and honestly so was I, but I wasn't going to lose my chance at winning Uncle Thomas over. Even if he had no idea who I was.

My father helped me up the stairs whispering, "I hope you know what you're doing."

"Me too," I muttered.

Once inside, I made a super fast trip to the bathroom because I wasn't lying. I really did have to go, but as I headed back down the hallway to Thomas and my father, I admired the house. *The detail in the woodwork was amazing,* I thought as I rounded the corner. *Someone here had a knack for carving.*

"You seem to like it here," Thomas said.

I turned, finding my uncle sitting at the end of the long table. The main room looked like a massive conference room, but instead of office chairs and plastic tables, this room had a large wooden table that reminded me of my dining room table back at home. A beautiful etching ran through the center, made of blue resin and some sort of tiny crystal. I had never seen anything like it really. Thomas's chair was the largest in the room to accommodate his wide size and behind him hung large antlers of what looked like elk. *Or maybe moose?* I had no idea, but the furs and other woodsy decorations gave this place a cozy, cabin feel. I was *in* love with it all.

"It's beautiful. Who did all the carvings?" I asked.

"My brother and I have a knack for woodworking. Make something good with our hands was what our father always taught us. This is our newest building. It serves as a dining/meeting hall. We don't have very much financially, but with what we do have, we make stunning," Thomas replied arrogantly.

I could hear the insults laced in those words, but I chose to ignore it. Snapping back at him wouldn't get me anywhere.

"You two are incredibly talented," I replied, with a smile.

"That we are, but I don't think you came all the way out here to look at my cabin. What is it you want, and why are you here and not your Alpha?"

I took a deep breath. *I could do this*, I thought to myself before I stepped forward. "May I sit?"

He nodded and gestured to the chair at the opposite end, looking amused again. My father eyed me carefully before sitting down next to my uncle.

Yeah, he doesn't take me seriously, I thought to myself. *Even after hearing I was the heir, Thomas clearly did not view me as a threat.* That thought alone solidified my choice in coming here myself.

"Thank you," I said as I sat down in the large chair and played the part of an ignorant young lady. I made myself nice and cozy before smiling wide at my father and uncle.

"I wanted to invite a few of my new bear shifter friends, and of course you," I quickly added, "to my wedding tomorrow."

"Your wedding?"

Both my father and my uncle narrowed their eyes on me.

Without letting my voice shake, I continued, playing with my hair as I said, "Yes, my wedding. I recently found my mate, but I wanted a wedding too. Bastian's been supportive of my wishes, and one of my wishes was to invite the friends I've made since moving here."

He put his hand up in disbelief. "You've made friends with bears shifters? A wolf doesn't befriend bears."

CHAPTER 16

"Well, I only *recently* found out I am a shifter. I don't share in any of the hatred I've heard about," I answered, fiddling my thumbs together.

Thomas gaped at me. Like I was enigma he couldn't figure out.

Get in line, dude.

"Your Alpha would never accept this," he finally said. "I'm assuming it's why *you're* here and not him."

"My uncle has given the formal invitation for you and my friends to enter our lands, which is silly to me by the way. A formal invitation," I replied, rolling my eyes. "But I wanted to be the one to invite you, and I asked him to come instead. The point is, I made a few friends here, and I'd like them to be apart of my special day. I don't understand all the fuss about it!"

Thomas slapped his hand down on the table, and I jumped in my seat. My heart thundered in my chest, but his booming laughter surprised me. *Okay— wasn't expecting this,* I thought to myself. *To become bear food, yes. Not making the clan leader roll with laughter.*

"Let me get this straight," Thomas spat out between laughs. "You drove nearly 30 minutes, breaking multiple laws when you crossed by the way, into bear country, while pregnant and alone, just to invite some of my people to your wedding."

He laughed again, and even my dad looked a little amused. He shrugged his shoulders when I looked to him for guidance. *I guess he wasn't expecting this either.*

"Well— I invited you too," I said quietly.

Thomas laughed even harder, and soon my dad was smiling.

"Well done, Shanely."

My eyes shot to my father, and he winked at me. My mouth dropped open, but his voice quickly made me close it.

"Not now, sweetie. Just focus on your uncle, but you're doing well. Thomas isn't one to laugh very often."

I slowly pulled my eyes back to Thomas, trying to forget the fact my father just sent me a mind-link. *This was his first link,* I thought to myself, but I did as I was told and focused back on my uncle.

Thomas slowly stopped laughing and wiped his eyes. "You are by far my favorite wolf, but I cannot allow anyone to attend. You understand, right?"

My face fell. "But why?"

I felt like a child all of the sudden as he stared me down. His stare was so intense and judgmental that it was crazy to think that I was related to this scary man.

"Simple. I cannot trust your wolves not to react harshly to my people."

"I *have* approval. No one will harm anyone there, and my Alpha will ensure that as well. You are welcome to bring your own enforcers if it makes you feel better too. My Alpha is honestly becoming very supportive of my choice of friends."

He scoffed then. "And what about your mate? You mentioned Bastian, as in Bastian Fenrir?"

I nodded, and my dad winced slightly. *Well, that can't be good,* I thought. I frowned, feeling like this conversation was tipping in the wrong direction fast.

"He's never liked bears before and has honestly been a thorn in our side for quite some time. Whenever there's a problem, Bastian's at the heart of it. He likes to stir up trouble, that one, and he's also a very large and powerful wolf. How could I feel good about sending my people to be around him and his brothers?" he asked as he crossed his arms.

"Look, I don't know everything Bastian's done to the clan, but I can tell you he's changed. He's very different from before and is trying to make amends with some of the shifters here. Just please trust me on that," I pleaded.

If only he knew the real truth, I thought to myself. I wasn't sure if I should tell him, and the way my father looked at me now, you could see he was warring with the same question. *Thomas could take the news either way, and if we chose wrong, then we'd had a whole mess of problems.* My chest warmed again, and my wolf seemed to nudge me along. She and I both knew that if he took the news well— it could mend so much between the shifters.

My uncle seemed pretty stuck in his ways though. *If I couldn't get him to agree on it; how could I bridge the gap between the groups? How could I change the warnings I have seen?*

CHAPTER 16

"Trust you? I don't even know you! I can't even figure out your scent. It's similar to a wolf, but it's different too, which makes me think you could be a mixer. That would be against the law and dangerous to my clan if anyone discovered you here. You're different, and different doesn't always mean safe. I will always choose what is safe for my clan before anything else."

I sighed heavily. "My scent is— complicated."

My father carefully shook his head no, and my face fell. *He must have made up his mind then.*

"Complicated? I don't like complicated when it comes to shifters. It tends to mean dangerous," Thomas replied, his eyes narrowing.

Suddenly, a loud commotion sounded outside. Snarling ensued, and Thomas and my father bolted outside faster than I could get out of my chair. I scurried to catch up.

"Oh no."

That was all I heard from my father before I passed by and found my mate in the center of a large crowd. Bastian was bleeding from his nose as he squared off with a bear shifter, and boy did he look pissed.

"Crap," I whispered.

Thomas glared at me, and I gritted my teeth. *Well, this was crappy timing,* I thought to myself. My uncle wouldn't believe a word out of my mouth ever again now. The bear shifter swung at Bastian again, but he dodged to the right and pushed the man aside. My mate had his fist raised, keeping an eye on the other shifters trying to trip him up.

Bastian's focus was firm on the stocky man in front of him and thankfully not at me. *God, this had gone from bad to worse.* No one had shifted yet, but I knew it was only a matter of time if someone didn't stop them.

The shifter continued pushing Bastian, trying to fight, but Bastian kept dodging each and every attack. He refused to put a hand on him and guilt ate at me. *He wasn't defending himself like I knew he could.* Shouting continued, and Bastian got in the bear's face.

"My mate is somewhere here! Back off, and tell me where she is!" he bellowed. I couldn't hear the shifter's response as the crowd roared excitedly. Violent speech about how this *Michael* should just cave in my mate's face sounded loudly, and my hands tightened into fists.

"And you say to trust you," Thomas snarled.

I glared back at Thomas, and a snarl burst from my lips. *Bastian didn't come here with ill intent. My uncle had ears and could hear what Bastian was asking, but it didn't matter,* I realized. *All Bastian wanted was me, and yet my uncle could only see what he wanted to.*

This was a mistake.

"I wasn't lying! Do you see what's happening? Your bear is involved too, and Bastian hasn't once swung at him!" I shouted back angrily.

My father carefully stepped in front of me as Thomas glared back at me, his eyes flashing red against me. Thomas gave a warning snarl, but I didn't care. I didn't care I was staring down the Clan leader. Rage burned through my veins, and I squared my shoulders, daring him to make a move.

"Shanely!"

I turned, finding my mate looking at me with relief in his eyes. He took a step in my direction, when Michael took advantage of the distraction and struck him in the jaw. Bastian dropped to the ground as the crowd roared again.

"Bastian!" I cried as I rushed towards him.

Caleb began pushing his way through the crowd, and I could hear my brother yelling for everyone to move, but they wouldn't listen.

That burning sensation struck my chest again, and my wolf howled. She was suddenly quiet as I turned on my heels to face my uncle. *He had to stop this!* I thought as my rage reached a whole new height. *This was his clan, and it was his responsibility to stop this before it got any worse.*

I shouted, "Bastian never hit your shifter! That shifter took it too far, and you know it! My mate is bleeding by one of *your* people. Bastian is just desperate to find me because I didn't tell him I was coming here, alright? You of all people should know how sacred mates are."

My uncle's nostrils flared, but I watched his eyes slowly return to normal. I waited for the command to come, but he didn't say anything, and my face fell. *He wasn't going to stop anything,* I realized. *Thomas will never accept me. He will never accept Bastian or the pack.*

CHAPTER 16

I gritted my teeth, throwing my hands up to walk away from the only family I had met that disappointed me. *I had done nothing but be kind and respectful, and he still won't listen! If Thomas wasn't going to stop the fight then I will.* My stupid inner voice, telling me this was the right course of action was wrong. *I should have never come here.*

My eyes found Bastian, who struggled to get through the crowd. Anger surged again as I shoved the ones blocking my path aside. Bastian jerked around, keeping Michael in his sights as he tried to get out of the circle. No one wanted to help him though. They were all to eager to see the action.

My mate easily evaded Michael. It was clear their training was not the same as Bastian used Michael's own momentum against him more than once. Bastian never once struck the man, and I knew it was for me. He didn't want to fight these shifters or even defend himself the way he should *because* of me.

My father shouted behind me. "Shanely— calm down before you do something rash."

I ignored him. Anger surged throughout my body, and my burning sensation only amplified. All I could see was that stupid man *still* trying to hit Bastian, and it infuriated me.

Caleb had finally reached the center, but Michael pushed Caleb aside. The others in the crowd grabbed Caleb and hauled him backwards again. There was nothing he do without shifting.

Bastian put his hands up, shouting something, but it wasn't working. No one was listening, and the pain I began to feel worsened. Something cracked inside my chest as I ran towards my mate.

"Bastian!" I shouted again, pushing through the crowd to the front. I was nearly to him, and once I reached him, we were *going* home.

Bastian's eyes quickly found mine, but before he could take another step, Michael struck him again. Another crack as Bastian hit the ground for the second time.

My vision suddenly glowed red, and everyone's head snapped to me now. The chanting stopped, and those around me wisely took a step back. Pain rippled in my body, and I took a deep breath, willing whatever was happening to keep going. Because I wasn't going to get in the way this time. *Oh no,* I thought. *I'm going to give that prick a lesson he won't forget.*

Bastian was back on his feet quickly, looking utterly shocked and downright scared. He didn't know what to do other than watch.

The bones in my body continued to crack and rearrange themselves within me. Something deep within was pulling through, and despite the pain, I was ready to meet it.

"Daniel, what is she?!" Thomas bellowed behind me.

I could hear their thunderous footsteps behind me, but it didn't matter. *No one was going to be able to stop me from protecting what was mine!* I screamed as fur slowly pushed through my skin, and my bones grew inside. My nails sharpened as everyone began to shout around me, but soon they were all drowned out by a roar.

A roar from my bear.

Chapter 17

Pain rippled through my body as my bones cracked and moved. My grizzly awoke and forcefully shoved my wolf aside and emerged. Fur coated my body, and I shook my head as my canines elongated, sharpening themselves and pushing against my lips. My paws landed on the ground, and my chest heaved. *I had shifted. I had shifted into a grizzly bear—*

The pain was instantly gone now that the shift was over, and I stretched my muscles and shook out my fur. I felt *powerful*. Like a door opened inside me and this monstrosity came out. *I had dual-shifter abilities,* I thought to myself. *My dad was right.*

While my wolf was cunning and cautious, my bear was bold and powerful. All that power was being fueled by anger though, and the need to protect what was *mine*. My bear aimed her attention right at Michael, whose eyes were wide.

I reared on my back legs, roaring as I slammed back to earth again. The ground shook, and everyone backed away to watch the fight. I loved how strong my senses were with my bear's ability. I could hear Michael's heart race, scent his fear, and see the sweat on his brow. My lip curled in disgust. *I was ready to rip him to shreds.*

Michael suddenly shifted, and his black bear landed before me. I snarled at him. He charged towards me, but I felt so good, I met him halfway. We clashed in the air, snarling as we tried to rip out each other's throat. Michael's bear was smaller than mine, and it wasn't hard to force him where I wanted him to go.

We side-stepped, and Caleb grabbed Bastian, pulling him away from us.

Bastian looked ready to step in between us, and I could see him struggling to stop his own shift, but Michael was mine to deal with. It was my fault we were in this mess, and I was going to stop it.

My bear pushed for more control, standing on our hind legs and shoving Michael back. I pushed back to the forefront again. *We are a team!* I shouted in my head, and my bear snarled but relented. We couldn't do this alone, and I made sure to keep my seat as co-pilot. I had to trust Caleb to deal with Bastian now. Keeping control of my grizzly and dealing with Michael was hard enough as it was.

The adrenaline coursing through my veins while we fought was hard to handle, but it surprised me how ease it was to fight as a bear. It was like second nature, and together we were easily *destroying* him. It was almost funny how weak he really was against me.

We managed to strike Michael hard enough I smelled blood. He stumbled to the ground, moving slower now, but I didn't care. All I could see was a threat to my family. All I could *feel* was the anger I felt watching Bastian drop in pain. Michael was a danger to my family, and I was going to eliminate that danger.

Michael struggled to his feet, and I roared again. My paws pounded the dirt, and I charged, not giving that bear a chance to get away, when Bastian suddenly flew in front of me with his arms raised. He didn't bat an eye as I skidded to a stop in front of him.

"Shanely, stop!" he shouted firmly. Anger flooded my system as I chuffed at him. He took a step towards me. "I'm okay. Just look at me, baby. There's no threat. There's no danger."

I threw my head up and down, roaring for him to get out of my way. *He had to move,* I thought as I began to pace back and forth. Michael was still alive, and therefore the threat to my family was still present. I tried to go around him, but Bastian stepped in my path every time. I barred my teeth to my mate, and he barred his neck.

"Shanely," Bastian pleaded. "Please shift back."

Michael had gotten to his feet and roared at me again. *This fight wasn't over, but Bastian was in the middle!* I thought in sheer panic. I tried to bolt around, but Bastian continued to get in my path. Michael charged, and my heart stopped. I snarled, when Caleb surprised everyone by running forward. He put his back against my mate and held his hands up to stop Michael.

"Michael, stop!" Caleb shouted. "Leave him alone, and she will stop. You started this by attacking her mate!"

I continued pacing back and forth, watching the black bear closely. Micheal hesitated, snarling as his gaze went from me to Caleb. I didn't trust him, and I wasn't about to let up and let him harm my family.

Bastian stepped into my view once more. "Shanely?"

I finally looked at him. I still wasn't happy he was hurt in the first place, but he seemed okay for the most part. His nose had stopped bleeding, but his lip was busted. *It wouldn't take him too long to heal,* I reminded myself. *The marks Caleb had given him had healed within a couple weeks so this was nothing compared to that.* I felt my anger start to subsided, and I took a deep breath to steady myself.

Bastian slowly moved closer to me before resting his hand against my head. I closed my eyes, letting him rub my fur and that amazing spot behind my ears. It was heavenly, and I finally understood why he never wanted me to stop when I would pet him. I nudged closer to him and relaxed into his touch.

"You're beautiful, Shanely," he said, with such admiration in his voice. I opened my eyes, and he smiled at me. Bastian rested his head against mine, and we stayed like this for a moment. The rest of the world disappeared around us, and for a moment everything felt right. Just *right*.

Thomas's voice broke the silence and pulled me from my bliss. "Michael shift. Everyone else leave now!"

Michael forcefully did as he was told, and it looked like it hurt too. Our eyes met, and boy did he look awful. A smirk crept up my face. I felt rather proud of myself, watching him glare at everyone before storming off into the woods. *Serves him right,* I thought to myself. Soon all that was left was us, and my smirk fell when I looked around. Thomas looked pissed and guilt slowly crept in. *I had really stepped in it now,* I thought to myself.

Thomas turned abruptly to my dad. "Did you know, Daniel?"

My father nodded. "She's my daughter, Thomas."

Thomas looked at me with such surprise, and I dropped my head. I could feel his eyes on me for quite some time, and no one spoke. I held my breath, waiting for him to speak again, but nothing happened. By shifting like this, I pushed my secret out to the entire clan. Everyone knew now, whether I wanted them to or not. *There was no hiding who I was now.*

Bastian stood in front of me, trying to block me from my uncle. I was three times his size though. He couldn't hide me if he tried.

"Who else knows?" Thomas asked quietly, and I stole a glance his way. I frowned. I expected rage not— sadness. He seemed hurt almost as he looked to each of his family that stayed behind. I was surprised to see Alana and Octavia stayed too.

"I do," Caleb answered proudly.

"A select few from my pack including my Alpha. No one knew if she'd shift into a bear though," Bastian answered for me. His hand never left me, and I was grateful. I needed his touch right now because I had completely made a mess of things.

Thomas looked to me then, and the sternness in his eyes returned. I swallowed hard.

"Can you shift back?" he asked.

My eyes widened. *I hadn't thought about that. I had no idea how to start a shift. It just happened before.* I made a chuffing sound and nudged Bastian. That's when I noticed my paws. They were white.

White?! I shrieked inside. My paws were entirely white. *Is that even normal for a grizzly bear?*

"I cannot force a shift with her. She's not a part of my clan, so I hold no sway over her or her animal," Thomas answered.

"I think I can help," my father replied. He held his hands up in front of him and slowly approached. Bastian stepped to the side to let him near.

"Shanely, my beautiful girl," my father whispered quietly to me as he admired the bear I had become. I let him rest his hand on my head while he continued, "You shifted because you were angry, didn't you? You were

CHAPTER 17

worried about Bastian and felt the need to protect him. That's your trigger for your bear. In time, I think you can call on her whenever you want, but protectiveness is what brought her forward now. You are the perfect mama bear. Just like your mama."

My heart swelled, and I laid my head on his shoulder. Thomas watched the whole exchange not saying a word. I felt awful for the position I just put everyone in. I truly didn't know how I was going to fix this.

"Now," Dad said, pulling back and gesturing to my mate, "look at Bastian. See that he's safe and calm your bear inside. She might retreat on her own and let the shift happen naturally. Just imagine being your adorable human self again, and the shift should start."

I focused on Bastian like my father told me too. His warm smile melted my heart, and he rested his head against mine saying, "Come back to me, baby."

My bear let go, slipping further into the dark as my bones began to crack. Pain rippled across my body as every bone excruciatingly crunched into place again. Without the adrenaline or anger blocking everything, it hurt to shift. I sucked in a breath as my body shuddered with the pain. My vision sadly returned to normal, and the fur shrunk beneath my skin as I shifted back to my human self. The world spun, and I gasped for air when my grizzly was finally back in her place inside my head.

"Catch her," Caleb cried out as I swayed on my feet.

Bastian was already a step ahead and had his hands around my waist, while I tried to get my footing.

"Easy, baby. The first shift is the hardest," Bastian whispered. I slowly nodded my head as the world slowed around me. Soon, I could focus on my beautiful mate again, and I smiled.

"Let's discuss the rest of this inside," Thomas said as he gestured back to the main building.

My smile fell.

What have I just gotten us into?

Back inside, we all returned to our seats without a word. Thomas motioned for my father to follow him to the back room, and I didn't dare go after them. I had already made a mess of things as it was, and Bastian needed me. His tight grip on my belt loop told me he wasn't letting me out of his sight anyways. I had to trust whatever was going on between Dad and Thomas would work out.

Bastian sat in the chair I previously sat in and pulled me on his lap without asking. He forcefully wrapped his left hand into my hair and buried his nose into the crook of my neck. He inhaled deeply. Bastian seemed a little anxious still as he ran his hands up and down my arm.

Worry etched my brow as I asked, "Are you okay?"

He simply nodded and took another deep breath like he was starved of air. I pursed my lips together, feeling bad that my grand plan fell through like this. I truly thought I was doing the right thing— *at the time.*

"I came back to the lodge to check on you, and I couldn't find you," Bastian said, pulling me from my thoughts. "Cade said he left you at the lodge, and your uncle hadn't seen you for almost an hour. It's was then I noticed the truck missing. I tried to use our bond, but it was faint and hard to get a good read as to where you went, but your uncle Cain figured out exactly where you'd be when I gave the general direction the bond was pulling me."

I nervously scratched the back of my head. "Yeah—"

Bastian gave an irritated look. "Shanely, we were *terrified*. You just took off all alone and didn't tell anyone where you were going. You are pregnant and marked by a rogue. A fact I didn't think I had to remind you of."

I winced. *Yeah— probably not my finest decision*, I thought to myself.

"I'm surprised the Calvary isn't here with you," Caleb chimed in quietly. I bit my lower lip.

Bastian sighed. "Cain thought it would be best if only I came after her. He's trying not to start a war."

His glare settled right back on me, and I groaned. I tried to sit up, but Bastian kept a tight grip on my hair, waiting for me to explain myself. I sighed and slumped against him.

"Cain and I didn't agree. I wasn't trying to start a war, but something deep inside was pushing me in this direction, Bastian. I can't explain it, but

CHAPTER 17

I *needed* to be the one to speak to the Clan Leader. I needed to be the one to try to mend some of these problems between us. Maybe it was my bear driving me or maybe it was my warnings— I don't know, but I didn't mean to worry you all or get you hurt. I thought I'd be back before anyone even knew I left," I replied and looked to the floor. "I am sorry, Bastian."

My father and Thomas joined the group, looking as pissed off as the rest of us. Bastian sighed but relaxed his tight grip on me.

"It's okay, Shanely," he said softly. "Just please, stop putting yourself in danger. You're giving me a heart attack on the daily. I don't know how much more I can take."

A sly grin formed on my lips, and I nuzzled back against him again. I felt his lips touch my cheek softly, and everything felt right with the world again.

"I am sorry, Bastian. I thought I could do this, and I didn't mean to mess it all up," I whispered, looking back at my uncle, who took his seat.

"It was always going to be messy when the truth came out anyways. You listened to your instincts, and I get that. I *am* proud of you for being so brave, but you have to promise me you won't do something like this again, especially pregnant. Can you do that for me?"

"I'm not helpless, Bastian. I can do things too, and we won't always agree on everything. But I do promise not to run off like that again. Next time, I'll shoot you a text before I take off on an adventure."

He laughed and smacked my backside. "A text message? Oh no, I don't think so, Shanely. You are never leaving my sight again. Nothing good comes from you being on your own."

I giggled, slapping his chest playfully. "Oh, stop it."

"Your bear is amazing by the way," Bastian whispered in my ear, and my smile widened. "I've never seen a bear quite like yours."

"Neither have I," Thomas said firmly, and my smile fell.

We both looked at my uncle, who's stern gaze was locked on me. He then glared at Caleb, and I swallowed hard. *I hope he wasn't in trouble because of me too*, I thought to myself. I reached out and squeezed his hand.

"*Thank you, Caleb.*"

He looked in my direction.

"Always."

"Your bear is quite large with colors not typical for a grizzly bear. In fact, they are extremely rare," Thomas said as he rested his head on his hands, watching me closely.

"What do you mean rare?" Bastian asked.

"Grizzly Bears aren't normally white. It is extremely rare in the wild and shifter communities around the world. From what I recall, I believe we've only had two known white grizzlies in our society," Thomas replied.

My dad nodded. "Both were before a war."

My eyes widened. "I'm not here to start a war," I said firmly.

Dad gave me a weak smile. "Of course not, but maybe the prophecies have more than one meaning, brother."

"Prophecy?" Bastian asked.

"It's not something we normally share with wolves, boy," Thomas said bluntly, "but seeing as you're mated to a bear, I supposed you can be trusted for now."

Bastian radiated tension, but he said nothing in return. My hand instinctively went to the back of his head and neck, hoping to rub any tension away before it grew too much.

"It's really just a legend," Thomas said, rubbing his beard. "Stories that have been passed from generation to generation really. White grizzlies became the sign of something big to come. When a white bear emerges, the clan knew to expect trouble. The last two we've seen brought about a war, and bear shifters barely survived. The last one was during the shifter wars, where we lost most of our land to you wolves, and had the Division breathing down our necks for decades. The last white grizzly died then."

"Shanely is new to all of this, brother. She's been through a lot since she came into these mountains. She's not trying to start a war," my father pleaded, but Thomas stared straight ahead to me, and I shifted uncomfortably on Bastian's lap.

"I'm not, I promise! I'm trying to do the opposite actually. I want to abolish the laws that say wolves and bears can't mix," I replied.

Thomas studied me. "Sometimes war comes even when you don't mean to start it."

My warnings suddenly came to mind, and I swallowed hard. I quickly shook my thoughts from those awful nightmares. *The last thing I needed was to give Thomas more ammo to assume the worst.*

"I would do *everything* in my power to keep both wolves and bears safe. They are both apart of who I am," I said firmly to my uncle. He just snorted in response.

"That brings me to the next point. Were you ever going to be honest with me, Daniel? Or did we stop being brothers that trusted one another?"

"Thomas," Dad growled, "I wasn't trying to lie to you. I—" Dad's voice trailed off, and I felt awful forcing him to talk about my mom when he clearly wasn't ready, but he sighed heavily and said, "I found my mate, brother."

Thomas's eyes widened.

"My mate is and *always will be* Mercedes McCoy, heir to the McCoy Pack. I found her when our father was still leader. It's why he gave you the leadership role. I was too distracted trying to keep her safe and a secret. Her father was brutal, Thomas."

Thomas lowered his head. Shame filled his eyes as he muttered, "He told me you hated the birthright."

"No, I did not," Dad replied, leaning forward. "I was hoping once I was leader I could keep Mercedes here with me in the safety of clan lands until I knew what to do with her father. Everything was difficult back then, and my heart broke when she just disappeared. I couldn't find her or see our bond anymore, and I just wasn't present enough for Dad, I guess. He gave you the birthright, and I could never challenge you for it. I still won't do that to you, little brother."

Thomas looked back at him. "It belongs to you though. How can I keep it when it wasn't rightfully mine to begin with?"

"Thomas, do you even remember me being at your ceremony?" Dad asked, and Thomas shook his head. "That's because I wasn't. I had gotten passed out drunk and didn't even feel when Dad stripped me of the birthright before giving it to you. My time to lead has passed, and I don't want it anymore."

Thomas slumped back in his chair, looking less and less scary by the moment. Guilt ate at me. *I forced them to deal with this,* I thought to myself.

"This is your birthright," Thomas cried out. "I am giving it back!"

"Tom, stop," Dad snapped. "I can't lead. Not anymore. I've done things I can't take back, Thomas, and I stand behind Shanely now. I *want* this alliance to work. I want to watch my grandchildren play and not have to worry about someone finding out, but I can't be the one to do it! It *needs* to be you."

"What did you do?" Bastian asked, narrowing his eyes.

My dad suddenly looked to me and then to Bastian. Hairs on the back of my neck stood as Dad sighed saying, "I let my pain guide me. That's all that needs to be said."

"No. You did something serious to the wolves and somehow managed to get away with it," my mate said in a low tone. "I have a feeling I know what you did, but I need you to say it."

"Bastian?" I gave my mate a look, but he wouldn't relent. He held my father's stare, and soon everyone looked confused.

Dad gave Bastian a pointed look. "If you already know then—"

"Because the wolves deserve to know who saved them."

My father scoffed. "The wolves won't take it that way, boy. We both know that."

"Take what, what way?" I asked as everyone's eyes widened. *What was I missing?!*

"Oh my God, brother," Thomas muttered, leaning back in his chair. He ran his hands over his face and groaned.

"That was you! Everyone heard about that story!" Caleb practically shouted.

"Guys, please just tell me," I pleaded.

My father spoke finally, "I killed your grandfather, Shanely. It was me."

My eyes widened. I never thought my father capable of doing something like that. *He seemed so patient and level-headed,* I thought to myself. I can't

CHAPTER 17

even imagine him angry. I didn't know what to say or how to even process this new tidbit of information. My own father *murdered* my grandfather.

My dad looked to the ground for a moment before addressing me. "I was blinded by my rage. Mercedes was just gone, and I couldn't even catch her scent. I feared the worst, and I stupidly made my way to your pack lodge one night. It was late, but your grandfather was outside alone, and that's when I scented her. Your mother. It was her blood, and it was on him somehow."

My heart seized as I listened closely. No one said a word as my father confessed his greatest sin.

"My bear took over completely, and I lost control of him. I went— feral. Just briefly, but when I finally came out of it, we were miles up the mountain, and he was already in pieces. What kills me was your grandmother was there that night.," he said, braving a look in my direction. My stomach twisted. *My poor grandmother,* I thought. *I couldn't imagine watching something like that.*

"My heart just stopped. She must have felt the bond snap and followed us, I don't know. I was covered in blood, her *mate's* blood, and I thought she had called the pack down on me, but she merely nodded her head and disappeared into the forest again. That was it. She never spoke a word to me or anyone else about that night, and I waited for someone to come after me for it, but no one ever did. I descended the mountain, and no one knew what happened. They were the only mate bond I have ever seen behave like that."

Bastian tensed beside me as I asked, "You smelled my mother?"

Dad nodded his head. "I didn't know about you though. I assumed he killed her, but I never felt the bond break like you were supposed to. It was just gone. Not like my bear would listen to anything at that point though."

"You went through all that alone, brother?" Thomas asked, covering his mouth in shock. He just stared at my father in disbelief, and I began to wonder if my first impression of my uncle was wrong. *Maybe he wasn't so cold after all?*

My father shrugged. "When I told you all those years ago that you were what the clan needed, I wasn't lying."

"No more. We are family, and we do things together," Thomas clasped his hand on my dad's shoulder before turning to me. "I guess that means you too, little bear."

He winked at me.

"So— I'll take it you'll come to my wedding?" I asked, grinning.

Thomas laughed, shaking his head. "I knew there was something different about you. I could smell it when you first arrived, but you must take after me. It's the only logical explanation as to why you amuse me so."

My father rolled his eyes, ignoring his brother as he turned to me. "Your Alpha is sure about this?"

"Positive," I replied.

"Then a small number of us will attend. Baby steps," Thomas said, leaning back into his chair.

I ran over to my new uncle and hugged him tight. "Thank you, Uncle Thomas!"

He tensed slightly but quickly returned the hug. He patted my back roughly before he finally scooted back and stood.

"Now, if you don't mind, I must deal with Michael and the others. I'll see you tomorrow, little one."

Thomas strolled out, and my father pulled me into the hug next.

"I always knew you had a bear. You are stunning, Shanely, but don't ever do that again."

"Oh, she won't be. I assure you," Bastian interrupted, and I stuck my tongue out at him.

"So, you knew I had a bear?"

"I had a feeling. I just didn't think it was going to show before your wolf though. Your wolf scent was so much stronger, and your bear was nearly nonexistent."

"Okay, can we address the fact that Shanely not only destroyed that prick Michael, but she also got away with hugging Uncle Thomas. Like if *I* had done that, he would have smacked me in the back of the head!" Caleb exclaimed loudly. Everyone laughed hard at him as he cried out, "It's not funny!"

CHAPTER 17

Eventually, he started laughing too.

"Go. I'm sure your Alpha wasn't too thrilled with your little stunt today. We'll be there tomorrow," my father said.

Crap, I thought as my anxiety grew. *I forgot about Uncle Cain.*

"Is he mad?" I asked Bastian nervously.

"He isn't happy, Shanely," he replied as he extended his hand.

"I'll see you soon," I said as I left with my mate. He helped me into the passenger side of the truck before sliding into the driver's side. He pulled his phone out and dialed a number.

"Cade?"

I could hear the conversation through the phone. Cade was practically yelling at Bastian, and I rolled my eyes.

"Do you have her?! You've been silent for a while man. Elijah and I were about ready to make our way to you."

"I have her, and she's safe, but you need to get the Alpha and head to the cabin. We have some new developments we need to discuss now. Bring her uncles and her aunt too as well as Ryder and Johnny."

"Thank God, man. You tell her she's getting an earful from me when I see her! I should have never left her alone! We're on our way."

He hung up, and Bastian put his hand on my thigh. "It's going to be okay."

God, I hoped so because now I definitely smelled like a bear. There was no hiding what I was now.

Chapter 18

Everyone was standing on the porch, already waiting by the time Bastian pulled into my drive. I groaned as we got close. *No one looked happy at all*, I thought to myself, especially not Cain. They all stared right at me, but his red eyes glared at me, and I slowly shrunk in my seat. I didn't want to leave the truck.

My aunt was moving before Bastian had even parked.

"Shanely!" my aunt cried as she opened my door and hauled me out. She about broke my back with the bear hug she gave me as she shouted, "Don't you ever do that again!"

"Oh, she won't. I promise you that," Bastian proclaimed, giving me a pointed look.

"Are you going to make that promise to everyone?" I asked coyly.

He just smirked as he walked around the truck. My aunt inhaled deeply, pulling back as her eyes widened. The other waited seemed to finally catch my scent too, and I winced as they all looked alarmed.

"Whoa— Shanely. You have a bear," Elijah said dumbfoundedly.

"There's no hiding you now," Cade chimed in as he made his way over to me. He gently scooted my aunt to the side to hug me. "We *will* be talking later, Baby Girl."

"What happened?" Uncle Cain asked. His wolf pulled through his voice, making it deeper than normal, and I shifted on my feet as Cade stepped away.

I frowned when I felt his Alpha power emerge. It was leaking all around him, and everyone stood to the side to get away from it. I jutted out my hip

CHAPTER 18

as I stood in front of my truck. *Okay, I get being mad, but using your Alpha power like this was a tad too much*, I thought to myself.

I stepped forward, when Bastian laced his fingers in mine. My brows rose in surprise that he was approaching with me. I knew he could feel the Alpha power, and this was entirely my fault, but it was comforting having him with me. I turned to face my punishment. It was just us and my uncle now.

"I invited the bear clan to the wedding like we talked about," I said. More sheepishly than I meant to.

"I also remember telling you not to leave pack lands. You disobeyed an order and put yourself and your baby in harm's way. Not to mention Bastian, who I can see was in a fight."

Cain's power came in waves, and I sighed heavily. *Oh boy, was he angry*—

"I wasn't trying to put anyone in danger. I just thought—"

He cut me off shouting, "You didn't think, Shanely! You blindly went ahead with your half-cocked plan, and it could have started a war! Thomas could have killed you for simply being on clan lands without an invite or kept you from us! He would have figured out how special you are to all of us and tried to ransom you or imprison you to ensure he got what he wanted from us. Any one of those options would have started a full-blown war between our kinds, and then the Division *would* have gotten involved! Your warnings would have come true!"

His snarl silenced the woods, and I pursed my lips together. *He wasn't wrong and had every right to be upset with me*, I thought as I looked to my feet. He stomped down the porch steps.

"You, Shanely," he snapped, his finger pointed straight at me, "you *alone* seem to hold the entire pack's future in your hands. But you went ahead blindly. You disobeyed your Alpha and put everyone in danger all for a wedding invite!"

Bastian promptly pulled me behind him, snarling, and Cain growled.

My mate growled right back. "Don't."

My eyes widened as I looked to my uncle. He had stopped dead in his tracks, glaring at my mate, who hid me from view.

"Bastian, move. I'm not going to hurt her," Cain said firmly.

"My wolf can't tell the difference right now. I suggest you stay where you are," Bastian bellowed. Everyone's jaws dropped when Bastian snarled loudly, pushing me closer to the truck. *This was turning from bad to worse,* I thought to myself. Cain just stared in disbelief.

"I understand you are angry, Alpha. I am her *mate*, and I'm pissed at what she did, but you cannot talk to her this way. I will not allow it, and I will not allow you to come any closer to my mate and child," Bastian shouted.

Cain's face suddenly twisted in anger. He took another step towards us then. "I said stand aside. That's a direct order."

His Alpha power surged to the surface, striking everyone nearby. The group had dropped to their knees and panic swept over me. *They're all in pain because of me,* I thought. *This was my fault— and yet I'm the only one who can't feel it.*

My aunt stormed over to Cain, shouting at him to stop, but he and Bastian were in a battle for dominance. No one was thinking clearly anymore and anger filled my core again. I tugged on my mate's arm, but he wouldn't budge. *Bastian was challenging him for me,* I realized. He, *again*, was going through something painful just to protect me. Guilt ate me up inside as I watched the two snarl at one another.

Was this all I was going to be for Bastian? I wondered. *Just another problem or a danger to him?* He was finally starting to feel Cain's Alpha power now, but he still refused to move, and I scrambled to figure out what to do to stop this. He should have dropped the moment he felt the Alpha's power, and it was amazing that he could even do this, but it was all stupid. *Just a pissing contest between the two.*

I barred my teeth and tried to move around Bastian, but he gripped me hard, forcing me to stop. His legs shook now, but he refused to move or look away. He wasn't going to give in. Suddenly, Bastian roared in pain, and my eyes widened. *That didn't sound like his wolf,* I thought.

Cain pulled his power back as he stared bewilderingly at Bastian. My mate's legs went solid again, and he rolled his shoulders to go again. My uncle blinked before barring his teeth and hitting Bastian with his power once more. I growled. *We were a family and families don't behave this way!*

CHAPTER 18

I yanked my hand away from my mate and got in between the two. I held my hands up shouting, "Stop it now! The both of you!"

I glared at them both, but neither one of them would budge. My chest warmed again, and my wolf surged to the surface. She seemed just as angry as I was and pushed something from the tips of my fingers. A new sensation bubbled forth from deep within my core and flung towards my uncle.

His face twisted in pain. For the first time, I could *see* the Alpha power from Cain and I. Cain's red power swirled with my white, and my eyes widened when I saw my power had coated my skin entirely. A solid white shield covered every inch of my skin, and Cain's power couldn't reach me. I had never seen anything like this before, and Cain winced again as my power struck him.

I looked to Bastian, who stood with a white shield around him as well, and I cocked my head to the side. *His was spotty*, I thought to myself. *Cain's power could still reach him but most was blocked. Was this why he's able to stand here as long as he did?*

I shook myself from those thoughts and turned to my uncle again. My wolf pushed for more power, and I trusted her guidance. I pushed more of my power from my fingertips, and Cain hissed in pain. His red Alpha power forcefully returned to his body, and I held my arm out until it was fully gone. My eyes widened when I tried to stop though. *It wasn't working*, I thought as I clenched my fist together. *I couldn't turn it off!*

Bastian's gripped my waist as I sucked in a deep breath and shut my eyes. *It's done*, I told myself. *Please just stop!* I tried telling myself over and over there was no more threat. Bastian was fine. I was fine. This was just a petty fight that pissed me off. I didn't need to lose my temper too. Going over the facts made my bear relent enough for me to shift back with the clan. *Maybe calming down would be enough to stop using my own power too?*

It took a moment longer, but my Alpha power slowly retreated back to me, and I released the breath I'd been holding. I opened my eyes, finding everyone staring at me with worried glances.

"I'm sorry, Uncle. I've never done that before, and it was too much. I don't know how to control it very well," I muttered, leaning back on Bastian for support. Today took a lot out of me, and I was thoroughly exhausted, but I felt bad for hurting my uncle. I felt bad for the whole day.

"Everyone needs to calm down. No more of this," shouted my aunt, "from any of you!" She gave her mate a very stern look, and he dropped his gaze, exposing his neck.

"You were right, Uncle Cain. I wasn't thinking about all the details. I just trusted my gut that this was the right call. That I needed to do this for the pack and clan. I think it was my bear guiding me, but whatever it was, I am sorry that I put everyone out and made you worry. You are my Alpha, and I didn't listen," I said as I turned to face Bastian. "And I am sorry you got hurt too. I never wanted to put you or this baby in danger."

My mate softened his expression and kissed my forehead as he tucked me back into his embrace.

"Bastian got hurt because he refused to fight the bear taunting him," I continued. "I was granted a meeting with my uncle Thomas and my dad before he showed up, but when I saw Bastian getting attacked, and Thomas was doing nothing to stop it, my bear came through, and I shifted."

"Into a white grizzly," Bastian added matter of factly.

Cade whistled, and my aunt put her hand to her mouth. Ash looked outright shocked as Aspen threw his hands in the air. Clearly, they all knew the significance of the color white with shifters. I was late to the game per usual. My uncle Cain remained silent though, still processing everything.

"My father said my need to protect Bastian is what pulled my bear out. It's my trigger until I learn how to shift on my own," I said, dropping my gaze. *I just wanted to sleep.* My body was wracked with exhaustion and stress, but I waited to find out what my punishment was for the little stunt I pulled today.

"She beat the snot out of the other bear, Alpha. She's a beast," Bastian added proudly. "Larger than Caleb."

"Good lord, and he's a tank!" Cade exclaimed.

Elijah nodded in agreement and ran his fingers through his hair as he looked to me. It took the three of them to deal with Caleb the other day.

CHAPTER 18

Cain finally spoke, "I take it the entire clan knows about Shanely then?"

At least he seemed calmer, I thought to myself. *But I knew better than to assume his anger had passed. The punishment was coming.*

"They probably do by now," I answered. "We drew a small portion of them out with my arrival and then again with the fight. Uncle Thomas knows everything though. About my parents and who I am."

Cain nodded slowly. "And what did he say?"

"That I apparently must take after him. That I amuse him," I replied with a sarcastic laugh.

"She seemed to soften him, Alpha," Bastian chimed in.

"Are they coming tomorrow?" my aunt asked.

I nodded. "He said a small portion would be present. Baby steps."

"You seem to be pushing us into a new era whether we are ready for it or not," Cain said softly. "There are no more baby steps."

I couldn't tell if he was proud or scared in that moment. Maybe a little of both. I wasn't sure, and I wasn't going to ask as I was still clearly in hot water.

"All I know is that the second that baby is born, Shanely is entering enforcer training! She can't seem to stay out of trouble," Uncle Ash practically shouted.

We all turned to look at him, surprised by his sudden outburst. It was enough to break the last of the tension though, and everyone started to laugh. Uncle Ash just threw his hands in the air.

"Well it's true," he muttered.

"I'm sorry, Bastian. I let my temper get the best of me, and my wolf saw you as a challenge and not as family," Uncle Cain said.

Bastian simply nodded his head towards my uncle. A silent response my uncle seemed to understand, and he smiled back.

"How did you two do that though?" Ryder asked.

Johnny chimed in, "Yeah, seriously that was painful. We couldn't even stand, and his Alpha power wasn't even directed towards us."

I shrugged. "I don't know. I've always felt my uncle's Alpha power, but it's never once hurt me or bound me like it does all you."

"I think being mated to Shanely seemed to help me. It wasn't as strong for me this time, but I can't really explain it. It was like we had a shield or something," Bastian said.

"Shanely has her own power," my uncle Cain stated sternly. "I felt it. It was strong and was pushing through mine with ease. It actually hurt me and made it hard to breathe."

"I could see your Alpha power, Uncle. Bastian was telling the truth about having a shield. It was like my power protected us from yours. Bastian's was just spottier than mine was, but I've never done that before."

"What does that mean, mate?" Aunt Cassia asked warily.

He rubbed his beard. "I don't know. I've never heard of a wolf being able to do that. Maybe it's because she's a mixer? But it's something to watch for and also best to stay between us. The fact that she's a white bear, makes me wonder if she will be a white wolf as well."

"I've seen her wolf, remember? She is a White Wolf," Bastian said calmly. "Her uncle told us about their own prophecy concerning the White Bear. It's a legend to them, I guess, as well as for us. They said it always signifies a great change."

Cain studied us a moment before looking at Aunt Cassia. "I've never heard of this before. She can't be the answer to both shifters, can she?"

Wait just one minute, I thought to myself. *The answer to what?* I wasn't here to answer some prophecy, if that's what they were all thinking. I didn't ask to be anything but me. I came here for a new life, adventure, and maybe to learn about the family I had. Not start a war or answer some prophecy. I wanted to stop my warnings from coming true and be with my family. For us all to be *safe*. The only way to do that was to blend the shifters together, which I was more than willing to fight for. I had already lost so much already, and I didn't want to give up anymore. But that *did not mean* becoming the prophetic answer to some legend I knew nothing about.

"What's so special about being white?" I asked sarcastically.

"White is just very rare in shifter society," Uncle Aspen answered. "It usually comes with a larger animal and a great deal of power."

CHAPTER 18

"She's meant to lead, Cain," Ash stated firmly.

"No, I'm not. I'm meant to get married and have this baby. I'm not challenging you, Uncle Cain. I don't want to be Alpha of the pack," I stammered.

Uncle Cain just looked at me with sorrowful eyes before lowering his gaze. My eyes widened as I had never seen him do that before. Not to *anyone* but Cassia.

"Let's not worry about anything right now," Cassia said as she approached me. She tossed her arm around me. "No one knows for sure what color your wolf is anyways. Come inside everyone, and let's just focus on the wedding for now. We need to iron out some details before tomorrow anyways. Bastian, Cade, and Elijah; your parents and sister are nearly here from the airport. They need to be informed of Shanely's status now before tomorrow. No surprises."

"When do they get in?" Bastian asked, with a shaky tone.

"Less than a half hour maybe. Enforcer Drake is bringing them here instead of the lodge, so we don't have much time," she replied as she ushered us inside.

Uncle Cain stopped me as I walked past, and without a word he hugged me tight. I hugged him back fiercely before following my aunt inside. Bastian and Cain spoke quietly before they followed too.

We all needed to discuss what to do now. Uncle Cain felt like he needed to inform the pack tonight before everyone was surprised by my new scent or by our new guests. He said this was big enough to call a special pack meeting, so he could announce it in person instead of using the mind-link. Cain and my other uncles left to deal with the pack shortly after that.

My aunt was looking in on my little one while we waited for Bastian's parents to arrive. The triplets seemed nervous about their parents showing up now, which did not make me feel better. They kept giving me sympathetic smiles, but they were whispering among themselves a lot. Bastian just looked stressed, and I was terrified that I just made everything worse by shifting into my bear, especially for them.

"I think you have a quick shifter in here," Aunt Cassia said, pulling my attention from the triplets.

"You think?"

"I do. You seem rounder than even this morning. I think because you're a mixer, it's progressing much faster than expected. I wouldn't be surprised if you go into labor early."

"How early are we talking?" I asked as my nerves began to unravel.

"I honestly don't know with you," she replied, pursing her lips together. "This is new territory for all of us, but Malin and I have been keeping a record of everything with you for future cases."

"You think there will be future cases like me?" I asked, sitting forward in my seat. That idea was something to think about. Shifters finding their mates wherever and creating more mixers with the pregnancies that would no doubt come from that.

"You seem to be changing everything, Shanely. Everyone who has learned the truth about you has changed. It's like you've affected all of us, and it's connecting us again. I can't help but wonder about this spreading throughout the world. We'll be ready for whatever happens though," she replied, with a smile.

I thought about that for a moment. Change could be good, but it's also nerve-wracking with the Division breathing down our necks. Things were smooth on that front, and I was not about to stir the pot with them. The world seems to have forgotten all about shifters, other than the made up stories and movies they created. I didn't want to deal with the Division nor do I want to put the pack or clan in harm's way, but the idea of combining our groups was something my heart wanted. Question is; how far will I push this? *Was I even supposed to heal the shifter world?* I thought to myself. My uncle's words rattled through my head again. *"Sometimes war comes even when you don't mean to start it."*

"You know you haven't come in to talk to me yet. Dr. Malin still wants you to talk about those dreams," Cassia said softly, and I slumped in my seat. "Have they been bad this week?"

I shrugged, not really wanting to discuss my warnings.

"She told me what happens in the dreams you mentioned. The fact that

CHAPTER 18

Bastian is having dreams too, makes me feel like this is more than just nightmares. I think you're sharing some of your new abilities with him."

My eyes widened. I didn't want Bastian to get this ability because it was just plain awful. I slowly looked his way. He was staring at the floor, completely lost in thought. *Haven't I cause enough trouble for him?*

"Malin mentioned seer abilities and what they mean, but honestly the whole thing scares me," I said, taking my eyes off my mate. "I've been getting dreams about our pack being annihilated by the Division, and then when I met Patrick, he triggered a new warning, except this one was years in the future. I have no idea how to prevent anything."

"I know, but the thing to remember is that it hasn't happened yet. It's not a guarantee anyways. You are listening to your shifter instincts, and as rocky as the path may be, it all seems to be for the best. Let's wait and see how frequent your dreams happen after your wedding. Maybe since you are mending relationships between the major shifter kinds here, it will change the warnings you are having."

I nodded, like it was really that simple. *There was nothing really to do but wait, I guess.*

"Can shifter's have more than one ability?" I asked.

She nodded. "It's rare to have more than one without a mate, but it's not impossible. You share through the bond."

"Bastian and I are both changing," I whispered softly. "It's frustrating because I haven't shifted to my wolf yet so our bond isn't complete, but I can sense everyone in the pack. Locating everyone is easy, no matter the distance for me. Now, I'm getting warnings, and Bastian has definitely grown in size, plus you heard him earlier. He sounded like a bear, and then there's the whole shield thing we have going on. I've never felt that power before. What exactly does this all mean?"

Cassia sighed as she reached for my hand. "I think it means you are a strong Alpha, Shanely. Bastian was too, and now because of your mating, the two of you are becoming something entirely new. We've never seen shifters like the both of you. Bastian does smell like a bear now, but I can't tell if it's because he's your mate and smells like you, or if he's somehow developed a bear to shift into as well. Your uncle and I have some theories, but even with those, we don't have anything concrete to guide us. There's no point stressing about everything right now, since we can't prove what your wolf is. It's not going to make you happy or be good for the baby."

I leaned back in my chair and thought about what she said. I thought about my life up until this point and how much it has really changed. Despite everything that had happened in my life, I was glad I was here. I finally felt like I truly belonged somewhere. I wanted to change things for the better for shifters, and I wanted to listen to whatever was guiding me inside, but I didn't want to take over the pack. I'm happy where I am. I just want to blend the family I do have, but Cassia was right. We didn't know anything, and we wouldn't until I shifted into my wolf. *Until then, I'm not going to worry about it,* I thought to myself. *I'm just going to be— me.*

"Aunt Cassia, can I ask you something?"

She nodded. "Ask away."

"What's the deal with you and your sibling's names?"

She laughed. "Our mother had a thing for tree names. Seemed to feel more at home in the woods than anywhere else. We all are named after a tree of some kind. I figured you were going to ask more about the White Wolf."

I shrugged. "I'm not sure I'm ready to hear it. A white grizzly has it's own prophecy, and it's a lot to carry. Right now, I don't want to be anything but Shanely."

She nodded solemnly. "I understand, but sometimes our destiny isn't as scary as it sounds."

Gravel crunched on my drive, and I turned to the sound.

"Your ears are getting better, my love," Bastian said to me as he extended out his hand. I took it and slowly forced myself to my feet.

"I guess so. This must be your parents?" I asked, and he nodded. We all heard the truck coming up the drive, and Cade and Elijah went outside first. I was grateful as it gave me and Bastian a moment.

"Are you ready for this?" he asked.

"As I'll ever be," I replied with a sigh.

CHAPTER 18

After the day I've had; what's one more thing?

Chapter 19

A black Expedition came to a stop as I stepped out on my front porch. My aunt passed me and stood in the front, being Alpha female and all, to greet our guests. A job I was glad I did not have right now because I just wanted to hide away in the safety of my home. My anxiety was already through the roof with the whole *white bear prophecy* and *"She is meant to lead,"* thing Ash said earlier. Meeting the parents of my mate was just icing on the cake, and now I scented like a bear. I wasn't sure how they were going to take the news of me being a mixer because there was no hiding it now.

The truck barely came to a stop before a thin, athletic girl bounded from the vehicle. She plowed into Elijah before turning to Cade. They were all smiling and talking at once that I knew right away she must be Bay. I couldn't contain my grin, watching the family reunite, and I nodded their way to Bastian, trying to give him a little push towards his sister. He simply smiled and remained by my side, turning his attention back to the Expedition. I frowned, noticing how rigid my mate was, and wondered if he was feeling nervous too.

Bay was gorgeous with long, brown hair in tight, kinky curls. She looked taller than I was but not quite the boy's height, and she had the same piercing blue eyes as Bastian. She wore jeans and a long sleeve shirt that fit her snugly, and she seemed unaffected by my scent. She was too busy greeting her brothers to notice me, and a small wave of relief washed over me. *Maybe they wouldn't care that I was a mixer?*

My relief was short lived though when a very tall, lean man with dark eyes stepped out of the back seat of the Expedition. I blinked, noticing

CHAPTER 19

how much my mate looked like him. *He was a spitting image of his dad*, I thought to myself. *But there was something off about him too.* Instead of Bastian's warmth, a haughty air clung to him, and I fell back a step, hiding in Bastian's shadows.

A small woman with perfect hair and a flowery dress stepped out of the truck then. The boys seemed to take after both parents as I saw many resemblances coming from her too. *The triplets got their eyes from her*, I thought as I smiled. She was pretty and held herself with dignity and respect. They were the Alpha pair in their pack in Denmark, and they behaved like royalty.

Both immediately recognized my scent when they inhaled deeply though, and their eyes found me right away. *Both* seemed alarmed by it, but Bastian's father looked down right angry after a moment. Tension filled the air, and when their dad stopped their mom from greeting Cade and Elijah, I just knew we were in for trouble.

My aunt tried to fill in the awkward silence by greeting them. "Liam! Michelle! It's good to see you again! Welcome back to McCoy lands."

They didn't respond. Bastian's father just glared at me, and then his eyes dropped to my rounded belly. I shrunk further away, covering my belly with my hands and feeling protective against his judgmental stare. Bastian's shoulders tense, and his eyes darkened.

"Mom, Dad," Cade said, trying to smooth things over. "It's good to see you!"

He and Elijah made their way over to their parents, and Liam momentarily took his eyes off mine to greet his boys finally. Bastian made no attempt to greet them.

Bay slowly made her way towards Bastian and I. She seemed cautious but not upset with me. I gave her a smile, which she returned, but before I could even say hello, Liam interrupted.

"That's close enough, Bay," her father commanded.

"Dad," Bastian growled out. "Let's be civil now."

"Civil?" Liam scoffed. "You freaking mated a mixer and didn't think to mention this? You could have saved us a trip, son."

My eyes widened as his father spoke. It felt like a slap to my face, and he sounded like he was just done with Bastian simply because *I'm his mate. Would he really give up his son because of me?* I wondered. The thought of being the reason why Bastian didn't have a family anymore tore at my heart. *Here I was, yet again, hurting Bastian, even if it was indirect.* I lowered my head in shame, wishing the ground would just swallow me whole, but Bastian wouldn't let my hand go. His grip only tightened, and I didn't know to do to fix this.

I stole a peek at him, but his murderous glare was directed at his father. His eyes were no longer blue but shifter gold with something else mixed in this time. There was a small hint of another color swirling in his eyes. I tried to look closer, when my aunt spoke.

"Liam, that's not fair—" my aunt said, but Liam wasn't listening.

"I trusted you with my sons!" he shouted, pointing his finger angrily at my aunt, "and this is what you allowed to happen? I was told he mated your niece! Not some mixer, Cassia. This was supposed to be what made Bastian finally take his birth right, but now—"

Liam glared in my direction, and Bastian pulled me behind him to shield me. I could feel Bastian's anger trickling from the incomplete bond, and I just felt worse. I leaned my head against his back as tears filled my eyes. *I've ruined everything for Bastian,* I thought to myself. I was glad he taught me how to block my thoughts because I didn't want him to know what I was feeling. It would just be one more thing he'd take blame for, so I shut our bond down tight. Bastian turned briefly to look at me, but I refused to look up at him.

Bastian turned back to his father, and I stole a peek around him. Cade pulled away from Liam, while Elijah did the same with their mother, who had yet to speak. She looked surprised, and almost proud of her sons, but the look was gone by the time I blinked. I don't think anyone else even caught it, but she quickly schooled her face to look stoic and unaffected.

Liam scowled as Cade and Elijah took their stance in front of Bastian and I. They both crossed their arms and glared right back at their dad. *Oh my God, they were making a choice,* I thought to myself. *I was making them lose*

CHAPTER 19

their family too.

"That's enough, Dad. You don't know the full story," Cade said angrily.

"She's more than just a mixer. You need to listen and hear Bastian out for once," Elijah chimed in.

"You've turned all my sons against me now?" Liam asked, tossing his hands in the air. "Against their natural wolf side, Cassia?"

"No one is going against you, but your tone and words are harsh and disrespectful to the rightful heir of the McCoy Pack. I suggest you restart and apologize," my aunt said forcefully. She sounded like a Queen, and I'll bet my uncle would be proud if he heard. *He should be here with her, but he's off putting out another one of my fires.* Guilt stabbed me in the heart even more.

Liam glared back at me. "She's no heir," he snapped. "She's not even a true wolf. Bay, get in the car."

"Dad—" Bay muttered, "stop *please*. Let's just hear them out and see what's going on first."

"Now you? Do I not have any loyal heirs left?" he shouted, and Bastian tightened his grip on my hand. To the point it started to hurt.

"Fine," Liam snarled, "if you want to stay and *listen* so badly, then you can live with your brothers and that thing! Michelle in the car now. We're going home."

"Liam—" Michelle's voice trailed off when Liam snarled at her. She dropped her gaze and promptly moved towards the Expedition, and my eyes widened.

God, he was a bully! I thought, clenching my fists together, but then I looked to my mate. My utterly perfect, loving, and kind mate. *Was this his childhood? Were we more similar than I realized?*

"So, that's it? You're just going to refuse to meet your own son's fated mate! You're going to walk away from your grandchild all because Shanely is half-bear?" Bastian snapped as he finally let me go. He was furious as he stepped down in between his brothers and snarled.

"That freak of nature in her belly is not my grandchild! I can smell it! It's just like it's mother," his father snarled.

"That is my child!" Bastian growled. "Being a father means more than just blood."

Liam rolled his eyes. "A mixer, Bastian? I mean *that's* what you're really going to tie yourself down too? What you're giving everything up for? She's beneath you and frankly shouldn't exist. You condemned yourself when you didn't reject her and take another."

Bastian's growl turned into a ferocious roar, and I heard a faint growl of a bear pull through. Cade and Elijah joined in. Not batting an eye over what their brother sounded like.

Michelle took a step back, and Bay looked equally startled at them. She put her hand to her mouth, and her eyes went back and forth between her father and her brothers, but Liam just looked disgusted.

"Careful now, Bastian. You're starting to sound like a bear," Liam replied coldly.

"Good!" Bastian bellowed as he pushed past his brothers. "I'm glad I do because it's one more thing to separate me from you! I sincerely hope it's an ability Shanely shares with me, so you can spend the rest of your life knowing that your *prized* son, the one groomed since birth to take the throne, is a *mixer*. That he's a bear shifter too, and that he doesn't *need* you. I want you to spend the rest of your miserable life knowing I want nothing to do with you or your throne ever again. You are no longer welcome on my land or near my mate!"

My heart broke. Bastian just cut ties with his family permanently, and it was all my fault. My stomach twisted as I shrunk further in the shadows on the porch, feeling more like a coward than ever before.

Liam's eyes went wide as he visibly shook with fury. Michelle put her hand on his shoulder, but he yanked it off and stepped towards Bastian.

"Fine with me. You are hereby stripped of your birthright," Liam replied harshly, and Bastian sucked in a deep breath. He grabbed his chest, and I could hear him struggling to breathe. I could almost *feel* his heart race in my own chest, and it was scary how fast it was.

I ran to him, throwing my arms around him as I searched his face. Bastian struggled for a moment longer, shutting his eyes tight as whatever Liam did ran through his system. Suddenly, his breathing leveled out, and when he opened his eyes, he merely gave his father a savage smile. My eyes widened. *He looked almost— relieved.*

"Elijah, you are next in line. Are you staying with this abomination or will you be smart and return home to take the birthright?" Liam asked, putting his hands on his hips.

Bastian's smile fell, and he finally took his focus off his father to look at his brother. His face softened as he whispered, "It's okay if you want to go back."

Elijah just gave him a pointed look right back before stepping forward.

"I reject the birthright," Elijah replied confidently.

My heart hurt as Elijah clutched his chest, breathing rapidly just like Bastian had. He staggered a bit before getting his bearings. *This was all my fault*, I thought as Elijah took his place next to me and Bastian. I extended my hand, and Elijah squeezed it tightly.

"Cade?"

"I reject the birthright," Cade announced without hesitation and grabbed his chest. A single tear rolled down my cheek as I went to my brother-in-law.

"Cade—" I whispered. He gave me a sad smile before kissing my cheek and tucking me back behind Bastian. Cade joined his brothers, drawing a line right in front of me. *They all chose me— they chose me over their own blood. I just ruined my mate's family.*

"Great," Liam muttered. "I have no heirs. No sons left."

"It didn't need to be this way," Bastian replied in a low tone.

"You're right. I should have never let you come here. None of this would have happened then," Liam replied.

"Dad? Did you give me the birthright?" Bay squeaked out. She rubbed her chest hard enough to make her skin turn bright red.

Liam just shook his head angrily. "I'm sorry Bay, but females don't lead. We still stick to our traditions unlike these wolves. You've been stripped of the birthright, Bay."

"Liam!" Michelle cried out as Bay dropped to the ground.

Elijah ran to her but couldn't catch her in time. She landed in the dirt with a harsh thud, groaning as her breathing increased. It looked like she was having a full blown panic attack, and my heart broke even further.

"Get in the car, Bay," Liam demanded, and I nearly snarled.

"Seriously? You're still going to boss her around after doing that to her? You know how painful that is!" Cade shouted angrily.

"She's my daughter, Cade! She knows that females don't lead. It's nothing personal," he shouted back.

"Not personal? She can barely breathe! You know the pain that comes with stripping the birthright!" Bastian yelled as he stepped closer to his father.

"Enough Bastian! Bay decide now because I have had just about enough of this place. Get in the car or stay here. I really don't care at this point."

She looked vexed by her dad, and I staggered on my footing. My jaw dropped as I watched the whole evening unfold into one of the worst evenings of my life. Liam was just abandoning all his children and said it didn't *matter* anymore. *How could a father do this?* I thought. Especially over something as silly as being a mixer. Suddenly, my bear rose to the surface, snapping her jaws, and wanting out, and it was all I could to do keep her back.

Bay narrowed her eyes as Elijah helped her stand, but she refused to answer her father. She just glared at him, and I felt horrible watching the family fall apart. Liam grunted, pulling Michelle back into the car without another word, and it slowly disappeared down the drive.

Silence filled the woods as that wretched man left our property, and I slowly looked to the Fenrir family. *Well, what's left of the Fenrir family,* I thought to myself. *I caused all this damage for them.* I *destroyed* their family. I looked to the ground, my eyes filling with unshed tears, and Bastian gripped my chin firmly. He tried to get me to look in his eyes, but I just couldn't. I gently pulled away, and he let me.

"Shanely—"

"I am so sorry," I spat out, wiping my eyes before the tears fell. "To *all* of you. I ruined your family. This is all my fault."

CHAPTER 19

Bastian frowned, tapping my chin so I'd look at him. This time I held his gaze because no matter how you looked at it, I was the one to blame. I was the mixer. I was the one who ran off the day before my wedding and shifted into a bear. I couldn't even wait until after we were married before doing something so reckless. Now Bastian won't have his family at his wedding. They won't be here for any of life's major milestones because I did a stupid thing and threw my scent off. Bastian's face softened as if he could read my thoughts and believed them. I looked away then.

Bay shook her head saying, "It's not your fault. Dad's never been good with change or other shifters for that matter. It's nice to finally meet you though, Shanely."

"You mean Dad's good at being a jerk," Elijah said in a snarky tone.

"It's good to meet you too, Bay," I replied, trying to force a smile to my lips.

Bastian walked over to me and placed both hands on the side of my face, stilling me as got close. "*None* of this is your fault, Shanely. There are things you don't know, but you didn't make us choose a side. He did, and I will always choose you, my love. *You* are my family, and I'm not sad to let him leave. I am so sorry you had to hear all those things though. He was wrong about you, Shanely."

My brows furrowed by his response, and my stomach twisted inside. All I could think was what horrors had my mate endured growing up? He seemed so happy that it was hard to imagine he had a rough childhood, but I felt like a fool for assuming. His lips suddenly kissed my cheek, and he leaned in close to whisper, "Open the bond up, mate. I'm not asking either."

My own breath caught at hearing his demand as I slowly dragged my eyes up his body until I met his gaze. His eyes were gold again with that extra color, and I noticed it was a reddish streak that mixed beautifully with the gold. Bastian was breathtaking.

"*And if I don't?*"

A faint growl emitted from his lips as he heard my link, and I smirked when he shook his head and smacked my backside.

"Cheeky mate," he muttered as he reached for Bay. He pulled her into a hug saying, "I'm sorry for dragging you into this. I didn't mean to get you kicked out, Bay."

"Dad kicked me out, not you. Honestly, I think he's been looking for an excuse anyways. I've not been the easiest to deal with lately," she replied sheepishly. "Besides he's wrong. He can't interfere with mate bonds. They're sacred, and he should know better."

Bastian nodded, and Cade hugged me, pulling me from their conversation. "You okay, Baby Girl?"

I nodded, but we both knew I was lying. Today had been too much, and I couldn't help but hear Liam's insults over again in my head. *"I had been in three fights or disagreements today. With Michael, my uncle, and now Bastian's father, and each one got Bastian hurt in some way. I was the worst mate ever."*

"Hey, ignore my father. He was wrong about you and our baby. You are the best thing that ever happened to me, okay? If my parents can't see that, then I don't want them in our lives anyways. And I'm fine mate. To me, it's an honor every time I get to protect you or take care of you. This is what I was made for," Bastian said, hearing my internal monologue. *I forgot I had broadcasted everything just now.*

My aunt Cassia walked up to our group. "I've informed your uncle, love. He's furious but said he would deal with Liam himself. Bay, you are officially welcome to join our pack. We would love to have you stay here with us. You will feel the sharp pain of disconnection as your brothers did when they joined, but it should pass quickly. Prepare yourself though as yours will be more painful than theirs were."

"Thank you for letting me join your pack. I appreciate you taking me in and all, but where will I live? Dad drove off with my stuff. I really don't want to be a burden to anyone and would like to make my own way," she asked.

"You're welcome here with us. Your brothers practically live here anyways, so it will be nice to have another girl around," I offered, with a smile.

"Aww, you know you love having us around, Baby Girl," Cade chimed in as he gave me a side hug. Elijah smirked, poking me in my sides and

CHAPTER 19

making me jump.

She returned my smile as she watched our interaction closely. "Thank you, Shanely."

"I should return to the lodge. This has been an eventful day, and we still have much to do. I'll see you all bright and early," Aunt Cassia said as she gave us all one last look before shifting and running home.

"I say let's end this day! I don't know about all of you, but I don't think I can handle anymore drama," Cade exclaimed.

We all grumbled and nodded in agreement. Bastian and I hung back some, letting the others go ahead of us.

"I think we need to add some new additions to the cabin, Bastian. Your brothers and sister can't sleep on the floor and couch forever."

I watched as Cade and Elijah led Bay into the cabin, excited to give her the grand tour. *Everyone seemed happy and content here,* I thought to myself. *If they felt like this was home, then I wanted them to stay.* Honestly, the idea of not having them so close gave me anxiety. I had become attached to all three of the Fenrir brothers, and I didn't want my family to stay anywhere else than with us.

Bastian smiled at me as he pulled me in close. "You want them to stay? Like live with us?"

"I honestly can't imagine my home without your brothers. I'm sure I'll feel the same with your sister. Besides, she just lost everything because of me. It's the least I can do," I replied. I turned to look at him now. "I mean, are you okay sharing the cabin with them?"

"I love the idea, mate. Just hearing you ask for them to stay means the world to me. I love you, Shanely," he whispered as he kissed my cheek.

"I love you too, Bastian."

But this time my lips found his, and I kissed him hard. I needed him, and he needed me, and I was going to enjoy this moment before something else ruined it.

Chapter 20

I awoke to a small knock on my door.

I cracked one of my eyes open and was nearly blinded by the sunlight. I groaned as I rolled away. The blinds were wide open, and I covered my head with my blanket. *I bet Bastian opened them on purpose.*

Another knock sounded, and I groaned again. I didn't want to get up. *Maybe they'll just go away if I stay quiet enough?* Silence filled the room, and I smiled as I buried myself even further under the blankets, until another knocked sounded, and my smile fell.

"Shanely? Your aunt called a few minutes ago. She said we're needed at the lodge now. Bastian and my brothers left a while ago to get ready themselves, and I don't really know where to go."

Bay. I had momentarily forgotten she was here. The events of last night replayed in my head. She awoke in the middle of the night in extreme pain. Her scream startled us all, and we were wide awake, trying to help her through the pain of losing her pack bonds. Her father permanently severed the bond but waited until the middle of the night to do it. The boys had it easier, I guess, since it wasn't an outright expulsion. They simply broke on good terms because the boys were supposed to return one day, but Bay's was completely different. She was in pain for a while before finally collapsing from exhaustion. No one slept well after that.

"Shanely? Are you awake?"

"I'm up! I'll be quick in the shower, and then we can head out," I hollered back, waiting until her steps retreated back to the kitchen. Now that I unlocked my bear form, all of my senses had improved. It wasn't perfect,

CHAPTER 20

but it was still something to adjust to.

I walked in the bathroom and gasped when I saw my reflection. My hands went to my belly, which was a whole lot bigger than it was the night before. *My little shifter was growing quickly, and it wouldn't be long before he or she was here,* I thought as I lifted my shirt.

I gave myself a minute to picture myself as a mom. Most of my pregnancy I've been apprehensive about the whole thing. I wasn't really sure how to be a mom, but I wanted to be a good one.

I frowned then, realizing Bastian and I had never even thought about baby names. We've been so busy, trying to juggle everything that was being thrown at us, that we never got a chance to discuss names. *We should have one ready,* I thought, pursing my lips together while I tried to come up with something. *I liked the name Benjamin for a boy. Maybe Cole? Or Bellamy.* I had always loved that name and wondered if Bastian would like it too.

The clock in the bathroom chimed, and I pulled myself from those thoughts. It was time to get moving. *It was my wedding day after all.* I smiled before I quickly showered and ran out to meet Bay.

"Whoa, you grew in size," she exclaimed, eyeing my belly.

I laughed. "I should be offended, but I did, didn't I?"

Bay laughed out loud. "I didn't mean it that way, sorry! My brothers say I have no filter."

"It's fine. I'm not easily offended," I replied as I grabbed an apple and quickly grabbed my sneakers. I frowned as I tried to lean down to tie them. My belly was actually getting in the way, and I turned, trying a different angle.

"Here," Bay said, with a giggle, "let me."

"Thank you," I replied, lifting my foot towards her. "So, you're 17?"

She nodded. "Yup. I turn 18 in like a month actually."

"Have you found your mate yet?" I asked casually.

She laughed again. "Thankfully, no. Otherwise, we'd be forever separated."

Bay had a point, I thought to myself.

"Well, who knows?" I said, with a grin. "Maybe he's here."

"I doubt that. My pack used to tease me that I was destined to remain alone because I'm so difficult. I'm thinking they might be right. Besides wolves drive me crazy."

"That's kind of cruel," I replied, taking another bite of my apple.

She shrugged. "It's fine. I was a terror growing up."

"You don't seem that bad," I countered.

"This is just the surface. The Bay I let everyone see now. Growing up, I always wanted to prove myself to my father. He favored the boys, and I had to be just like them. Then when they left, I just seemed to struggle to find my place. Well, up until about a year ago. I found a hobby that I'm really good at. It's a good outlet for me, especially back home, but I don't think most could handle who I really am," she replied as she stood up, helping me to my feet.

I pursed my lips together. *She seemed a little guarded, but I don't think it had anything to do with me,* I thought as she gathered her own shoes and jacket. She seemed almost as lost as I was growing up in the system, and I felt for her. I was happy she found something to help her through it all though, but I wanted to do whatever I could to help her here.

We locked the back door and made our way down the trail to the lodge. I was proud of myself for knowing how to get there all on my own.

I was surprised to find no enforcers waiting around to guide us though. I tried my senses first, and I didn't smell any wolves nor did I see anything. *Maybe Bastian trusted us to get there on time without any issue?* I beamed at that thought. I hated being a burden to the pack here, and I know they watched over me more than anyone else. But a nagging feeling in the back of my mind had me using my new skill anyways.

I had gotten fairly decent at switching it on and off and pulled on the pack bonds. I saw four wolves, two on either side of the trail, slowly following us, and I rolled my eyes. *I should have known he'd send someone,* I thought to myself. I almost giggled, and Bay eyed me funny. I just shook my head, not really able to explain it without it making zero sense.

I decided to keep her talking instead. I was curious about her and her life with her brothers back in Denmark, and I hated how she viewed herself. I hated she seemed so lost like I used to feel so I nudged her gently. "You don't really seem like the rebel type. No offense."

"You'd be surprised. Looks can be deceiving after all," she smirked.

"Try me."

"You really want to know?" she asked, raising a brow.

I carefully stepped over a root, making sure I didn't trip. *That was the last thing I needed.*

"Yeah, I do. We are family after all, and I'd like us to be close. I never had siblings until I came here, but you are my first sister so tell me. What's this hobby of yours that you're so good at?"

We had made it half-way down the trail already, and I could see she wasn't sure whether she should say anything or not. She studied me for a moment, and I raised my eyebrows. *How bad was it?* I thought to myself.

"Alright, but don't mention it to the triplets, please. They'll just go all caveman on me, and I don't want them to interfere with anything right now. I'm going to just figure out my new life here for now, and they'll feel the need to lecture me over it. I can't do anything with it right now anyways. Deal?"

"I don't really like keeping secrets from Bastian. I have in the past, even just briefly, and it always hurts him. I don't want to lie to your brother, Bay. You have to promise to tell them at some point."

She thought about it for a moment. "Deal. I turn 18 soon anyways, so I only need the secret until then, and it would be nice to have someone to tell. I'm pretty excited about it really, but I'm a cage fighter. Like a *really* good one. I've made a name for myself back home."

"You're a what?"

My jaw dropped. I was expecting something like she's an artist or something, not *this*. She did *not* look like she was fighting for a living. She looked strong and athletic, sure, but not a fighter.

"I found the ring one night after I left the compound. I was angry and stumbled upon the underground ring. They were short a fighter, so I volunteered. No one believed I could fight though, and they all laughed at me. When I insisted, they said why not and started making bets against me. They all lost a lot of money that night, and I got to release a whole lot of stress. Plus, seeing their smiles fade quickly was the best. I annihilated their fighter in less than a minute and even made decent money too that night. I fight in the human's underground ring occasionally but mostly just in the shifter ring."

"Wait, you fight as a wolf?"

She eyed me cautiously, and I could hear the shift in her tone. "It's really not that bad, Shanely. I have Alpha traits, despite what my father says, so my wolf is larger than most. The only ones I really keep an eye on are tigers. They're crazy strong."

"Whoa, back up. You're fighting tigers!? And you want me to keep this from your brother, my mate? I mean, do you really not know Bastian? He'll sniff out a secret like this in no time!" I stammered on, and she rolled her eyes.

"I knew you wouldn't handle this well."

"Hey, I'm handling this all just fine, thank you very much. It's a little shocking to hear, but seriously Bay, you need to be careful. I think your career is over though. There aren't any rings around here."

She smirked again, and I could see the wildness in her eyes. A bad feeling hit the pit of my stomach then.

"Oh, there are," she said, with a grin. "I've heard of them, but don't worry about me. My parents disowned me, but I was doing alright, even under their thumb. Now, I'm a free woman! I don't need anyone deciding my fate ever again, but I do love knowing my father was always intimidated by Mor'du. He never knew it was his own daughter."

"Mor'du?" I asked.

"That's my fighting name. It's Scottish like from that one kids movie," she replied as I slowly grinned.

"What?" she stammered. "I loved that movie growing up, and I couldn't give out my real name!"

"Isn't Mor'du a bear though?" I asked, chuckling to myself.

She laughed hard. "It was just icing on the cake really. Another slap towards my dad."

I completely lost it then. I was laughing so hard my sides began to hurt, and soon she was laughing too. By the time the lodge came into view, we were both crying from laughing so hard.

"Thank you for sharing with me," I said as I hugged her. "I don't think I've ever laughed that hard before."

"Just please, don't tell them? Not yet," she begged me.

"Alright. Just don't fight before telling them. They mean well, and I'm sure you all can come to some kind of understanding. Plus, then I won't be lying when I tell him you only told me about back home stuff," I said.

She nodded and whispered, "Thank you, Shanely."

I gave my new sister a smile before looking around the lodge. There were a great many people running about now, and they all had jobs to do. Some were carrying flowers or trays of food, while others carried heavier items like folding tables and chairs. I felt bad that I hadn't really done anything to help set up. Everyone was smiling and seemed cheery, but this was my wedding. *I should help somewhat,* I thought to myself.

I started towards a few guys carrying chairs with Bay right behind me. I turned many heads as I walked by. They tried to pretend they didn't notice my belly or my new scent, but even I knew both were shocking. Some even congratulated me as they passed by, which was a pleasant surprise.

"Can I help you guys?" I offered.

They smiled at me before their eyes dropped to my belly. They both looked kind, but I could see the look they passed between themselves.

"We appreciate the offer Miss, but you best not be carrying any chairs. You're already carrying precious cargo," the one on the left said as he picked up another chair.

"I don't mind!" I went on as I tried to take a chair, but the wolf pulled away.

"We're happy to help, Miss Shanely. Thank you, but we've got it. Besides, Bastian would be pissed if he found out we let you carry the chairs down the hill. No offense, but I don't want to make that wolf mad," he said, with a laugh.

"Ain't that the truth. Go, Miss Shanely. We are honored to help make your day special, and we look forward to getting to know you better too."

The two wolves smiled once more and carried on their way as I turned to Bay defeated. She just chuckled and pushed me to the lodge. "Seems big brother has a reputation. Come on, let's go!"

I looked around to see if anyone else needed help, but she kept pushing me forward. We entered the lodge, which was just as busy inside as it was outside, and my aunt spotted us right away.

"There you are! Come on. Let's get ready upstairs before the boys come out. They're getting ready downstairs," she said, pushing us to the stairs.

I had plenty of time to get ready, I thought to myself, but my aunt wasn't having it. She ushered us quickly to the bedrooms on the second floor, and I finally gave up trying to help. *No one would let me anyways.* Bay looked a little uneasy as my aunt opened the door.

"You okay?" I asked before going in.

"Yeah, I'm fine. I just don't know where to go now. I don't even have a dress," she said, looking to the floor then.

"Bay, you belong here with me," I said as I hugged her. "You're going to stand with me, right?"

"Really? You barely know me, Shanely. Wouldn't you rather have your friends?"

"Bay, we're sisters now. I'd love you to be up there with me," I replied.

She quickly wiped her eyes. I hated that she felt so out of place right now, and it made me so angry to know it was all because Liam dumped her here. *How a father could do that to his child was beyond me.*

"I don't even have a dress, Shanely. My father kept my bags," she said quietly.

"Yes, you do!" my aunt cried through the door. I pulled Bay inside as my aunt carried a few dress bags in from the closet.

"I had an extra brought in from the shop this morning. With everything going on, I forgot to mention it!"

"This one is Shanely's," she said, handing me the largest bag. "Here is the one for Bay, and this one is mine."

"Who's the other dress for?" I asked as someone knocked on the door.

CHAPTER 20

"Come in!" Aunt Cassia hollered, without answering me.

The door opened, and Alana peeked her head in. "I was told to come up here."

"Alana!" I ran over and hugged her.

"Whoa, you got big!"

I laughed. "I think the baby wants out!"

"Good thing we went with the dress we did. I knew there was something different with you. Just being part of my family wasn't my first thought," she giggled.

"Alana, your dress is here!" my aunt said as she handed her a bag.

"Thank you, Aunt Cassia," I whispered as she passed. She just winked at me.

"How was it entering wolf lands?" Bay asked, and I noticed she seemed fairly alright with Alana being here with us. I smiled softly to myself.

"It was a little awkward, but no one was rude or anything," she said. My brows rose as I turned to my aunt.

"The vast majority of the pack took the news rather well. I'd say considering," Aunt Cassia said.

"The vast majority?" I asked.

She sighed. "You can't please everyone. Some are not joining us today."

"Let me guess Derek and his evil spawns?"

My aunt just gave me a small smile but didn't answer. *Fine with me!* I thought to myself. *I really didn't want to see Emma or her family anyways.*

We spent the next couple hours getting ready and snacking. I was so thankful my aunt had someone bring up food because I was starving and that apple just wasn't cutting it. I snuck a peek out my window once my dress was on, and my hair was done, and saw the bear clan just starting to arrive. My uncles, Ash and Aspen, were all out front greeting everyone and leading them to the back yard. *Everything was going smoothly,* I thought, when someone knocked at my door.

My father popped his head in, and I giggled as his hand covered his eyes entirely. "Everyone decent?"

I laughed. "Yes, come in!"

He dropped his hands and stopped dead in his tracks when he saw me.

"Shanely, you look beautiful. Just like your mother," he said as he smiled at me.

I gave him a twirl, and he chuckled. "Thanks, Daddy."

I hugged him tight, and my heart swelled in joy. *Everything was perfect now,* I thought to myself. His eyes suddenly dropped to my necklace, and he stilled. His hands started to reach for it, but he decided against it and dropped his hands to his side.

"What is it?"

His brows bunched together as if lost in a memory, but he answered, "That's the necklace I gave your mother."

My eyes widened. I grabbed my necklace, studying it like I had a thousand times. Emotion gripped my heart as I asked, "This came from you?"

Dad nodded slowly. "I didn't notice it before. I thought it was lost with her, but I gave it to her right after we found out we were mates. I wanted to give her a ring, but I couldn't so I bought this instead. I figured no one would ever question it."

"It was left to me when I went into the foster system. I've always had it with me," I replied as tears formed in my eyes.

He gently rubbed the side of my face before saying, "She would have wanted you to have it. It's a way for her to be apart of this day with us."

"It belongs to you though. You need to have a part of her too," I said as I started to take it off.

My dad stopped me. "No, please. It's where it should be. Besides, I do have a part of her still and that's you."

He kissed my forehead, and I held onto my dad for a while. *I needed this. I needed him my whole life, and I can't believe it took me this long to find him.* It just wasn't fair, but at least I had him now.

"Your uncle Cain told me about your request that he initially denied, but seeing how this is no longer a secret— may I have the honor of walking you down the aisle?"

I nodded yes, afraid I'd start crying if I tried to speak, and he gently wiped a tear away. *I was actually getting to live out one of my dreams since I was a little girl*, I thought. My biological father was about to walk me down the aisle. This was nothing short of a gift. One I would cherish forever. Dad beamed at me and extended his arm out.

"I never thought I'd have this privilege, Shanely. It's all thanks to your grandmother for dragging you back to my world again. I wish I could thank her for all she's done for us."

"Oh no, no! No tears! We don't have time to fix your makeup! It's time to go!" my aunt Cassia interrupted as she ushered us out into the hall.

I chuckled, trying to pull myself together, and smiled wide when I saw Alana and Bay. Both were stunning in the black, strapless, flowing dresses my aunt picked out. *They were simple, yet stunning. My aunt did a great job with the selection.*

We made our way down the stairs, where Cade and Elijah were already waiting. They looked gorgeous in their white tuxes, and they both *oohed* and *awed* at us girls before kissing our cheeks. It was crazy to know that these wonderful gentlemen came from such a wicked man. They didn't take a single trait from him, and I was proud to call them family. I would *never* abandon them.

We quickly lined up and made our way to the back doors. Alana walked down with Cade, while Elijah escorted Bay. Everyone looked so lovely together, but I was anxious to find my mate though. I missed him.

Soon, it was our turn, and I saw so many faces turning to look at me. My eyes widened as my stomach lurched itself into my throat. I dug my heels in, freezing as the entire pack and clan stared at me.

My father wrapped my arm around his and gave me a wink before forcing me to the doorway.

"I've got you," he said softly. "I will always be here for you."

My heart swelled, and some of my nerves faded. He patted my hand, and we stepped outside.

The aisle was long to accommodate both the pack and clan. The pack had put screens up on the outside of the chairs, so the ones in the back could still see the ceremony clearly. Cade and Alana had made it to the end by the time we finally started walking.

As soon as I stepped on the white pathway, I heard the song. Our pack's sacred song. Everyone stood and started to sing.

My mother told me someday I would buy
Galleys with long oars
Sail to distant shores
Stand up on the prow
Noble barque I steer
Steady course to the Haven
Hew many foe-man
Hew many foe-man

"Just breathe baby," my dad whispered, but I was lost in their singing.

My chest warmed as my wolf beamed inside. She felt happy, so ridiculously happy, and I wished she'd come out to see the pack herself. Maybe not in this moment, but soon because this was beautiful.

The bear clan started to stomp and clap to the song's beat, along with the ones playing the music. They sang a different song, harmonizing with the wolves well. My heart swelled, seeing them contribute to our special occasion. I smiled at everyone that we passed, but soon my entire focus zeroed in on one person. Bastian.

He was breathtaking in his tux, and by the look on his face he was captivated by me too. His tux was all black, and his hair was freshly cut and styled. It looked messy but sexy. His beard was trimmed too and was a lot shorter and closer to his face than before. Everything about him just screamed sexy, and it was hard to focus on anything else. I couldn't believe *he* was all *mine*. My cheeks turned red from his intense stare. His eyes seemed to tell me he had only one thing on his mind as they raked up and down my body.

"You're beautiful, Shanely."

Unable to contain my smiles, I answered him.

"*You look pretty good yourself, Mr. Fenrir.*"

He gave me a crooked grin.

CHAPTER 20

"I can't wait to officially call you Mrs. Fenrir."

I felt like I was going to burst from the joy I was feeling. *How did I get so lucky to have him for a mate?*

My uncle Cain stood at the end as we approached them. I smiled, seeing my brother Caleb standing directly next to Bastian, which I thought was incredibly sweet. *He must have walked in with Bastian,* I thought as my eyes drifted back to my wonderful mate.

The girls stood off to the left, while the boys were on the right. All my immediate family were in the front few rows, regardless of which shifter they were, which was the way it should be.

My dad kissed my cheek and handed me to Bastian before standing next to Thomas. Bastian's eyes suddenly flashed gold before he quickly yanked me forward and kissed me. His lips met mine, and it felt like the rest of the world just disappeared. It was just the two of us, and I didn't want to come up for air. I wanted to stay tangled up with him forever.

Uncle Cain cleared his throat as everyone started whistling and catcalling. It broke the fantasy we were in, and I pulled back, blushing as I hid from the crowd. Bastian just gave everyone a boyish grin.

Bastian gave my uncle a shrug. "I couldn't wait any longer."

The crowd around us *awed* at that comment, but my uncle proceeded to roll his eyes.

"Anyways— we're here today for the marriage between Shanely McCoy and Bastian Fenrir. Now officially connecting them together in every way possible."

He spoke for a few more minutes about how sacred mate bonds were before he asked who gave this woman to be married. I've never seen my father so emotional and proud as he stood up in front of everyone and declared, "I do."

Then Uncle Cain had us recite our vows. I jumbled through mine, struggling to put into words how much Bastian meant to me, even though we only knew each other for a short amount of time. It was like I had so much to say, and it all needed to be said at the exact same moment, but Bastian didn't seem to mind as he gently stroked my cheek. I leaned into his hand, needing his touch as much as he needed mine.

Next was Bastian's turn. Bastian's vows were pure and full of love. He spoke with such confidence and kindness and to hear how he truly felt about me was something I will always cherish. Especially after all the hate I've received just for existing.

"Do you Bastian Lee Fenrir take Shanely J McCoy to be your lawfully wedded wife? Your mate and protector?"

"I do, sir."

I smiled back at Bastian, and my uncle asked me the next question.

"Do you Shanely J McCoy take Bastian Lee Fenrir to be your lawfully wedded husband? Your mate and protector?"

"I do."

"Bastian, do you have the rings?" my uncle asked.

I gave Bastian an odd look. *He never mentioned getting rings for us*, I thought. Shifters go either way when it comes to rings. Some wanted them, while others just wanted the bond. They didn't want human traditions, and I told Bastian that he could decide what he wanted when it came to them, but he never mentioned anything to me before. Bastian simply winked at me, and I cocked my head to the side, wondering what he was up to.

"This is my gift for you," Bastian whispered as Caleb handed him a small box. He opened it and inside were two *beautiful* rings. His ring was thicker than mine, but they were both matching silver. Bastian had vines etched into the sides of his ring, with two golden wolves on either side of the small amber that sat in the middle.

My ring matched his, but instead of the vines, my ring had a wolf on one side and a bear on the other. Three beautiful square diamonds sat in between them, and my hand covered my mouth in awe. They were beautiful, and I was in absolute love with them. I have never really worn a lot of jewelry, but these were *perfect*.

"Remember when you questioned what I did for a living, and I told you that I would always be able to take care of you? Well, this is just something I am able to do with my trade. I made these for you, Shanely, with diamonds found near these mountains. Even the amber on my ring was found right here. These mountains are your home, and I wanted to make them a part of our union today. I've been working on these rings ever since I found out we were mates."

"Bastian, you made these? They're beautiful!"

"I did, my love," he replied as he slipped my ring on my finger. It fit perfectly, and he handed me his. "Now everyone, shifter or human, will know you are taken."

"I love you, Bastian," I replied, slipping his ring on his finger.

"I love you too."

"Then by the power vested in me, by the State of Washington and as Alpha of the McCoy pack, I hereby declare you husband and wife!"

Everyone stood and cheered as Bastian kissed me again, this time much harder than before. He thankfully didn't dip me. I don't think I'd be able to with my belly now, and with this dress I doubt he could even see how big I've actually gotten.

"Let's hear it for Mr. and Mrs. Fenrir!" Cade shouted, amidst the hollering. It was loud, and I swear I could feel the earth shake from all their cheering.

"Receptions at the barn!" Cain shouted as everyone surrounded us to congratulate us.

I was blown away by the reception. Everyone was just excited and happy, and no one cared they were smashed up against a different shifter. The large crowd slowly made their way down the small trail to where the big red barn stood. Bastian and I stayed back and greeted everyone as they passed by on their way to the reception, and Cade and Elijah never left our side. It was great getting a chance to personally greet the clan and pack. I thanked them all for all their assistance in making this day perfect and for sharing in our special day. I even saw the two wolves I tried to help earlier with their own families. They winked at me after congratulating us, and Bastian gave me a funny look. I laughed and shook my head. He didn't press me about it.

Soon, we greeted the last of the guests, and the four of us made our way to the barn too. The creek ran to the left of the barn, and everything was decked out in twinkling lights and lanterns. Both doors on either side of the barn were wide open, letting in a perfect fall breeze. I was in awe again. Everything was decorated and just beautiful. Lights hung from the ceiling, and the band played off to the side. They had even laid down a nice hardwood flooring so everyone could dance and not walk on the normal dirty barn floor. There were plenty of seats for everyone, and the food was already set up. Gorgeous white and black flowers decorated the area, and I smiled looking at them. *Bastian used my favorite color throughout the whole room and adding the white amongst it was stunning,* I thought as I took it all in. Everything seemed to symbolize something between Bastian and I, with either bears and wolves or our initials.

"Did you do all this?" I asked, with a wide smile.

"I thought you'd like it. I had a tremendous amount of help to set it all up, but it was my design. I tried to make it everything you would have wanted and mentioned to me before," he said as he squeezed my hand.

Everyone clapped as we walked in, and Bastian led me straight to the middle of the floor. The band started to play a pretty song, and without warning, Bastian slipped his hand behind my waist and started twirling me. He guided me around the dance floor to our first dance as everyone took pictures, but I hardly noticed them. I was *lost* in Bastian. *He really thought of everything and went all out for me to have the perfect wedding. I just wish my mom was here to see it too.*

As the music finally stopped, he kissed me again. Everyone had joined in with their own partners, and we continued to dance amongst our families and friends.

We grazed on the food as the evening went on, which was so delicious that I went back for seconds. Everyone danced most the night away as we laughed and just enjoyed ourselves. We had no interruptions, no looming danger. The awfulness of yesterday didn't even come to mind as we celebrated Bastian and I.

The pack and the clan seemed to be mingling fairly well too. I kept a close eye just in case. They each sat on opposite sides, but no one seemed angry with one another. I had even seen a wolf ask a bear to dance. Everyone seemed surprised at first, but it opened the door for the two shifter kinds

CHAPTER 20

to blend even more.

It was starting to get late when my uncle Thomas made his way over. You could tell he was still a little on edge, but he smiled as he approached me. He had worn a nice gray suit and pulled his long hair back into a nice, neat braid. He also had a small gift in hand, which I was not expecting. Gift giving at a wedding wasn't apart of shifter tradition, and I didn't want anyone to either. It was the one thing I asked for when we talked about the planning. I simply wanted their company on my special day, but here he was, with a small box in hand.

"Here, Shanely. I wanted you to have something to represent your bear heritage and as an apology for yesterday. I was arrogant, and I let it blind me to what a member of my own clan was doing, and for that I am sorry. Your father just told me of the necklace you have on already and its significance to the both of you. I thought this might actually be perfect, even if it was not planned," he said, handing me the box.

I opened it to find a beautiful silver bear with a black diamond where the heart should be sitting inside. My mouth dropped. "Uncle, you got this for me? You didn't have to buy me anything!" I touched the pendent, tracing the outline of the bear.

"This actually belonged to your aunt Hannah. I bought her three necklaces over the years, and I have saved them for my girls after she passed. They each have one, but this one— this one still needed a home. I did not know whom to give it to until I met you. It seemed fitting to keep it within the family, and I wanted my niece to have this. I wasn't kind to you or your mate yesterday, and my Hannah would be mad at me for the way I treated one of my own, even if I did not know right away. Besides, I'd like everyone to know what your other half is," he said before he leaned in close to whisper, "your better half."

Thomas grinned and winked at me before walking away. I giggled at my ornery uncle, and Bastian gave me a funny look.

"What's so funny?" he asked.

I shook my head. "Nothing. Can you help me add this to my necklace?"

He helped unfasten the chain on my necklace to slip the new pendant on. I was planning on saving the other chain in case anything happened to this one. Both pendants fell against my chest, and I held them in my hands smiling. *It was both halves of me.*

"It's beautiful, Shanely. You're stunning," Bastian said before he kissed me again. He guided me to the dance floor and wrapped his arms around me. Getting as close as my belly allowed him to, we danced.

My brows furrowed when I noticed Elijah jogging up to us from the other side of the room. "Heads up, brother. We have company."

Bastian looked puzzled. 'What are you talking about? Who's here?"

Cade joined us then. "The cops. Patrick is here."

I shot Bastian a look as a wave of panic rolled through me. "Why is he here?!"

"I don't know, but you need to stay away from him. Go sit by your dad, please. I'll go with the Alpha and see what's going on. Cade stay with her too."

He kissed my forehead before pushing me to Cade. He and Elijah quickly met up with my uncle, who was already on his way out the door. I could see Patrick just barely through the doors, heading down the hill with another officer in tow. *What could they want?* I thought anxiously.

Cade dragged me further into the room, and we quickly found my dad and brother talking to my uncle Thomas.

"What's going on, boy? You look a bit serious for a wedding," Thomas jokingly said.

"Officer Patrick is here. We aren't sure why, so we're moving Shanely farther away, without looking like we're straight up hiding her."

"Well— are you hiding her?" Thomas asked, eyeing the two of us.

"Seriously? Good lord, what is this guy's problem?" Caleb stammered as he stepped in front of me, blocking me from view.

"We think Shanely is a seer, brother. This cop seems to keep triggering warnings for her, but he's too interested in her anyways, and he's the son of our Division leader," my father replied, giving me a weak smile.

Thomas swore. "Anything else I should know about?"

"No, I think that's it," I replied, with a sly grin. "You're all caught up,

CHAPTER 20

Uncle."

He gave me a pointed look and turned back to the front doors. Bastian and Cain were talking to the cops now, and they both looked pissed. Patrick's head was on a swivel, and my eyes narrowed. *What could they possibly need at my wedding,* I thought to myself. I straightened when his eyes found mine, and he *smiled.*

Patrick turned back to my mate, and the two seemed to argue for a bit. I watched as Uncle Cain finally stepped in between and gestured to the rest of the reception. Bastian threw his hands up and started to walk my way, but Patrick stopped him. *What was happening?* I thought. I couldn't hear what was being said, but Patrick simply gestured to his partner, who had a pad and pen out. Elijah stepped back while they argued and disappeared in the crowd that formed.

"Hang tight, Shanely," Elijah said through the link. "I'm on my way. Stay with Cade."

"What's going on, Elijah? Why is Bastian not allowed to leave? Why are they even here?"

"Someone called the cops on us. They complained of the music being too loud, and then another call came in about possible drugs being on the premises. Seems like someone wanted to disrupt your wedding, and Patrick volunteered to come and check everything out. They're bringing a dog in to go through the barn, and since this is Bastian's wedding, he's responsible. He's being detained there while they check."

My eyes widened. Elijah was nearly to us now, and I looked back to Bastian. He was still talking to Patrick's partner, but his eyes were on mine.

"Bastian?"

"Shanely, I'm so sorry. I'm stuck here, but I'm watching everything, I promise. I have to go right now, but don't leave my line of sight, please."

"I won't. Just be careful, and please don't leave with them!"

"I love you." he whispered softly.

"I love you too."

Another cop slowly made his way down with the drug sniffing dog, and they started moving throughout the reception. Patrick moved around as well, but he wasn't checking the room like he should. Instead, he made his way straight to me.

Elijah stepped in his path. "Shanely, there you are! We forgot to take pictures by the cake. C'mon!"

He dragged me away towards the cake on the opposite side of the room, and I could see Patrick stop to talk to my family from the corner of my eye. I let out the breath I'd been holding as Elijah pulled out his phone. We pretended to take pictures of the cake and then with each other, all while watching Patrick from afar.

Suddenly, Patrick was moving again, and Elijah pretended to be ignorant of his surroundings and shoved me towards a table of older wolves in the back. He and Cade took turns moving me around the room, keeping me far away from Patrick and the drug sniffing dog. Patrick looked entirely pissed as I kept just out of his reach, but we were running out of things to do. *Hiding would be the best choice,* I thought to myself and turned to my brothers.

"I have to pee," I said, with a forced smile.

"I'll just hide in the bathroom," I said through the link. *"Just let me know when they leave."*

They nodded and lead me to the left of the barn, where the two bathrooms were located. I went straight to the one designated for ladies, closing the door as I slipped inside. I took a deep breath and walked to the mirror to inspect my dress. Cade had stepped on it during our little game of Keep Away, but it didn't seem to be torn or anything. I dabbed my runny eyeliner and adjusted my shoulder cuffs, when a loud commotion sounded outside the door.

The door suddenly clattered open, and Patrick stood in the frame, eyeing me before he step inside with that dog.

"This is ridiculous!" Cade hollered as the officer pushed him back. "That's the ladies—"

My eyes widened when Patrick shut the door.

"Shanely. You seem to be a difficult woman to say hello to," Patrick said, with a soft smile.

CHAPTER 20

"And you're in the ladies room, Officer," I replied as I tried to step around him and the dog.

The dog barked aggressively at me, and I stepped backwards. My eyes widened as Patrick whistled, letting the leash go, and the dog ran right for me. I flew back against the wall as she barked and snarled at me. Any movement made her snarl more, and my breath caught in my chest. I didn't know what to do without getting bit, and I was stuck in the corner, unable to move.

"Seems like she found something. Maybe I just need to search you to find what I'm looking for?"

I gave him a vicious look before snarling right back. "Control your dog! There is nothing on me. Whoever called you tonight gave a false report, and I'd like you to leave now!"

Patrick whistled again, and the dog stopped barking, but stayed right in front of me. I gritted my teeth together in frustration. My wolf surged to the surface, eyeing the creature from within. She was not threatened in the least. I, however, *was*.

"Oh, I don't have to go anywhere for the moment. But there's something I just can't figure it out," he said, crossing his arms.

"And what's that?" I snapped.

"You," he answered plainly. "You seem so different, Shanely. Unlike anyone I've ever met. It seems like everyone else here thinks so too, seeing how they're practically hiding you away from me."

"No, I've just told them how uncomfortable you make me feel, and they're trying to keep me safe!"

"Me? How have I ever made you uncomfortable?" he asked, stepping closer to me.

I glared at him. "Really? You have me trapped in the bathroom with you and your dog, and you can't see how creepy you're being right now?"

He rocked his head back and forth, and a smirk slowly appeared. "Okay, fair point there, but it didn't need to be this way if you had just talked to me out there."

Another loud commotion startled the both of us as Bastian's voice boomed through the door.

Patrick rolled his eyes. "I guess lover boy's finally noticed you're in here with me. Guess I'll have to do this the hard way."

Patrick whistled again, and the dog started to snarl and bark at me. I pressed myself further against the wall as the door flew open. Bastian looked feral.

"Care to explain why you have my wife locked in a bathroom with you, Officer?"

Patrick gave me one last look before turning to his partner. "Sable's found something. She checked the room but won't leave the bride alone. I need to do a body check."

My eyes widened as Bastian got in Patrick's face. "You will do no such thing. My wife doesn't have anything on her!"

Patrick tsked at my mate. "Careful now. You don't want to be arrested for threatening a cop, now do you? Besides, I'm just doing my job."

"Mr. Fenrir step aside, and let Officer Patrick through. He legally has the right to check now, and if neither of you comply with us, you will both be arrested. If nothing is found then we can leave you all in peace," the other officer said, and I scoffed.

"You've got to be kidding me?!" Cade hollered. We had drawn a crowd outside the bathroom now and both the pack and clan looked angry. *This needed to end before someone shifted.*

"You did this on purpose, Patrick," I said angrily.

"I have no idea what you mean. Now, Garrett, why don't you hold the groom here. I think he's going to be a problem."

His partner walked in and pushed Bastian aside. He looked so close to shifting, and I was afraid of what would happen if he lost control.

"Bastian?"

My mate looked at me, and his face softened slightly. "Shanely, I don't know what's going on—"

I put my hand up to ease him. "It's okay. I know I'm innocent here, and I will demand apologies from everyone when they see for themselves."

Patrick smirked as he stepped forward. The dog retreated to the other

CHAPTER 20

officers as Patrick forced my hands up. He made sure not to leave the tiniest gap as he felt my arms and neck. He went through my hair next before making his way down my body. His eyes gleamed as they slid up and down my waist, and I gritted my teeth, but I forced my anger aside. Bastian was already breathing heavily. *The last thing I needed was to give him my rage too.* I tried to keep his focus on my eyes, but he was glued to Patrick.

"Careful," Bastian snarled as Patrick felt my lower half.

Patrick grinned back at Bastian before continuing on. The officer had to push Bastian back after that, and Elijah came to assist. He whispered something in my mate's ear, and Bastian relented some.

"There's a lot of dress here, isn't there?" Patrick asked coyly.

"Let's go, Officer," I snapped as his hands pushed the dress in between my legs. He felt up and down each one before turning me around to do the backside again.

"Maybe I should do a more thorough search here? The dress is very full, and I might have missed something. I should just go underneath to make sure," Patrick stated to his partner as he tried to lift my dress. I yanked my dress out of his hands, glaring.

"That's enough! Get your hands off my wife!" Bastian bellowed, and Officer Garrett looked a little nervous.

"Patrick, I think it's enough. She's clearly not carrying anything, and we should go and file the false report. We need to have the trainer look at Sable when we get back too. She was wrong tonight," he said as Patrick glared at him.

At least someone here was thinking with a lick of sense, I thought to myself. I straightened my dress back out and ran straight to Bastian. He forcefully pushed past the officer and wrapped his arms around me tightly, whispering how sorry he was.

Patrick slowly stood and whispered as he passed by, "Congratulations on the baby, Shanely."

Bastian about snapped when Patrick winked at me before walking out. My mate slammed the door shut behind the police, and I could hear my uncle yelling at them through the door. Bastian locked the door and bolted right back to me.

He snarled as he got close, and it startled me. It sounded vicious, and I looked into his eyes, trying to figure out what he was thinking, because Bastian would never snarl that way with me.

"You reek of him," he said gruffly. His eyes shifted gold.

I tried to get a whiff of what he was talking about, but I couldn't smell anything but Bastian right now. He was lost in his own thoughts though, and I didn't try to pull him out of it. Bastian rubbed my arms up and down, touching every bit of my skin as he could. He buried his face in the crook of my neck, breathing heavily, while running his hands throughout my hair. It was then I realized what he was doing. *Bastian was re-scenting me, taking away the smell of Officer Patrick.*

And I let him. I loved that he was removing any trace of the creepy man. Patrick was repulsive, and I hated his hands had even been on my body in the first place. *I don't know how he rigged tonight,* I thought to myself. *But I would love to know who made that call.*

Bastian knelt down on his knees as he ran his hands across my legs, sending shivers up my body. I lifted my dress slowly for him, exposing my leg just a little, and he stopped moving. He slowly looked up at me as he licked his lips.

"Don't miss a spot, Bastian. Make sure you cover every inch of my skin," I said calmly, and he gave me a wicked smile. His hands went underneath my dress, and I felt him slowly touch my leg. I closed my eyes, focusing on his touch as he went slowly up and down my body. Bastian was a gentleman though and stopped them before they climbed too far up.

"I am officially yours now, my love," I said, as I looked down at him longingly.

He carefully rearranged my dress before standing up. Then he towered over me, commanding my attention before replying in a deep husky voice, "You've always been mine, my love, but I don't have it in me to start something and not be able to continue. And I will not have our first time be in the bathroom at our reception. I am so sorry you had to go through that though."

CHAPTER 20

"I wasn't going to give him a reason to arrest you. Like in our vows, I'm here to protect you too," I replied quietly.

"It should never be with something like *that* though. When I find out who made that call, I swear I'll kill them," he snarled again.

I gripped the sides of his face, making him look at me as I said, "Bastian, it's okay. It could have been way worse, but I'm alright, and I—"

I didn't get a chance to finish my sentence as I was snapped into another warning.

Chapter 21

Patrick came home, and he slammed the door shut, making me jump.

"What's your problem?" I asked, irritation lacing my tone.

"You," he replied. "You are my problem! I'm getting really sick of waiting on you to accept me. I've been patient and kind, and I'm taking care of you, but you are *my* girl. I need more from you."

I scrambled to my feet, trying to put more distance between us.

"Patrick—"

I couldn't finish my sentence because with two large strides, he grabbed me and kissed my lips. He forced his tongue in, and I about gagged, so I did the only thing I could. I bit down.

He yelled out in pain, tearing himself away from me. He cursed before pushing me against the wall. His eyes were wild, and he was angry. So very angry with me. I could see the blood in his mouth as he spoke.

"Shanely, I know Bastian isn't the father to your first kid. If he can play pretend then so can I. You just have to accept me."

Patrick stood over me as rage coursed through my veins.

I glared back at Patrick. "You killed my mate, and now you want to be my children's father!? You honestly think you can replace Bastian?"

"I told you the Division made the call to deal with you all. I stuck my neck out to save you and your kid. The least you could do is be grateful!"

"Grateful!? Calvin told us everything, Patrick. This is all your fault! We're not even friends, Patrick, and yet you wouldn't take no for an answer. You maneuvered everything, so you could justify killing Bastian! I will never love you! I will never be anything but a prisoner to you!"

CHAPTER 21

Patrick gripped my neck so hard and so abruptly, I didn't even register it was about to happen. I clung to his hands, struggling to breathe as my feet left the ground. Then I felt the cold steel of his knife on my stomach, while his eyes slowly went up and down my body.

"Let me try this again. Either get on board with the idea of being mine, or I will cut these babies out of you to make room for my child. Do you understand? The twins will only live if I get to be the father, and you play the loving wife. Either way, I still get what I want."

He dropped me, and I gasped for air. I collapsed on the floor as his clunky boots walked across the room. He opened the door before turning to me.

"Think about it, Shanely. I'll give you five minutes with the kid before I require a decision. Oh, and tonight, I demand some attention."

* * *

"Whoa, baby! I got you!"

I heard Bastian's voice before I could see him. I was breathing hard, and I clung to Bastian as my vision cleared. A sob escaped my lips, and I fell against my mate.

"Shh— baby, it's okay. That won't happen, I promise you! Okay? None of that will happen!" Bastian shouted. He sounded as panicked as I felt.

I pulled back, wiping my eyes and ruining the make-up Cassia put on me. "I'm sorry, they just feel so real. I don't think I can talk about it right now."

"You don't have to. I saw everything through our mind-link."

My eyes widened as I turned to him. Bastian's eyes looked so sad, and my heart broke even more. *What was I going to do?*

"I'm so sorry, Bastian," I mumbled as I tried to calm myself down.

"Shanely, you don't have anything to apologize for. Remember, *none* of these are set in stone, and trust me when I say *none* of that will ever happen. Well, I mean there is one thing I plan to make happen as soon as you are ready."

I eyed him funny, and he kissed my nose. "I plan to make your belly swollen again as soon as you're ready to have more children. You are going to be the perfect mother, Shanely, and I want lots of kids with you."

I couldn't contain the grin on my face, and I kissed him again. It was better than trying to find the words to express how much I loved him. Bastian's hands went back in my hair, and he pulled me close. We stayed lost in each other for awhile before he finally broke our lips apart.

"I love you, Shanely."

"I love you more, Bastian," I replied.

He grinned down at me. "Do you want to finish the reception? I understand if you rather go home, but I do believe we never got any cake."

"Oh, cake sounds delicious!" I replied before looking in the bathroom mirror. I quickly adjusted my hair and wiped beneath my eyes, hoping to fix the mess I just created. Once I was finally better, I let Bastian lead me out of the restroom. Cade and Elijah were waiting still, and they looked relieved when they saw us.

"Shanely, I am so sorry! I tried to stop him—" Cade stammered, but I cut him off.

"Guys, it's okay. I'm alright. Bastian and I just needed a moment is all."

"I wasn't going to let her spend the rest of the evening smelling like that douche bag," Bastian stated firmly.

Elijah laughed. "I don't blame you. We figured it was something like that."

"Well, not the whole time," Bastian said, with a boyish grin that quickly turned sour. "Shanely had another warning."

"Seriously? Was it bad?" Cade asked in a hushed tone.

"It wasn't good," I replied.

"Was it Patrick?" Elijah asked, looking at me with concern.

I nodded, and he swore before replying, "He's going to be a problem, Bastian."

"I know," he replied grimly. "What happened out here?"

"Cain let them have it for everything and escorted them off the property to make sure Patrick actually left. Some wolves followed him back to town to the precinct. He's officially gone tonight, and he wouldn't say who called. Said it was police business," Elijah replied, rolling his eyes.

CHAPTER 21

"Yeah, I bet it was," I said sarcastically as my father walked up.

Everyone came to check on us, and I reassured everyone that I was okay. I insisted we not let this spoil our night, and I made the band start back up. Bastian left me briefly in between his brothers to grab a slice of cake and promptly set me in a chair to eat with him.

I looked around the room, taking in as much as I possibly could of this night, while trying to pretend the middle wasn't just awful. I was grateful we stayed despite everything as this was the best distraction from my new warning. From here, I could get a great view of everyone as I munched on my delicious slice of cake.

Johnny kept his eyes glued to Alana the whole night, I noticed. She stood mostly with Octavia and Bay, all three munching on cake as well. I felt bad for him as I watched him pine after her. He seemed smitten with her, but he never told us there was a bond or anything. As a wolf, he should have been able to tell since they've made eye contact before. It was just sad to watch.

Cade and Elijah both had girls on the dance floor near us. The girls seemed on cloud nine, and the fellas were all laughing and enjoying themselves. I sighed in relief.

Caleb talked to my uncle Cain and my dad, and they seemed to be having a decent time together too. That was a sight I don't think anyone would have thought would happen. My father asked me for the next dance, and then my brothers all asked for a dance. I danced with everyone in my family as did Bastian, who had asked Bay, Alana, and even Octavia to dance. She gave him such an uncomfortable look but said yes anyways.

My poor feet were sore by the end of the night, and I soon collapsed in a chair with another slice of cake and propped my feet up. I didn't want to move anymore and was perfectly content to watch everyone else around me. Most of the pack and clan said their goodbyes around midnight, and it was just my inner circle of friends that was left.

Ryder and Johnny were now talking to Caleb, while Bay and Alana huddled close. Johnny was still hyper focused in the girls direction. I sighed and left it alone. There was nothing to do if there wasn't a bond, and I didn't want to make it harder on him than it needed to be. *They'd be a cute couple though,* I thought to myself.

Cade and Elijah were talking to the band as they were packing up to leave too. Bastian made his way over and sat across from me to start rubbing my feet. I tried to protest, imagining how black my feet must be since I kicked off my heels long ago, but he held my leg firm, giving me a look that said not to fight him on this. I noticed he gave me this look a lot. *I was going to have to learn how to do it,* I thought to myself. I finally gave and thanked my mate, and God, his hands were like *magic*. I groaned as he rubbed them, making him laugh.

A smile curved on my lips when Bastian leaned forward with that look in his eyes. His eyes dropped to my lips then. I smiled and leaned forward, ready for his kiss, but instead he gave me a wicked grin right before he stole the bite of cake off my fork.

"You did not just do that!" I exclaimed, tipping my head back to laugh hysterically.

He shrugged. "Consider it payment for the foot rub, mate."

I playfully pushed him, when a loud commotion sounded behind me.

"Don't touch me!"

Emma. I instantly knew who it was without even having to turn around. *First Patrick and now her?* I thought to myself. Bastian looked pissed as he stared ahead at the mess unfolding. I managed to twist my head around to see her stumbling into the barn. I rolled my eyes. *She looked drunk.*

Emma pushed past Ryder as he tried to stop her from entering, and Bastian gently set my foot back down on the floor.

"Let's go, Shanely," he said as he slipped my shoes on for me. Emma came barreling into our view, giggling as she knocked a chair over.

I glared at her. "You shouldn't be here, Emma."

She staggered further into the room, ignoring me.

"You've met Emma?" Bastian whispered.

"Unfortunately," I replied.

I narrowed my eyes to her and repeated myself a bit louder, "You shouldn't be here, Emma."

CHAPTER 21

"I'll go wherever I want to, I'm afraid. You are not my Alpha, so I really don't have to listen to you. Besides, this is a party after all! I came to mingle! Although, I'm surprised anyone is still here. Wasn't this supposed to be shut down?" she said, hiccuping.

"What do you mean shut down?" Bastian demanded as he stood abruptly.

Her eyes lit up when they settled on my mate. "Bastian! There you are! Won't you dance with me?"

I rolled my eyes as he asked again, "Did you call the police on us?!"

Emma stumbled towards Bastian. "I have no idea what you're talking about."

She hiccuped again before giggling, but Bastian was fuming now. I reached for his hand, tugging on him gently. He helped me stand, and I glared at the drunk girl before me.

"So, let me get this straight. First, you tried to sabotage the reception, and now you want to crash it? God, Emma just go home. You weren't invited in the first place," I replied sarcastically. I was done playing nice with this girl and her family. They were in for a rude awakening if they thought they were going to get away with trying to ruin my wedding.

"I was too! Alpha Cain invited us all!" she stammered.

"Nah, I'm pretty sure no one wanted you here," I countered.

Everyone had stepped towards Emma now. She was drawing in the crowd, and I think she took it as a good sign because she beamed at the boys, batting her eyes as she whipped her hair around. She had no idea they were just waiting for her to biff it bad. *She could barely stand,* I thought to myself. *How much did she have to drink??*

"Emma, you need to go home. You're drunk," Elijah said, with his hands raised defensively. As if he expected to have to catch her at any moment.

"Oh, I'm fine! Besides if the smelly bears get to stay, then I most definitely get to stay."

She spun abruptly around, spilling whatever was left of that bottle of hers, and I quickly pulled my dress back to avoid getting it soaked in alcohol.

"Back off, Emma," Johnny growled, making his way closer to the girls.

Alana, Caleb, and Octavia said nothing but stared annoyingly at Emma.

Octavia merely rolled her eyes and shook her head with a smile when I mouthed *sorry* to them.

"You can't tell me what to do, Johnny! I'll tell my dad if you try to even touch me," she said, giggling again.

My wolf snarled within me. She was pissed with Emma's behavior and completely ready to do something about it, but I shoved her back down. *I wasn't the Alpha, and it wasn't my place to correct her like that,* I scolded myself.

"No problem there, Emma. No one wants to touch you," he snapped back, and everyone muffled their laugh.

Her face turned beat red as she glared. "Oh, screw you, Johnny!"

"I believe I just said I don't want to."

We lost it after that. I couldn't help it and laughed hard as her nose scrunched up in disgust. Emma stumbled again, nearly taking out Caleb and the girls. Alana and Octavia quickly stepped to the side to avoid colliding with her.

Emma snarled and shoved Alana shouting, "Get out of my way, you filthy creature!"

She stormed away, throwing the bottle on the ground as she went. Alana flew to the side, barely missing the table next to them, and Johnny bolted forward and caught her before her head hit the ground. They tumbled, and I released the breath I'd been holding as Johnny slowly helped her sit up. *Oh, thank God he was standing so close,* I thought to myself. *That would have been a nasty fall.*

"Oh my God," Alana whispered as Johnny sucked in a deep breath.

"Nice catch, Johnny!" Cade shouted, but Johnny didn't respond. The two stayed frozen on the ground just staring at one another. *What in the world was going on?* I thought, expecting him to help her up already. Suddenly, he was kissing her.

"Whoa. What just happened?" Caleb asked as he slowed his pace towards them.

"Oh my God!" Octavia shouted, rubbing her chest frantically.

Everything clicked into place as I realized what was happening. "OH MY

CHAPTER 21

GOD! You're mates!"

Everyone whipped their heads from me to them. Johnny finally came up for air, and he rested his head against hers, beaming from ear to ear. She whispered something to him, but our group roared with excitement, rushing towards as Johnny finally helped her stand.

Caleb slapped Johnny on the back before Ryder gave him a hug. I went straight to Alana and pulled her into my arms.

"Congratulations, Alana! And you too, Johnny!" I cried excitedly.

"I wondered why your dress shop smelled divine when we came in with Shanely," Johnny proclaimed.

"You did?" she asked, her face crimson red.

"Yeah, it was driving me crazy, but I couldn't figure it out. I never felt the bond when I looked at you."

"Because for bears we need touch for it to connect," she laughed before scooching back into his embrace. "You must need both with mixed matings."

"Well, that explains it then. Oh lanta, I never thought I'd say this, but I am so glad Emma was here!" Johnny bellowed as he wrapped his arms around Alana.

We all roared with laughter. Johnny kissed Alana's forehead, and she seemed so content and happy now, like everything was just complete in her life. *I knew the feeling well,* I thought to myself as I smiled up to my own mate.

"She finally did something good for once!" Elijah said excitedly.

"We should call our parents and my brother. He would have felt the bond form, even from Russia," Alana said sweetly. She was on cloud nine, and I couldn't be happier for my friend.

"We're heading to the lodge to call everyone. Goodnight everyone!" Johnny said as he dragged Alana towards the lodge. She giggled the whole way.

"Goodnight!" the group shouted together.

"Man— none of that would have happened if Shanely didn't move to town," Caleb announced proudly, and I blushed.

"I didn't do anything, guys," I replied bashfully. They all winked at me, giving me a knowing grin before Bastian pulled on my waist.

"Come on, babe. I believe you owe me something back home. I've been patient long enough," Bastian whispered in my ear. Heat crept up my face, and the fellas laughed at me.

"On that note, we're heading to the lodge as well. We're staying here tonight," Elijah said, with a wink. I covered my face in Bastian's chest as they all continued to snicker at my embarrassment.

We parted ways with the others, and with every step I took, my nerves rolled in my stomach. *God, I was so nervous,* I thought as we started down the trail towards home. I hoped I'd be everything he imagined. I hoped I wasn't a disappointment.

The boys had set up twinkling lights along the path for us, making for a pretty walk through the woods. It felt like a fairy tale as I walked with my beautiful gown in the forest with my drop-dead gorgeous mate.

We sauntered up the porch steps and into the house. I swallowed hard when Bastian locked the doors behind us, but when he turned to face me, his eyes glowed gold. We had lived together long enough that I knew when his wolf was at the surface, and right now, Bastian looked ready to shift.

I gulped and slowly stepped backwards. He noticed, and a sly smirk formed on his lips. "What did I tell you about backing away from me?"

I gave him a playful shrug, biting my lower lip as he watched my every move.

Bastian stepped closer saying, "Don't you know that wolves enjoy the hunt?"

I felt my wolf come alive at his words, and I let her instincts move me. She wanted to *run*. I bolted as fast as my sore feet could move, feeling the need to give chase, but I shrieked as I barely made it out of the kitchen before he cut me off. Bastian had vaulted over the counter and stalked towards me again. My dress was so long it was difficult to move quickly in.

"This isn't fair. I'm pregnant and in a long dress. It's too easy for you to catch me," I playfully teased. Bastian gave me a devilish grin as he picked me up and turned quickly towards our bedroom.

"Don't you worry about it, my love. We'll have plenty of chances for you to try to outrun me. You never will though, I can promise you that. I would have thrown you over my shoulder, but it seems like I'll have to wait until the baby gets here for that."

"I promise you once this baby's out, you won't catch me next time," I said confidently.

Bastian whipped his head to mine, and his eyes shimmered red this time. "Is that a challenge, mate?"

I held his gaze. I had never seen his eyes solid red before, but they were just as beautiful as his oceanic blue. Feeling confident, I leaned in close to whisper, "It's a promise."

Suddenly, this overwhelming sensation filled my chest, and my wolf pulled herself to the front on the controls. My teeth sharpened painfully fast, and before I knew it, she had pushed me to his neck, and I bit down hard.

He groaned, resting against the wall as I held onto his neck with my teeth. Bastian's ragged breath was the only sound in the room before our bond began to glow. It glowed brighter and brighter, and I felt more connected to Bastian than ever before. I could feel his joy as clear as if it were my own emotion. It was pure and exciting, but it quickly changed into something far more primal, and I realized I still had my teeth in him. I blinked, letting him go and covering my mouth with my hand. A mixture of shame and guilt filled my heart as blood slowly trickled out from the wound.

"Shanely," he whispered gruffly between breaths. I didn't even realize that I had bit him that hard, but it left a definite mark.

"I'm so sorry, Bastian. I don't know why I just did that. I couldn't stop myself."

Bastian set me down gently before gripping my chin gently. "Don't apologize, mate. You marked me, and it felt amazing. God, you're so sexy."

Bastian slowly kissed my neck as he made his way to my lips, then he was pushing me backwards. A thousand different questions flooded my brain, but none of them mattered in this moment. Right now it was just him and I.

Bastian never broke the kiss. His hands gripping my hair as a guide, and

I let him push me towards our room. He was in complete control, and he slammed the bedroom door closed behind us. I struggled for air by the time he finally broke our kiss, and my eyes widened when he chucked off his tie.

"Will you mark me too?" I asked, and the question made him groan again. The thought of Bastian marking me about did me in, and my wolf howled inside. *Would this mark remain forever?* I wondered. *God, I hoped so.*

"Oh, I plan on it. Twice actually," he finally answered. His voice was husky now as he gently moved my hair out of his way.

"Twice?"

"Mmhmm," he replied, slightly preoccupied with kissing my neck now. "I will in both my wolf and human form just like you did right now."

My eyes widened. "In your wolf form? When?"

Bastian chuckled softly before replying, "Don't worry about it right now, love. My wolf will wait until he sees yours before marking you. Now I, on the other hand, will not be waiting. You are mine tonight, Shanely. Now, no more questions."

"But Bastian—"

He gripped my chin firmly. "I said no more questions."

And then he kissed me.

Chapter 22

We didn't leave the cabin for two weeks after our wedding. That night was pure bliss in more ways than one. Bastian and I have spent every second together, and no one bothered us. Where everyone was or what they did, I didn't know. And honestly, I didn't even care. All I wanted to focus on was my mate.

Bastian and I remained in our honeymoon bubble, and it was perfect. The weather was quickly becoming cold, but that just made our cabin that much more cozy. I looked for my own mark every time I passed by a mirror too. It laid perfectly at the base of my neck, and every time I saw it, I thought of the moment when he put it there. That feeling was unlike any other and connected another strand to our mate bond. His mark burned against my skin, and now it stayed forever. No one will ever be able to separate Bastian and I. This was one tattoo I could get behind.

Like a proud peacock, Bastian strutted around everywhere we went, showing off his mark and never once covered it up. Even when we broke out our hoodies for colder weather, he still made sure his neck stayed exposed for the world to see. Slowly but surely, our mate bond was becoming whole.

When we weren't tucked away in our *bedroom*, we spent most of our time on the back porch, just like we did when we first met. Bastian spent most of it in his wolf form, being lazy around the cabin. He had no responsibilities but to be with me, and for a little while we could forget about the rogue and Patrick. The rogue hadn't made any appearance since the day that Caleb picked me up in his truck or if it had, I had no idea they were even there. Everyone was completely baffled by it's behavior. It was not how rogues usually operated, and no one knew what to do to find them. My uncle Aspen wondered if joining the pack was enough to scare the rogue into moving on, but we were still being cautious just in case. I was safe as long as I stayed with Bastian.

I was past the point in my pregnancy to shift now, and that was disappointing. I only got to shift once, and I was back to waiting again. All I wanted to do was run through the woods with my mate. Give him more of a chase than I had the first time. I craved seeing that wild look in his eyes right before he came after me. Who knew I truly liked possessive and dominating behavior? It was probably the fact that I was finally with the right person that I discovered how much I *could* like that behavior.

And boy did I like it.

Bastian wolf had grown more too, and his paws had turned solid white. Malin assumed because I was a mixer, it was somehow changing him too, but we didn't have any concrete answers as to why he looked so different. I couldn't help but wonder if maybe my bear had changed as well, since he marked me, but I can't shift to even check. I'm stuck waiting until I give birth, which was getting closer and closer by the day.

Bastian said he noticed a change within him too that started around the time I first discovered my bear. He can't figure it out but something just feels off. We're keeping quiet about it for now, but I wonder if I'm beginning to share more than just my abilities with him. He said it was just an odd feeling, like an empty space deep inside that shouldn't be there. Doubt was creeping in that I affected him more than anyone ever realized. The question was, would he be okay with the changes happening to him?

My wolf never changed. She's always there, watching and guiding me, but I can't figure out what her trigger was. I'm stuck waiting until after giving birth to even try, but I have no idea what to even do to start with. I know my dad said my protectiveness over the ones I love was my bear's pull, but I didn't know what to do to pull my wolf out. Time will tell, I guess.

Two weeks soon turned into two months. Time was passing by so quickly, and everyone was busy preparing for the harsh winter. We were thrilled for Johnny and Alana's mating, and we had a small ceremony for them at the

CHAPTER 22

clan's lodge. Alana didn't want anything more than that, but it was still gorgeous and extravagant. Even her dad, my stubborn, wolf-hating uncle, seemed to welcome Johnny into the family without hesitation. He knew how sacred mate bonds were, and after finding out what happened to his brother and my mom, he didn't interfere. He even gave them a small cabin on his land to use when they stayed there, so just like me, they had two homes now.

Slowly, the hatred between the bears and the wolves were dissolving. Alana and Johnny's mating just pushed everyone closer together. I may have been the tip of the iceberg, but they were the snowball that kept everything rolling. We've started seeing everyone mixing on both lands now and new friendships were forming over the old mistrust and hate. We had very few that really weren't happy with the new changes, but like my aunt said, we couldn't please everyone. I was sure eventually they'd come around or leave like some have already.

It wasn't as crucial to monitor the lands like before, so some of the enforcers took up different jobs in the meantime. The triplets, along with Bay, who was fitting in quite nicely with the pack, started work on my cabin. They had a lot more free time now that the patrols had been laxed. Well, other than those sent to patrol around my cabin in search of the rogue still, but I wasn't too worried about it anymore. I hadn't noticed anything amiss lately. It was like the rogue was just— gone. And I was okay with that.

My uncle didn't understand the thought process behind this wolf though. Most rogues were relentless with their marks. They didn't have a pack to help keep them in check, but this one didn't seem to operate the same way. Usually, they take it as a slight against their skills as a wolf if their hunt gets away and could be extremely temperamental over it. This one was just gone, and no one could find him or her. They usually had a vile smell to them as well. Because they didn't belong to a pack that would mask over it, the evil within them would come through to warn others of their true nature, but no one had even managed to catch its scent. I didn't know what to think, but I've been so busy with everything in my new life, I was starting to forget about the rogue.

The triplets started working non-stop between their main job at their machine shop and working on the cabin. The nursery is now complete, but I haven't been able to see it yet. They were waiting for the baby to be born before they finally showed it to me, but it drove me crazy just waiting for them to let me in! I would stare at the door, debating whether or not to just go in without them knowing, but I didn't. I didn't want to ruin their surprise, so I'd sulk away and try to preoccupy myself with other tasks.

The boys were building on another section to the cabin for everyone to have their own rooms as it was too small for all of us. Caleb and my father came by often to help out too. They were very skilled at what they did, and soon all five guys fell into a good rhythm together. They wanted to seal everything up before the really cold weather hit. Looking at the building plans, I realized it nearly doubled the cabin's size now, as well as adding an entire second story. They had a lot to do, but my dad offered to use his crew to help speed everything along. It was coming along rather nicely.

As happy as I was with the new edition, I'd catch my father frequently lost in thought as he worked on the cabin. I'm sure building here again was difficult for him, and I tried to occupy his time while he worked, talking to him about whatever he wanted to talk about. He'd smile as I'd follow him around, wherever he was working for the day, but at a certain point Bastian kicked me out, saying it wasn't safe for me to be waddling around all the tools and construction material. I rolled my eyes as my dad laughed, but Bastian didn't care. He'd escort me back to the other side of the house before going back to work. My mate was on the lookout after that, and I wasn't able to sneak back very often.

I was a balloon now and waddled everywhere I went. It was difficult to do anything honestly. I wasn't used to being so big, and I often dropped things on the floor. Squatting down was tricky, and once or twice I lost my balance and found myself landing on my butt. I was able to get back up on my own for a while, but lately I've just given up, waiting until someone walked by to help me stand. Bastian always worried when he'd find me on the ground, but Bay would laugh and tease me relentlessly. *Just wait till she gets pregnant.*

CHAPTER 22

Without any effort, Bastian would haul me off the ground and plant me on my comfy rocking chair or the porch swing with a bundle of blankets. I'd kiss him as a thank you, and he'd be distracted for a little while before he'd get a call or someone would come looking for him. I'd simply wink, and he knew full well what I was doing every single time. Everyone else would roll their own eyes and pull him away back to whatever task they were in the middle of, but I didn't care. I missed my mate!

Dr. Malin checked me over often, and she seemed to think that because this baby's blood was composed of two different shifter kinds, it was causing the baby to grow at twice the speed considered normal, which was fine with me because I was so ready for this kid to be here. Daily life was a real struggle, but Malin reassured me it would probably be any day now.

Emma, one hundred percent, denies even being at my wedding, let alone drunk out of her mind. She insisted she wasn't the one to make the call to the police either, but we were positive it was one of them. Bastian practically growls whenever Emma or one of her family members comes near, and they've wisely kept their distance. There is always tension with that family now, but because no one could actually prove it was them, my uncle couldn't rightfully punish them. Her father tried to blame me for starting rumors about Emma being drunk at my wedding, despite what anyone said to defend me. I rolled my eyes at Derek during that meeting and decided to just ignore him. Nothing anyone said was even going to make a difference with that man, so why bother? He really wasn't too happy with me, but then again, he really wasn't happy with anything I did.

Derek and his family seemed to pull further away from the pack, and I wondered for how long they'd actually continue to stay. We already had a few families move away, and join other packs for different reasons, and I was surprised Derek stayed as long as he had. No matter what I did, Derek found a way to blame me for some slight against the pack. Everyone knew he was grasping at straws, just trying to play politics against me, but I was waiting for the day they either left or hopefully he'd finally just give up and accept the fact that I'm apart of this pack now.

And I wasn't leaving.

Snow had finally begun to fall, and I stood outside to watch the first snowfall of the year, grinning the entire time Bastian let me stay out. Pretty soon everyone was buried under a foot of the stuff. Being in the mountains meant more snow than usual, but it was gorgeous outside. I loved watching the snowfall as I curled up with a book near the fireplace. Indiana got snow, but it was nothing like this.

Most of the pack wore their furs instead of their human form during this time of year, especially when completing work around the land or checking on the pack and clan, as some of our members lived farther up the mountains than the main lodges. We were in the middle of stocking up, so we could avoid going into town too. Driving was tricky way up here in the winter, so the pack tried to be prepared for the bad weather that always came, which meant I was staying at the lodge now to be closer to Doctor Malin.

I couldn't shift anymore, and Bastian was nervous about me going into labor quickly. He seemed anxious about labor in general, and it was sweet so I let him fuss over me. Honestly, I was terrified at the idea of giving birth, but my aunt said she would stay with me to help in anyway she could. I felt better knowing I had people whom I loved helping me through it, and I tried really hard not to stress about it. Not until the time came, then I'd let myself freak out.

But I did realize that I was having less and less warnings at night. They started off becoming less vivid and detailed before I noticed some nights I didn't even have one. I was finally getting real rest again without the constant nightmares, which is fantastic because I was exhausted from carrying this kid already. I napped all the time, and I had never felt so lazy before. Apparently, it's normal for the expectant mother to sleep a lot right before the baby comes. Just another sign it was nearly time.

And that bringing the pack and clan together was a big enough change to stop my warnings from happening. That was a relief unlike any other.

One bright, and surprisingly sunny day, I was hanging around the lodge reading a book, while Bastian attended a meeting in my uncle Cain's office.

CHAPTER 22

Being this close to giving birth, he thought me staying out of some of the meetings and stress they brought would be better, and I was okay with it. I was too tired to really put much effort into anything lately, let alone pushing to attend pack meetings. I was curled up next to the fireplace reading, when I heard a loud voice shouting through the door of the hallway. *Someone was clearly not happy right now,* I thought as I turned back to my book. The door slammed, and I jumped when Derek stormed out and stomped right over to me. I honestly hadn't seen him in awhile, and boy was he upset.

"This is all your fault!" he screamed at me. Derek's face was beat red again as he jammed his finger in my face.

"Derek, that's enough!" Cain hollered back, and Bastian crossed the floor in no time, standing in front of Derek to block me from view. Derek looked angrily between Bastian and myself before storming off.

I sat up and asked, "What was that about?"

My uncle sighed, running his hand through his hair. "He's just angry and wants someone to blame."

"About what?"

Cain looked at me, giving me a small smile. "We made a decision today to give some land back to the bears and demolish the border between us for them to roam. Legally, they would be allowed to build on the land we'd donate, and then the clan could have more roaming land to use when needed. The land selected is in the back part of his section, where his family likes to lay claim."

"Really?! Thank you, Uncle Cain!" I cried out, grinning wide. "I'd hug you, but I can't stand right now."

Amused, he replied, "It should have happened a long time ago. It's not even his land, so I don't understand why he's so angry. He still seems to hate bear shifters and probably blames you for being part bear."

"Don't worry about Derek. He'll get over it," Bastian stated firmly. "Cade heard his family is planning to leave anyways."

"We need to alert the pack though," Cain told Bastian, and I frowned.

"You will have to send a hive-link out," Bastian replied.

"Wait, for what? And what's a hive-link?" I asked, curious about what was going on now.

"Alphas can contact the entire pack with the mind-link, but this is all at once. It's called a Hive message. There's a winter storm coming through tonight. We have a few feet of snow heading our way," Bastian answered.

"Really?!" I asked excitedly. I wanted as much snow as possible this winter. I was ready for it!

Bastian nodded, giving me a knowing smile. "Which is why we need to warn everyone. Make sure they prepare for the next few days quickly. Dr. Malin will be on her way within the hour, and she's staying here in case you go into labor. She may not be able to make it to the lodge in weather like this even as a wolf. I want to play this safe."

"Well, I'm off. I need to let everyone know what's going on and then find my mate. We'll need to run into town before the storm hits to pick up the packages we've ordered. I need that part to fix the back up generator. Stay safe, you two," my uncle said as he headed out the door and to his truck.

"So— are you busy this afternoon?" I asked coyly to my handsome mate. His smirk about did me in.

"Nope! I'm all yours. What do you want to do?"

"Honestly, at this point eat or sleep. Actually, sleep. I'm exhausted," I replied, stretching my arms out. I set the book down on the coffee table, even though I desperately wanted to know what came next in the fantasy book I was reading. I just loved a good Assassin story, and I was dying to know what happened to Margo.

"Well, c'mon love. Let's get you to bed," he said, reaching for my arms to help me stand.

"Can't we just stay here?" I begged. "I'm so tired, Bastian, and the couch is cozy. Plus, there's a fire."

He smirked again before forcing me to sit up a bit. Bastian slid in behind me and laid me back against him.

"Of course, honey. Get some rest. I'll watch over you," he whispered.

I snuggled against him and pulled the couch blanket over us. Within a few minutes, we heard uncle's hive-link about the storm. The lodge stayed cozy and quiet, and it didn't take long for my eyes to become heavy enough

CHAPTER 22

that I succumbed to darkness.

* * *

I was startled awake when someone started to move me. I slowly opened one eye to see Bastian sliding out from behind me.

"Hey baby," he whispered. "I didn't mean to wake you."

The lodge was completely dark, and the wind howled loudly outside. I blinked furiously as I sat up.

Still disoriented I asked, "What's going on?"

"The storm hit a little sooner than they called for, and the power went out. Henry, the older wolf just down the trail, his generator won't kick on, and he needs it for his oxygen machines. The boys and I are heading down together to help him out."

"Oh no," I said as my heart sunk. "I hope he's okay. Are you sure you'll be safe though to travel through the storm?"

The wind was loud outside, and you could hardly see past the snow falling. This storm was going to get bad fast, and I worried about Bastian and his brothers being out in it.

"Don't worry, it isn't far. I'll be back before you know it. Dr. Malin is here, and your aunt and uncle will be back soon. They got stuck in town getting that part, so it's taking them longer to make their way back. Might have to travel by fur."

He winked at me as his brothers showed up. They quickly closed the door, keeping the wind and snow out the best they could. It still made me shiver.

"Dang! Storm's picking up. We need to go Bastian if we're going to make it back in time," Cade said, shaking the snow from his hair and coat. His eyes softened when they found mine. "Hey, Baby Girl. How's my niece taking the storm?"

"He or she is doing good. Just snack hungry," I replied, with a grin.

"Well, go feed my nephew! We'll keep an eye on your mate," Elijah said, smiling.

I stuck my tongue out at them and kissed Bastian goodbye. I slowly got to my feet as they left out the back. Passing the hallway on the left, I saw Dr. Malin's light on at the end. It was weird being at the lodge that was basically empty. It was usually the main hub, with people constantly coming and going, but ever since winter hit most in our pack stayed home. I didn't blame them, as it was cold and just easier to stay closer to home, but I did miss the constant movement of people in and out of this place. I liked how busy it usually was.

I opened the cabinet in the kitchen and pulled out the box of cookies I stashed away when Bastian wasn't looking. *A few wouldn't hurt,* I convinced myself. Even though I knew I should avoid the sugar. They just sounded amazing, and what baby wants, baby gets.

I made my way to Dr. Malin's room to offer some to her, when I heard a grunt. I stopped dead in my tracks, not really sure what I heard, when a growl followed by a loud crash came from Malin's room. My eyes widened, and I ran to her, pushing my way inside the door. Dr. Malin was unconscious on the floor.

Standing behind her was a very large man in a mask. Panic rose inside me, and I dropped the box of cookies. I watched him step over her casually before bolting as fast as my pregnant legs could go, but he was quick. I made it to the end of the hall, when he grabbed my hair. Before I could scream or send my mate a link, he covered my face with a cloth. It smelled funny with a hint of something sweet. It nearly gagged, and my heart thundered in my chest. The masked man kept it firmly over my mouth and nose. I tried to scream, but everything grew fuzzy, and I felt my body begin to sway, just as everything went black.

Chapter 23

The thrumming in my head wouldn't stop, and I groaned as I rolled to my side. *Why does everything hurt?* I thought to myself. My memories came rushing back, and I forced myself to sit up. My eyes widened as I looked around the dark room. I was laying on some musty cot on the ground in a room I had never been before. *Where was I?* I thought as my heart skittered in my chest.

"Someone took me," I whispered to myself, seeing my breath in the air. I pulled my knees to my chest, trying to savor what little warmth I had. *I had to get out of here—* I groaned and clutched my head, unable to finish that thought. My head pounded in my skull, feeling *fuzzy* for some reason. Muddled and messy, it was hard to think clearly, and I rubbed my temples, hoping the drug they use to knock me out would wear off soon.

The wind howled outside, shaking the room I was in, as the snow storm raged on. My body shivered harshly from the cold, and I pulled my long-sleeve shirt down further. *This wasn't going to cut it.*

I had to move before the person who took me came back, but my eyes drifted to the raging storm outside. *How was I going to survive in that?* I needed help.

"Bastian??" I said through our link. I waited a moment as I forced myself to my feet. Nothing happened, and I frowned, searching further. *"Bastian!"*

It was then I realized I was alone in my head. Like *entirely* alone. My wolf and bear were gone and panic surged within me. I was desperate. Fear rattled my core as I scoured my mind for my lost animals, but the search only made my head hurt worse. I clutched my head as the pulsing became too much. *I was going to pass out if I wasn't careful.*

I was empty inside. As odd as it first was when I discovered my animals, I had grown to love them. I relied on them for everything, and now that they were gone, I felt incomplete and human again. And I absolutely hated it.

I began to pace the too small room, trying to sort out what to do. *My mind-link wasn't working, my animals were gone, and I was stuck in some shack in the middle of a snow storm, wearing maternity pants and a long-sleeve shirt—* My options were not looking good. I clutched my fists together as my anger surged. *There has to be some way out of this!*

I looked around, hoping to find maybe a radio or something I could use to call for help. *This must be a hunter's shack,* I thought, due to how primitive it was. *There had to be something I could use.* There was only a small table with two chairs in the corner and a bucket in another. A very large window was behind the table and chairs, and I could see nothing but white snow falling quickly in the dark. My shoulders fell. *I'd been unconscious for some time.*

I slowly crept towards the window, when suddenly a large black shadow moved across it. I froze as the door swung open, letting in a burst of cold air and snow, as a stocky man in a large overcoat walked in. My eyes widened as I glared at my kidnapper.

Michael.

He took one look at me before grabbing his phone. It rang twice before someone picked up and he said, "She's awake."

Michael slammed it shut before the other person could respond, and I glared at him. He stomped his boots out, kicking snow everywhere, and then shook the snow from his coat.

"Comfortable?" he asked me sarcastically.

I remained silent. I hadn't seen him since our fight when my bear woke up. He didn't come to the wedding, and I honestly had forgotten all about him. *Was he seriously this upset because I showed him and his bear up?*

"You're not going to talk?" he asked. "Funny. You had plenty to said the last time we saw one another."

"Why are you doing this?" I demanded, crossing my arms. "Didn't get enough of a beat down the first time?"

CHAPTER 23

He snarled before he shoved me backwards, and I landed on the cot. He plopped down in one of the chairs against the wall then, grinning like a mad man.

"So, she does speak. Do I need more of a reason than that I just really don't like you? You showed up my bear, but now the whole clan loves you because you're *the White Bear*, and I can't challenge you again. Thomas has so many new rules about what we can and can't do to you and your freaking wolves now that the whole clan has changed. It's not the same, so when someone dangled a little money in my face, and your name came up, I just couldn't help myself," he smirked.

"Bastian will kill you," I said confidently.

Michael laughed heartily. "He won't find me. I'm leaving once the storm passes, and besides he'll be a little busy planning your funeral."

My heart began to race within me. Assuming their plan and hearing it out loud were too very different things, and I tried to control my breathing. I wanted to show him that he didn't scare me. That I was confident my mate would find me and shred him to pieces, but my body betrayed me. I had no idea where I was or how I was going to get out of this. Anxiety grew as I realized I was no match for Michael. *If I could shift that would be a different story*, I thought to myself. *But I can't shift.*

Michael looked all too amused with himself right now as he slapped his knee. "Don't worry! I won't be the one to kill you. That one's on his way."

"Who's coming?"

"You'll see," he replied before propping his feet on the table. I listened to some ridiculous game play on his phone, trying to come up with a plan to escape. I sent a thousand different mind-links to Bastian and his brothers, but no one answered me. My heart felt heavy as we waited for this *mastermind* to finally show.

"I have to pee," I said after awhile.

"Bucket's in the corner," he replied nonchalantly. Michael never removed his eyes from his phone, and I gritted my teeth.

"I'm not using a bucket in front of you!"

"Suit yourself. Just don't piss your pants because then I'll be pissed, and you'll be soaking wet. How long do you think you can last like that?"

I rolled my eyes but gasped when a brown wolf suddenly appeared in the window. My eyes widened. *I knew that wolf!* I thought to myself. *That was the wolf that attacked me on my first night here. It was the rogue everyone had been searching for.* I glanced at Michael in bewilderment. *How was the rogue here? How did he know the rogue!?* My mind raced with a thousand different questions on how this could be. *No one had picked up on its scent. No one had seen it once, and we all thought it moved on!*

"Ah, there he is!" Michael stated as the door flung open, and the rogue stepped in. My eyes widened when I realized how very wrong we all were. Because it wasn't a rogue at all. It was Derek.

"You—" I said quietly in disbelief. "It was you that attacked me that first night! You're the rogue everyone's been looking for!"

Derek rolled his eyes at me, shaking the snow from his coat. "You've been a difficult one to get rid of, that's for sure."

"Why did you attack me that night, Derek? Why are you doing this now!?" I demanded, and he leaned against the door.

"Being a mixer isn't enough?" he scoffed. "I scented you in town, well before you even made it up these mountains, and when I realized you weren't a full wolf, I decided to do what was best for the pack. But your aunt just had to cross paths with me that night, and I couldn't dispose of you then. I couldn't finish the job!"

"You're sick, you know that? What kind of a monster could do that to another person?" I shouted as I scurried to my feet. My fists clenched at my sides.

Derek snarled as he backhanded me across the face. Stars burst through my vision, and I fell back on the mattress pad. He suddenly yanked me up by my hair, and I stifled a scream. His hot, rancid breath reeked of rotting flesh, like he had just gone out for a hunt before coming to see me. Bile rose to the back of my throat as I struggled not to empty my stomach.

"I'd be quiet if I were you. I have had just about enough of you and that stupid mouth of yours," he growled.

Derek threw me to the floor then, and I landed hard on my side. I swore

CHAPTER 23

under my breath as pain shot down my leg from my hip, and he flipped me over abruptly, stepping on my neck so I couldn't move. Air was immediately cut off, and I tried to push against his boot. Panic surged again, and I instinctively tried to call on my animals, but everything was quiet still. That unforgiving pain throbbed against my skull, and I shut my eyes tight.

"Trying to shift?" he asked, with a chuckle. I pushed harder against his boot, but he only applied more pressure.

Derek laughed. "Yeah, that won't happen for a while now. We drugged you to make sure you couldn't use your shifter abilities. I mean, weren't you the least bit curious as to how *no one* was able to sense me when I was after you? Why no one was able to figure out where this rogue was?"

My eyes bugged out of my head. My lungs were screaming for air, and I felt my face turned purple before Derek finally moved his boot. Gasping for air, I rolled to my side and coughed uncontrollably. My vision swayed, and I blinked tears away. *Don't cry, Shanely,* I thought to myself. *Don't let them see you break.*

"Every time I've gotten close, you landed yourself smack in the middle of everyone. Stupid unexpected things would happen like that bear shifter showing up in his truck, or the real bear stumbling upon you by your cabin. I wanted this to be a quick and clean kill, you see. Just dispose of you deep into the mountains where no one would find you, but you had to go and make everything difficult by attaching yourself to overzealous shifters. First Cassia and the twins, then Caleb, and then Bastian and his annoying brothers."

I rubbed my throat, wincing as I swallowed. "How were you hunting me this whole time?"

Derek laughed again, like it was so clear, and I was just too dumb to understand. He sat down in the other chair, grinning wickedly at me. "That drug is highly effective in large quantities, but in small doses it merely hides you. I was always able to shift, but no one would be able to see me with the pack bond or pick up my scent. It let me go all over really. It cost me enough, that's for sure, but it was well worth it as you can see. I always get my marks, Shanely. I will always do what is best for the pack, even if they can't see that."

"All this because I'm a mixer?!" I growled out. My throat was hoarse, and it hurt to speak. I glared at Derek. *If I was a seer then where were my warnings for any of this?* I thought angrily. *I never received a warning about Derek or Michael!*

Derek threw a wad of cash on the table, ignoring me. "There. That's the final payment since you actually delivered. How did you manage getting in without alerting everyone?"

Michael laughed, tucking the money inside his coat pocket. "Because that abomination has everyone so relaxed, no one bats an eye to a bear in the woods now. Plus, they were all running around with the storm coming, so I went ahead and made sure they'd be busy for awhile."

Derek smirked. "Smart for a bear."

I looked at Michael with wide eyes. "*You* destroyed the generators?"

Michael snarled but said nothing as he got to his feet. "Are you going to kill her soon?" he asked, completely ignoring me as well.

I rubbed my neck and tried to scooch further away from them both. My belly started to hurt, and I was worried how the baby was doing. He had moved a moment ago, but now it was quiet. *Too quiet.*

"Just debating how," Derek answered. "Go. I have no more need of you."

Michael shrugged and left the hut, leaving me alone with Derek. *Maybe if I could keep him talking it would give my mate time to find me?* I thought to myself. It was the only hope I had honestly. Despair was slowly trickling in that he wouldn't find me in time though.

"Bastian will find me. He's probably already out looking," I replied, faking every bit of confidence that came out of my voice. My face throbbed, and my neck felt like he crushed my windpipe, but I hid the pain the best I could, giving him the nastiest glare I could muster.

Derek smirked, almost amused with me, and it shook my confidence that much more. "Yeah, I doubt that, but I'm banking on him dying in this storm with the rest of the failure that is this pack."

My heart stopped. I didn't think about that. *Bastian will freak when he won't find me at the lodge,* I thought as panic surged through my veins. *He'll*

CHAPTER 23

be out in this storm looking, and everyone else would be helping him. I was going to be the death of my family.

"This pack started to go downhill the moment you showed up. I knew we'd have problems the moment I saw you. You took my cabin on the border. You've let the bears into our lands. Shoot, you're even one of them! And now they've taken my land. I've had enough. You've got everyone wrapped around your little finger, and I'm done dealing with it," Derek snapped as he stood and looked out the window. "I've made a deal with Liam, and I'm moving my family to join his pack instead. It's clear I won't be advancing in this pack, and honestly I don't want anything more to do with a pack like this. Once I kill you, I'll be leaving for Denmark. Just got to wrap up a few things, and then I'm gone. The pack can tear itself apart looking for you. Eventually, they'll find some of the pieces, but it's hard to say when. Maybe they never will. I mean, we are extremely far up the mountain side."

"Did Liam ask you to kill me?" I whispered, fearing his answer. *Bastian would be devastated if Liam was involved in this.*

"Nah, I just needed to get my mark before I left," he answered, "but then again I doubt he'd mind. He doesn't seem to like you much either."

I scurried back as Derek stormed towards me. My back barely hit the wall when he suddenly yanked on my legs and pulled me towards him. He towered over me, gripping my wrist so tightly they burned in agony.

I was *helpless*. Utterly *useless* and at the mercy of Derek. I couldn't keep my fear from showing as my eyes welled with tears. They slowly ran down my cheek, and he gave me a wicked smile.

Derek knelt down slowly to whisper, "The storm's moving quick. I think this next part will be easier with you unconscious."

My heart thundered right before he struck me hard across the face. My head rebounded off the ground, and I was out like a light.

Chapter 24

My body was frozen solid.

Frozen solid and wet.

My head bobbed as I slowly came to, groaning with every jolt and bump my body felt. My head pulsed like never before, and I tried to open my eyes, but only my right would open. My left just seemed swollen shut and stuck together. *God, what did Derek do?* I thought as a harsh wind pierced my body. My teeth clattered together as I shivered, and goosebumps covered my entire body as I looked up at the dark sky.

The snow had stopped falling, but light was barely beginning to appear through the trees. I groaned as a sharp tingling sensation hit my arms. Panic pulsed within me when I realized my arms were tied above my head. I couldn't move them, and God they hurt like crazy. My head lifted, looking around to the passing trees and brush that I didn't recognize. *I was being dragged,* I thought as anxiety rushed through me. I tried to yank down my arms, but the tension from the rope forced them above my head, and I groaned, feeling my wrists burning like the skin was getting peeled underneath. *God, the pull was killing my arms, and I was soaking wet from the snow. Everything* in my body hurt.

I jerked to my side, hoping to stop Derek from dragging me even further, when suddenly I did something I never thought I would do.

I peed my pants.

My nose scrunched in disgust, when my stomach suddenly cramped. I sucked in a breath as the worst stomachache hit me.

But then my eyes widened.

CHAPTER 24

It wasn't pee, I thought as the cramp slowly subsided. *Oh my God— my water just broke.* I barely kept the sob from escaping my lips. Derek didn't seem to realize I was awake, and I was terrified he'd knock me unconscious again because I awoke too soon. *How was I going to get out of this?* I was already soaking wet, and my water breaking just made everything worse.

Another contraction hit, and I whimpered slightly. *Oh God, was this what contractions felt like?!* I thought as a tear fell down my cheek. My body already felt broken. *How was I going to escape while in labor?*

I tried my mind-link again because I needed help. I couldn't do this alone, and I prayed the drug was already wearing off. My animals were still gone, but maybe it had worn off enough for the link to work?

"Bastian!?"

Nothing. My heart sunk.

"Bastian!" I screamed inside my head.

"Cade!"

"Elijah!"

"ANYONE?!"

The silence was deafening. I felt like I was going to throw up. *No one could hear me,* I thought. *No one was coming to save me.* Anger coursed through my veins as I silently cried. Derek continued to drag me through the brush, and there was nothing I could do. *I was never going to see Bastian again. I was never going hear him call me love or kiss those too perfect lips again.* I had no idea what my death would do to him or if he would be just like my father and never know what happened to me. My heart ached for my mate. *I was going to die, and so was my baby.*

He or she would never take their first step or say their first word. Their life was about to be stolen from them all because I was different. My mother left the pack for this very reason, and I didn't follow her example. Now my child was paying the price, and I hated myself more than anything because I *should* have done more to protect them. I foolishly stopped worrying about the rogue, and I would pay the ultimate price for it.

Derek suddenly stopped pulling me, and I sagged in relief as I forced my arms below my head again. Blood flowed through my veins painfully, but

I didn't care. I was too busy watching Derek, trying to figure out what he was doing.

Derek was hunched over on my left with the rope. My eyes followed the line, and they narrowed when I realized he had tossed it over a thick branch above. I tried to roll over to my knees, when Derek pulled on the rope again, making me fall backwards. It was hard enough to knock the wind out of me, and it seemed to trigger another contraction. My whole body arched with the pain as Derek dragged further back and hoisted me in the air.

My eyes widened when my feet just barely touched the ground, burning my wrists bound by rope. I couldn't stop twisting in a circle, and bile rose the back of throat as the world spun. Derek laughed hysterically, watching me spin around helplessly.

This was funny to him?! I thought as my eyes flashed with rage.

"There," he said, helping me spin again. "This should work out just fine, I think."

I opened my mouth to spew venom, when another contraction hit. I groaned, hunching forward from the pain, and breathing heavy from my mouth. My vision blurred as agony rippled through my body, letting a small whimper escape my lips.

"Babies really do have terrible timing," he replied sarcastically.

I gritted my teeth, spitting in his face the moment I could breathe again. I was pissed and ready to tear him apart with my bare, *human*, hands!

Derek slowly wiped his face off, looking calmer than I thought he would, but when he pulled out his large hunting knife that was hidden on his hip, my eyes widened, knowing I had made a grave mistake. He sliced me across my legs before I even had a chance to beg him not to. I screamed as the pain became too much, and Derek brought the knife to my cheek. It was dripping wet with my blood, and he pushed into my skin ever so softly.

"Next time that happens, I slice across the belly. Understand?"

I barely nodded. He knew my weakness, and there was nothing I could do but wait. Wait to *die*. I looked down, watching my blood slowly drip off my leg and into the white snow below. I must be delusional because all I could think was how pretty the crimson blood looked against the pure

CHAPTER 24

white snow. My head swayed, and I blinked furiously to stay awake.

Derek abruptly pulled on the rope again, and my legs dangled freely in the air. I was completely suspended off the ground, and I watched Derek tie the rope off once more.

"There," he said with a grin. "I don't think you'll be going anywhere now."

Another contraction hit again, and this time I did cry out. I stopped caring about him watching me fall apart. The pain was getting worse, and I knew that meant I was running out of time.

"Bastian—"

Still no answer.

"You've got a nice puddle of blood happening below. That should be enough to attract all sorts of animals, and I think this will be more fun," he said as the wind shifted me slightly. "I mean, sure I could kill you myself, but can you imagine your mate stumbling upon this mess? You hanging what 6 or 7 feet off the ground? With your lower half missing or entirely mangled and half-eaten, no baby in sight. Yeah— this will do nicely."

The man was sick, I thought as my mouth watered. *God, I wanted to throw up*. Bile just sat at the back of my throat, and it was all I could do to keep myself from getting sick. *Derek was a cruel and disgusting man that needed to be removed from this earth.* But I couldn't do any of the things he deserved. I could only watch as he simply wiped the blood off his hands, my blood, looking almost proud of his work. It disgusted me.

"You will die, Derek," I muttered through my labored breathing. "I guarantee that."

He laughed. "Have a wonderful death, Shanely. I have a plane to catch."

Derek shifted before disappearing into the woods, leaving me alone. *If I never see that man again, it will be too soon*, I thought to myself. I tried to wiggle my arms around, hoping I could slip a hand through, but I could barely move them. Everything hurt, and I started shivering uncontrollably now. The only warmth I had was the blood coming out of me, and I knew I wasn't going to last much longer.

A contraction hit again, and this time I screamed. I screamed until my lungs wouldn't work. Hanging here for so long was restricting my air supply, but I couldn't figure out a way to get down. It felt like an eternity had passed since Derek strung me up here. My legs didn't want to move, and my arms were dead already. The only thing helping me keep track of the time was my contractions, which were coming closer and closer together.

I sobbed as I hung there. *This was going to be a slow death*, I realized. *I may even be alive when a predator finds me dangling here.* I cringed at the thought of being eaten alive. To feel every bite and tear of flesh as a wild animal consumed me.

"Bastian?" I begged through the link. *"Please hear me!"*

"Bastian!" I screamed with the last little bit of energy I had left. Silence *answered* me.

A heart-wrenching feeling hit me the moment I finally gave up. *No one was coming.* No one would even find me in time, and I knew if I passed out there was no waking up again. The nausea was unbearable from the blood loss, and I tried not to focus on it, but I was weak. Weak, in pain, and exhausted. I just wanted it to stop. I just didn't want to feel *this* anymore, and my eyelids slumped with heaviness.

Suddenly, I heard a howl off in the distance, and my heart stopped. I waited, listening carefully in case I was wrong. *Maybe I was just losing it now*, I thought to myself. *But it sounded like a wolf.* I just prayed it wasn't wild. It was eerily quiet in these woods, and I waited.

But then I heard it again! The howl was much closer this time, I was sure of it, and I cried out when I finally recognized it.

It was Cade!

I tried to call out his name, but I couldn't get any sound to come forth from my mouth. Nothing but tears came as I swung there. *He would surely smell the puddle of blood beneath me, right?* I tried to reassure myself that help was coming! The howl pierced the air again, but I couldn't quite tell which direction it was coming from.

"Cade—" I whispered, my throat burning.

Cade's wolf burst through the trees, and he jolted to a stop when he saw me. He howled again before charging towards me. Elijah shot through the trees moments behind him, and they both shifted. My eyes searched for Bastian.

"Shanely! Oh my God!" Cade shouted. "Elijah, cut the rope! I've got her."

Elijah ran to the rope and slid in the snow immediately with his knife at the ready. He started cutting it, while Cade grabbed me by my legs, pushing me up to give my arms relief.

"Oh my God, Shanely— there's so much blood," he muttered in shock. "Hurry up, Elijah!"

"I'm trying!" he shouted back. The rope snapped, and I collapsed against Cade. Everything swayed hard as I clung to reality, and Cade carefully laid me on the ground and tore off his coat. He wrapped it over me and then inspected my legs as Elijah ran to us.

"She's been sliced across her legs. She's lost a lot of blood, Elijah, and she's frozen solid," Cade cried out.

Elijah gritted his teeth as he ripped his coat off, tucking it underneath me. "What happened, Shanely?? We went back to the lodge, and you were just gone!"

"The baby," I whispered as another contraction struck. I cried out, and my back arched again. Cade pulled me close, trying to comfort me, but this was unbearable. I couldn't breathe as it rippled through my body with such sharpness before it slowly turned to an ache. I fell against him.

"Crap, are you in labor?!" Cade asked in a panicked voice. He never panicked. Cade was always the goofball of the three. He was upbeat and positive all the time. Nothing rattled him, but the look on his face scared me. It scared me half to death.

"What are we going to do?" Cade asked his brother, holding me tightly.

"I don't know. We're way too far up this side of the mountain, and everyone's spread out too far to use the mind-link. No one can hear us right now, and I've got no signal. This isn't good, man," Elijah answered as he ran his hand through his hair.

"Come on. There's an old abandoned hunting cabin to the west of us. We'll take her there and figure it out from as we go. Shanely, how far apart are the contractions?" Cade asked, hauling me off the ground.

"I don't know," I somehow managed to answer.

Cade made sure the coat stayed under me, while Elijah adjusted Cade's coat over me. I was sandwich between thick linings of fur, but I felt awful because they were left with nothing but their shirts. Cade's shirt didn't even have sleeves, but the boys didn't even seem to notice. They started moving quickly through the woods once I was in Cade's arms.

"Cade, this is dangerous this far up the mountain. You know where we're headed, right?" Elijah asked. He kept checking over his shoulder and scanning the woods as if something would jump out at us any minute.

"You got a better idea?" Cade muttered as he moved through the thick snow. In their human form, they moved a lot slower, and I felt horrible. I was already shivering and being carried in between their coats. They'd die from exposure before anyone would even find us.

"What about you guys? You'll freeze," I stammered.

"Shh, Baby Girl. Don't worry about us. You just stay under the coat. Elijah, check your phone. Do you have a signal now?"

He shook his head. "Not this far up the mountain, Cade. I have the timer ready though. We need to time her contractions."

"Do you know enough about childbirth to guide her through this?"

"Between the three of us, we can manage, I think. How much farther?" he asked, looking back at us. His eyes softened when they met mine.

"A couple more miles, I think. Just keep an eye out," Cade snapped before looking down. "Shanely, what happened? All Malin remembers was getting knocked in the head. We found her at the lodge but not you. That was two nights ago."

My eyes blinked slowly as exhaustion swept over me. "Michael, that bear I fought at the clan's land, drugged me with something. I tried to run, but he was so fast. He brought me up the mountain to Derek. He was the rogue."

Elijah growled viciously as his head whipped to mine. "Derek? He was the rogue? How is that even possible?"

"He used a low dose of the same drug, so no one could see him move

CHAPTER 24

around in his wolf form. He wanted to kill me because I am a mixer. A mixer who was letting the bears take everything, according to him."

"I am so sorry, Baby Girl. I knew he didn't care for you, but I *never* thought he'd do something like this. We should have figured this out, Elijah. That's on us," Cade snapped, and Elijah's eyes flashed gold. I didn't want them to blame themselves though. *No one could have seen this coming.*

"I can't believe he was even capable of something like this. He will die. I promise you, Shanely," Cade said as he stepped over a fallen tree.

"Do you know where he went?" Elijah growled.

"He left—"

I gripped Cade's shirt as the pain of labor hit me again, but this contraction hit me harder and seemed to last longer than the rest. Pressure was starting to build down low, and I tried to breathe through the pain, but it was really difficult. I slumped against Cade when it finally stopped.

The brothers looked at me nervously. I doubted they expected to be anywhere near me when I gave birth, let alone actually delivering my baby for me.

"Hang on, Baby Girl. I see the cabin now," Cade whispered as he rested his face against mine.

I snuggled against him, craving the warmth he had from his wolf. A part of me felt like I was fading away. My heart hurt missing Bastian, and all I wanted was to have him here with me. An overwhelming sadness draped over me as I thought of my mate.

"Bastian?" I whispered, and Cade just held me tighter.

"We'll find him. We'll find him," he whispered back.

"That's four minutes, Cade," Elijah said, and Cade nodded. My eyes grew heavy, and all I wanted to do was let my head fall back so I could sleep. I was too tired to hold it up anymore. I was too tired to do anything right now.

"Whoa, Baby Girl. You got to stay awake for me, okay?" Cade said nervously as he gently rubbed his face against mine.

"I'm awake, Cade. I'm awake."

The cabin was locked surprisingly, but Elijah had no problem kicking the door open, and Cade rushed me inside. There wasn't any electricity, and I didn't see a fireplace sadly. It was one large room, but at least we were out of the harsh wind. There was a couch on the left and just some random storage boxes on the right, with plenty of trash scattered about. Elijah slammed the door closed before turning back towards us.

"Set her here on the couch," Elijah commanded as he dragged the couch closer to us. It looked extremely old and loaded with dust. I'm sure it had been sitting here abandoned for years, but at this moment that couch looked like a 5-star hotel.

Cade set me down on the left side, propping me up against the back pillows before sitting down across from me. He lifted my legs, which had become stiff and extremely sore.

"Baby Girl, I need to remove your pants, okay? We need to prepare for the baby. Your contractions are really close together now," Cade told me, waiting for my response. I nodded as Elijah dug through the boxes around us.

"This ends my knowledge of child birth, Elijah. I hope to God you know more," Cade exclaimed as he started to pull my maternity leggings over the wounds on my leg. His face twisted in anger when he saw my exposed legs. I leaned forward slightly to see, and I had to admit they looked bad. *They were deeper than I thought.*

"I'm going to kill him. I swear to you, Shanely. I'm going to kill him."

"Get in line," I muttered, trying to lightened the mood. It didn't work.

Another contraction hit, and I sucked in a breath as it ebbed and flowed. Elijah came running over with an old blanket. He covered me and sat down next to us. He froze momentarily when he saw my legs too before focusing again on the task at hand.

"I found fishing wire for the cord, and I have my knife. This was the only blanket though," he mentioned as Cade grabbed my panties. He hesitated again.

"I'm going to take these off now," he said softly, looking at me with such intense sincerity that I knew he felt awful for me right now.

I nodded, giving him permission. I was in too much pain to even care that he was about to see all of my business. Cade slipped them off quickly and tossed them aside. Elijah moved his arm behind me to help hold me up before kissing my forehead. I rested my head back against him so grateful that they found me. His scent soothed me. It smelled so close to Bastian's, with just a small difference to it. I needed every ounce of comfort they could give.

Elijah gently rubbed my left eye, which was finally starting to open. He traced my wounds with his finger, trailing down to my neck.

"Cade—" Elijah muttered.

Cade looked up briefly and grimly nodded back. "I know. I saw that carrying her here."

"It's a boot mark," Elijah hissed as he gritted his teeth.

I pulled their attention away from my neck as another contraction hit. I cried out in pain, and Elijah never let me go. Cade spoke softly to me, but I couldn't even begin to understand what he was saying. *It was too much. It was all too much, and I just wanted to go home. I wanted my mate. I needed him!* I collapsed again after it passed. *I couldn't do this much longer,* I thought to myself.

"Elijah, you need to leave. Go get help," Cade stated firmly.

"No, I can't leave you two! You can't deliver a baby and then defend them by yourself. You know where we are, Cade!" Elijah shouted right back.

Outside, I could hear the wind picking up again. It was howling just like last night, and suddenly I feared another storm. *What if we are never found?* I thought as my anxiety rolled again. *What if another storm hit, and we were stranded up here?* We were clearly in a place that the boys feared, and that was saying something, but my baby wouldn't survive in these temperatures.

"Elijah, take a look around. This cabin looks like it's been abandoned for a long time, okay? She isn't going to last long being this cold and *this injured*, plus what are we going to do to keep this baby warm?" Cade said, giving him a pointed look. "This side of the mountain is full of large cats and high winds. She's bleeding like crazy, and it's freezing here. Something big is going to find her soon if we don't end up trapped by the weather again. We have no signal, and we're too far to mind-link anyone. We need help. You need to get Bastian," Cade pleaded.

Elijah looked torn. "I can't just leave you two though. My wolf is going crazy at the thought of it."

"Look, neither of us know how to deliver a baby. I'm praying mother nature just takes over here, but we're all going to die if you don't go. Bastian went opposite of us, but he can't be that far away. He's feral enough that nothing's going to go against him, and he's by far the largest wolf in the pack now. We *need* him to guide us down with Shanely, and he's also the closest wolf to us right now. Just go down far enough for the link to work, and you can call him. Just anything that will alert him to where we are! I've got Baby Girl."

Elijah glared a minute longer before abruptly kissing my forehead and shouting, "I will be right back, you hear me? Do not leave this cabin!"

Cade nodded, and Elijah bolted through the door before I could even say goodbye. I could hear his wolf howling in pain, getting quieter over time.

"Shanely, your body knows what to do, alright? So, when you feel pressure or like you need to push, just listen to your body."

Cade leaned down and grabbed Elijah's coat and recovered my chest. I had a few more contractions before I felt immense pressure and a whole lot of burn down below.

"Cade!" I yelled, and he gripped my hand tightly.

"You can do this, Baby Girl!" he shouted. "Just breathe!"

I obeyed my body like Cade told me too and pushed with all my might. What little strength I had left, I used right there. My whole body pulsed with pain, and I screamed, grabbing the back of my knees as I pushed with each contraction.

"Come on, Baby Girl! I can see the head. You're doing great! Just push!" Cade hollered. He gripped my hand, and I used him as a brace almost, pulling as hard as I could. He was a rock, never once moving or letting me go.

"One more, Shanely! Okay? The heads out already. We just need one more big push!"

A sob escaped my lips. "I can't, Cade. I'm too weak! Bastian should be here! I should be home, safe at the lodge, not dying in these mountains! This isn't fair! Why is it never fair for me!?"

I sobbed harder as I fell against the couch. *I couldn't do this anymore,* I thought to myself. *I'm done.*

Cade gripped my chin like Bastian always did, pulling me forward to look at him, and my heart broke even more. *He should be here! My mate should be here.*

"You can do this, Shanely. You are by far the strongest girl I know, so don't give up. Your baby needs you, so push!"

He forced his hand back in mine, and I listened to him. I pushed again, feeling such fiery agony before a rush of liquid came out, and I cried out in relief. The pain was gone instantly, and I heard the most beautiful sound I have ever heard before. A baby's cry.

"Baby Girl!" Cade cried out, grinning like a banshee. "You did it! Oh my God! I'm so proud of you!"

He quickly wiped the fluid off the baby's face with his sleeve and wrapped Elijah's coat around it. A sly grin crept up his face as he turned to look at me again.

"I was right by the way," he said smugly.

"What?" I said, laying my head back. Too tired to lift it anymore.

"Here, hold your daughter."

With that, he placed this tiny, and just perfect, little baby in my arms. *A girl,* I thought to myself. *I had a daughter! A beautifully little girl.*

"Oh, look at you little one," I muttered, placing my finger in her hand. "Couldn't wait a few more days, huh?"

Cade wrapped the fishing line tight around the cord and then used Elijah's knife to cut it. I was mesmerized by her. She looked just like me, and I couldn't believe she was really here.

He knelt closer to us, getting a better look at her, and he smiled wide. "She looks just like you, Baby Girl. Well done."

Cade kissed my forehead as he slipped his arm behind us, giving me more support to sit up, and I rested my head against his shoulders.

"I wish Bastian could have been here for this. He missed it," I whispered sadly. Tears welled in my eyes because he missed our daughter's birth.

"I know," he said solemnly. "Bastian will find us though. We'll get out of this."

"How is Bastian doing?" I asked quietly.

Cade looked sad for a moment. "It's not been good, Shanely. He just about snapped when the bond disappeared."

"You said he was feral?"

Cade sighed. "Pretty darn close. He blames himself for not staying with you in the first place, but it was all our fault. When you were just gone, we didn't know what to think or even where to start looking. His wolf took over in a lot of ways. Feral is a nice way of putting things."

I sighed heavily. My mate was hurting, and I honestly don't know who had it worse right now. I couldn't imagine being in his shoes. Not knowing what happened or if the other was safe.

"I'm sorry, Cade," I whispered.

Cade brushed away the hair fallen on my face. "Shanely, you have nothing to be sorry for. You've had a horrible few days, and someone tried to kill you. Don't apologize for that monster. I'm just glad we found you when we did. Elijah will find Bastian, and before you know it we will be back home snuggling with this little one."

He smiled down at me, and while hearing what he said made me feel better, I still felt horrible for all the worry and pain I put everyone through. Especially my mate. My stomach started to cramp again, causing me to worry, and I sat up a little more.

"Cade, something's wrong."

He flew back to the other end of the couch.

"What's going on? Another contraction?" he asked, completely oblivious to where he was looking or how exposed I really was, but now that the pain of labor was gone, I was fully aware.

"Milder. Is it the placenta?" I asked, trying to get my embarrassment under control.

"The what?!"

My stomach cramped, but it was nothing compared to the actual contractions, and I felt a wet goo slowly fall out of me.

"What is that?" he asked, his face looking slightly pale.

I laughed weakly. "The placenta. The baby grew in that. I'm so sorry to ask this, but you need to make sure it's all there."

"How do I do that?!" Cade asked, looking mortified. I think the adrenaline was wearing off the both of us because he was completely freaking out now. *If I wasn't hurting so bad, I think I'd be doubled over laughing.*

"I don't know! I just know if a piece is missing then I can bleed out!"

He poked the placenta around, twisting and turning it, while making a weird face. I felt awful as his hands were now covered in my blood, but it had to happen.

"It looks all there, but I'll be honest, I have no idea what it's supposed to even look like. I could be wrong."

"Well, we will know in a matter of minutes then," I said grimly.

"Hey, don't lose hope. You have survived so much, Shanely. I know we're all going to make it home safely," he replied as he covered my legs back up. Thankfully, the bleeding seemed to be slowing down, but I was still weak from what blood I did lose.

Cade instantly whipped his head to the back of the cabin, and he put his finger to my mouth to shush me. *I didn't even try to say something,* I thought to myself.

I listened carefully but couldn't hear anything but wind. He was hyper focused though and slowly moved his head to whatever he was listening to. That's when I heard a growl. It was very faint, but still there, somewhere in the distance. Cade inhaled a deep breath before muttering something to himself. I couldn't smell anything, and I opened my mouth to ask him a question, but he shook his head no. I snapped my mouth shut and hoped my baby stayed asleep. I pulled Elijah's coat over her head to shield her as much as possible from the cold.

Cade abruptly stood and tried to look out the windows. He looked alarmed, and I could see his enforcer training start to kick in.

"Did that sound close to you?" I finally asked, because I just couldn't take it anymore. I was trying to keep the panic from rising anymore than it already was, and I was seriously praying Cade would relax and tell me it was just my mate.

"Something must have your scent, Shanely," he replied quietly, and my heart stopped.

"What do we do, Cade? I can't walk, and it's so cold. She'll die in this weather! She doesn't even have a name, and she's going to die!"

I started crying all over again, and Cade rushed to me. He grabbed my chin, forcing me to look him in the eyes as he said, "Neither one of you will die, I promise you that. We'll stay here for now. I only heard one lion, so if I need to, I can step out and kill it."

"Don't leave us!" I pleaded with him.

Cade smiled at me and said, "Never, Baby girl."

And that's when a large mountain lion crashed through the window behind us.

Chapter 25

Glass flew everywhere.

The frigid cold air hit my lungs as I dove into the couch to shield my baby. Cade toppled over me, and I heard a hiss coming forth from the lion. My eyes widened as Cade slowly stood. *I had never seen a lion up close like this before,* I thought to myself. My heart began to race as a second, *much larger,* lion jumped through the window.

"Shifters," Cade snarled, and I held onto my baby tighter.

The two cats shifted into men, and I scooted back against the couch. Both were of average height and wore clothing that blended in well with the snowy woods outside. One was bald, while the other had hair down to his shoulders. Both were unremarkable, but I knew better than to judge a book by its cover. *This was not good.*

The long-haired man nudged his friend, grinning as he pointed at me and said, "Guess we could have used the front door after all."

His friend snorted. "What do we have here?"

"Trespassers, I'd say."

"Just passing through gentlemen. We just made a pit stop is all," Cade replied. He slowly knelt down beside me and picked me up off the couch with my daughter in my arms. I dragged that blanket with me, tucking it in to keep the cold from hitting my daughter further.

"You know I really don't like trespassers, David," the long hair guy said, and the other grunted in response.

"Since when do mountain lions work together? You all are lone hunters usually," Cade asked, inching backwards towards the front door.

David scoffed. "When it's mutually beneficial, that's when. You know the bounty we collect on wolf heads? The Tiger King *loves* to hang a wolf."

The other one took a deep breath, eyeing me closely. "What is she though?"

"She is none of your business. I'm warning you, lion. You come any closer to her, and I promise it will be the end for you," Cade snarled. His eyes flashed red, taking me by surprising. *I had to give it to him,* I thought to myself. *He was every bit as fierce as Bastian.*

"Frank— it seems we have someone important here. I bet we'd get more from the King for her."

"That's what I was thinking," Frank replied, and my stomach twisted. "Plus, I smell a pup."

Cade stepped backwards before barring his teeth at them. "One *last* chance. Walk away and live or die right now!"

"Hey, you're on our land! You're just asking for trouble being here," David snarled.

"This is Dead Man's Hollow!" Cade hollered back. "No one owns it. You are just the only ones stupid enough to stay here, but it doesn't make it your land!"

"Name calling now? And you say we're dumb," Frank tsked away. David just looked pissed as his hands clenched together in a tight fist.

"I will kill you if you don't leave now," Cade growled, his wolf pulling through his voice, and my heart began to thunder in my chest. *He can't fight them both,* I thought. *He's out-numbered and—*

"And what exactly do you think you're going to do with her in your arms?" David asked, pulling me from my thoughts.

Cade hesitated before he took another step backwards.

"You know everyone says how stupid cats are, but I didn't believe them until now," he said before flinging the door open and bolting out of the cabin.

Cade ran fast for not being in his wolf form, and I jostled around in his arms. I clung to my baby as Cade stumbled slightly, righting himself, and bolting to the left in an attempt to ditch them. I could hear the snarls and growls gaining on us and fear gripped my heart. *Cade had major stamina, but he wasn't going to last forever, especially when we ran into deep snow*, I thought as I tried to peek over his shoulder. The lions had shifted and were moving easily in the snowy terrain.

A screeching wail pierced the air, and my little girl began to cry. Cade's lungs heaved as he continued to run, and I felt awful for him. *This was too much*, I thought as my brother-in-law bolted left again and ran down a hill. He slid in the snow, and I squealed when we went down, but he landed on his knees and slid the rest of the way down.

Cade grunted as he stood again, shifting me in his arms before running down the trail. I could see Elijah's tracks in the snow, and I prayed he was close. Cade's head snapped to the right, and he swore before bolting off the path again.

Suddenly, a lion shot out before us, and Cade ground to a stop, breathing hard. It screamed at us, and the larger cat soon made its appearance too. The lions just paced back and forth before us, and tears had filled my eyes. I searched for my bear or my wolf but neither were there and panic crept in. *I wouldn't be able to help him fight the lions—*

Other than my daughters soft cries, the forest was silent. As if waiting to see what the other do first, the three men just glared. Cade shifted on his feet, and I could see the panic in his eyes. For a brief second, he looked to the left, but soon his attention was back on the threat before us. He scented the air next, and I realized what he was doing. *Cade was looking for his brothers*, I thought, praying they were close.

David shifted back. "Leave them, and save yourself, wolf. We'll be happy with just those two!"

Cade's eyes narrowed in anger, but he sighed before lowering me to the ground. He propped me up against the tree and kissed my forehead.

"Tell my family I love them, okay Baby Girl? Promise me?" he said softly, and my eyes widened. He looked so sad, pleading with me to say yes, and my heart snapped as I understood what he was doing. *Cade was saying goodbye. He didn't think he was going to make it out alive.*

I gripped his shirt tightly and pulled him close. "Cade don't. You walk away right now. Do you hear me? Walk away, and find my mate. I will be okay while you do."

A tear slid down my cheek, and he softened with me. His hand slowly reach and untucked my grip on his shirt. I couldn't breathe as he gently wiped my tear away and smiled.

"Tell Bastian I am sorry too," he whispered, leaning down to give my daughter a kiss. "Take care, Aerith. Your uncle Cade loves you very much. Make sure she knows that too."

Without another word, he stood and faced the mountain lions courageously.

"Cade—" My voice trailed off as he took a few steps forward, never once turning around to look back at me.

"Well—" Cade snapped as he tossed his hands in the air, "what are you waiting for? An invitation? If you're too stupid to walk away, then you deserve everything that's coming to you!"

Cade ran, howling as he shifted to meet the lions. David shifted mid-jump and collided with Cade with a sickening thud. I could do nothing but *watch*. Watch as my best friend fought to protect me. I tried to summon my bear or my wolf again, *begging* them at this point to finally come back and help me, but both were gone, like they never existed in the first place. I felt completely human, and I *hated* it.

"Cade behind you!" I shouted as one of them tried to grab Cade's back leg.

Cade jumped out of the way in the nick of time and bit down on the lion's shoulder. He hissed back and started bucking, trying to throw Cade off, but Cade hung on. He shook his head until I heard a sickening snap. The lion's leg went limp and blood started to pour from the wound. *It looked like Cade was trying to tear it off completely.*

My heart stopped though when the other lion slammed into Cade, pinning him to the ground. The lion took a swipe with his back paws and cut Cade deep along his side. I screamed when blood appeared all over Cade's belly. He snarled back at him and snapped his jaw around the lion's leg. It howled loudly as Cade tore into his flesh, but the other lion suddenly bit down on

CHAPTER 25

Cade's leg, causing him to let go.

"Cade—"

I sobbed in the snow, unable to do anything to help. *I was watching my best friend die, and there was nothing I could do to save him.*

The lion slammed into Cade, forcing him back as he slid across the snow. This time Cade didn't move. He just whimpered as blood pooled around him. The lion paced back and forth, watching Cade closely, while the other started limping towards me. Cade snarled again but stayed down.

"Cade— please," I begged him, staring into his blue eyes. The snow around him turned red, and I suddenly snapped. "Please don't kill him!" I begged. "I'll go with you willingly if you just leave him alone!"

The lion circling him turned to face me as Cade snarled loudly. His gold eyes told me he was screaming down the bond at me, but I didn't care. I would gladly go if it meant Cade would live.

The two slowly crept my way, and I held my breath. *They were taking me up on my offer,* I thought as relief washed over me. Cade growled loudly, struggling to stand again, but he slumped over in the snow. My lips puckered as I watched his body fail him.

"Cade don't—"

Suddenly, the lion with the limp snapped his jaw around my foot and pulled hard. I screamed as his teeth punctured my ankle, and he dragged me into the clearing. I clung to the blanket, keeping it around me and my baby, as the lion continued to drag me. The other hissed loudly, and he finally let go. They snapped at one another, and I tried to push myself up. I only had the blanket around my lower half and a new kind of fear crept in. I had barely rolled to my side, when the large lion hovered over me. I held my breath as he barred his teeth. Saliva dripped from his mouth, hitting me on my cheek, and I stifled a sob.

Cade snarled again, but this time he sounded weaker than before. I couldn't turn to look as the lion growled in my face loudly, and I screamed as he pawed at the blanket.

I shut my eyes tight, when a rush of air passed over me, and the lion was shoved away. My eyes widened as a black blur crashed into him, and the two tumbled in the snow.

"Bastian!" I cried out in relief.

My mate looked back at me, and his eyes filled with instant relief, but I laid there gaping at him. His wolf looked wild and feral. *Exactly the way Cade described him earlier.* Bastian didn't look like his normal self, and I put my hand to my mouth in shock.

Bastian's eyes were solid red just like an Alpha's should be, I thought to myself. Bastian barred his teeth to the lions as he stood protectively in front of me. I glanced to Cade, and my heart stopped when I noticed his eyes were closed, and he didn't look like he was breathing. *No, no, no!*

"Cade's not breathing!" I shouted.

Bastian howled loudly, while the cats hissed. They charged forward, and my mate met them halfway.

It was then I realized what Bastian had done. Elijah suddenly flew into the clearing and into the large cat's side. All four were rolling on the ground fighting, while I slowly dragged myself towards Cade. I made sure Aerith stayed covered in my arms as I painfully made my way through the snow, ignoring the throbbing pain in my legs.

There was blood everywhere, and I inspected the long wound on his torso and belly. I shimmy out of the coat I wore, shivering harshly when the cold air hit again, and pushed it against his wound, hoping to slow the bleeding.

"Please Cade," I whispered. "Please open your eyes."

But Cade's eyes stayed shut. No matter how many times I begged for them to open. A faint howl sounded in the distance, and the largest cat suddenly shifted. The fight ground to a halt.

"I'm warning you, wolf. You're picking a fight you can't win!" David snarled, looking haggard and beaten. Bastian simply growled back in response.

"What?" David snapped. "You not going to talk to me now? I think you'll want to hear my deal though."

Frank shifted now and looked out of breath. His arm looked mangled, and I gritted my teeth. *I wish Cade had just ripped the stupid thing off.* Elijah slowly made his way in front of us, snarling as he went.

CHAPTER 25

David looked to Elijah, then to Bastian, and finally back to Cade. "This girl must be pretty special to get such protection from all three of you."

Frank smirked. "Have you seen her, brother? She's absolutely delicious, especially without that blanket."

Bastian shifted instantly. "Don't talk about her like that!"

My eyes widened. *His human form looked as feral as his wolf did.* His hair was all over the place kind of messy and blood caked his skin. *That wasn't fresh,* I thought to myself. His chest heaved as he started to pace back and forth in front of me.

"I think we found the mate, Frank," David said, chuckling to themselves. Frank's eyes gleamed with amusement before settling back on me.

"You three are not going to win this. We've been collecting wolves for some time, and that one's nearly dead. The Tiger's King already been informed we're bringing in the best haul we've had in a long while from this wretched place, so there's no point trying to fight it," Frank said casually.

"But we can make you both a deal though. Same deal we gave that one," David said, gesturing to Cade, and I tightened my grip on his fur. David slowly dragged his eyes back to Bastian saying, "*Run.* Run for your lives, and we won't mention anything to the Tiger King about you two. You might even save that one over there, but the girl and pup comes with us."

My breath caught in my throat. I had never heard of the Tiger King before, and by the looks of the brothers, he was a new threat to them too. My eyes slowly drifted to Cade. Blood seeped through the coat still, and my heart cracked. *He was going to die,* I thought to myself. *It took two to carry Elijah, and Cade was the same size. They couldn't carry us both.*

I knelt down and kissed the top of Cade's head, knowing what I had to do.

"Just me!" I shouted, and the whole group turned to me.

Bastian stole my attention though. His feral eyes shot to mine and then to our baby. His jaw locked when he noticed the blood, but that was good. He needed to see how dire Cade was to accept what I planned on doing.

I looked to David saying, "You don't get the pup. You can take me to the Tiger King if you promise to leave these three and my child *alone.*"

Bastian roared, but I kept my gaze on David. He was thinking, contemplating, but Cade didn't have that kind of time. Elijah shifted, staring at me in utter shock, but it was Bastian who startled me. His eyes had darkened to the point I didn't recognize him anymore. His fists had clenched so tightly that blood would fall if he didn't let up. I turned to my mate, hoping to reason with him.

"I'll be okay, my love," I said softly as tears filled my eyes. "But Cade's dying, and I won't let your brother die. You can't carry us both so please *save* him."

A soft cry escaped my lips before I could stop it, and Bastian barred his teeth. Bastian's anger was overwhelming, but it stung when he ignored me. *He had to know why I wanted this?* I thought as I searched his face for any sign he understood. *He had to know I loved him more than anything, but I couldn't live with myself knowing I had a chance to save Cade and didn't take it.*

Bastian simply turned around. Never once saying anything to me.

"Done," David cried out. "You've got a minute to grab your brother and the kid, and move on."

"Why do you even want her so badly?" Elijah demanded.

Cade's chest moved slower now, and the pain I felt in my heart grew unbearable. He was barely breathing, and I didn't know what to do. I couldn't help *anyone.*

"She's different. Plus, look at her. Even with all that's broken, she's still the sexiest thing we've seen in a long time," Frank said. "She'll cut our debt in half once the Tiger King sees her."

Bastian roared again, and my eyes widened. I watched my mate closely, and even Elijah looked alarmed. *That didn't sound like his wolf—*

David studied Bastian as his eyes furrowed. He pointed at my mate then. "You— you're just like her, aren't you?"

Bastian shook where he stood, and I held my breath as a new color of fur appeared on the back of his arms.

Frank took a step back, looking warily between my mate and I. "Maybe we should just let it go, David."

David narrowed his eyes. "And bring nothing to the Tiger King?! No, the deal was made, and that slut's coming with us!"

CHAPTER 25

Bastian stumbled forward, roaring so loud, it shook the trees. His bones cracked and shifted in a different way than I had ever seen, and my jaw dropped. Gray fur pulled through his skin, and his shoulders grew massive as black claws dug into the snowy earth.

Elijah backed away from his brother, looking more afraid than I had ever seen him look. He came for me. Never once taking his eyes off his brother, and my heart started to thunder in my chest. *It can't be—*

In an instant, the mate I knew had changed into something new. The dark paws of his smokey gray grizzly shook the earth as he landed, and he roared again. Frank flew backwards, landing hard on his back, and he scurried to get to his feet. The stench of fear filled the air, but I couldn't believe what I was seeing.

"My God," Elijah muttered. "Bastian's a bear shifter."

"He's a mixer," I added softly, as my hands tangled in Cade's fur tightly. I held onto my best friend, trying to steady my ragged breath.

And then Bastian charged.

He went for Frank first, and David bolted out of the way. Frank screamed as he tried to shift, but Bastian caught him on his back and slammed him to the ground again. Frank's head bounced off the ground, dazing him.

David hissed as his cat ran to attack my mate from behind, and my heart seized. Bastian swung his large paw, shoving David aside as if swatting a fly, and my eyes widened. Bastian's jaws suddenly clamped around Frank's neck, lifting him off the ground as blood rolled down his body. His gut-wrenching screams filled the air until a sickening snap sounded, and Bastian finally let him go. Frank fell to the ground, eyes wide open, and did not move again.

I rolled to the side and emptied my stomach. Frank's dead eyes churned my insides violently. I could still hear the fight continue behind me, and I wiped my mouth clean as my body shook.

Elijah pulled me into arms, whispering over and over, "I've got you, Shanely. I've got you."

David's cat screamed, echoing throughout the forest, and he charged again. Bastian roared as he ran to meet him. All it took was one swipe of his paw against David's spine to drop him. I looked down at my own hands, remembering how sharp my bear's claws were when I fought Michael. *That cut went deep,* I thought as David struggled on the ground.

His back legs were useless, and he cried out in pain, writhing in the snow. Bastian stalked towards David, and even from here I could see the pure hatred in that lion's eyes. *He wasn't sorry,* I thought. He was pissed and going to stare death straight in the face until the bitter end.

Bastian bit the back of his neck and shook violently. David's eyes rolled to the back of his head, and my mate dropped him, roaring so loudly I covered my ears. But then he reared back and slammed his paws down on the lion's body. My eyes widened, and I gave Elijah a worried glance. Bastian repeated this, slamming his heavy frame against David as he continued to roar. *Was he feral?!*

Suddenly, my family burst through the trees and skidded to a stop when they saw the massacre. Bastian paid them no mind and roared a final time before finally leaving David mangled in the snow. I stared at my mate, who finally turned to face me. His fur was covered in blood, but I watched his red eyes fade slowly to blue, and I sagged in relief. *He saved us— he saved us all.*

Without a word, he ran to me and shifted as he slid in the snow. He tore his coat off and forced it on me. Warmth immediately surrounded me as a sob escaped my lips. He grabbed my face, pulling me closer, and I held my breath as his eyes flashed gold.

"Don't you ever ask me to leave you again," he growled. "Do you understand me, Shanely? I don't want to hear those words leave your mouth *ever* again."

His gruff voice captivated me, but the longer I looked into his eyes, I realized they weren't filled with anger but *fear.* Bastian looked ready to break as he waited for my answer, so I simply nodded my head, giving him the answer he needed. He kissed me hard then, and I melted into him. I was desperate, but soon I broke our kiss when my overwhelming emotions took control, and I started to sob.

"Bastian—" I whispered, my voice breaking ever so slightly. "I didn't

CHAPTER 25

think I'd ever see you again."

"I will always find you, Shanely," he whispered, when he noticed the little one squished between us. "And you. I will *always* find you too, Little One."

The corners of my mouth rose as I leaned against his head. Our baby rooted around under the coat, entirely oblivious to what just happened.

"Bastian, how did you do—" Elijah stammered, but Bastian just shook his head.

"We need to move. Shanely's still bleeding, and the baby's getting too cold. Cade's unconscious too," Bastian stated as he turned to the others blatantly staring at him. "I said move!"

The group moved abruptly, and my eyes widened. Cain and Cassia said nothing to the snarly command, and I watched my family shift to help us. *Cain's wolf must understand the stress Bastian is under to forgive the disrespect,* I thought to myself.

Cassia slid in the snow next to me, placing her hands on Cade, and I exhaled the breath I'd been holding when her eyes began to glow. "Go Bastian," she said firmly. "Get her and the baby back to the lodge, and we will meet you there. I need to close some of Cade's wounds before he can be moved. I've got him, I promise!"

Bastian gave her a grateful look before hauling me into his arms. I groaned when my legs dangled low, and Elijah forced him to adjust.

"Don't look," he commanded my mate. "Just keep your arm here." Bastian gave him a look, but Elijah shook his head saying, "Trust me."

I held my breath, tucking my knees up for relief, and wondering if Bastian would look anyways. His whole body was tense, but to my surprise, he adjusted his arms and pulled me in close. With one last look to Cade, Bastian bolted down the trail.

He was swift through the woods, and I pulled the blanket over the both of us to hold in as much warmth as I could manage. That bitter wind was brutal as Bastian ran through the woods towards home, and I needed to make sure our baby stayed warm until we got to safety. Her whole body was pressed against my skin, trying to give her as much heat as I could, and she seemed alright. I, however, could feel my entire body wanting to shut down with how cold I was, but she seemed perfectly fine against me. *I'm grateful their coats had a thick fur lining,* I thought to myself. *It was probably the only reason why she was alive right now.*

Bastian moved fast down the mountainside, and it didn't escape my notice that he wasn't tiring out the way he should. Cade was breathing hard by this point, but my mate kept going. *Was this because he's a mixer now?* I wondered to myself. I placed my hand on the torn part of his shirt, feeling his warm skin against mine. His heart thundered in his chest, but he kept his breathing even and steady as he ran through Dead Man's Hollow.

He was suddenly slowing his pace, and I stole a peek from under the blanket. He had stopped at a handful of snow mobiles that were parked under the trees.

"Everyone took a snow mobile so far before tracking on foot. We'll get home much faster now, baby," Bastian answered, and I looked up to him. I realized he had spoken more to keep his wolf in check than for my benefit, but it didn't bother me. I was safe with him, and I knew we'd reach home again. I gently reached up and touched his cheek. His eyes closed for a moment as he leaned into my touch, but the comfort was short lived as he abruptly moved again, choosing a snow mobile to drive us down.

Bastian carefully tossed my injured legs over the seat and climbed aboard behind me. I sat upright, wincing as we got adjusted, but I stilled when I noticed him staring at me. It was like he was finally seeing my injuries, and his eyes flashed with emotion.

"Oh my love—"

It was the hesitation in his voice that threw me. *I must look absolutely horrible for him to stumble like that,* I thought to myself. I dropped my head, pulling the blanket over my face so he wouldn't see anymore. I heard his heavy sigh then.

"Are you strong enough to hold onto me while I steer us home?" he asked softly.

I nodded my head and adjusted our daughter in my arms. I carefully positioned her between the two of us and wrapped my other arm around

CHAPTER 25

his neck. I was snug against him the moment he gripped the handle bars, and I felt the warmth of his breath when he leaned down to whisper, "Hang on, baby."

Bastian slowly took off as we heard howls coming from behind us. Relief washed over me, knowing Cade and the others weren't far behind. Soon, I heard nothing but the snow mobile as Bastian drove us home. *Bastian was right,* I thought to myself. *We definitely were going to get home a lot faster with this thing.* It was a tricky pass to drive through, and some spots he had to slow way down just to get through safely, but my mind couldn't help but wonder how Michael managed to bring me up here in the first place.

I heard the pack long before the lodge came into view. The enforcers swarmed the snow mobile, howling as they ran on either side to protect us. The gratitude I felt was overwhelming, and I smiled when I stole a peek at them.

Bastian slowed the snow mobile down, and I watched a good chunk of the enforcers bolt back into the woods. *Going to escort Cade and the others down,* I thought to myself as we made the last little stretch towards home.

I couldn't contain my smile. This place had truly become my home. *The only home I ever wanted to have,* I thought to myself. I leaned against my mate, smiling, as Bastian pulled up to the lodge and stopped the snow mobile.

Chapter 26

I groaned as Bastian lifted me off the snow mobile and carried me inside. A multitude of voices sounded the moment we rushed in, but it was the warmth on my skin that held my attention. *God, they must have cranked the heat just for me,* I thought as I exhaled deeply. I wiggled my toes, trying to get feeling to return and regretting it immediately when pain pulsed from my legs.

Bastian didn't say a word to anyone before taking off to the back rooms where Malin's exam rooms were. He kicked the door closed, silencing the voices demanding to know what happened and where everyone else was. Only then did I untuck myself from the blanket, giving him a grateful smile. *I didn't want anyone to see me like this.*

My mate set me down carefully on the left bed before rushing to the cabinet across from it. Dr. Malin had plenty of warming blankets ready in the cabinet, and soon Bastian had put every single one over me. I sighed into the unbelievable warmth and let my eyes close. *I was home— I was alive and home.*

My eyes fluttered open when I heard Bastian yanking every drawer open then. His shoulders were still tense as he slammed cabinet after cabinet, grabbing supplies he needed to help me. My heavy eyes drifted to our little girl though. She was still rooting around, and I knew the intense cry was coming.

"Bastian—" I said softly, "she needs to eat."

Bastian stopped dead in his tracks, turning to me slowly as he asked, "She?"

CHAPTER 26

It was then I realized only Cade and I knew the gender. I smiled wide, nodding my head as I pulled the blanket down so he could see her face.

"You have a daughter, Bastian, " I answered. "Meet Aerith. I'm sorry, Cade named her before he fought the lions."

The familiar smirk I had grown to love crept up his face, and he shook his head. "Way to be dramatic, Cade, but I like it. Aerith Fenrir."

That ghost of a smile quickly fell before he raided Malin's tall cabinet for formula. He read the instructions on how to make the bottle as I gently rolled her off my chest and laid her next to me. The cries came then, but I was so exhausted, I was afraid to drop her if I didn't set her down. My body was crashing, and it was all I could do to keep my eyes open.

Bastian shook the bottle as he dug around in another cabinet, when I whispered his name. My mate looked over, and his eyes looked heavy with grief when he understood what I needed. He scurried over and took her from me, wrapping her in one of the warming blankets for now.

Aerith latched quickly for her dad, and he seemed in awe of her. I had finally let my eyes close to rest. *She was safe. I was safe, and we were finally where we belonged*, I thought as I let myself go. A soft hand pushed my fallen hair aside, and when the bed dipped, I opened my eyes to find my mate looking ever so broken at me. The pain in his eyes was too much to bear, and I rolled to my side, placing my hand on his leg.

"Do not blame yourself for this," I said softly, and he dropped his gaze from mine.

"I'm so sorry, Shanely. I never should have left you alone that night," he muttered shamefully. It broke my heart, and I tugged on his shirt. He slowly looked back to me.

"Bastian, none of this is your fault. You saved me *again*," I said, giving him a pointed look. "No one knew what Derek was planning. He was the rogue."

He gritted his teeth saying, "When I get my hands on Derek, I swear—"

Panic surged within me at the idea of him chasing after that wolf. Tears filled my eyes as I tightened my grip on him. "Please, don't leave me."

My voice shook softly, and he softened his rage. Bastian scooted closer, burying his face in my neck, and I inhaled his scent. It was an unbelievable comfort, and I took several deep breaths, trying to permanently burn that scent into my brain. The floodgates open then, and I sobbed against his shoulder, clinging to my salvation, and he never let me go. He stayed until my tears dried themselves, and I pulled back to kiss his cheek.

Leaning his head against mine, he said with a quiet voice, "Shanely, I need to look at your injuries."

I nodded my head, knowing this was going to suck, and he gently laid Aerith in the bassinet with the warming light above. My shifter abilities were slowly returning, but the drug must still be in my system because I wasn't healing fast enough and both my animals were gone still. Infection was sure to set in if I didn't get the wounds cleaned and stitched together.

A haunted look appeared on Bastian's face as he turned to face me, but when I blinked it was gone. He grabbed a warm, wet rag and sat down next to me again. He inspected my face first, turning my cheek in both directions as he wiped the blood and grime away. His eyes darkened when his hand reached my neck. "What happened here?"

"Derek's boot," I replied, with a snort.

His eyes met mine, flickering gold as he asked, "His boot? He *stepped* on your neck?"

The mood in the room shifted, and I placed my hand over his, keeping him calm and tethered to me. It wouldn't surprise me one bit if he lost grip over his animals and they sought out revenge. We hadn't even gotten to the worst part, and he was already hanging on by a thread.

"I'm okay, Bastian," I said softly. "It will heal, I promise."

He said nothing, but he didn't leave either, and I took that as a win. He continued addressing the wounds on my body silently, wiping my skin as clean as he could get for now. I had small cuts and minor bruises here and there, and some discomfort from delivering Aerith, but my legs were the worst of everything. I knew they would be the hardest to look at.

I winced as Bastian removed the blanket from my legs and saw the open wound. He stilled as his eyes flashed to solid gold, and I quickly covered them back up. Bastian visibly shook, fighting the shift from happening, and

CHAPTER 26

apparently losing when fur began to appear on his arm. I was afraid he'd lose control and run off to hunt Derek, but he stood abruptly and yanked open the cabinets again. I watched him closely as he got what supplies he wanted, setting it on the small table between the two beds.

"Your legs need to be cleaned before they begin to close," he said gruffly, his wolf's voice twisting with his words.

"You really don't need to fuss over me, Bastian. I'll heal— just be with me now," I pleaded with him. *I didn't want him to deal with my wounds,* I thought to myself. *Not when they hurt him so.*

A look I did not like appeared on his face when he said, "If I had just been where I was *supposed* to be, none of this would of happened. I have to fix this, so please just let me take care of you."

My heart sank, and I placed my hand against his cheek. I held his gaze saying, "Only if you promise to stop blaming yourself for this. This wasn't *your* fault. Call it a compromise."

His eyes filled with despair, remaining gold as he answered, "Shanely— I don't know how I will ever not feel horrible for this."

My shoulders sunk, knowing full well there was nothing I could say to change his mind. So I let him fuss over me. Anything to ease his wolf and help him feel better. He uncovered my legs from the mounds of blankets again, and his eyes darkened as he got a better look.

I looked down and winced. *My legs looked gory,* I thought to myself. There was dried blood everywhere as two deep cuts ran across my legs. My shifter healing had started to close the wounds, but it wasn't enough. *They needed stitches.*

I notice Derek didn't cut me in a way that I would have bled out quickly. He wanted me to suffer, and he wanted me to be *alive* when a wild animal found me. I shuddered at that thought. It didn't take long for those mountain lions to find me and Cade in that hut. If the Fenrir brothers hadn't found me when they did, then those two would have, and I'd already be on my way to the Tiger King.

Bastian started to shake again the longer he stared at my wounds. His breathing labored, and he shut his eyes tight for a moment. *He was trying to regain control,* I thought, and I slowly leaned forward and squeezed his hand.

Bastian's eyes opened as he let go the breath he was holding. In a raspy voice, he whispered, "No one will ever touch you again."

Without another word, he got to work at cleaning the wound. He filled the basin with warm, soapy water, and my body recoiled when he placed the rag against my skin. Pain engulfed every cell in my body as he gently wiped away the dried blood. Everything burned, and I slumped back on the bed, unable to take it anymore.

Once my legs were as clean as they could be for now, he wiped away the blood on my head that I didn't even know was there. He wiped everything away and helped remove all the wet and ruined clothing. Thankfully, I had spare clothing already stashed here for when I went into labor, and Bastian helped dress my upper half and grabbed me my extra set of panties as my old ones were back at that hunter's cabin. That was tricky getting my underwear and shorts past the wounds on my legs, but we managed as the faint sound of snow mobiles sounded in the distance. *They were close.*

Bastian quickly realized Aerith was still in her blanket, and she had peed through it. He seemed frustrated with himself as he rushed to grab her what she needed, and I wished more than anything I could help him. The wound on my legs pulsed so badly, I was worried I'd pass out if I tried to move them. I had to watch as he gently cleaned her up as well, removing all the goo and blood from birth the best he could until she could get a proper bath. He then threw that blanket in the bin and put her in an actual diaper with a sleeper outfit before setting her back down on a clean bassinet. Bastian laid a baby blanket over her this time, since we were in the room with her, and she just slept like a rock through it all. A small smile formed on my lips. *She wasn't bothered by the noise or with Bastian moving her around,* I thought to myself. *Did I just get lucky and have a golden child?*

The snow mobiles roared just outside our windows and shouting ensued as soon as they cut the engines off. I looked to my mate, who's body was tense listening to them rush Cade inside. It pulled at my heartstrings, and I hated we had to leave them behind.

CHAPTER 26

Cain and Elijah walked in, with a still unconscious Cade in his wolf form in their arms. His belly faced my way, and I could see the wound was just barely closed. *At least he wasn't losing anymore blood,* I thought, but my heart hurt just looking at him. Cade was only like that because he refused to leave me.

My aunt was right on their heels and started working again on Cade's wound. My uncle put his hands on Cade as well, and I realized he was using his ability too. *It must be really bad if Cain was getting involved.*

"I chose the wrong side," Bastian whispered, and I turned to find him rigid against the wall. He just stared with sorrowful eyes at his brother, and I didn't know how to fix this for him.

"What?" I asked.

"When we couldn't find you, and Dr. Malin said she was attacked, I was frantic. We needed to split up to cover our lands. Your dad and Uncle Thomas scoured their lands and their side of the mountain, while a small number of us wolves took this side. Most were stuck in their cabins because of the snow, but we all had to wait until the storm had passed because it was a white out. You couldn't see anything, and it wasn't safe to be out in the storm. The waiting was *awful*, Shanely. I wanted to leave right then, but there were no prints or anything to track. You were just gone, and my wolf was beginning to act feral when we finally were able to check the rest of pack lands. My brothers and I took the furthest mountain, while your uncles took the river. That mountain peak, we split. I went alone because I'm faster than my brothers, and I didn't want to wait. I couldn't wait for anyone or anything, and I hastily chose a direction that forced them into the other. I *chose* the wrong side. Cade and Elijah searched the left side, where they found you. If I had just picked the right path then that wouldn't have happened," he said, gesturing to Cade. His anger flared, and he clenched his hands into tight fists. My heart broke watching him in such pain. *This wasn't his fault—*

"*I* should have found you, but if we want to get right down to it, I should have never left you alone that night in the first place. Derek would have never even gotten close to you if I had just stayed by your side!" he snapped angrily, tossing his hands in the air. "*This* is all my fault, Shanely."

Silence filled the room, and I sat there gaping at my mate. *How could he even think that?* I thought to myself. *He had no idea this would happen. No one thought the rogue was someone from the pack, but it wasn't his fault that Derek did what he did.* But when my mate's eyes suddenly filled with tears, I knew this was not just unbelievable rage over everything. Bastian felt guilt and shame over what Derek did to me. To us. *Two emotions he shouldn't feel with this,* I thought to myself. I opened my arms, reaching for him, and he rushed towards me. He buried his face in the crook of my neck and wrapped his arms around me tightly.

"God, I was so scared," he whispered. "I couldn't even feel our bond anymore. I couldn't track you or send a link, and I thought I lost you for good. Will you ever forgive me, Shanely?"

"Forgive you?" I muttered, pulling back to look him in the eye. "Bastian, you saved me and our daughter. You saved your brother, and we are all home safely because of you. From the bottom of my heart, thank you for rescuing me."

I pull him in and kissed him hard. His hands gripped the back of my hair as I melted into him. *I will gladly spend the rest of my life making sure he never blames himself for this,* I thought to myself as we finally broke apart. I smiled wide as he laid his head against mine and sighed. *Bastian was my hero and always will be.*

"None of what happened is anyone's fault but Michael's and Derek," I said, giving him a firm look. Bastian shook his head and kissed my cheek.

"Michael? That bear shifter you fought?" Uncle Cain spat out.

"He's the one who actually took me from the lodge. Michael brought me to some shack way up in the mountains until Derek was able to meet us. Derek paid him to grab me because he had never been able to. He's the rogue everyone was looking for."

"I'm sending Johnny a link now. Let your father and Thomas find Michael, and I'll send the enforcers back out to look for Derek. We will find them both, Shanely. I promise," Cain said confidently.

"Don't bother looking for Derek," I muttered as I leaned back in bed.

CHAPTER 26

"He's long gone by now."

"What do you mean? Do you know where he went?" Uncle Cain asked.

"Derek fled to Liam's pack with his whole family. He made a deal with him, and because of their hatred of bears and me, it aligned their interests. He's joining their pack," I said, and Bastian tensed as his eyes widened.

Fury filled his eyes as he asked, "My father called a hit on you?!"

"According to Derek, no. He wanted to get his mark before he left the pack," I answered before yawning.

Cain shook his head in disbelief. "I'll have the enforcers check their area and see who's left. We'll search the airports as well. This is among shifters, so it's within our right to deal out justice to Derek and anyone else who supports him!"

Cain was yelling by that point as he paced the room back and forth. *He was struggling with his wolf too, it seems,* I thought to myself. *The pacing seemed to help though.*

I yawned again, blinking ever so slowly as my body feel into pure exhaustion. I could hardly stay awake, and Bastian gently lifted me forward and slid in behind me. He laid me against his chest, and I sighed with relief. Bastian was so warm, and I felt safe with him so close. No one could touch me while he was here, and I turned to my side to get more comfortable.

I frowned when I noticed my aunt. She was in her own head now as she continued to help Cade, but I didn't like how weak she looked. Her shoulders were hunched over, and her eyes had deep bags under them. Cade's injuries were significant, but my aunt could only do so much before she'd collapse from exhaustion too.

"Derek nearly killed Shanely, which put Cade in the path of those lions. This is unacceptable, and I'm not leaving it up to chance! Anyone have a picture of this guy?" Bay asked, and I turned to face her. I didn't even know she had walked in with Ryder, and I gave them both a small wave. Ryder couldn't bring himself to smile as he waved back.

Elijah kissed my cheek as he collapsed in the seat between the beds. He gave his brother a grim look before turning away to look at the floor. I could see tears in his eyes as well, and I knew he was angry with himself for leaving us in the first place. *He felt guilty too—*

Cain walked up to Bay. "I can get you one. Do you have friends back home that can help?"

She nodded, and I felt my mate stiffen. I slowly stole a peek at my mate, and Bastian just stared at her with a blank expression. His finally shook his head and asked, "Who do *you* know that handles stuff like this?"

Bay looked to her brothers nervously. Her eyes slowly found mine, and she groaned. "Well, I wasn't planning on telling you any of this but— I have plenty of friends in the underground ring that should be able to take care of him."

"The underground *what?*" Elijah asked, with a clipped tone.

"You're looking at the one and only Mor'du!" she said as she mockingly bowed, and I let out an unflattering snort. *The Fenrir family had a flare for being dramatic,* I thought to myself.

"You're Mor'du? You're the champion from back home?!" Elijah cried out. Bastian's jaw dropped and had yet to close. Everyone else just looked confused.

"Wait, who is Mor'du?" Cain asked.

"He, or well *she*, is a very well known fighter from back home. There's an illegal underground ring that my brothers and I would go watch before we came here. Mor'du is legendary back home, and his reputation has spread throughout the shifter nation. Undefeated and scary as can be in his fights. Or I guess *her* fights," Elijah answered, shaking his head in a huff.

"What has Dad been allowing you to do?!" Bastian demanded.

Bay dropped her head in frustration, and I got why she didn't want to tell them. I could only imagine what would happen when Cade found out.

"Guys, take a breath," I said quietly.

"Yeah, chill," she muttered.

Elijah looked at Baby, half in awe and half terrified. I don't think the brothers really knew how to accept this new piece of information about their baby sister. *But Bay was nearly grown,* I thought to myself. *I still thought it was crazy but to each their own.*

"What are we going to do with you?" Elijah muttered as he crossed his

CHAPTER 26

arms.

"Let's just use this to our advantage. Call them but be discreet," Cain said, and she nodded before leaving the room.

Bastian leaned down, giving me a knowing look. "You don't seem too surprised by this."

"I'm not," I said, and his eyes narrowed. "One; I'm new to everything so I had never heard of Mor'du or all the details of her reputation. Two; she told me a while ago, but I wanted *her* to be the one to tell you guys. I made her promise not to fight until she talked to you three first though. And three; I'm injured, so you can't be mad at me."

Bastian smirked before kissing my forehead, and I smiled. I had missed that face he always made when I amused him. I leaned back against his chest as he wrapped his arms around me again. I sighed as I listened to the sound of his heart beating steadily in his chest. It was the best sound in the whole world.

"I love you," he whispered.

"I love you too."

The room grew quiet, while everyone worked and settled in. Elijah made his way over to the bassinet, smiling as he stole a glance at our little one.

I watched my aunt continue to work on Cade. She was seriously starting to look pale, but she never took her hands off. She never stopped working. My uncle switched gears and put his hands on my aunt's shoulders instead. Some color returned to her cheeks, and she straightened her shoulders and continued to heal my brother-in-law.

Dr. Malin came in shortly after and asked for the baby first. She had a bandage on the side of her head and explained that she was with the group checking throughout town, so it took her a minute to get back once she heard the Alpha's call. Malin checked Aerith over and helped clean the cord well before redressing her. She was fine despite everything, and Malin laid her back down in the bassinet. I gave Cade and Elijah all the credit with her. Cade was the one who cut the cord and delivered her, while Elijah knew what was needed in the first place. She was alive and well because of them, and a slight blush crept up Elijah's face. He settled back in the chair next to us, and I grinned, watching him all flustered.

"Now, let's see your legs," Malin said, pulling me from my thoughts.

I groaned as Bastian helped carefully pull the blanket back, and they still looked awful. He had managed to clean them thoroughly, which helped her see the wound clearly, but my shifter abilities weren't kicking in fast enough. I already knew they were going to need stitches.

Malin leaned down to examine the wound closely. "You should be proud, Bastian. I imagine that wasn't easy keeping your wolf in check long enough for me to arrive."

"I'd be proud if I had—"

"Bastian," I scolded, giving him a firm look before turning back to Malin. "He means thank you."

She chuckled softly, but then her eyes narrowed. "Your shifter healing abilities should have kicked in already," she said quietly. "I'll have to heal you myself."

"Probably for the best because I don't know when they will fully come back to be honest. I can feel it, but it's really weak right now," I replied.

She frowned. "What do you mean?"

"Derek had Michael drug me," I replied. All eyes in the room turned to me. "It basically made me unable to shift or use any of my abilities. It's why I was never able to fight back or call any of you."

Everyone looked alarm. Malin turned to Cain and said, "I have never heard of something like that before."

"It's how he was able to move around like a rogue too. He took a very small dose of the stuff when he was hunting me, so no one would be able to see him as he moved about. It was enough to somewhat mask his smell, I guess. He came close a few times after the initial attack, but I was never truly alone, so he reached out to Michael instead."

"Cain, how is that even possible?" Malin asked as she placed her hands on me. Her eyes glowed, and soon my skin started to slowly stitch itself back together. I winced and looked away. Elijah wiggled his eyebrows as my stomach churned. *This just felt so weird*, I thought as my skin pulled itself together again.

CHAPTER 26

Cain shook his head. "I don't know. I've never heard of anything that could trick the pack bond like that. I never *once* suspected him as the rogue."

"There's more. Has anyone heard of the Tiger King?" I asked.

Uncle Cain turned around, giving me a look of alarm. My anxiety rolled as I realized he knew the man.

"What does he have to do with anything?" Cain asked.

"Those mountain lions, Frank and David, mentioned him a lot. He has a bounty on wolf heads, and they wanted me and Aerith badly," I answered. "I don't know why."

"Is that why you left the cabin? Elijah and I made it there, but it was a mess. I followed the tracks until I heard the fighting," Bastian asked.

I nodded and winced again. "They broke through the window. Cade ran as fast as he could but carrying me slowed him down. They caught up to us quickly, and they kept trying to get Cade to abandon me and Aerith, just like they offered you. They said the Tiger King would be very interested in finding me. That it would pay off their debt."

"For now, let's just fall back into the shadows. The Tiger King is a brutal young tiger that hates wolves. We don't go south of town because of him. It's just safer for the pack," Cain commanded.

"Alright, I've done everything I can, Shanely. You just need to rest now, but I'm so glad everyone is safely home," Malin said as she patted my feet. I looked to my legs and smiled. I didn't care I had two long scars now. I was just so relieved to be home.

"I'm done too. I can't do anymore for him right now. Let's let them sleep, guys," Aunt Cassia said.

"I need to rest, but I'll take over in a little while," Malin said, and my aunt nodded gratefully.

Cassia had deep bags under her eyes and looked exhausted. Even my uncle looked entirely drained and rough. *They were in no condition to do anything but sleep,* I thought to myself.

"I called your dad and Caleb. They should be here soon, but it might take them a little bit to get back," Cain said to me, and I nodded softly. He turned to my uncles then. "Ash and Aspen, you two are in charge until your sister and I come back downstairs. We're going to recover in case Cade or Shanely takes a turn for the worse and needs one of us. *No one* is allowed in this backroom. Ryder, you and Bay will guard the door, and send the enforcers to surround the lodge. I don't know who knew about Derek's plan or not, so I'm not trusting anyone but those in this room. Understood?"

Everyone nodded as they left the room, and I turned to look at Cade. His wound was a bright, healthy pink and fully closed now. His breathing had evened out, and soon I was sure he'd shift back to his human form. I was grateful that he was okay, and I laid my head back against my mate.

"I'll stay and watch my niece," Elijah chimed in.

My aunt was the last to leave, and she rested her hands on my feet. She smile softly as I could feel her start to drain me. Everything felt heavy, and I could barely keep my eyes open.

"Sleep, my love," Bastian whispered. "I've got you, and I'm not letting go."

Chapter 27

I woke up to the sound of low voices around me. I was still wrapped between Bastian's legs, with his arms snuggled around my middle. *He wasn't lying, I thought to myself. He never let me go, and I was in the exact spot as I fell asleep in.* As I was about to open my eyes and say hello, I heard my name.

"I don't know, man. What Derek did to Shanely was twisted." *Elijah. They were talking about how they found me,* I thought to myself.

"What happened exactly? Elijah didn't go into much detail when he found me, and I don't want to ask Shanely," Bastian asked quietly.

I stayed so very still. The last thing I wanted was to interrupt this conversation or let them know I heard in the first place.

"I heard something faint, so we followed it just in case. It wasn't long before Elijah smelled her blood, and I mean *a lot* of blood, brother."

Cade. My heart nearly burst to hear his voice again. *He was awake and alive.* I couldn't believe I nearly lost him too.

"Her hands were tied above her head, and she was hanging like 7 feet off the ground, maybe? She was just hanging there, soaking wet, and a puddle of her blood lay on the ground just below," Cade went on. "It was like a scene from one of my video games, dude. Shanely's lips were blue, and her eye was swollen shut. She looked dead already."

Bastian flinched, and my heart just broke. Hearing their thoughts over what happened was unnerving. Living it was a whole different matter, but I was hoping to just put it in the past entirely. I never wanted to think about it again.

"I don't think I will *ever* get that image out of my head, Bastian. It was like he wanted her to die a slow, painful death or at least leave a gruesome-looking body for us to find," Cade said, and Bastian's breathing began to change. I could feel his wolf emerge ever so slightly, and I don't think he even realized he was squeezing me tighter.

"I've never seen anything like it either. It honest to God scared me, Bastian," Elijah chimed in. "I started cutting her down as Cade grabbed her body. She looked— I don't know, spacey? Like everything was difficult for her to focus on, which I'm sure was because of the blood loss, but she managed to tell us about the baby. She screamed during that first contraction we were there for, and I thought for sure something was wrong with the baby too. We made a last minute decision to run through Dead Man's Hollow. We didn't have another option, Bastian."

My mate said nothing. He just listened, but I could feel every muscle tense when they said where they took me. *It must have been a bad place for Bastian to react this way*, I thought to myself. I was so curious as to why though.

"We were almost in the thick of it anyways. The contractions were close enough together that we couldn't make our way back to you. She was in too bad of shape, Bastian, so we took her to that hunter's cabin we found a long time ago. The cabin was empty, and we didn't scent anything nearby, but to be honest we could have missed something. We were scrambling, trying to just deliver this Little One safely," Cade continued.

"We had nothing though. No mind-link or service. Just nothing," Elijah continued before sighing deeply.

"I thought maybe we could stay hidden long enough until he found you so I made Elijah leave, but those lions found us really fast. In hindsight, I shouldn't have pushed him to go, but I didn't know what else to do. I didn't hear or scent anything dangerous, and I *thought* we'd be okay. The lions must have been minutes behind Elijah and I though," Cade said solemnly.

"Scares me to think what would have happened if we didn't find her when we did," Elijah chimed in, and the three brothers got quiet after that.

Finally, Cade broke the silence. "She was so brave though, Bastian. Not only did she deliver Aerith beautifully, but she stayed strong despite it all.

We don't even know everything Derek did to her, other than what marks we could see. I really didn't do anything other than hold her hand for the birth, which was by far the scariest thing I have ever done in my entire life. How she was even able to do that is beyond me, but you would have been proud if you saw her."

"You two found her, and not once did you think of yourselves. Don't say you guys didn't do anything— you guys did *everything*. You both risked your own lives when you took her to Dead Man's Hollow, and we all know how dangerous that place can be. Cade, you carried my mate and child miles in the snow on a dangerous mountain, while being chased by lions, and Elijah, you risked going alone through the mountains just to find me. Neither one of you took the easy way out. I can't thank you two enough for being there when I couldn't be."

"She's family, Bastian. We'd do anything for her and this Little One. We're just extensions of you anyways, you know that. We made that deal as kids, and we're sticking to it. It will be the same when Elijah or I find our mate," Cade went on. "Although, I pray we *never* have to go through something like that again. This was the worst thing I have ever been apart of."

"No kidding," Elijah huffed, "but seriously Bastian, you have one tough mate. Not many could have gone through what she did and survived."

I felt Bastian's kiss on my forehead gently as he whispered, "I know, and I can't believe she's mine."

Everyone stayed quiet after that. It was strange knowing they thought I was brave and strong. I sure as heck didn't view myself that way. I mean, I was the one that needed rescued in the first place. But after years of listening to Peter beat me down, it felt so good to hear the Fenrir brothers talk about me the way they did. Peter was nowhere near the sort of men they were, and they were in awe of *me*. It really showed what sort of men the Fenrir triplets were because they had no idea I was even awake, and yet they still praised me.

Their words warmed my heart, and I couldn't help but repeat them over and over again in my mind. Eventually, I fell back asleep.

***

I awoke to sweaty bed sheets and a crazy sore body. I moved my hips, trying to find a cozier spot on the bed, when I noticed I had space. Like *plenty* of space in this bed, and my heart raced inside my chest. *Bastian wasn't here like he promised,* I thought as I shot forward and opened my eyes.

I scanned the room and found my mate standing by the bassinet with Aerith in tow. He had made another bottle and smiled when he turned around.

"Hey baby," he said softly. "You're awake. How are you feeling?"

I slumped backwards on the bed and sighed. "I'm good. Just incredibly sore."

My legs still hurt, but I could move them better than before, and I promptly kicked off the mountains of blankets. I was roasting and probably needed a shower at this point.

I looked towards Cade, who was awake and watching me. My heart leapt for joy as he smiled saying, "There's my Baby Girl."

"Cade! You're okay!" I cried out, reaching out for his hand. He leaned forward and took my hand in his, squeezing it gently and running his thumb over mine.

"I told you everything would be fine!"

I snorted, giving him a pointed look. "I believe *I'm* the one who said that. You were saying your goodbyes!"

My smiled fell and tears suddenly filled my eyes as I remembered that awful moment. Listening to him accept defeat just about broke my heart, and I couldn't stop myself from crying.

His face softened saying, "Oh, Baby Girl—"

Cade dropped my hand, reaching over to pull my bed towards him until it lined up with his. My eyes widened in surprise. He must be in a lot of pain, but he didn't seem fazed by it. *At least it had wheels to make it easier.*

Cade pulled me close, wrapping his arms around me, and I cried into his shoulder. I could feel the bandage wrapped around his chest, making me feel even worse. I let go of the pain I felt over the last few days, and Cade simply held me until I finally managed to calm down.

"Don't you ever do that again, Cade," I sniffled as I pulled back to glare at him.

"You are the bravest girl I have ever met Shanely, and I am fine really," he protested. "Please, don't cry over me."

"You three always get hurt because of me though," I said, grabbing tissues from the box behind us.

"Hurt? Please!"

I gestured to the bandage that wrapped his entire torso, giving him a pointed look. I vividly remember that lion slicing him open and him dropping in the snow. *And the blood— there was so much blood.*

"What this? These are battle scars, Baby Girl! You don't understand what a gift you've given me. All the ladies will want me now and besides— I just thought you could use a buddy in here," he said as he wiggled his eyebrows at me.

I couldn't help but laugh hard at how ridiculous he looked like right now. I playfully pushed him saying, "You didn't need to join me in here! You could have just visited instead of nearly dying."

"Ow, ow, careful! I'm still healing," he said, holding his chest as he winced in pain. Guilt overwhelmed me, and I gently placed my hand on his shoulder.

"Oh, Cade! I'm so sorry. I—"

His sudden laughter interrupted me, and a scowl covered my face. I pushed him even harder then. "Jerk."

"Okay, okay, I'm done! Now, give me my niece!" he playfully demanded, and Bastian just rolled his eyes at the two of us.

"And what if I want my daughter?" I asked, jutting out my bottom lip.

"Too bad. I've been waiting for my turn for a while now," he said, sticking his tongue at me. I tried to snatch it, but he was too fast.

Bastian walked over and gently laid her down between us. "Here, just share, you two. Oh, and since when did you get permission to name my kid, Cade?"

Bastian slid into the bed behind me and held onto my waist. His nose immediately went to the crook of my neck, making me smile. All four of us somehow managed to fit between the two beds.

"Hey, I was going to die man! I decided to give her a name before I did. I just didn't expect you to keep it!"

Cade rubbed Aerith's little nose before letting her grab his finger with her tiny hand. Her arm was the length of his finger, and it was adorable seeing how smitten the two of them were with her. She cooed and looked around, not really settling on anyone in particular.

"It's pretty!" I defended. "I've just never heard of it before. How did you even come up with it?"

Aerith looked around with her pretty little eyes, and I smiled. *She did look like me.*

Cade started laughing before muttering something under his breath, and I narrowed my eyes.

"What?" I asked, watching him scratch the back of his head nervously.

He muttered again, and I rolled my eyes. *Oh lord—*

"Dude, we can't understand you," Bastian said, with a clipped tone.

Cade winced slightly. "Um—" he said softly, "from a video game."

"From where?!" I shrieked.

Cade's face turned a bright red, and I leaned my head back, rolling with laughter.

"You named my daughter after a video game character?" Bastian asked, somewhat amused.

"Only from the best Final Fantasy installment to date! She's an awesome character too!" Cade defended. "Like I said— I didn't think you'd keep it."

"I'll have to play it, I guess," I replied.

"It's a good game," he said before turning his attention back to Aerith. He wasn't really listening anymore after she had latched onto his finger again.

"Has my dad gotten back?" I asked quietly, and Bastian gently rubbed my arm. He was honestly making me sleepy again, and I swore he had magic hands or something because he'd knock me out every time he rubbed me.

CHAPTER 27

"Your dad was here earlier when you were sleeping. He held Aerith for a long time before Thomas called him. They found Michael. Thomas, Caleb, and the rest of the bear clan stayed out until they caught his tracks well into Canada. Honestly, if it wasn't for Johnny's mate bond with Alana, we would have been too far to alert the bears in time to find his scent. It would have been lost in the snow, and we may not have ever found him again."

"Wait, I thought you had to be somewhat close for the mind-link to work?"

"For wolves you do, but bears aren't pack animals so their link extends out farther than ours do. Either way, it doesn't matter with mate bonds. You can always reach me, no matter where you are in the whole world. Fortunately for us, Johnny was with Ryder, searching this side, while Alana was with her father."

"Huh. That drug must have messed with the bond then," I said, thinking back. "I tried to call you and the pack, but it was radio silent for me."

"Dr. Malin drew some blood while you were out. We're still trying to figure out what Derek did. I have never heard of it before," Bastian answered me.

"Where is everyone right now?"

"Your aunt and Malin are resting. They were pretty drained between healing you and Cade. Some of the other pack members needed mending as well, but not for anything as serious as you two. Bay has been on the phone dealing with the underground ring back home to find Derek. No luck yet, but she's been keeping us posted," Bastian replied.

"And before you ask, yes, we've been cool about the whole thing," Cade chimed in, and a small smile crept up my face.

"Alpha Cain is with Thomas here at the lodge, discussing what to do with Michael. Because of his and Derek's betrayal, we don't know who to trust in either the pack or clan, but it sounds like one of the bears has a special ability that can help us. Thomas is furiously trying to start going through the clan first, and then the pack, on who's trustworthy and who isn't. Caleb has refused to leave Michael. He's making sure he stays— docile," Bastian smirked, and my smile fell. *I didn't want to think about him.*

"He stopped by to meet his niece and see you, but you hadn't woken up yet. He went back to guard Michael, but it seems your uncles are all in agreement that he should die for his crimes against you. Because Michael is a bear, it falls to the clan to deal out justice so your father has that special privilege. It has been decided already that when we find Derek, he will fall to me to deal with, if you choose not to deliver justice yourself. Oh, and Ryder and Johnny are just behind that door, standing guard here, while Alana has been running around making sure everyone has plenty of food."

"You and I have been in and out of it for a few days now," Cade said, booping my nose.

I blew out a loud breath as I mulled over everything he just said. "Is life ever going to go back to normal?"

Bastian sighed as he said, "Yes, it will! Because I'm never letting you leave my line of sight. Nothing good ever comes of it!"

Cade laughed as he nodded his head. "Ain't that the truth!"

"Shut up! It's not like I go looking for trouble," I replied, laughing.

"I know, baby. We're only teasing!"

The four of us stayed curled up in bed like that for a while. Everyone filed in and out throughout the day, checking on us all. Bastian was the only one who never left the room. His wolf was extra jittery since they found me, and I often woke up to him curled up on my feet in his wolf form or lying in front of the bassinet. I loved seeing his wolf again.

Everyone was so smitten with Aerith that I barely got a chance to hold her. Dr. Malin finally said I was strong enough to go home with the baby after about a week in the exam room. I was allowed to leave before Cade, but I felt horrible for leaving him there by himself. I started to protest, when Cade told me to get home. He was only going to be a day or two behind me, but I needed to get back to civilized life again. I just rolled my eyes. These boys exasperated me, but I loved them anyway.

Cade ended up with a long pink scar along the side of his chest. It went all the way from his hip to shoulder. He and I would always have a physical memory of this moment, and a small weird part of me was glad I wasn't alone in that. It was hard to look at my legs and see the mark, but knowing

CHAPTER 27

Cade had one too made me feel oddly better. I wasn't alone, but I still wish it never happened to him in the first place.

Dr. Malin kept him a couple days longer, just to ensure he was completely healed and ready to return to work. Bastian carefully drove Aerith and I home, followed by a tremendous amount of enforcers. I swear my uncles, Ash and Aspen, practically lived in their wolf forms as they patrolled our cabin and the land around it constantly. No one was taking any more chances as Derek had yet to emerge in Denmark.

Bastian stayed true to his word and never let me out of sight. He even tried to come into the bathroom with me, but that was where I drew the line. *I wanted to pee in peace, thank you very much!* He finally relented when my wolf snapped at him. I was thrilled to finally be back in my own place again, and Elijah had set all the flowers and get well cards from the pack and clan on the table for me to look at the moment I stepped inside. It was a sight to see as my front entrance and back table was covered in stuff.

The triplets finally showed me the nursery they had done for Aerith once Cade made it back home to join us, and it was beautiful! Since they didn't know the gender, they went with a neutral tan color as the base and hand-painted wolves and bears on the walls. I didn't even know the brothers had artistic talent, but they did a great job. They made the animals doing all kinds of things like running, howling, and some even looked like they were playing. It went along the middle of the wall like a border. There was one white bear and one white wolf in the mix of them all, which I thought was incredibly sweet.

The crib was a dark stained wood, and it was lined with the softest sheets I had ever felt. That part was a gift from Caleb and my father as they made it themselves at their woodworking shop. A small glass mobile hung over the top, with the moon at its center and wolves hanging around it. A dresser and a comfy rocking chair completed the room, and it was stocked entirely by clothes and gifts from the pack and clan. It immediately became my favorite room in the whole house, and soon I was painting my own room with the same colors.

My uncle Thomas stopped by and apologized profusely for Michael. He had no idea what was even going on, and it killed him that one of his own harmed someone in his family. Apparently, it was his daughter Octavia that had a hidden talent not many knew about. She could sense when anyone, shifter or human, lied. My uncle Cain and Thomas have been going through the pack and clan for anymore traitors, but it was taking some time to do it. It wasn't the easiest thing for Octavia to do, but she worked hard to get it done quickly.

Most of Derek's family left with him. They searched his home and land, but it was empty and completely cleared out. A few from his family stayed behind though, which was surprising. They wanted nothing to do with Derek ,and even gave up his Council seat to show they weren't here with malicious intent. Unfortunately, a certain someone stayed behind as well, and I scowled when Ryder told us who. I didn't trust Emma one bit, but Octavia didn't pick up on any lies or ill intent, and Emma denied any involvement in her father's plans. She explained that she was just jealous of me but didn't wish me dead or anything. She was *working* on her feelings towards the bears, and my uncle reluctantly chose to believe her. He warned her that she was on thin ice because of everything with her dad though. She chose to stay within our pack, even though I thought it was all baloney. Guess I just had to deal with it.

Since mingling with the bears, and opening up the borders between our lands, we've had quite a few matings happen. Surprisingly, Uncle Ash found his mate amongst the bear clan. Everyone was still adjusting to the fact that you needed touch to find your mate amongst bear shifters because with wolves they felt the connection when their eyes met. It didn't work that way with bears though. Until they touch, skin to skin, the connection wouldn't form. Everyday it seems like someone new has found their mate.

The first time I met my new great-aunt was at the lodge when she delivered food while we were still in recovery. She had never left clan lands before, and she was excited to explore and meet new shifters. But boy was she out-going. She talked nonstop and was the sweetest person I think I had ever met. She just bounced from person to person, talking all about the chili she made and how there was a secret ingredient buried inside.

CHAPTER 27

She challenged that no one would be able to figure it out, which Cade took personally, and Bastian and I just grinned watching her talk to everyone.

But then she came right up to Ash and shook his hand before he could object. The bond instantly snapped in place, and for a moment, the room grew silent. His eyes went wide just before he kissed her. It was the most emotion I had ever seen from my uncle other than anger, and it was absolutely adorable when he would not let her go for the rest of the day. We congratulated them, and she just talked and talked about how she had given up on the idea that this would ever happen. Ash simply smiled, saying nothing. They were complete opposites, but it seemed to be exactly what they both needed in a mate. It's been really joyous on both sides, and she moved in with my uncle here on pack lands the next day.

Bay has been struggling lately. She been working hard with her contacts back home, but Liam's locked everything down tight. She hasn't really said much about Derek either. Just that she's handling it and not to worry, but I rather her just let it go. She looked stressed, and I hated seeing her like this. We all assumed that Derek made it to Liam's pack since the pack's been under lock down, but his ties to *our* pack have been permanently severed, and my uncle has put out a reward for any information on the whereabouts of Derek to the World Council. We just have to wait to hear back from them.

Both of my animals finally came back. It took time for the drug to fully clear out of my system, but they emerged again, and I felt whole once more. Malin was able to identify some of the components from the blood sample, but it was going over our heads a little. I was just thrilled to feel my bear and wolf again. I still wasn't able to shift into my wolf, but she was at least there, guiding me like she always had.

Bastian and I took long walks together in the snow in our bear forms. Having my fur was so much easier than my skin with this weather, and I blended in so well with winter that most had a hard time seeing me. It was fun sneaking up on people and scaring them silly. Eventually, it became a game, and then a tactical experiment. Everyone started joining in to learn how to better fight and defend themselves against something they couldn't see, and I got in some training that I so desperately needed as my uncle Ash told me, *repeatedly*.

The boys were finishing the renovations on the inside of the cabin to make room for everyone. Caleb even decided to stay at the cabin with us, so he didn't have to be so far away all the time. He said it was just temporary, but it was closer to work, and he wanted to spend more time together, especially with Aerith. I didn't mind one bit. I was glad to have him in my life everyday.

Everything was coming along rather nicely, and it felt like we were becoming our own mini pack. Ryder and Johnny didn't move in but were over nearly everyday. Even Octavia came around every so often. Her and I were slowly getting adjusted to one another, but it wasn't what it used to be.

In the meantime, I stayed busy. I started sitting in on meetings with my uncle a lot more, trying to learn everything I could about how the pack operates. He was teaching me how the finances worked, and what he did with the investments to keep the pack running smoothly. It was a lot, but I was catching on. Bastian was slowly taking over as Head of the enforcers too. Ash and Aspen were stepping aside, letting the younger wolves learn the ropes, and my mate was their first choice. I was incredibly proud of Bastian.

Aerith seemed to grow like a normal child would. Humans couldn't tell anything was different with her shifter blood, so the Division would never know as long as we laid low, and continued making amends with other shifter kinds. I'd rather have friends than enemies any day. There were no signs that our little Aerith had any shifter abilities, but Dr. Malin insisted it was a bit early to know for sure. We all anxiously waited to see if her scent would ever change, but to me she was perfect. Regardless if she ever gained the ability to shift.

I was going to make sure she had the life I always wanted. The life every child deserved. She'd wake up everyday, knowing how loved she was, and I never wanted her to doubt that. She had an amazing family, and she would never question where she came from like I did growing up. My little girl was going to grow up happy and safe, and that was *all* I wanted for her.

CHAPTER 27

At this point, after everything, I was simply grateful for the peace and quiet.

I never thought my life would have amounted to much of anything, but I'm so thankful I was wrong.

Bonus Chapter

Bastian

Bzzzz

"God, Bastian," Cade mumbled. He glared at me from his bunk next to mine. "Will you shut that stupid phone off?!"

Bzzzz

I rolled over as my other triplet, Elijah, glared before burying his head under his pillow.

"I'm trying," I snapped as I fumbled around in the dark. The other enforcers began to emit a low growl of annoyance, but one snarl from me shut them up. *This was part of the job,* I thought in a huff.

"Hello?" I answered gruffly, still pissed I was woken up in the first place. I glanced at the clock. It was well past midnight.

"Bastian?" Alpha Cain said in his typical deep voice, and I sat up, picking up on tension as well. "I need you."

"What's going on?" I asked as I stole a peek outside. No warning sound came from the group selected for the night run. Nothing seemed wrong, but the way my Alpha spoke had my wolf a little spooked. Cade and Elijah sat up as well.

"There's been an incident," Cain said, sighing. "I need you and one of your brothers present for a emergency Council meeting."

My eyes widened. "Seriously? No one said—"

"This wasn't broadcasted," he said firmly. "My wife made a discovery, and we need to keep things quiet for the moment until we figure this out. She's on her way to the lodge already, and I need you to get a move on. Full gear tonight, and send three grunts ahead. I need extra support for this meeting. Have your other brother run an additional patrol too. We may have a rogue."

"Yes sir," I answered, motioning for Cade to hit the lights. *Everyone's getting up now, especially if we were dealing with a rogue*, I thought to myself. "I'll be there soon."

Cain hung up the phone as my brothers stood, grabbing their gear.

"Just one," I said firmly. They both gave me a sour look. "Cain's orders. I need one with me, and the other needs to lead a patrol. Alpha thinks we have a rogue."

Elijah swore before dropping his gear. "I'll do the patrol since there's a possible rogue. I'll sniff it out faster than Cade."

Cade rolled his eyes but put on the vest Aspen gave us when we got promoted to Alpha Cain's personal enforcers. It's more for intimidation anyways.

"Fine," I answered, turning to the other wolves waiting for orders. "Ryder, Johnny, and Xaden. Gear on, and head to the lodge. Alpha has a council meeting and needs security. The rest go with Elijah! We have a possible rogue in the area, and I need to know how it got inside our territory without us knowing! Move out!"

The wolves scattered then as I grabbed my own vest. Something was gnawing at me about this whole thing. The patrol Ash sent out tonight never said a word about a rogue wolf coming in. *So what in the world was going on, and how did it get passed us?*

"We'll figure it out," Cade said, pulling me from my thoughts, and I shot him an annoyed look. He merely chuckled. "Every thought is written on your face, Bastian. But seriously take a breath. We'll figure everything out once we get there and get the rest of the details."

I muttered my agreement as I laced up my boots.

"I just don't understand why our patrol didn't say anything," I said, giving one sharp whistle to the wolves taking their time. They picked up the pace as Johnny and Ryder took off to the lodge, with Xaden chasing after them. They didn't have the gear we did, but we'd only be minutes behind. "Did you hear anything?"

Cade shook his head. "Nope, and I linked Henrik while you were on the phone with the Alpha. It's been quiet."

I grunted my annoyance as we finally strolled out of the room. Cade merely slapped me on my back then.

"Don't worry, brother. You're still the best of us all," he said, with a grin. "This doesn't change anything."

I rolled my eyes. "I'm not trying to be the best, Cade, but if we do have a rogue then that means it slipped past our defenses somehow. That's a big deal, especially when we were sent here to learn."

Cade raised an eyebrow. "Like you really care what dear ole Dad thinks."

I shrugged. *He wasn't wrong—*

"No," I finally answered, "but I don't want to be a disappointment either."

Cade gave a low chuckle. "Yeah, well I don't see how you're going to get around that when you tell him you aren't coming home."

My stomach twisted as I thought of the conversation I had been putting off. My mother already suspected what I wanted, but I had yet to actually admit anything to my dad yet. We're supposed to return at the end of the year.

The lodge came into view, when suddenly I got a faint scent of *honey*. I slowed in my tracks as I tried to find the source to this delectable smell. Cade turned, giving me a look, and I chastised myself for getting distracted. I scurried after my brother, trying to get my head in the game, but that scent grew stronger. I couldn't figure out where it was coming from, but God it smelled good.

Putting a scowl on my face, I strolled into the conference room, with Cade hot on my heels. I took my place behind Cain's chair and forced myself to stand at attention. All while keeping my wolf from tearing the room apart in search of that intoxicating scent. Cade, Elijah, and I were the Alpha's personal guards, and our job in these meetings were to face the doors with our head held high, and to eliminate *any* threat to the Alpha and his mate. Not run around chasing some scent. Even if it drove my wolf mad.

"Well, she's a doll." Cade's voice pierced my mind, and I snarled.

"Focus, Cade."

"I'm calling this emergency meeting to order. I thank each and everyone of you for coming in so late and on such short notice. We have a few things we need to discuss, but first, everyone here needs to understand that what's about to be said *will* stay within these walls. Some very serious problems have come up, and this is not news for the pack, or anyone else until we know how to handle this. Understood?" Cain asked sternly.

Nosy bunch of shifters. Each and everyone was clearly dying to know what was going on, and I was a little irritated I was finding out with the rest of the Council. *I should have known first being Cain's enforcer,* I thought to myself. That honey scent permeated my nose again, and I quickly shook my head before I got lost in it.

"Good. First things first, I would like to introduce my long-lost niece, Shanely. This is Mercedes's daughter, and Willow's granddaughter. She now knows about shifters."

Pure shock shot through my system as I finally broke protocol and snapped my head to the left. My wolf *howled* within me as I struggled to gain my composure. I couldn't breathe as I stared at the most beautiful, redheaded girl next to Cassia I had ever seen. My wolf pushed against my skin as I finally found the source to that intoxicating scent.

But— no bond snapped in place, I thought as my world came crashing down around me.

"Willow didn't have any grandchildren."

"How can that be?"

"Are you sure? She doesn't smell like a full wolf."

Everyone started talking at once, but I couldn't stop watching the mystery girl before me. She looked uncomfortable sitting there quietly in her seat, while the rest argued loudly. My heart went out to her, and all I wanted to do was help her feel better. *How did we not know about her? She's a freaking McCoy! How could we let something like this happen?!*

"We know she doesn't smell fully like a wolf. While we don't understand why that's the case, we all can admit she does smell *somewhat* like a wolf. She is also in Willow's private will. We sent off the sealed original right after Willow passed away to the lawyer who had it drawn up, but it's been months. We hadn't heard anything, so I just assumed it was left to the family like it was always talked about. I checked the copy he sent me when Ash called in the incident, and sure enough, her name is on it," Cain said, sighing.

"How did we miss this?" Kyle asked.

"The only thing the lawyer told me was that he would handle all the affairs for us and just send us copies of everything. With everything we've had going on lately with the Medvedev clan, I haven't had the chance to open it until tonight. The lawyer must have contacted Shanely here about the cabin and set the whole thing in motion. Willow left her cabin and the land to Shanely," Cain continued on. "I know this will come as a disappointment to you, Derek. The land will not be sold to you anymore, and I am sorry about that. I shouldn't have started that whole process until I knew for sure what her will stated, but I had no idea there was an heir. Willow knew by law the land stays within the family."

"Unless it is agreed upon by the entire family," Aspen chimed in.

"Which can only mean Shanely is her next of kin," Cassia said, and Shanely slowly looked to her aunt. Her breathtaking green eyes flashed with sadness before she schooled her face to show no emotion at all. *Something she seemed all too familiar doing,* I thought to myself. It only pissed off my wolf even more.

"Dude, you're staring."

I nearly snarled at my brother right then and there. His glare forced me to straighten my shoulders and look forward again. *Like I was supposed to—*

But then Cain seemed almost hesitant to continue speaking, and I began to wonder what else was going on.

"I don't understand why she only smells faintly of a wolf, but there are only two possibilities," Cain said, pulling me from my thoughts. "Shanely either doesn't smell like a wolf because her wolf's been dormant for so long, or it's because her father isn't a wolf."

My eyes widened as the whole room erupted. *Not a wolf?!* I thought as my mind reeled. *My God— that would make her—*

Cassia interrupted my runaway thoughts saying, "We know Mercedes was a wolf shifter, but she left so suddenly and told no one why. It makes sense if she was pregnant by another shifter."

"But that would mean she broke our second law!" Derek shouted.

I took a step towards him when he glared at Shanely but quickly shook myself from my murderous thoughts. *I had to get it together,* I thought to myself. Thankfully, that gorgeous girl didn't notice my slip-up, but Cade did. My brother's brow rose ever so slightly, and I quickly stood attention.

"Wait, what is the second law?" she asked, and I nearly melted right there.

Her voice was heavenly, I thought to myself as my whole body relaxed. She soothed my aggressive wolf, relaxing me to my bones, and my mind started to run amuck again. *She feels like my mate, but where is the freaking bond?!*

"Are you okay?" Cade asked through the link, but I ignored him.

"We only have two universal laws between the shifter nations. One is with the Division; we are not allowed to harm humans or interfere with them, meaning we don't marry humans or deal with any issues with them ourselves. The other law came about after the shifter wars though. When humans discovered shifters, and the whole werewolf term came about, wolves were the only known shifter kind to humans. We were the primary target and were hunted at great lengths by people. This was all happening world-wide, Shanely," Cain said, leaning forward to explain our history to her, "and it was an awful period in our pack's history. Our pack was greatly affected, and the Alpha back then fought hard to rectify what happened. During that time other shifter kinds, specifically the bear clan neighboring us, decided to take advantage of the situation with the humans, and they attacked our pack, taking over the land in these mountains."

"They stole them, you mean," Nathan muttered quietly.

"The Alpha turned the tides and told the newly created Division that we weren't alone. Wolf shifters are the dominant shifters in the world because we have far more numbers than any other kind, and while wolves managed to hold their own against the humans, other shifters did not. They didn't have the numbers to protect themselves and many died because of the human's fear," Cain went on, leaning further back in his seat.

My eyes were glued to Shanely, who seemed genuinely interested in everything my Alpha was saying. *God, I just wanted to be closer to her,* I thought as I shifted back and forth on my feet. *To breathe in her scent and just hold her. I would never let her go too.* It was then I realized we hadn't even gotten to the rogue yet, and I sucked in an agitated breath, wondering how she was wrapped up in that. *Please for the love, don't let her be a mark.*

"Eventually, we struck a deal with the Division," Cain continued. "We had one leader from each known shifter kind meet with the Division team at their headquarters. They wanted us to disappear and never interfere with humans again. To become forgotten, and the best way to do that was to keep us a secret and hide us in plain sight."

"They helped rid the world of our memory, and kept tabs on all of us making sure we followed the rules, but the second law came about after the Division's leader left," Cassia continued.

"We had too much trust broken and way too much blood spilled that no one wanted to mix our kinds together anymore. We separated all of shifter kind and started a rule that you do not marry or mate with other shifters. Shifters keep to their own kind. We separated after that and took the large portion of land back from the bears that they stole during the wars. The Alpha of our pack and the leader of the bear clan divided the town and created the neutral lines, and we haven't mixed since."

"Enough with the history lesson. She's an abomination and shouldn't be here!" Derek shouted again.

My eyes turned red as I glared at that bald-headed prick. I have never liked him and calling her an abomination just *permanently* put him on my bad side. My wolf was determined to make him pay for that.

Cain slammed his hand down on the table, making it shake violently. Shanely nearly jumped out of her seat, but Ash put his hand on her shoulder, halting her from fleeing. She looked alarmed, and I couldn't help but step closer to her. Cade's eyes widened, as if yelling at me to cool it, and I forced myself back to my post. My brother studied me closely, but I couldn't answer him.

I had no idea myself.

"*Dude, what is going on?*" Elijah asked through the link, but I ignored him too.

"Derek, you will show me, *your Alpha*, some respect. Do not speak to me or Shanely this way again. Is that clear?" Cain growled.

Shanely's face turned to pure panic when Cain's wolf pulled through, and my heart sank. *God, she's seen our other form already,* I thought as my wolf whined within me. It had to be the case because she looked terrified right now. She did not want Cain to shift, and panic slowly crept into my own head. *What would she do if she saw me? Would my wolf scare her too?*

"Yes, Alpha," Derek gritted through his teeth.

I barred mine, and he narrowed his eyes. *Yeah— he and I were going to have words later.*

"Now, *no one* will call my niece an abomination again. We don't know anything concrete anyways, so there is no point flinging accusations. We may never know exactly why Mercedes left, but my heart breaks to know she didn't trust any of us to stay and deal with whatever was going on. This pack is a family first, and we are all going to start acting like it, despite the rule. Shanely is here, and I will not lose another family member. Whatever Shanely is, we will deal with it within our pack, understand?"

I stood tall, glaring each and every council member into submission. I was one hundred percent behind my Alpha's declaration, when a timid voice came from the other side of the room.

"Alpha?" Alice said softly. "The thing is, she will have to be a secret. If the other shifters find out, it could start another war. Who knows how they will twist this. You can't trust them, especially the bear clan."

"For now, we know there is some wolf DNA in her. We stick to that— no, we will insist on it. She grew up human, so we'll say she doesn't smell like a wolf completely because she's dormant. Everything else will remain private. We don't give the other shifters any reason to attack. We control this area because of our numbers, and the size of our territory, but we will prepare just in case," Cain replied confidently.

Yes, we would, I thought to myself. I shot my brother a firm look, who gave me one in return.

"*We* can scent she's different. Keeping her a secret will be almost impossible, I fear," Alice countered, and everyone started talking at once again.

Derek rolled his eyes but said nothing, for which everyone was thankful. *Why he's still allowed on the Council, I'll never understand,* I thought to myself, and I crossed my arms, listening to everyone debate this. But there was nothing to debate really. We would protect this girl with our lives because she was *one* of us. A McCoy. And that meant something to me.

And that didn't have anything to do with the fact that she pulled me in like a moth to a flame. My head was spinning with the thought that maybe she was my mate. *Maybe—* I thought to myself. *Just maybe, she was mine.* My wolf growled in agreement.

"This is not the only issue we have to deal with. Shanely was attacked tonight in McCoy territory," Cain said, and I couldn't stop my wolf from snarling.

I bit my tongue to stop myself from shifting as I stared at the girl once more. Pure rage coursed through my veins at the thought of *anyone* attacking her. *That was unacceptable, and the enforcers at the barracks were going to hear about it.*

"What?" Alice asked in disbelief.

"What do you mean attacked?"

"Shanely was chased into our lands tonight by a wolf. She was in bad shape when we found her, and I healed her enough to come here," Cassia stated matter of factly.

Agony hit me in the chest. This stunning girl nearly died because a rogue wolf slipped through the cracks. *This was on me.*

"She said something bolted out in front of her, causing her to crash, which forced her to walk the rest of the way home. Ash and I went back to check her truck, while she was unconscious, and it was a mess. She's lucky she had her seat belt on when she crashed, Alpha," Aspen added in.

God, this just kept getting worse and worse, I thought angrily. I clenched my hands in anger, feeling the familiar warmth of blood trickling out where my nails dug in. My wolf was too close to the surface. I had to rein him in.

"We found wolf tracks near her truck, Cain," Ash continued.

My wolf snapped.

"Was it a shifter?" I gritted through my teeth.

Cade raised a brow in my direction. I know this was completely out of standard protocol, but I didn't care. I needed answers before I went hunting.

I was going to kill that rogue *tonight.*

Everyone turned to face me, but my eyes were glued on Shanely. She finally looked me, and when our eyes met, all the air from my lungs was ripped from my chest. My wolf purred inside as some sort of connection hit between us, but no bond. *No freaking bond.* I didn't understand why this was happening, but my wolf and I were in agreement. Bond or not, she was ours.

God, she was beautiful, I thought as my eyes roamed over her. Beautiful and fragile, and she needed protection. *She needed us.* My wolf hummed in agreement as Cade's voice pierced our mind.

"Did you get a bond?"

I looked at him from the corner of my eye as I straightened and got control of my temper. I ignored my brother when I realized my Alpha watched me with extreme interest.

Interest I didn't want him having.

"We don't know," Cain replied, "but by the way everything looked tonight, we are assuming a rogue went after Shanely."

My wolf roared inside, and I felt him slowly begin to emerge as I lost a small resemblance of control. Shanely looked terrified as I paced behind my Alpha, but I had to *do* something, otherwise I was going to shift and find the prick that tried to kill her. I couldn't keep my eyes from turning gold. I couldn't keep my eyes off of her.

Shanely sat wide-eyed as she rubbed her chest hard enough to leave a mark. I could feel her anxiety from here, and all I wanted to do was run to her. Run and explain how she didn't need to worry. That she was safe now. *She was safe with me.*

"Blood will spill—"

I looked to my brother, who was just as pissed as I was, and gave him a firm nod. Anger fluttered down my bonds, and I felt Elijah in the back of my mind.

"What is happening in that meeting?!"

I couldn't answer as our Alpha Female stood abruptly and silenced the room once more.

"Everyone! Please settle down and remember this is all still new for her. She had no idea about our kind before tonight. Now, I know we haven't had a rogue in our territory since my father ran this pack, but what we need to figure out is how he got in undetected. Not lose our heads over the fact that one is here! This wolf managed to crash her truck and chase her deep into our territory without *any* of us knowing. That's a huge problem! My brothers and I only found her because she lost a decent amount of blood," Cassia bellowed.

We all dropped our heads out of respect for our Alpha Female. *She was right,* I thought as I checked my temper. *This was on us.* I tried to settle my rage, but then that douche spoke.

"So your so-called niece just shows up and lures a rogue into our land? She's brought danger to the whole pack by attracting one here! It probably followed her from wherever she came from, and how do we even know she's telling the truth? This girl could be lying about who she is, and then by right that cabin should still be mine! *Everyone* here knows this girl isn't worth sacrificing the safety of actual wolves—"

I *snapped.*

The moment those words left Derek's mouth, I flew over the table and picked him up by his throat, slamming him up against the wall and tightening my grip. I heard my brother swear as he rushed to stop me, but I refused to let go. My wolf was ready to kill him with our teeth for the insult against what was ours, but I was just content to see if I could pop his head clean off his shoulders.

My wolf pulled through as I snarled, "Don't you *ever* speak about her that way again."

"Bastian, let him go! That's an order!" Cain shouted.

Anger flooded through me, and for the first time in my life, I didn't want to listen to my Alpha.

"Bastian, let him go or Cain will throw you out," Cade warned, and I barred my teeth.

Leave it to Cade to be my voice of reason. I snarled before finally relenting and dropping Derek to the ground, straightening as I turned to face my Alpha.

"Do you need to take a walk, Bastian?" Cain asked sternly.

This was the best I could do to force my wolf to relent, but my eyes were still gold. He was staying at the surface, and there was no pushing him away. I slowly glanced towards Shanely and frowned. *I did not like the look on her face right now,* I thought as my wolf whined within me. *I frightened her.*

"I'm not leaving this room," I replied in a softer tone as that prick scooted further away from me. I needed everyone to understand that there was no way I was leaving her right now. I just couldn't.

Ash and Aspen stepped in front of her, effectively putting a wall between her and I. It pissed me off, but I didn't challenge them over it like I wanted too. I didn't want to scare her even more. Her frantic eyes shot back and forth across the room. I was dying to know what was going through her mind right now. *Was her fear just because we were shifters? Or was it because of my temper and Derek's insults?*

"Then control your temper. Do not make me regret allowing you to stay. Return to your post," Alpha Cain yelled, and I knew I was in trouble. *Yeah, I was going pay for this later.*

My wolf finally retreated at the Alpha's command, and I looked to my girl once more. She peeked around her uncle's shoulders, waiting to see what I would do, but I wasn't going to harm her. *I would never harm her,* I thought to myself. *And I needed to prove that point.*

Without a word, I walked the long way back to my post. Ash snorted as I passed by them, but I held my head high, crossing my arms once I stood behind the Alpha again, and glared at the douche who sat back down at the table.

"Don't mistake my calmness for acceptance, Derek. This is the second time you have disrespected my family tonight. I will throw you off this Council and out of this pack if you do this again," Cain said, glaring at him.

Cain's Alpha power hit everyone in the room then, including me and my brother. It licked my skin, sending my wolf into submission, and I lowered my head. *Cain was pissed.*

"You just had to piss him off," Cade muttered, and I shot him a glare.

My Alpha finally killed his power, and I exhaled a sigh of relief, when I suddenly noticed Shanely. She stood rigid and backed further away from everyone. *From me—* I knew the look on her face. *She was going to bolt.*

Ash picked up her chair, while I bounced on my feet. She was going to run, and I couldn't let that happened. Anxiety welled up inside, and I could hardly sit still. She wouldn't take the seat, so Ash decided to stand with her. *It should be me standing next to her. I should be the one to comfort her.* To ease her worries and fears away, but I couldn't.

It would be the last thing she'd want.

"Since we have no way to figure out where the rogue went, we will just have to double up the patrols and maybe set up other security measures. Shanely will need extra protection too, seeing how she managed to get away. She's marked now," Cassia said.

God, hearing that term about killed me. *Marked.* Rogues were relentless with their marks— My wolf growled within me. *I won't let anything happen to her.*

"No, I won't," Shanely snapped back, and my heart stopped.

"Shanely dear," Cassia pleaded with her, "you can't shift right now. We need to make sure you're safe."

"No. From this meeting alone, I can see I'm nothing but a problem to you all. An *inconvenience* and a threat, and I refuse to cause you all harm or be a burden in any way. Look, I needed this escape, but I can move on just as well. If you allow me to stay in the cabin for a little while until I can save up enough to leave, I would appreciate it. You don't need to worry about protecting me. I'll do just fine on my own," she countered.

Every word she uttered forth was like a dagger to my heart. I couldn't contain the fierce growl that came from deep within me. My wolf was pissed hearing her say she'd just *move on*. Leave and never come back. And then there was the issue of why she came here in the first place. *What was she running from?*

I couldn't help but stare at her in disbelief, but this time she stared right back. It startled my wolf, which only made me fall harder. *How could she do this?* I thought to myself. *How could she have zero faith in our ability to protect her? We were the largest and strongest pack for a reason, but she wants to just give up?*

My wolf was a strong Alpha, but she never once squirmed or dropped her gaze. It pleased my wolf to see her strength and determination, and my blood suddenly heated. But then she spoke again, crushing me all over.

"Just leave me alone, and I'll be gone before you know it. The pack can return to normal then," she said quietly, but her eyes never left mine.

As if saying this directly to me. My jaw locked, and I forced my wolf aside. She was scared, and I never wanted to make her afraid of me. Of us. But I refused to let a rogue harm what was mine. *I was going to keep her safe, even if I left this pack just to follow her.*

"Shanely, you're family. What happened to you is inexcusable, and you deserve to live here with your family and your own kind," Aspen said as he put his hand on her shoulder. It didn't seem to help. Only worsened what she felt.

"No," she shouted loudly, stepping further away from her uncle. *From me.* "You all barely know me, alright!? I'm not a wolf. I'm not a shifter. Look, I won't say anything about you guys, but I don't want to be a burden either, and I certainly don't want anyone to get hurt because of me. If the rogue is coming back for me then it's better I be alone anyways and away from all of you."

My heart broke, hearing her words leave her lips. The room erupted again, but I was just stuck on the pain of her wanting to go. My pain turned to rage at the fact she wanted to risk her life just to make the pack's life *easier*. Her eyes met mine briefly, but I couldn't control my own emotions anymore. I have never been so out of control before, but she was my undoing. She took another step back.

"You have no idea how badly I have wanted to know my family and where I came from, but it's clear my mother ran away because of me. Maybe she was ashamed of who I was? I don't know, but she made it clear she didn't want me here. I'm not worth all of this fighting, trust me," she said, and I snapped again.

"You're giving up just like that?" I growled out, unable to keep the hurt and anger from my voice. "No one can even try to find this rogue or offer to protect you. You're just going to *leave* and never come back? All because of one fool in this room that doesn't think you belong here. Do you seriously think so little of yourself that you're willing to risk meeting this rogue again all on your own? Because we all know how well that turned out the first time, now don't we?!"

"*BASTIAN!*" Cade bellowed through the link.

My eyes widened as I realized how harsh that all came out. My brother glared at me as I watched the aftermath of my temper unfold. She looked devastated, which only made me feel like a further puke. *God, I was screwing up left and right with this girl*, I thought as my heart thundered in my chest. And when she took another step back, my heart broke a little further.

"I can't do this anymore," she croaked out as tears formed in her eyes. *I did that. I didn't— I would never—*

My wolf finally relented, and I took a step towards the girl. I had to fix this, but Cade got in my way.

"You've done enough."

I didn't fight him because he was right. She bolted out the door and panic filled my chest, watching her leave.

"Shanely!" Cassie hollered, chasing after her.

The rogue— I shoved passed Cade, when my Alpha suddenly threw his power out in the room, hitting my chest hard.

"You," he snapped, and I slammed to a stop, "you've done enough. Ash and Aspen, go follow her. Make sure she gets home, and then leave her in peace. The rest of you go home and keep everything to yourselves while we sort this out. Cade, send word to double patrols around the cabin and make sure the rogue can't get close!"

BONUS CHAPTER

Cade gave our Alpha a nod, watching me closely as he left the room. I gritted my teeth, waiting for the verbal backlash that was coming. Everyone left before I turned to my Alpha.

"What is God's name do you think you're doing?!" he snapped, and I winced at the aggression in his tone.

"Alpha, I didn't mean—"

"No," he snapped, cutting me off. "You don't speak! Shanely had a horrible night tonight. She was thrown into our world headfirst, and her first night in these mountains, she stumbles onto a rogue. Then she has to sit here and listen to Derek berate her, and you snap at her like that when she gets scared?! That is unacceptable, Bastian!"

I dropped my head, feeling every bit of a lousy puke right now. *I didn't mean to add insult to injury,* I thought to myself. I couldn't stand the thought of someone marking her or her leaving Diablo forever. *But it doesn't excuse my behavior.*

Cain dropped in his seat, sighing. "We were devastated when Mercedes disappeared, Bastian. And then to find out she had a daughter like this? Cassia's been beside herself since she called it in. We need to welcome her in the pack. Make sure she knows she's safe with us. Not blow up on her."

I slowly looked to my Alpha, whose brows had furrowed with worry.

"I am sorry, Alpha," I said quietly. "And I promise I will apologize when I go to her tomorrow."

Cain's eyes flashed red, making my stomach twist in knots. "You will do no such thing. You crossed the line tonight, Bastian, and I'm not chancing *anything* with my niece. It is clear your temper is out of control, so I'm putting Ryder and Johnny on security detail until she's more comfortable."

My eyes widened. "You can't—"

"I can!" he bellowed. His Alpha power hit me straight in the chest again as he said, "Bastian, you are to stay away from Shanely until I give the word. You will not come within 50 feet of my niece for your lack of control tonight."

The command coated my wolf, and suddenly, it was as if chains held us down. I stood there in shock as the reality of what he just commanded hit me. My eyes met his as an icy rage filled my chest. It was strong, and my brothers hovered in my mind because of it.

My rage was bleeding through our bonds.

"Find this rogue and kill it," Cain commanded again before dismissing me for the night.

My wolf studied our Alpha closely and then barred his teeth. I was slightly at a disadvantage going head-to-head with his wolf, but I forced my wolf to submit, knowing there was an easier way. *Let Cain assume he has me so he'll leave me alone. Command or not, I am going to see Shanely.*

A vicious burn coursed through my veins as I turned around and strolled out of the room.

Bonus Chapter

Bastian

"Hey, you're alive!" Cade said as I forced my way into the bunkhouse. "Didn't think you'd be standing once Cain got ahold of you."

I rolled my eyes as Elijah leaned against the bunks. "What in the world happened tonight?"

"Bastian lost control," Cade teased, grinning like a banshee, and I snarled at him.

"He never loses control," Elijah said, giving me a look. I sighed, collapsing on my bunk. Morning was just around the corner, but all I wanted to do was go to her. Make sure she was safe, but that stupid command ground me in my spot. *At least Ash said she made it home safely.*

"Oh, Bastian got himself all in a tizzy over the Alpha's niece," Cade went on, and Elijah's eyes widened.

"What happened in that meeting?" my brother asked again, and Cade filled him in, enjoying every second of it. I didn't have it in me to explain anyways.

Elijah slumped down in his bunk. "Good Lord. Is she your mate?"

I stilled at the question. Cade leaned forward, waiting for my answer too, and I sighed before answering, "I don't know. I think so, but the bond never clicked in fully. All I know is my wolf and I claim her as ours."

They looked to one another slowly. I didn't blame them. Shoot, this was confusing to me too, but I knew how I felt about her. Something was drawing me to her. I don't know why the bond hasn't happened yet, but I didn't care. *She is mine.*

"So what do we do about it?" Elijah asked quietly.

Cade looked to me then. *This was all on me,* I realized, and I straightened my shoulders. "Mate bond or not, I am going to protect that girl with my life."

Cade smirked saying, "And what about your Alpha command? How are you getting around that one?"

I frowned, standing to look out the window. Aspen was outside already with the recruits, going over what needed to be done with today's patrol. The patrol that *I'm* supposed to lead. Suddenly, a brilliant idea popped in my head.

I turned to face my brothers. "I need your help."

* * *

"Are you positive Aspen won't notice?"

Elijah's voice shot through my mind as I quietly stalked past the guards stationed nearby Shanely's cabin. Cain's orders were to stay far out of sight, but there was a large tree near her creek that I had every plan to pop a squat and watch her from. *No rogue was getting past me.*

"Dude, it's fine," Cade muttered. *"I've played the broody brother multiple times. Nobody's caught us yet."*

I snorted, leaping over a log and ducking downwind towards her cabin. I could smell honey from here, and it was all I could do to go slow.

"Quiet, you two," I snapped. *"Look, I already know at some point Cain will catch me over this, but I don't care. I just need to know she's safe."*

"How exactly are you even doing this right now?" Elijah asked. *"Cain put that command—"*

"I know," I answered. *"The 50 foot mark's coming up. I can feel it."*

"And how are you going to get passed it?" Elijah countered.

"I don't know."

Alpha Cain's power grazed against my skin. A growl slipped passed my lips before I could stop it. *God, this hurt.* I lifted my paw, but it slammed back down on the dirt. I could just barely see her cabin past the trees, and I grounded my teeth in anger. *Shanely is all alone in that cabin,* I thought to myself. *She needs me.*

My body shook under the pressure of my Alpha's command as I lifted my paw again. *Shanely needs me,* I thought again. *I have— to— protect— my— mate!*

Suddenly, I leapt forward as I broke through the command. The weight fell off, and I could breathe again. I had no idea how I managed to that, but I wasn't about to question anything. I took off towards the cabin and into the hiding spot. I had a clear shot of her entire backyard and cabin, and I exhaled a sigh of relief. *God, she was right there. I could fix everything between us and apologize for lashing out.*

"I'm here."

"*You made it passed the command?!*" Elijah asked in surprise.

"*I did. I'm going to check and make sure she's alright. How's it going Cade?*"

"*Not now. Aspen's getting ready to leave.*"

"*I'm at the shop now,*" Elijah said. "*Let me know how it goes.*"

I left my brothers and darted towards the cabin. *I owed them big time after today.* I bounded towards her door, but the deck boards creaked loudly, and I froze. Nothing happened so I decided to press my luck and move closer to the window. *I just needed to see her,* I told myself. *I just needed to make sure she was alright.* I leapt up on the sill and stole a peek inside.

Shanely lay in a tumbled heap on her bed, completely sound asleep. I exhaled, fogging the window up slightly. I couldn't help but stare at her. She was so beautiful. Just peaceful, and I wanted it to stay that way. Forever. I just wanted to make her happy for the rest of my life. That's the only thing that mattered anymore.

A sound came from behind, and I squinted my eyes. A patrol was circling around, and I shoved off her window and hid back under the mulberry brush. The fruit would be enough to mask my wolf's scent, and I'd be able to stay and watch her. *She may not want me around right now, but it doesn't mean I won't keep her safe from the rogue.*

I surprisingly stayed put for the entire day. Cade was doing a good job of being me, and with the help of our other friends, the Alphas and leadership were none the wiser. Shanely never once moved though. She slept so soundly, I was beginning to get nervous. I watched the house as the sun set and night came. Elijah joined me then. I was grateful he took over the night shift, so I could sleep. He or Cade were the only ones I trusted, and Cade was off being me. So far we were keeping up the ruse.

And I got to be with my girl.

Elijah left me to take care of our machine shop early the next morning. Shanely had finally woken, and I could see her moving about her house now. I watched her clean and unpack her belongings. Every step made me relax. *If she was so determined to leave, she'd be packing up already. Not settling in.* My wolf and I took that as a good sign.

She opened her bedroom window then, and I stilled as she looked around outside. She scented the air, and I cocked my head to the side waiting. I wasn't sure what she was doing, but she left the window open, and I continued to watch her. I was itching to bolt across the creek. I wanted nothing more than to rush to her, but I forced myself to stay put.

"Uhh— Bastian? Cain's joining the patrols."

I swallowed my snarl, knowing my time with Shanely was running out.

"Just stick to the plan," I said firmly.

"Roger that."

Shanely opened the backdoor as Cade left my mind. My head shot up as I watched her collapse in the swing. That thick honey scent filled the air, and my wolf shuddered. *I had to move,* I thought as panic slowly crept in. *I had to see her. Before it was too late.*

I shot to the brush closest to me and stilled. Shanely moved so swiftly towards her door. My stomach launched into my throat, and I moved again. I couldn't let her leave.

I came out of my hiding place, moving so slowly so as not to spook her more. She stilled when she saw me, and I saw her chest moving slightly erratically. She was nervous.

Yeah, well— so am I.

My nerves grew worse the longer she watched me. She seemed to relax some, but I had never felt so subconscious before. *God, this was killing me.* I couldn't help but move towards her just a tad. She was my flame, and I was determined to get burned.

BONUS CHAPTER

The creek was the pack's boundary line though. *I shouldn't cross it without her permission,* I thought to myself. I didn't want to push her again, so I sat down on my hind legs and waited. My eyes pleaded with her to let me in, hoping she understood what I wanted. It was killing me to wait though.

She watched me for awhile before deciding my fate. My heart broke when she put her hand on the door to go back inside. I slumped to the ground, covering my snout with my paw. I couldn't keep the whine from escaping my throat, and I waited for the door to slam. *God, I was dumb,* I thought angrily. *She wants nothing to do with me because I was a tool to her.*

I heard her door close softly, but the sounds of her breathing were there still. I moved my paws, cocking my head to the side in surprise. She was still there, watching me intently.

She stayed.

My heart leapt from my chest as I abruptly sat up. *Maybe there was hope yet. Maybe she doesn't hate me.* Finally, I heard her angelic voice speak.

"I'm assuming your wolfy ears can hear me, but you can come over."

She didn't have to tell me twice. I bolted over, jumping the creek with one swift motion before grinding to a halt at her stairs. I didn't want to scare her further than I already had, so I forced myself to go slow. She studied me with such intensity I actually had to pay attention to my feet. I was going to trip on my face and humiliate myself if I wasn't careful. I took the steps slowly as Shanely sat back on the swing. She patted the seat next to her.

"You can sit with me," she said softly, and I nearly leapt for joy. I started to shift back when she said, "but I don't want to talk. You can be here though if that's what you want."

I stopped my shift abruptly. *She doesn't want to speak with me.* My shoulders sunk a little as I approached the swing. *This was a win,* I reminded myself. I am grateful just to be with her, and I stopped just before her. Her eyes widened as she looked up to me, and I debated how I was going to do this. *This swing was built with shifters in mind, but how could my wolf fit on here without laying on her?* I wasn't exactly a little guy. I wanted her to know I respected her, and I would never put her in an uncomfortable position she wasn't ready for.

She shrieked when I jumped up, shifting the swing abruptly as I tried to balance my large frame on it.

"I didn't mean literally next to me! Can the swing even hold your wolf?!"

I chuckled through my wolf. *God, she was adorable,* I thought to myself. I jerked my head towards the ceiling, where the massive bolts held the swing upright before adjusting my tail away from her. She pursed her lips together, and we sat in silence for a moment. My heart thundered in my chest as I experienced pure happiness for the first time in my life. I had never felt anything like this before, but by God, it was hard to stay on one side of the swing.

I was too large honestly. It would have been easier if I shifted first, but she didn't seem too keen on seeing me just yet. I honestly thought my wolf would be the form she didn't want to see, and I wasn't sure how to take the truth. But it was impossible not to brush up against her, and every time we touched, a shiver shot through me. She made me so nervous. So ungodly nervous that I struggled not to be awkward. I have never had trouble with ladies before but this girl— this girl was my undoing.

The swing jolted as I tried to readjust, but Shanely surprised me when she patted her leg saying, "It's okay. You can rest your head here, otherwise I think you'll fall off."

Did I just hear her right? I thought as my heart thundered in my chest. I cocked my head to the side, and she turned about fifty different shades of red. *I did hear right*— she was *allowing* me to rest my head on her leg. I never in a million years thought something like this would happen. Nervous energy shot through my system, amplifying what I already felt inside as I watched Shanely.

Embarrassment flooded her face, and I decided to take her up on her offer before she changed her mind. The honey sweet scent filled my nostrils the second I laid my head on her knee, and I struggled to keep my wolf in check. *He freaking loved her scent.*

We stayed quiet then, just rocking back and forth together, and I was utterly in heaven. That is until I felt her rub the fur on the back of my neck. When her finger gently scratched the sensitive part behind my ears, I realized *this* is what heaven felt like. *God—*

"I'm sorry!" she stammered. "I was zoning out, and I—"

Her words pulled me from my blissful thoughts as she yanked her hand away. I whined, pushing back against her hand. I knew I was being ridiculous, but I'd do anything to have her hands on my neck again. *To have her hands anywhere—*

"You *want* me to pet you?"

I pushed again, hoping she understood my answer, and she gently scratched again. I nearly shuddered but settled back down, closing my eyes as the girl of my dreams pet my wolf. My ears perked up, twitching her way when I heard her stomach growl. *I needed to feed her soon.* I'll have to send one of my brothers a message to bring something because there was no way I'd leave her now.

I owed my brothers a lot actually. They had no idea the gift they gave me by covering for me. This was not how I expected this morning to go. I honestly thought she'd chew me up and spit me out for my behavior, but she didn't. Her too good nature just asked for space, and I'd give her anything to make her feel better. Another reason to believe this girl was supposed to be mine.

"Dude—" Cade said through the link, and I stilled. *"We are in trouble."*

A branch snapped in the distance, and I looked into the woods. Dread filling my core as I searched for my brother.

"How close are you?" I asked solemnly.

"Close."

Crap. I rolled my eyes, knowing my pleasant morning was about to come to an end. My ears twitched towards the trail that led to the lodge. I could hear their paws hitting ground, already knowing exactly who was coming. I had *moments* left with this girl. *It wasn't enough,* I thought. *It would never be enough.* I looked to her one last time, my eyes heavy with sadness. Her breathtaking eyes looked confused for a moment, and my God, I could get lost just looking in them. But then my gaze dropped to her full lips, and it took everything in me not to just shift and kiss her.

Cain had every right to seriously punish me for disobeying an Alpha command. It pissed me off because it wasn't fair, but there was nothing I could do. I wasn't Alpha. I licked her cheek, the closest I could get to kissing her goodbye, and hopped off the swing.

She followed, and the Alphas and their family poured out of the woods. I sat down at the top step and waited.

Waited for my demise.

Everyone shifted, including my brother, who gave me a grim look. I gave Shanely one last look as my Alpha flung his power out, hitting me in the chest.

"Bastian shift now," Cain demanded.

I shifted, shoving my wolf beneath my skin painfully, and stood before my Alpha, breathing hard. I could feel Shanely's eyes on mine, but I didn't dare look up from the ground. Cain was pissed.

Really pissed.

"You realize you disobeyed an Alpha order, right?" Cain asked gruffly.

I did the only thing that was wise in the moment. I nodded my head and stayed quiet.

"Sorry, man. I held out as long as I could," Cade muttered in my mind.

"I ordered you to keep your distance from my niece. You pushed the line with her that night, and we were *all* giving her space. You also skipped out on your job and responsibilities to the pack. Have you been here this entire time?"

This time I lifted my head to reply with confidence. I did disobey, but I would time and time again for her. *He needed to understand that.*

"I have been Alpha," I answered, "but I didn't cross the creek line until this morning."

"Wait, how long have you been here? How long was I asleep for?" she asked, and I finally turned away from my Alpha.

"You slept sound for nearly 24 hours. I stayed close enough to keep an eye on you but far enough to not be seen or heard. I couldn't leave you alone out here. Not after everything."

I looked to my feet, feeling bad I had watched over her without consent. *I did it for the best of reasons though.* Her intense gaze stayed on me, and I nervously stuck my hands in my pockets.

"Why?" she finally asked. I cocked my head to side. She wasn't angry. No, she seemed more curious than anything.

"Why what?" I asked in a softer tone.

"Why risk whatever punishment Cain's going to give you to watch me? You don't even know me," Shanely said, and I shrugged. I didn't know how to explain this without freaking her out, so I went with the easiest option. A half-truth.

"My wolf does, and what happened to you is inexcusable. Wolf shifters don't attack people, and if I can't kill the shifter responsible then I'll make sure he never comes close to you again," I said, finding my resolve. *I needed her to understand this too.* "You don't need to leave your home because of a rogue, and I'm going to make sure you're safe. That's my ultimatum, and I refuse to budge on that."

Her eyes widened, and I could hear her heart skip a beat inside. She looked completely shocked by my words, and my eyes narrowed on her. *Someone broke a part of her,* I thought to myself. That look only comes from someone who's been broken by a person they trust. Someone Shanely should have been able to rely on but failed her completely. *I didn't like it.*

"Regardless of why you did what you did, you broke an Alpha command," Cain bellowed. My head dropped, waiting for the punishment to come.

"Shouldn't that be impossible?" Aspen said quietly, but Cassie shushed him.

"Cain? Or Uncle Cain? Or Alpha? I'm sorry, I really don't know what to call you," Shanely stammered nervously. I watched the Alpha softened as he turned to her.

"You are the only person that can call me Uncle Cain instead of Alpha and get away with it. These two don't seem to be having kids anytime soon."

Aspen wasn't amused when he replied, "Yeah, well not everyone is lucky enough to find their mate at 13."

"Anyways Shanely, you haven't officially joined the pack, even though I have vocally claimed you as one of my own. Technically, you aren't even required to call me Alpha yet."

"Even when that's the case, we will always be your aunt and uncle first," Cassia chimed in.

"Well then, Uncle Cain, I understand what Bastian did was wrong, but can you give him a warning or something this time?"

My head snapped to hers, and the corners of my mouth rose slightly. *This girl was something else,* I thought to myself, when Cade's annoying voice interrupted my thoughts.

"Aww she likes you—"

My lips pursed together in a tight line as I remembered we had an audience. I didn't want to question how she felt in front of everyone or why she was sticking her neck out for me. But Cade's words rattled my mind. All I could think of was the word *mate,* and I couldn't get my head to stop saying it.

"It's just that it was really kind that he stayed with me this whole time. No one's ever done something like this for me before, and I think it's probably why I was able to rest for so long, even if I didn't know one of your pack members was there," she rambled on, and I couldn't contain the small smirk on my face then. *She was adorable when she rambled.* She straightened herself, trying to gain her composure as she went on. "I was safe here at least. I— uh— I don't know. I just feel bad about him getting in trouble over me. I'm not trying to overstep, but I just wondered and technically I did invite him to the house, so he really did give me some space."

My eyes widened, drifting back to my Alpha. Cain looked almost *amused* with her right now. *God, this girl* was *my saving grace,* I thought as my heart fluttered in my chest. I knew full well that he was going to tan my hide the moment he found me, but Shanely seemed to soften his anger. *It seems after this is all over, I owed her too.*

"I appreciate the request, but Bastian broke a big rule. He's not allowed to go against an Alpha command. He still will receive punishment just like everyone else," he replied, but my eyes were still stuck on her. She seemed bothered that I would be punished right now. It made my wolf— *happy.*

"However," Cain continued, "due to the circumstances, I do appreciate him looking out for you and at least *waiting* to be invited in. I'll make the punishment fit the crime. "

I smirked, watching her eyes dart back and forth from me to her uncle. *She was so freaking adorable right now,* I thought to myself. I didn't even care that I had stopped listening to my Alpha by now. I was so mesmerized by *her* that I couldn't focus on anything else.

She turned to ask, "So, what happens now?"

"Bastian," Cain said firmly. His Alpha Power struck me hard, and I winced in pain, forcing myself to look at him. But I refused to show weakness in front of this girl, so I forced myself to hold my head high, despite the throbbing in my head wanting me to obey and expose my neck. "For disobeying an Alpha order, you will be relieved of your responsibilities as an Enforcer for the next two weeks. You will not be allowed in the High Council's meetings nor will you be my personal enforcer. Once your two weeks are up, you will be allowed in again."

I took a deep breath as the new command hit me. One I'd gladly obey. I gave him a firm nod as his voice pierced my mind.

"I am forgiving you today, Bastian, because of her and her alone. This cannot happen again."

I froze, understanding the warning in that tone. I seriously messed up disobeying my Alpha, and she saved me from his wrath.

"Now, seeing you'll have some free time on your hands, I'd like you to watch over my niece. That is if she is comfortable with that?" Cain asked, and I turned to Shanely.

She cocked her head to the side, jutting out that adorably sexy hip of hers as she responded, "I really don't need a babysitter, Uncle. I'm sure Bastian would rather do anything else with his time—"

"I'd be happy to," I interrupted, with a devilish grin. *I was going to already.*

"Shanely," Cain said, pulling her attention back to him, "the Council and I all agree that you deserve to remain *here* with your family. We are actively hunting the rogue, and I promise you I will find him, but we want you to stay with us here as part of the pack. Your scent is changing, Shanely, and you smell like a wolf. Even from the first night I met you, your scent is stronger, which makes you a target because you're not human. Until you shift though, you *will* be defenseless. You'll scent like a shifter without the abilities you need to protect yourself. Other shifters will be able to scent you out now, and you would be safer attached to a large pack. Hiding you amongst the pack would be the safest way to blend you in until we get more answers. Keep your cabin, your grandmother wanted you to have it, and no one feels right taking it back from you. We have some terms though we'd like you to agree on."

"What are you all thinking?" she asked nervously. *At least she wasn't saying no.*

"The Council and I discussed it at length after you left, and we came up with three things we'd like to start today. One; you do not go into town alone. Even though it is neutral ground, the rogue may be blending in, and it would be easy to snatch you there. Bastian is an Enforcer, which is our pack's security, so he can escort you or one of us will. Two; we would like you to train with us. You can learn to defend yourself and try to awaken your own wolf. We all feel her, so it's only a matter of time before you do too. The goal is to get you to shift, so you can protect yourself. No matter where you are in this world you will be safe, and you won't be such an easy target for the rogue then."

She nearly recoiled at Cain's words. It happened so fast, I barely caught the expression before it was gone again, and now more than ever was I curious to know what happened to her. I crossed my arms, forcing my wolf aside. *I needed to figure this out.*

"And lastly; you will need to officially join my pack. That way we can always be able to reach one another if something were to come up. Technically, right now you are unclaimed, which might be why the rogue chose you in the first place. The rogue would be able to sense you are now a pack member, and that comes with protection. He would be less likely to come after you now that you are no longer alone," Cain replied.

Shanely rocked back and forth on her heels, debating what to do. I could see the wheels turning in her mind, and when her nose scrunched up, I knew she had made her decision. *She's just lucky it was one I liked.*

"Alright deal, but I also don't want everyone to change their lives trying to keep me safe. I love the idea of training and unlocking my wolf, but I don't need a babysitter. I don't *want* one. I wont be a burden, Uncle."

How could she think she'd be a burden to us? I thought as my arms fell to my side. *To me.* I was really beginning to see such low self-esteem coming from her, and my wolf and I were going to fix that. *She'd see her worth,* I told myself. *I'd make her see just how special she was.*

"You will never be a burden, Shanely. This is what it means to be part of a pack, part of a family," Cain said, interrupting my train of thought. "Now Bastian, I'm trusting you to keep her safe. She is in your care now. Bring her to the lodge tonight at 7."

"But Uncle Cain—"

Cain simply ignored her and shifted back into his wolf. The others followed suit, except Cade, who was grinning from ear to ear. It didn't escape my notice how she blushed when her aunt gave her a wink before leaving, but I kept that little tidbit to myself. *No need to embarrass her further.*

I stuck my hands in my pockets as I turned towards Shanely. It was then I realized how easy it was earlier in my wolf form. I couldn't speak then but now— I exhaled slowly. Now I had to open my mouth and try not to fumble my words.

"Shanely, meet my brother Cade."

Cade crossed the creek to meet us at the steps. He was in his typical good mood, and I envied his confidence right now. God knows how nervous I was at the moment.

"Nice to officially meet you, Shanely," he said as he stuck his hand out to greet Shanely. His hand swallowed hers entirely, and I smiled softly to myself. *She was just a tiny thing.*

"Hi, Cade," she said quietly. "Nice to meet you too."

He turned to me then. "I covered as long as I could, brother. Cain seems to sniff out trouble quick, and once they realized I wasn't you, the gig was up. He knew *exactly* where you'd be."

"It's okay. I appreciate your help. It gave me a bit more time," I said, rubbing the back of my head. I chose my words carefully. *She's not ready to have that conversation with me,* I thought. *Not yet.*

"You guys swapped places?" she asked. I couldn't contain my grin then.

"Once in a while, when it's really important," Cade replied, with this twinkle in his eye.

Shanely narrowed her eyes, but soon seemed to zone out with her thoughts. I took a moment to check with Cade.

"Did you get in trouble?" I asked quietly.

"Don't worry about it, Bastian. It's just for half the time you got," he answered, and I sighed heavily. "Besides, you've got a hunch, and your gut is never wrong. She's worth it."

"Are you guys twins?" she interrupted.

Cade laughed, and I smiled wider. She had zoned out over us entirely, and now blushed profusely for interrupting us. That thought made my wolf feel content inside me.

"Triplets actually," Cade answered. "Though I'm the youngest and best-looking brother."

I smirked and playfully shoved Cade. He was such a freaking goofball, but it got a laugh out of her. She seemed to like watching our interaction, and I just took it as another sign she was my mate. My mate had to be okay with my brothers. *We were a package deal after all.*

"I'm only older by four minutes!" I jested before turning to Shanely. "Our middle brother will be around later today. His name is Elijah."

"Yeah, we thought we'd come hang out with you today," Cade said, moving towards the door, "if that's okay?"

Her eyes widened like she didn't know what to say. I felt bad when he put her on the spot like that, but Cade either didn't care or didn't seem to notice. My vote was on the latter.

"Listen," she said, crossing her arms over her chest. "I know my uncle asked you to watch me, but please don't worry about me. I'll get some sort of security out here soon, but I'm sure you have other pack responsibilities to handle."

"Nah, I want to spend my day with you. Besides Alpha Cain gave Elijah and I the week off too, so we have nothing going on," Cade replied casually.

"He did?"

"Well—" Cade said, chuckling, "in a way he did."

I snorted, crossing my arms and taking my familiar enforcer stance. I do it without thinking half the time, but right now it was helping ease my nerves. I said, "They both got suspended for assisting me. Just for half the time."

Her face fell as she exclaimed, "Cade, I'm so sorry. I didn't mean to get you guys in trouble!"

Cade raised an eyebrow as he replied, "Why are you apologizing? You didn't even know, Baby Girl! It's this fool that always ropes me into his shenanigans! He's the one to blame!"

I shot him a glare.

"*Careful,*" I warned him. He rolled his eyes.

"If I recall, Elijah and I have pretended to be you too on more than one occasion," I countered, and Cade bumped into me. He winked at Shanely again and managed to pull the biggest smile I had ever seen from her.

"Well, look at that, Bastian. I think she's gotta have the best smile I've ever seen!" Cade said, grinning.

My wolf loved seeing her happy as much as I did. *God, she was perfect,* I thought. *Utterly perfect.*

"She does, Cade. I'd like to see that smile more often."

She blushed, dropping her head, but I caught it. This utter joy shot through me then, and I don't think there has ever been a time where I was this happy. Not even when my father dropped me off at this strange pack.

Cade headed for the door then. "C'mon, let's see what there is to do for fun in here."

I couldn't contain the nervous grin from appearing as I rubbed the back of my head. I was going to have a freaking bald spot by the end of the week if I wasn't careful.

"Sorry, he's very— outgoing. After you," I said, gesturing to the door.

She didn't exactly say yes to spending the day with us, but I wasn't going to point that out. I watched every sway of her hips as she made her way inside, and my wolf emitted a low growl.

We seriously approved of our mate.

Bonus Chapter

Bastian

Cade was already in the hall closet, looking around inside, and I about died of embarrassment. *If only our mother could see him now—* I thought as I glared at him. *She'd tan my hide as well.*

"Cade, you're being nosy. Get out of there!" I hissed as he popped his head out with a sheepish smile. He simply shrugged and stepped out of the closet with his arms full of games and puzzles.

"No, it's fine really. You guys are welcome to go wherever. Most of the stuff here isn't mine. I was just trying to organize and clean up. It's kind of a mess really. I'm sorry about that," she replied as Cade set the games down on the table.

I took a look around, frowning. There was a lot to do yet. I didn't like knowing the place was so dirty for her.

And empty, I thought. *It was really empty in here.*

"Well, how about we help you fix the place up then? We can play these when we're done," Cade offered.

"Oh no, guys. It's okay—"

I couldn't stop myself from reaching out to comfort her. I had to help. She *had* to let me help. My fingers grazed her arm as I said, "Please, Shanely. Let us help out."

She froze, nodding her head softly, and I wondered if I was coming on too strong. I dropped my hand, trying to slow down for her. This was by far the hardest thing I had ever done though.

I strolled around the massive table and pulled out the broom sitting in the corner. Cade followed suit, and it took the pressure off my girl. She loosened up as we cleaned, and it was amazing every time she laughed. If I could listen to it all day, I would. It was the best sound in the world, and I tried everything I could think of to make her laugh again.

Cade insisted we play a game once everything had been done, and she seemed so eager to hear about our life growing up. I told her story after story, watching her eyes light up with each and every one, but to my dismay she was really vague when I tried to ask about her life. And each question only seemed to kill her mood. It was like watching a small piece of her die inside, and I could barely stand asking her *anything* at all. But it was killing me not to know. I needed to know how to heal her.

Cade's stomach roared loudly, making Shanely giggle. I stole a peek at my watch. *God, time flies.*

"Cade, your stomach sounds like it's a vicious animal," she said, making her way to the outdated flowery couch. Cade followed as I pulled out my phone to send Elijah a text. We needed food.

"Baby Girl, you have no idea. Agh, I could eat a bear right now."

"Not an actual bear though, right?" she asked as Cade roared with laughter. Even I couldn't contain my grin as I watched the two goof around. It made my wolf happy to see them become friends too.

"You're hilarious, you know that?"

She blushed, and suddenly my wolf pushed me forward. Cade was never a threat, but if she was going to blush over anything, then it was going to be over something *I* said or did. I pushed myself between the two, half sitting on my brother as I plopped down on the couch.

"Geez, Bastian. You could have just said scooch over!" Cade cried out, pulling his leg out from underneath me.

"*Dick,*" he muttered.

"Huh," I said with a grin. "I didn't see you, Cade. I was too busy ordering everyone dinner."

Cade's ears perked up, and I knew I had him. He could out eat everyone I knew. My phone buzzed.

```
"Sure thing. Picking it up now."
```

"Really? Whatcha get?" Cade asked, leaning into me. I shoved him off and pocketed my phone.

"Elijah's bringing a couple pizzas. Calm down," I replied.

"I feel bad, you guys. You got suspended because of me, then you spend your whole day cleaning and organizing my cabin, and now you're buying me food? You don't have to do that!"

"Baby Girl, we need to feed you. Do you see how skinny you are? You clearly aren't eating enough, and we're going to fix that. Besides, you have literally nothing to eat in this cabin. I checked," Cade replied, beaming back at Shanely.

I frowned, looking towards the kitchen.

"Wait, there's no food here?" I asked, looking to Shanely. She seemed almost *shameful*, and my wolf bristled inside. *I definitely didn't like that look.*

"Nope. It's totally empty brother. Didn't you notice when we cleaned the kitchen?" Cade asked.

"No, I wasn't being nosy like you," I replied sarcastically.

"What? I had the munchies," he said nonchalantly. I rolled my eyes but quickly shoved my brother's annoying stomach aside.

"Did you eat anything this morning then?" I asked her. My wolf was alert now. *When was the last time she ate something?*

"Bastian I'm fine," she answered, dropping her gaze, "really."

She didn't want to look me in the eye when she answered. I frowned, trying to do the math myself.

"If you didn't eat earlier then the last meal you had was before the rogue attacked you, wasn't it?"

She shot me an annoyed look then, and I knew I had her. *God, she must be starving right now*, I thought to myself as my wolf snarled at me. *I should have checked on her earlier.*

"It's not that big of a deal," she protested. "I'll eat when I can get back into town. You really don't have to buy dinner for me."

"Oh no, I'm getting dinner. I'll tell Elijah to bring groceries too so you have stuff here. You can't go without food, Shanely," I said, pulling my phone back out. I sent him a long message with a list of groceries I needed him to buy. I was just about to hit send, when she placed her hand on my arm to stop me.

"Bastian, don't do that," she pleaded with me. "You don't have to spend money like that on me. I doubt my uncle expected *this* when he asked you to stay here with me today."

I studied her for a moment, deciding how to answer her. Cade just went from me to her, and suddenly it felt too crowded in here. I gently pulled her hand off my phone and hit send. Her eyes widened, and she tried to pull away, but I held firm saying, "Come with me for a minute."

I didn't give her a choice as I pulled her from the couch. Cade gave me a knowing look, and I heard his link before we had gone two steps.

"Don't do anything I wouldn't do."

The jerk.

I shut the door as anxiety filled my chest thanks to Cade. I shuffled nervously on my feet, trying to get the words to come out. All I really wanted to do was scream *you're my mate!* I wanted to wrap my arms around her, tell her that everything's going to be okay because now I was here. I was here, and I was going to take care of her. Actually, what I really wanted to do was grab her waist, shove her against the wall with her hands above her head, and kiss the crap out of her but— that wouldn't go over well at all. She didn't know about shifters and mates. Shoot, I *barely* knew about this stuff, but I didn't wanna scare her away just when she was starting to let me in.

"Look, I really wanted to say this when I first got here, but you weren't ready to talk, and that was okay. I can be patient," I said, shoving my hands in my pockets. "Well, with you I can be patient."

God, I was flubbing up my words now like a complete idiot.

"Dude get it together. I can feel your nerves from here," Cade muttered, flustering me all over again.

"Shut up, Cade."

I sighed saying, "I am sorry for my reaction the night we met. I let my temper get the better of me with Derek, even though everyone knows he doesn't do anything unless it benefits him, and then I snapped at you. I'm *most* sorry about that. I was upset hearing what had happened in the first place, and then when you said you were going to just leave the mountains, I just—"

I dropped my sentence as she looked up at me with those big doe eyes of hers. *They were so green,* I thought to myself. *So green and so gorgeous.* I struggled to get it together as Cade put it, and I debated what to even tell her. *Do I tell her about mates? Do I even try to have this conversation now?* My brother hovered in my mind as I debated what to do. She crossed her arms nervously, and I sighed again. Fear won out, and I just couldn't do it. I couldn't spring this on her. *Not yet.*

Shanely seemed nervous with this conversation as it was and started playing with her hair. My eyes followed her every movement.

"Thank you for your apology," she said softly, "and for everything else you've done for me, but really don't worry about me. I'm not your responsibility nor do you have to spend all this money. I know my uncle asked you to watch over me, but I'll be okay on my own too. Joining the pack will help keep me safe, and I'm sure my uncle will find the rogue quickly. I'd like to be friends, but I don't want you to feel responsible for me. I'm sure your girlfriend or family will need you at some point, if the pack doesn't already."

I frowned. "I don't have a girlfriend, Shanely, and my family is back home in Denmark other than my brothers. Besides, I'm right where I want to be."

She stilled when I took a step closer. *God, I just wanted to kiss her. To hold her close and never let her go.* I took another step, feeling my canines start to enlarge.

"Bastian, I—"

My eyes dropped to her neck, widening when I saw a freaking *hand-print* on it. My wolf shot to the front, and I growled. I couldn't help it, and she staggered back a bit.

"Who did that to you?" I demanded, pointing to the yellowish-blue bruise on her neck.

She promptly covered it back up with her hair and stepped further away from me. My wolf was pissed.

"Bastian, it's nothing."

I followed her until her back was against the cabin. *I will slaughter the prick who did this to her,* I thought angrily. *I just needed a name.* I snarled as I said, "It's not nothing. It looks like a *handprint.* Who did this, Shanely?"

"It's just a bruise, alright?" she snapped back. Her defiance put me on edge. *She must be terrified of the man who did this to her.* "I'm fine, I promise."

"Shanely, did this happen before you came to Diablo or was this from someone in town?"

I had to know. I assumed this came from wherever she came from, but I had to know if this was another threat I needed to take care of. *If it was one of the Medvedev freaks, I swear—*

"It wasn't anyone in town," she replied softly before looking at her feet. She was shutting me out again, and I couldn't blame her. To her, I was just a temperamental wolf she barely knew but to me— to me she was so much more.

"Then who did this to you?" I asked in a softer tone. I sighed heavily when she wouldn't respond, and I pushed again. I pushed because my wolf wouldn't let it go. "Please just talk to me, Shanely."

"Bastian, we barely know each other. I don't feel like airing out all my problems to someone I barely know, okay? This is just a bruise, and it will heal so *please* drop it," she snapped, crossing her arms.

It killed me. Every word out of her mouth was like a dagger to my heart, and I took a step back. I was coming on too strong. Too harsh. *But couldn't she see I just wanted to help? Or did this man break her so bad that she couldn't see anything but a threat?*

I stuck my hands in my pockets because I didn't have great control over my wolf right now. She wanted space, and I had to give it to her. I was trying to give it to her.

"I'm sorry," she said abruptly. "That was harsh, and I didn't mean for it to come out that way."

I gave her a soft smile replying, "I didn't mean to pry. I just want to keep you safe, and it looks bad."

"I know my uncle asked you to watch me, but this isn't something you need to worry about. I don't mean that harshly either, but *no one* here needs to worry about it because it's in my past now."

"Will this be a problem in your future though?"

The look she gave me hurt, but I held my ground. She may never want me as a mate, but it doesn't mean I won't protect her with every fiber of my being.

"Bastian, really don't—"

"Shanely," I said, interrupting her again, "please just answer me that for now. Will it be an issue I need to watch out for in the future?"

She sighed, her big green eyes softening as she said, "No, he won't be."

"Thank you for telling me, Shanely," I gritted through my teeth. I struggled keeping my wolf at bay. I didn't even want my eyes to flash gold and scare her more than I already had. I *had* to get control. I had to show her that I would never harm her, and that I listened to what she said. She wanted this to stay in her past, and as long as that prick never showed his face around here, I could give it to her.

Silence filled the back porch, and I truly didn't know where to go from here. I didn't want to push this girl away, but I couldn't do the things I really wanted. I couldn't trust my wolf's instincts right now because every option he gave would just result in scaring her off permanently.

"You do know at some point I won't be your responsibility, right?"

That question rattled me, and I frowned even more. My eyes narrowed because I didn't like the idea of her not being my responsibility. I didn't like that that is what she was thinking.

"I don't know if this is a pack thing or what, but I'm sure my uncle will be putting you back on your normal responsibilities after your suspension. You aren't required to waste your time trying to keep me safe, and *none* of that requires you to buy food for me. Let me pay for it, please? I'd like to be friends, and not just a job."

Shanely offered her hand, and I just stared at her. She was such a stubborn, little thing, but I didn't know how to be *just* friends with her. I wanted to spoil her rotten. To care for her in anyway she needed. But what scared me most was what if this was all she wanted to give me? What if she rejected me as her mate because to humans soulmates are things of fairy tales? Shanely may be a shifter by blood, but she was human through and through. I was about to take her hand, and just accept what she was giving me for now, when I heard my saving grace.

Her heart began to race, and I slowly dragged my eyes to meet hers. *She was lying to herself,* I realized. *She was lying to me.* She felt *something,* even if she has no idea what it was. I could hear it. I could see it on her face now. Shanely may be telling herself that we can only be friends, but I can *see* she wants more. My wolf yipped excitedly under my skin. He was beaming inside, and just like that, I knew what I needed to do.

I'd give this girl all the time she needs to accept me and my wolf, but she was most definitely mine. *All mine.* Somehow, we were mates, even though the bond didn't snap in place.

I took her hand and yanked her towards me. I just wanted to hold her once before I let her set the pace. I wrapped my arms around her tiny frame and felt her tense up against me. To my utter delight, she relaxed and held onto me too.

I whispered, "I'd do anything for you."

I bit my bottom lip, regretting the words the moment they left my lips, while she tried to pull away. *I shouldn't have said anything.* She had just started to relax a little, and I pushed again. It was too much too soon, but I just *needed* a second more. That intoxicating honey scent filled my nostrils like a drug. I was instantly addicted to it so I begged, "Please stay. Just stay, Shanely."

I really thought she shove me off, but she settled back against me. I exhaled deeply, feeling content and happy as I held onto her, when suddenly she sucked in a harsh breath. I pulled back as she clutched her chest.

"What's wrong?" I demanded, but she couldn't speak.

Suddenly, I felt her pain. *God, this was awful,* I thought as it burned under my skin. I yanked her close again, rubbing her back in hopes to ease her pain. I shut my eyes tight as my blood burned inside my veins. Cade flew through the door then.

"What in the world is happening?!" he demanded as I exhaled slowly through the pain.

"It isn't me," I gritted through my teeth.

His eyes widened, and we both looked down to Shanely. She was pale as a ghost. Her eyes glossed over as if stuck in some sort of trance, and *my* eyes flashed gold as I struggled to keep my wolf at bay. I felt my canines sharpen once more, and I pursed my lips together to keep Cade from noticing. *This wasn't supposed to happen*, I thought. *Not yet.* I looked to Cade for answers, but he suddenly gripped his chest and looked just as lost as I was.

"What in the world is that?" Elijah's worried tone came through bright and clear as he sent a link.

"Something's wrong with Shanely," I answered.

"But why am I feeling it?!"

"I don't know."

She seemed to get her breathing under control, and I felt that burn slowly fade away. Thank God, because I didn't know how much more I could take.

"Are you okay, Shanely?" Cade asked nervously. She simply nodded, but I knew she was the furthest thing from okay.

"What happened? You gasped, and then my wolf felt your pain," I said, forcing her to look me in the eye.

This freaked me out. *I can take a threat head on no problem, but this? How was I supposed to protect Shanely from something like this again?*

Especially when I feel her pain too.

"What?!" Cade bellowed, giving me a look.

"I don't know Cade, but I could feel that burn, and so did my wolf. It was coming from her," I said truthfully. "He was pushing me hard to shift because something happened with Shanely."

"The bond didn't form though," he said firmly. "How can you feel her pain? How could Elijah and I feel her pain?"

I didn't know what to say. This wasn't how mate bonds work. Eye sight was the only thing you needed, and when you were of age, it all just clicked in place. *How do I make the bond with someone who doesn't have a wolf?*

"Guys, I don't know. It was just painful," she interrupted, rubbing her chest.

"Wait," Cade said as this strange sensation hit me. My wolf was alert and on edge again as I felt the presence of another Alpha draw close. "Do you feel that?"

"Yeah, I do," I answered as another feeling hit. I smiled, feeling that connection appeared slightly. *It wasn't complete, but it was there. It was freaking there.*

"I can sense your wolf Shanely, and it's strong," I said, unable to stop myself from grinning. "I think she's waking up on her own."

"Bastian, I can—" Cade started to say, but I cut him off. He and Elijah were feeling the connection too. *It only proved me right.*

"I know, Cade. I know."

"She is your mate."

"Somehow, she is. But don't say a word yet, Cade. I don't want to scare her, when I can't prove it yet. She clearly isn't feeling it."

"How is this even possible? Mate bonds are instant. Not gradual."

"I don't know. Maybe it's because her wolf is dormant? Look, please just don't say anything to anyone. Not until I can prove my claim."

Cade sighed inside my mind. *"Fine. I won't say a word and neither will Elijah."*

Elijah bellowed from inside the cabin. "Guys! I bring pizza!"

"Food! Thank the lord you're here, Elijah!" Cade shouted as he bolted to the back door. "I honest to God felt like I was going to wither away from starvation."

I smiled at my brother. *Way to break the tension*, I thought to myself. I turned to my mate and asked, "Are you sure you're okay?"

She nodded her head, but I could still see the turmoil in her eyes. She was scared, and honestly so was I. I had never heard of a shifter behaving this way.

"I'll talk to Cain about this. Everyone's wolf is different, but we've never had someone like you before. I'm not sure what to even tell you, but I'd watch out for signs of your wolf emerging. Your hearing and sight should start to improve too and even your speed and stamina. Those all improve with being a wolf shifter," I said with a grin. "Just tell me if something more happens or if that burning feeling comes back. We'll help you with this, Shanely. I promise, my brothers and I got your back. You're more than just a job, okay?"

Emotion flashed in her eyes, but I meant every word. *She would never be just a job to me.* I let her have a moment and followed her back inside, finding Cade carrying a whole pizza box to the couch. It was nearly empty already.

Elijah laughed when he saw the look on my girl's face.

"Don't worry," he said, chuckling. "I brought a lot of pizza. We're all used to Cade's stomach by now, but we'll feed you too, little one. I'm Elijah by the way."

He pulled her into a bear hug then, and I smiled. *She was meeting the most important people in my life,* I thought to myself. I knew the connection was forming for him too, and he shot me a look when she wasn't looking. I gave him a firm nod before moving to the paper plates. He seemed to understand and moved on from the conversation we *needed* to have later.

"So, I brought what you asked. It's on the counter over there," Elijah said as he pointed to bags of groceries. I nodded my thanks, feeling way better she had a fully stocked kitchen now.

"You really didn't need to buy me anything, guys! I should be taking care of you since you guys spent the whole day here cleaning and are stuck keeping an eye on me. I can pay for those, Bastian. Just tell me what it cost, please," she stammered nervously.

Elijah looked to me as my eyes immediately dropped to the bruise on her neck.

"*How do you want to handle this?*" Elijah asked.

"*Delicately.*"

"Oh no, you're not paying me for those, Shanely," Elijah said, with a smile. "We're taking care of you, *little one,* and besides Cade will be apart of the security team that's getting set up to watch you while we hunt this rogue. We need to make sure there's enough to feed him *and* you. We take care of one of our own."

"One of your own?" she asked, her eyes furrowing. My whole body tensed up as I shot Elijah a warning look. "Oh, because I'm about to be a part of the pack?"

He just winked as he replied, "Yeah, sure. Because you're pack."

I shoved him forward before he'd let anything more slip. *God, they were going to scare her away for me.*

Shanely promptly went to the groceries on the counter, but I could hear her stomach rumbling from here. I stacked four slices onto a plate before pushing it her way. Her stubborn self tried to protest, but I let her see the gold flash before my eyes briefly, and she finally caved and sat down to eat. I put everything away, filling every cabinet and drawer in her fridge and pantry. My wolf beamed at the sight.

The pizza was gone in minutes with Cade around, but I made sure she had a few slices for later if she wanted. When the games came back out, I shot daggers to my brothers, warning them I would pay them back for every embarrassing story they told about me. It was of *little* use though. She laughed at every word they said, and once that happened, they went out of their way to keep it going. I grumbled but finally relented. *If it made her happy, I'd allow it.* Even at my own expense.

She seemed a little off every so often, but I didn't blame her. Adjusting to a wolf being inside your mind and body at the age of 19 must be weird. We were born with our wolves so I've never experienced a time without mine. But Shanely— *I couldn't imagine being in her shoes.*

"So you're not originally from here then?" she asked, munching on her crust. We played that stupid game of buying ridiculously named properties that I completely sucked at while we talked.

"Nope!" Cade answered as he rolled the dice. "We moved here when we were teenagers, and now we have dual-citizenship."

"Why?" she asked, and I smiled softly to myself. I liked that she wanted to know more about my brothers and I.

"Well, Bastian here is next in line to be Alpha," Cade answered, wiggling his eyes brows at me. My smile fell.

Elijah looked between us two as he chimed in, "We were sent here to train. We're supposed to go back home at some point."

My eyes went straight to hers. She seemed bothered by that thought but abruptly stood to toss her plate in the trash. It was a little hard to read how she felt about that. *Did it bother her to know I was supposed to return to Denmark?* I couldn't help but feel a little good if it did, but I didn't want to spoil her mood. She grabbed a pop from the fridge as I sighed.

"It's your turn, Elijah," I said firmly, giving my brothers each a look. They winced.

Yeah, enough talking about me.

We played that game for another hour, but she just seemed distracted. I hated it, and I glared at Cade and Elijah every chance she wasn't looking. I couldn't get her good mood back. She just seemed lost in her own head, even when she smiled or answered us. *They didn't need to discuss home with her. It wasn't going to happen anyways.* Cade finally won, plopping on the sofa, when Shanely walked over to me. She held out her hand.

"Here," she said softly. A crisp one hundred dollar bill lay in it, and I gave her another look. Her shoulders fell. "Please, Bastian."

I smiled, loving every time my name left her lips. I could listen to her say it all day, but I took a step away from her, shaking my head.

"Don't offer again," I commanded, and her eyes widened. I winked before turning to sit by Cade.

Her cheeks flushed as she stuffed the money back in the pocket of her jeans. I grinned again, loving that I could get to her like that. I liked watching her squirm.

Elijah came out of the back of the cabin then, and I gave him a look now. *What was his problem now?* I turned, asking Cade about how the patrol went yesterday, when Elijah spoke.

"Shanely. Who's Caleb?"

My wolf bristled as I turned to look at my girl. She seemed surprised by his question.

"Elijah—"

"Just someone I met at the Den the night I was attacked," she answered.

"He was super nice, and he towed my truck home for me. Why?"

My wolf was on red alert now. *The Den was not a place where wolves were welcome, and that family was not someone I trusted.* I exhaled slowly, shoving my wolf aside. I couldn't shift now. I couldn't snap at her again like the other night. Even if none of my anger was directed at her, she'd only see it as an attack.

"You mean the bar in town?" Cade asked for me. "We don't really go there, Shanely."

I clenched my fists together so tight my knuckles turned white. I knew *exactly* which Caleb she was talking about now. *That prick gets on my ever-loving nerves—*

"Wait— Caleb Medvedev?" Elijah asked firmly. "He works at the Den, Bastian."

"*I know,*" I snarled to him. *Breathe,* I told myself. *In and out. In and out.*

"Then do something," he growled. "Caleb is dangerous."

I nearly shifted right then.

"I'm not sure," she replied cautiously. "I never got his last name. I met his cousin Octavia too, though she wasn't too thrilled to meet me."

"I'll bet," Cade said, frowning. He shot me a glare then, and I barred my teeth. They didn't understand, and there's not been time to have this discussion either. But this was *my* mate, and this was not what she needed.

"Back off, Cade."

"He left his number Bastian, hoping to meet up later, and he offered her a job at the Den," Elijah said as he passed me the note.

I studied it carefully before I started pacing the floor, needing to move or I wouldn't be able to keep my wolf at bay. *Caleb Medvedev was dangerous, and he was getting too chummy with my mate,* I thought as rage burned through my veins. *I had to protect my mate!*

"Were you going to call him?" I asked firmly. A little too firmly, I guess, because she tossed her blanket aside in a huff, narrowing her eyes at me.

"I can't even if I wanted to," she snapped, and alarm bells went off in my head. "I had to ditch my phone when I came here, so I don't even have a way to contact him. Caleb was *nice* to me. He was kind enough to bring my truck back for me, and he's offering me a job, which I desperately need right now. What's your guy's problem?! Why don't you like him?"

"Wait, ditch your phone?" Elijah asked, but I ignored him.

My wolf was agitated and downright scared out of his mind. *She didn't get it,* I thought as every awful possibility ran through my mind. *She just doesn't understand how dangerous that whole clan is. They'd kill her, especially once they figure out who she is and how much she means to me. They didn't exactly like me very much at all.*

Fear won, and I rubbed my face agitated. "He was nice? Shanely, Caleb's a bear shifter! They aren't nice, and you cannot trust him! You're staying away from him *and* Octavia. You can't work there."

I knew deep down I was being too harsh, but the fears my wolf and I felt blocked every sort of reasonable thinking. *I can't let her go back,* I thought. *I can't let her be around them ever again.*

"She's right though, Bastian. Her truck's outside with tools around it. I saw it when I came in earlier, but I just assumed someone from the pack towed it back. I didn't smell Caleb when I came in," Elijah mentioned.

Caleb had freaking been here?! I thought as rage filled my core. *This close to the border too.* My eyes flashed red as I stormed over to see for myself. *I was going to kill him. I was going to freaking—*

"You don't get to decide who I spend my time with, Bastian," Shanely bellowed, squaring up to me. I froze when she jabbed her finger against my chest. "I'm not your girlfriend or even your family. Caleb didn't treat me badly. He was a complete gentleman, and he even told me about the McCoys. He's the one who told me my mother's name, and he didn't spew so much hate like you all are doing either! I *need* his help, Bastian. I have less than $300 dollars to my name, and I won't last the month without the job!"

"Shanely—"

My voice broke as all the fight left me. I watched tears form in her eyes again, and it killed me to hear how much she was struggling. She was too thin as it was and knowing it was because she didn't have enough money broke me. *I had to fix this,* I thought as my stomach rolled with anxiety. *She would never go without again.* I slowly reached for her, but she quickly wiped her eyes and shifted away.

"You're going to put yourself in harm's way by getting involved with someone like Caleb," Cade said as he crossed the floor.

Shanely shifted on her feet nervously, and I narrowed my eyes. "Caleb won't hurt me."

"How do you know that Caleb isn't planning something behind your back because I can promise you, he could scent what you were," Cade asked as he stood over her, "and what better way to get back at the McCoy Pack than with *you*. You're making yourself an easy target by getting involved with him, especially since he knows you're a direct heir to the throne now."

"Cade—" I hissed, glaring at him.

"Shut up, Cade. Now."

Shanely visible shook at my brother's word. She reacted the same way earlier with Cain, but now it was way worse. Way, *way* worse.

"Wow Cade— it's good to know how you really think of me. Don't stop now. Go ahead and tell me how stupid I really am for believing he was a nice guy. Let me know I'm nothing but an idiot who can't do anything right," she snapped sarcastically, turning from us all, and heading back to the kitchen. My brother chased after her.

"Cade, stop!" I shouted through our link. He ignored me, and I quickly followed them. *God, I'm getting sick of Cade's mouth.*

"I don't think you're dumb, but how can you seriously trust Caleb? You don't know him like we do, and you are weaker right now without your wolf. You couldn't *even* handle the rogue, so how do you expect to deal with a grizzly? He's probably plotting against the McCoy pack right now, and he'll use you to do it!"

"Cade!" I bellowed. "That's enough!"

I've never commanded my brother publicly like this. I've never corrected him like a child because *we're equals.* It doesn't matter that I'm born to be Alpha. Cade is the same as me, but right now he was way out of line.

Tears fell down her face as I shot daggers at my brother. I needed to fix this with her, but she opened her mouth, saying two little words that stopped me dead in my tracks.

"Get out."

My eyes widened as my brother began to stammer, "No, Baby Girl. I didn't mean it like that. You're just new to all this and still human in most ways—"

"Get out! All of you!" she shouted, and the three of us stumbled.

"Shanely," I said quietly, "please—"

I reached out for her, but she side-stepped me and went straight to the door. *I was going to kill Cade. Kill him and his big fat mouth!*

"All of you out now!" she shouted. "I would never do anything to hurt my family or this pack, but if you think so little of me then leave and don't come back! I am not weak nor am I some charity case for you to fix. I do not need *any* of you to buy me anything. I'll figure it out on my own!"

With a fire in her eyes, she stomped over to me and shoved a wad of money in my hands. I just knew this was every dime she had, and she forced me to take it. Her entire life's savings sat in the palm of my hand, and raw emotion flooded my face. I couldn't help it. She was breaking my heart.

But Cade suddenly shoved past me, pointing at her neck.

"What's that then?" Cade demanded.

"Leave it, Cade," she replied, shrinking back. That wicked fire diminished some as she tried to cover the mark some prick left on her. I could feel my brother's rage seep through the bond then, and he stepped even closer to her.

"That's a handprint," Elijah said sternly.

"So someone else managed to harm you already. God forbid what happens if the rogue catches you or Caleb and his filthy clan steals you out from under our noses. See this is what I was trying to say! You don't understand what you're doing in the shifter world, and you're going to get hurt if you don't listen to us!" Cade bellowed.

My wolf roared inside, and I shoved him to the side as I got between them.

"Cade, shut up!" I bellowed back, getting in his face. "This isn't how we handle things!"

Cade's eyes were solid gold when he turned to face me.

"You knew about it, didn't you?" he snapped. "And you're okay to just let it go? Someone harmed our—"

"I am not letting it go!" I snapped angrily. "But yelling at her isn't the answer! She is new to—"

"Shut up, you two," Elijah snapped angrily. "Something's wrong."

I turned, finding my brother hovering over Shanely, who looked to be in shock. She wouldn't focus on him, so I shoved past him and started rubbing her shoulders. Anything to get her to snap out of whatever hateful thing was spewing in her mind right now.

Cade swore. "I didn't mean to—"

"Just stop," I snapped. I couldn't deal with my brother at the moment. Elijah, on the other hand, could.

"God, Cade. One of these days you need to learn to control your mouth. We are better than this!" he snapped angrily. "We have no idea the life this girl's lived and—"

"I'm sorry!" Cade shouted back. "My wolf is so heavily involved right now— I didn't mean to hurt her."

I pulled Shanely's chin up, searching her eyes for any sign of life in there. *C'mon baby. Talk to me.*

Suddenly, she snapped out of whatever was haunting her and jerked away from me. My wolf whined as she calmly walked to the back door and opened it.

"You're right, Cade. I am pathetic and weak, especially these last two years. I have been abused in every possible way before escaping here. He told me I was an easy target too, and if you both are saying it, then it must be true. I let myself stay with someone who treated me horribly because I believed him when he said I couldn't do any better than him. That I owed him for everything he's done for me. From giving me a place to stay when I lived in my truck, to feeding me because I was starving and had no money. I stayed trapped in that relationship for a long time because of how he made me feel. Because I couldn't see that I deserved better. When I finally gathered the courage to try and leave, this is what I got in return," she said as she lifted her shirt to show a 3-inch scar on her belly.

God— that was a knife wound.

"Or this when I didn't listen and obey what he demanded of me," she said, pointing to the bruise on her neck.

I felt sick inside. Bile rose to the back of my throat as she showed off nearly every mark she had. I stood there horrified as other scars started to appeared before me. With my wolf's sight, I could see *all* the damage that prick did. Rage burned in my veins, and my eyes flashed red as she went on to break my heart further.

"You want a list of injuries I've had from him, Cade? Do you want to hear all the stories from living in the foster system? All the awful homes I've shared with dozens of other kids all struggling with their own problems. Shall I continue on?" she snapped as another tear rolled down her cheek. "I told myself that I'd be different here. That I deserved better because I wasn't what he always said I was. I wasn't dumb or helpless or an *easy-target*. But thank you, Cade, for reminding me he was right. Thank you all for making me speak about something I never wanted to discuss again. For making me feel so bad about doing something for myself like becoming friends with Caleb or getting a job. Now please, all of you leave, and don't come back."

She stormed away, slamming her bedroom door behind her. We stood in stunned silence then, and I didn't know what to do. What I *wanted* was to run to her. To beg her for forgiveness, and do whatever she needed me to do, but it wouldn't be what *she* wanted. I turned to Cade.

"You're a dick," I said, and he dropped his head.

"I never meant—" he said softly, and I felt anguish in our bond.

"We know," Elijah said, and I glared at him. I really wasn't ready to forgive Cade just yet. Not until Shanely did, but Elijah gave me a pointed look right back. "None of us handled this situation right, and we need to fix it."

I sighed heavily as Cade winced.

"God, she's crying," he muttered. I turned towards her door. That *killed* me.

"Go," I finally said. "The both of you. I'll stay until she's ready to talk."

Cade looked at me with sorrowful eyes. "I need to apologize, Bastian. I don't know why my wolf snapped like that. I don't know why I lost control, but she matters to him. She matters so much, but I never meant to make her feel like that. I just want her safe."

I gave him a slow nod before heading towards her bedroom door. Their quiet steps receded then, and I settled down against her door. There was no way I could just walk away, but listening to her soft cries through the door was excruciating.

Shanely Thomas was my mate.

And I promised myself right then and there, my brothers and I would *never* make my mate cry again.

Series Order

The Shifter Series
Shifter Awakened
Shifter Prophecy
Shifter Deliverance
Shifter Sacrifice

The Nightlocke Series
Realm of Darkness
Island of Horrors

About the Author

M. L. White is a Fantasy Romance writer who is obsessed with wolf shifters and all things dragon related. She loves to read and actively seeks out books that suck her in and make her feel like their world is better than reality, and she is determined to spread that same joy to others with her writing. Her books are like movies in your head with characters you can't help but fall in love with.

When M. L. White is not writing, she's chasing after her three children and taking care of her wonderful husband. They're her whole world so she's pretty busy spending as much time with them as possible. You can find her walking the trails with her two dogs or gaming with her husband and son in her free time as well!

You can connect with me on:

🌐 https://www.authormlwhite.com
🐦 https://x.com/Author_MLWhite
🔗 https://www.instagram.com/author_mlwhite
🔗 https://www.tiktok.com/@author_mlwhite

Subscribe to my newsletter:

✉ https://dashboard.mailerlite.com/forms/1169872/137001126070322601/share

Also by M. L. White

* *Trigger warnings*- No sexually explicit content or graphic violence can be found in any of M. L. White's books. All available books do contain violence and death, grief and loss, and some abuse or mentions of abuse.

Realm of Darkness is darker in nature with fantasy monsters and may be disturbing to some readers.

Shifter Awakened has pregnancy/birthing moments and kidnapping but are not in grotesque detail. No foul language or graphic themes can be found in any of M. L. White's publications. These books are written for YA/NA age range. Read at your own discretion.

Shifter Prophecy
Nothing else matter when someone threatens to hurt your family. Not even going head-to-head against a crazy Tiger King who slaughters any wolf he finds.

Life is good for Shanely, Bastian, and their family. The only thing that could make it better for Shanely is finally unlocking her wolf. But until she figures out how to do that, Shanely's just enjoying her quiet and peaceful life.

Unfortunately, all that is about to change when Shanely discovers that her sister-in-law, Bay, has made a deal with sadistic shifter known as the Tiger King. And there's nothing she can do when he takes her and her two cousins, Octavia and Alana, hostage.

Now the race is on for Bastian and his brothers to complete the Tiger King's list of demands to rescue their girls from his clutches. As the boys work nonstop to pull them out alive, Shanely begins to see a new side to the Tiger King. One that he rarely lets others see.

Things come to a dangerous head as Shanely and Bastian struggle to navigate this new threat while trying to find a way back to one another.

Foretold prophecy mixed with Femme power; SHIFTER PROPHECY is a story about knowing your worth with Damsel out of Distress vibes.

Shifter Deliverance
Everything's about to change.

Shanely has finally done it.

She's found her White Wolf, but by doing so she has accidentally taken control as Alpha of the McCoy pack. Every wolf in the world has felt the White Wolf emerge, and now it's time to take control of the World Council.

But they aren't so willing to let their power go.

Now it's a battle between the two as Bastian and Shanely try to save everyone from the Council's wicked ways.

Meanwhile, things are getting heated with the Division back home. The Division Head for the McCoy pack isn't happy with the change in leadership and begins changing the rules on the Fenrir family, making demands he has no right to make.

Can Bastian and Shanely battle it out on two different fronts? Or will the whole White Wolf business permanently split them apart?

"I'm just as afraid as you are Shanely... just promise me at the end of the day you keep getting back up. You dragged me into all this, so don't bail on me now."

Shifter Sacrifice

And just like that... *Everything* fell apart.

Shanely and Bastian have stood together side-by-side through it all. From uncovering the truth about Shanely's past to tackling the power hungry wolves in the shifter community, they've taken charge and are forcing shifters into a new and peaceful era whether they like it or not. The prophecy of the White Wolf is coming true...

Until an old threat resurfaces.

The Division has become aggressive with Shanely and her pack. Other disgruntled Alphas have come forward wanting to go to war with the human organization that keeps the shifters under their thumb, and it's up to Shanely and Bastian to stop the bloodshed before it happens. But Calvin Jennings has threatened to make matters worse if they do not comply with his one demand.

Her.

The Jennings want her, and unless she goes willingly, the McCoy pack will be annihilated. Will Shanely be able to stop the war before it happens? Or will her warnings come true and she'll lose everything she holds dear?

Find out in Shifter Sacrifice!

Realm of Darkness

What would you do if the shadows were alive? What would you do if they were trying to kill you?

The darkness is a dangerous place, and it's all because of the Nightlocke. Born of shadows and King of all things wicked and evil, the Nightlocke is a monstrous beast seeking those to torture and kill.

The kingdom of Odemark is barely surviving because of it. The land destitute, the Queen murdered, and no Lightspark to save anyone. The kingdom *needs* a Lightspark. The only person able to heal the land and the people within. But the Nightlocke made sure to kill her long ago.

But Kymra has a plan. A plan to save her family from starvation and death. And everything's going well... until she comes face to face with the Nightlocke himself.

To her surprise, he steals her away instead of killing her on sight. Now she's a slave to a new master and has no idea how to escape. But as she starts to see the Nightlocke in a new light, she begins to wonder if she even wants to leave now.

Maybe she's crazy. Maybe she's officially lost her mind, but one thing's for sure. Everyone's might just be wrong about the Nightlocke.

Beauty and the Beast meets dark fantasy. This enemies to lovers story is perfect for those who love dark romance or villain gets the girl tropes.

www.ingramcontent.com/pod-product-compliance
Lightning Source LLC
LaVergne TN
LVHW091653070526
838199LV00050B/2166